A self-confessed bookworm,
at university and then went on
later, headteacher of a seconda
retiring, she turned to crime-
since. *Death by the Sea* is the sixth book in her much-loved
Anglian Detective Agency series.

*By Vera Morris and available from Headline Accent*

*The Anglian Detective Agency series*

# DEATH BY THE SEA

## VERA MORRIS

ACCENT

The right of Vera Morris to be identified as the Author of
the Work has been asserted by her in accordance with the
Copyright, Designs and Patents Act 1988.

First published in 2022 by Headline Accent
An imprint of HEADLINE PUBLISHING GROUP

2

Cataloguing in Publication Data is available from the British Library

ISBN 978 1 4722 8368 9

Typeset in 10.5/13pt Bembo Std by Jouve (UK), Milton Keynes

Printed and bound in Great Britain by Clays Ltd, Elcograf S.p.A.

MIX
Paper from
responsible sources
FSC
www.fsc.org   FSC® C104740

Headline's policy is to use papers that are natural, renewable and recyclable
products and made from wood grown in well-managed forests and other
controlled sources. The logging and manufacturing processes are expected
to conform to the environmental regulations of the country of origin.

HEADLINE PUBLISHING GROUP
An Hachette UK Company
Carmelite House
50 Victoria Embankment
London EC4Y 0DZ

www.headline.co.uk
www.hachette.co.uk

For Trevor, forever in my heart.

And all the people who live on that stretch of Suffolk coast from Southwold to Orford, who have helped me to create the six crime novels that form The Anglian Detective Agency series: fishermen, fish and chip shop owners, members of the Aldeburgh RNLI, the RSPB Minsmere, the NT Orford, owners of the Aldeburgh Bookshop, and residents of Aldeburgh and Thorpeness.

Thank you for your help, friendliness and wonderful stories.

Death is a meeting place of sea and sea.

Conrad Aiken


Love rests on no foundation.
It is an endless ocean,
With no beginning or end.

Rumi

# Chapter One

Friday, 13 April, 1973

Judge Neville Hanmer, sitting on the loggia of his bungalow in Thorpeness, shivered. The air was cooling after a sunny morning and a stealthy breeze was creeping in from the North Sea. The local people still addressed him as Judge, but he no longer deserved the title; it was as false as calling this house a bungalow, for it had three stories and five bedrooms.

He went inside and sniffed; the smell of the meal Mrs Hegarty had cooked him lingered, mixed with the more pleasant smell of paint from the watercolour he'd finished before lunch. The drying colour washes always reminded him of damp beach towels. In the sitting room, light pouring in through the uncurtained window, he examined his work. He'd painted from a sketch of fishing boats beached on the Aldeburgh shore. He nodded, yes, he'd caught the scintillations from the recently rained-on shingle. Not a bad effort.

How he wished he'd never gone into the Art Gallery in Aldeburgh, never met Tucker, never bought any paintings from him. That association had been his downfall. Although he swore to them he'd never accepted the frequent invitations to visit Tucker's house for the weekend, they didn't believe him. He was forced to retire. He hadn't been given a choice.

The smell of lunch won over the smell of paint. It had been a rather fatty lamb stew, more mutton than lamb. Mrs Hegarty's cooking was adequate, but rather plain and uninspired. 'Goodbye,

1

Judge,' she called after washing the dishes. 'Remember, I won't be in on Monday. See you Tuesday.' She lived in Aldeburgh and cycled from there each day, to wash, clean and to cook lunch for him, if he was in. He liked her and her cheerful chatter; on some days she was the only person he talked to. He opened the kitchen window.

Time for his usual walk. He put on a tweed jacket and red woollen scarf, pausing before the hall mirror and trying unsuccessfully to smooth his crinkly hair, once dark and thick, but now thinning and shot with grey. But, not bad for seventy-one, he thought, at least his eyebrows were dark and he hadn't run to fat, like some of his contemporaries. He shook his head; what use was his charm and wit now? Living here, isolated from his beloved courts and the companionship of his fellow lawyers and judges. He picked up his Malacca cane from the umbrella stand, opened the front door and stepped down into the garden, and out onto The Benthills, a rough road separating the six bungalows from the beach and North Sea.

The brown-green water slithered over the shore, deceptively calm, undulations replacing waves, sucking at the pebbles and hissing as it retreated. The slight breeze gently rustled last year's bent-grass stalks in his front garden. He'd left it as it was originally planted: the grass, tamarisk and gorse, blending into the sand dunes the houses were built on.

He frowned. What should he do? He *must* make a decision while he walked. If something dreadful happened, how would he be able to face the consequences of his inaction?

He turned away from the sea, walked down The Dunes, past South Cottages, crossed the road leading to Aldeburgh, and stood near the boathouse looking over the wide waters of the Mere. He thought of all his boyhood holidays in Thorpeness, in the house his parents had leased when the holiday village was built before the First World War. It was now fully his; he'd recently purchased the lease-hold when most of the estate was sold to pay death duties.

As a child, he remembered one year coming by train from London to the newly built station; it wasn't much of a station, only three obsolete old Great Eastern passenger coaches adapted to form a ticket office and waiting room, but when their trunks were unloaded from the train, and men wheeled them away, the family following behind them, it was special and exciting. The railway was long gone, no trains ran to Aldeburgh, and there was only a short stretch of track at Leiston, used to bring spent nuclear fuel from Easterspring power station.

He leant on his cane as he watched the boatman helping two children into a rowing boat, their parents nervously making suggestions and telling them not to row too far. The elder child, a boy of about thirteen, grasped the oars and competently rowed away, the younger girl waved to her parents. He studied the boy – a straight nose, determined chin, already showing promise of a handsome face. Why were the parents worried? They must know the Mere was only two and a half feet deep over its entire sixty-odd acres.

When *his* parents told him he was going to Never-Never Land, the home of Peter Pan, for his holidays, and Daddy would row him in a special boat over the Spanish Main, to Peter Pan's island, and he would see Wendy's house and visit the Smuggler's Cave, he'd been so excited he couldn't sleep at nights. Later in life, he'd learnt how Ogilvie, the railway magnate, inspired by his friend Barrie, the author of *Peter Pan*, had built this fantasy village. He still loved the place, but now it was his permanent home, he felt restricted. Perhaps it was time to buy a larger house with a good-sized garden? He'd ask Pamela to keep an eye open for any suitable properties near her.

He frowned again. This wasn't helping him to come to a decision. Was he being paranoid? Perhaps he should ignore the problem, if there was one. He gnawed at his lower lip. Should he follow Pamela's lead, and get help? He'd many former contacts in London, but wasn't sure if they would welcome his enquiries. Dear Pamela. She was the only true friend who lived nearby. When he'd lived in London, he'd revelled in their visits to The Royal Horticultural Society's shows; she'd persuaded him to go with her to Chelsea last year, but although he'd enjoyed her company and their discussions on the merits of the various show gardens, all the while he'd been

3

afraid he might bump into someone from his former life and be humiliated when they snubbed him.

Pamela knew he was a homosexual, but all he'd ever done was to admire and desire at a distance, apart from one sordid instance at boarding school, when he'd been forced by an older boy. Since then, he'd never touched, or been touched, by another boy or man sexually. The whole messy business of sex, whether with men or women, was abhorrent to him. Even when he'd weakened and pleasured himself, afterwards he was filled with self-disgust.

How he missed his former life. As a barrister he'd had a successful and lucrative practice, mainly dealing in litigation and libel. Much more fun than defending criminals. But taking silk, being a judge – it had been the fulfilment of his dreams. How proud his parents would have been if they'd lived to see that. He remembered the feel of his judicial robes; preferring the winter black robe, faced with fur, with its scarlet tippet, to the summer violet robe, lined with silk. He'd been told he cut an imposing figure in them.

The young boy continued to row vigorously; the girl dangled a hand into the clear water. 'Robert,' the mother shouted, 'that's far enough.' The father frowned at her. 'Do be quiet, Mildred. Stop making a fuss.'

Neville Hanmer smiled and walked away from the Mere. He turned north, up the Sanctuary into Old Homes Road, turning once more seawards, then left up North End Avenue. His guts clenched. Damn. Walking towards him was David Pemberton. When he heard Adam Pemberton, and his new wife, Ann, who'd been his former housekeeper, had bought a house in Thorpeness his heart sank. David Pemberton. In 1969, Adam's thirteen-year-old son had been kidnapped and held for two years by Tucker. In the City there were rumours of a paedophile ring and the deaths of Tucker and his assistant, Hagger, fuelled the gossip. The full truth of the scandal never surfaced, but his dear friend, the barrister John Butterfield, came to see him at his London home. He told him how he'd accepted Tucker's invitation to a weekend visit at his house near Aldeburgh, there he'd been attracted to a young man, another

4

guest. He'd been secretly photographed in bed with the boy. What had followed had been blackmail, not for money, but information. He couldn't face the humiliation if he was prosecuted. Three days later John committed suicide. Or was he removed? Shortly after, Neville was summoned to the Lord Chief Justice's offices and told to resign. His friendship with John and his connections with Tucker were enough for him to be deemed unsuitable for his position. It was that, or he'd be removed from his office. He was told to leave London and live a quiet life in the countryside. He'd come to his house here in Suffolk; perhaps he should have moved where he wasn't known, but although the scandal had happened a short distance from here, somehow the people of Aldeburgh and Thorpeness didn't associate him with it. But he was sure David Pemberton did.

He couldn't turn round; it would only confirm the boy's suspicions. My God, but he was beautiful: tall, rangy, with broad shoulders and narrow hips; as he matured and muscled up, he would have an athlete's body. His face was arresting, like a boy in a Caravaggio painting, oval, with pale skin and dark blue eyes; he'd inherited his looks from his beautiful mother, Carol.

'Good morning, David? How is your father?'

The boy's eyes were cold, like the winter's sea, his mouth unsmiling. He nodded and did not reply.

Neville's stomach contracted, but he nodded back, and continued on his walk. As soon as he thought David was out of view, he turned and headed home. As he came to the Country Club, situated just before his house, he decided to turn in there; if he was too late for afternoon tea, he'd have an aperitif. Mrs Hegarty had left him some sandwiches and a salad for his evening meal.

Glass in hand, he made for the balcony on the west side of the Club. There were two couples on the tennis courts: a pair of women playing a vigorous game, and on the other court a tall, blonde woman having a coaching session with Carlton Mavor. He knew Carlton didn't like him, he suspected he'd caught him staring when he had started coaching at the Club three years ago. Carlton didn't hide his dislike.

5

Goodness, the woman was good, hitting a sizzling backhand down the line. Carlton put down his racquet and applauded. They laughed. Carlton looked smitten. The woman turned and he recognised her. It was a sign.

As soon as he got back to his house, he looked for his telephone book; it was next to his diary on the desk. He found the number Pamela had given him; it was late in the afternoon to ring, especially on a Friday, but if he didn't do it now, he might never get round to it.

'Good afternoon, the Anglian Detective Agency,' a man said. 'Frank Diamond speaking. How can I help you?'

# Chapter Two

Monday, 16 April, 1973

In the office/dining room of Greyfriars House, Frank Diamond, one of the senior partners of The Anglian Detective Agency, frowned and looked at his watch. Where was Laurel? She'd said she'd be at the eight-thirty meeting, even though she was officially on holiday. They'd recently decided, as the Agency was doing well, they could afford, in rotation, to take some leave. She'd been with her parents for a few days, and now spent most of her time at the Country Club in Thorpeness, having tennis coaching from a young man she described as 'dishy'.

'Any idea where Laurel is?' he asked Dorothy.

Dorothy Piff, the Agency's administrator, former school secretary, and owner of the Tudor house, paused as she placed blotting paper and pencils at five settings on the table. 'She was up early, had her breakfast and took Bumper out for a walk.'

Bumper was Laurel's black Labrador.

'It isn't eight thirty yet, Frank. You sound tetchy. Couldn't sleep last night?' Dorothy asked.

Frank shrugged. 'I always sleep well.' He'd missed Laurel last week and wished she was coming with him this morning on a preliminary visit to a possible client. Instead, Stuart was lined up for that job.

Stuart Elderkin, once detective sergeant to Frank's detective inspector, eased his considerable bulk into a chair, looking relaxed, pipe in hand, the top of the bowl glowing red. He raised it to his lips and inhaled deeply, then puffed blue smoke to the ceiling. '*I've missed Laurel.*' He eyed Frank and raised his eyebrows, as though inviting a comment.

A door opened, a click and the sound of the kitchen radio died. Mabel Elderkin, Stuart's wife, one-time Mabel Grill, school cook and former owner of the famous Aldeburgh Fish and Chip Shop, bustled in, untying her apron and settling in a chair next to Stuart. 'I do like that new DJ on *Breakfast*, Terry Wogan, he's got a lovely voice, but I wish he'd stop playing Cliff Richard, I can't stand him.' She took a deep breath. 'Well, that's lunch prepared. You'll be back for it, won't you?' She directed the question to both Frank and Stuart.

'I'm sure we will, love,' Stuart replied. 'This is a different kind of case. We've not dealt with one like it before, have we, Frank?'

'I'm looking forward to it; I've heard the gardens are beautiful, and Pamela Gage sounded an intelligent and pleasant woman when I spoke to her on the telephone. I can't see any reason why we can't help her. But we need to find out what she wants, bring the facts back, then we can all make a decision.'

The outside kitchen door opened; sounds of claws skittering on the stone floor.

'I've just mopped it down,' muttered Mabel.

Hearty lapping and splashing of water.

Stuart laughed. 'There's Bumper, cleaning up after himself.'

Mabel smiled and dug him in the ribs.

Laurel Bowman, all five eleven of her, burst into the room, bringing with her smells of the seashore. 'Whew, didn't think I'd make it, Bumper was acting up today, chasing seaweed in the waves.'

She looked the epitome of health and happiness, face glowing, blonde hair shining. Was she just happy to be alive, or was there some other factor? Such as an attractive tennis coach? He was too young for her, must be ten years her junior. He tapped his watch. 'Shall we start?'

Laurel sat in the seat next to him. 'Did you have a good weekend? How's the love life going? Getting serious?'

He glared at her, then turned to Dorothy. 'Have you the agenda?'

She gave him a quizzical look over her blue spectacles. 'Have I failed you yet?' She passed a sheet of A4 paper to each of them.

He didn't reply, although he knew he should apologise for his brusque manner. He'd started dating a woman in Aldeburgh two months ago. Emma worked in the cinema's office, arranging the films and the other events the cinema hosted. He'd met her at an exhibition of a local artist's work. She was small, slight, with brown eyes, a pixie haircut and a nice sense of humour. He liked her, but she wasn't Laurel. He'd decided it was useless hoping Laurel would change her mind. He'd accepted she didn't fancy him; they were good friends and that would have to do, but when he'd seen her with Carlton Mavor, the tennis coach, having a drink with him and some of the other tennis players in The Cross Keys in Aldeburgh, the sour taste of jealousy invaded his mouth. He didn't like that feeling. It wasn't so bad when she didn't have any romantic entanglements . . . but who was he to talk?

They worked their way through the first two items on the agenda.

'Number three, financial report.' He waved to Dorothy.

She passed them another sheet of paper. 'You can see the out-goings and income for the last two months. I hope you'll be pleased with the last figure.'

There were noddings and sounds of satisfaction from all the other members.

'Gosh, this is very good, Dorothy, even better than before,' Laurel said.

'Excellent,' Frank said. 'We're more than holding our own.'

'Cliché,' Laurel cried. 'We certainly don't want to hold someone else's!'

Dorothy smiled, leant over the table and rapped Laurel's knuckles with her biro. 'And you a respectable former teacher!'

Frank didn't smile. 'Next item. Pamela Gage, who owns Yoxford Hall Gardens, contacted us to see if we could help her with a problem she has. She was cagey—'

'Not Gagey!' Laurel interrupted, dimpling at him.

9

'Idiot,' he replied, laughing, although he didn't want to.

'You're sharp this morning,' Stuart said. 'I think having a holiday has done you good.'

'Can we get back to business?' Frank asked, trying to look stern.

'Sorry, Frank,' Laurel replied, 'it's romping with Bumper, I get as mad as him.'

'To continue, Mrs Gage was unwilling to say too much over the phone. I had the impression someone was in the room with her, and she didn't want to be overheard. She said it was something to do with her plants.'

'She must have heard you had a degree in botany, Frank. Perhaps she wants you to advise her on plant propagation,' Stuart said.

Frank went to his home-town university, Liverpool, before he joined the police force. 'For God's sake, what's the matter with everyone this morning? As soon as this silly meeting comes to a conclusion, Laughing Boy Stuart and I will drive over to Yoxford and see her. Shouldn't take too long, I can't imagine what the problem is, but I can't see it can be that serious.'

'I'll have lunch ready for one thirty,' Mabel stated.

'Excellent. The last item is the visit by Neville Hanmer, who phoned me late Friday afternoon.'

'Judge Hanmer? I've seen him at the Club,' Laurel said.

'Not a judge any more,' Stuart said. 'Heard there was something funny about his retirement. This chap, a lawyer, told me they couldn't understand why he retired, he was at the peak of his career. He was well thought of, a popular judge, strong, but gave fair summing ups, this man said.'

Frank nodded. 'I rang Nick Revie and asked if he could tell me anything about Hanmer.' They'd met Detective Inspector Nicholas Revie on their first big case, when they searched for the missing teenager, David Pemberton. That case had repercussions for many important people, and the Agency's silence was bought by offering the future cooperation of the Suffolk police, with Nick Revie as their contact.

'And?' Stuart asked.

10

'He wasn't sure, but he thought although Hanmer wasn't involved in the David Pemberton case, he had friends who were, and he was tainted by association,' Frank replied.

'That's so unfair!' Laurel said. 'Goodness, if we were all judged by our friends, I think several of us would have to go into purdah.'

'You'll be all right, Frank, being as you haven't got any friends,' Stuart chortled, as he resumed puffing on his pipe.

Frank ignored him. That remark, plus the seductive aroma of tobacco smoke, irritated him. He decided he wouldn't offer to stop at The Eel's Foot on the way back from Yoxford.

'Can we get on?' Dorothy said. 'I promised the vicar I'd do the flower rota for next month. If some of the ladies don't have at least two weeks' notice, they can't cope.'

Frank rapped the table with his biro. 'Like Pamela Gage, he was unwilling to discuss why he wanted to see us. When I suggested I could come over to Thorpeness, he became agitated. "I don't want anyone to know I'm consulting you," he said. I tried to winkle a few facts from him; all he would say is he'd possibly ask us to discreetly make enquiries about a certain local person.'

'Intriguing,' Laurel said. 'Someone who lives in Thorpeness?'

'He gave no more details. He's due here at three o'clock. Hopefully he'll elucidate then.'

Stuart got up and knocked his pipe out on the ashtray, resulting in a tiny Mount Vesuvius of smouldering ash.

'I do wish you'd give it up,' Mabel said. 'Cigarettes are bad enough, but I'm beginning to hate that smelly pipe.'

Stuart looked hurt, his bottom lip protruded and his cheeks sagged, resulting in the return of his bloodhound look.

'I'm sorry, love. I know you enjoy your pipe.' Mabel paused. 'But it isn't good for you, you've only just got over that nasty cough you had for most of the winter.' She shook her head. 'You're all I've got left, Stuart.' Mabel's only son, Matt Grill, by her first husband, had died last year. She was making a good recovery, but the hurt was just beneath the surface.

Stuart sighed, then blew out his cheeks. 'I know you're right; I've

11

been lectured by these two often enough.' He waved the stem of his pipe at Frank and Laurel. 'I tried once, but I was a nervous wreck after a couple of days.' He turned and pointed at Dorothy. 'What about you, Dorothy? If I try to give up my pipe, will you give up your cigarettes?'

Dorothy looked affronted. 'They got me through the war, with a little help from Mr Whisky. What would I do with these,' she waved her hands, 'if I couldn't hold a cigarette?'

'A bit more gardening?' Frank asked. Not waiting for the acid reply, he nodded to Stuart. 'Let's get going, we need to get to Yoxford for ten. See you all at lunch.' As he passed Laurel, he touched her shoulder. 'Or are you heading for another tennis lesson with the handsome Mr Mavor?'

She looked up at him. 'No, I'm staying here, I want to hear what Mr Hanmer has to say.'

'Working in your holiday? What dedication. Learnt all you can from Mr Mavor?'

'I'm sure there's a few more things he can teach me.'

'Such as?'

'He says my net play needs improvement; I lack subtlety.'

Frank grinned. 'I question his judgement.'

'Are we going or not?' Stuart said testily.

Laurel looked thoughtful, Dorothy puzzled and Mabel worried. 'Goodbye, my lovelies, see you all soon.'

As Frank got into his Avenger GT, he smiled as he imagined the ensuing conversation.

# Chapter Three

'I've never been to this place; have you?' Frank asked as they passed through the small town of Yoxford.

'No, I haven't. It's always the same, you never visit places right on your doorstep. Mind you, it hasn't always been a nursery and open to the public,' Stuart said.

'When did it change?' He glanced at Stuart as there was no instant reply.

Stuart pushed out his lower lip and frowned. 'About ten or twelve years ago.'

'Quite recent for these parts.'

'Less of the sarcasm. Us Suffolk folk are slow but steady.'

'I'll go along with the slow. Going back to the hall and gardens, why did it change? New owners?'

'No. The house and garden have been owned by the Bangham family for, oh, I don't know, three hundred years?'

'But we're going to meet a Pamela Gage,' Frank said as he took the A1120 out of Yoxford.

'For once you've remembered who we're going to see. *She* was a Bangham.'

Frank laughed. 'I bet she was glad to change her name to Gage. She inherited the house?'

'That's right, and because of death duties Mrs Gage had to sell most of the contents of the house and hand over money and shares. Then she had to find a way to pay for the upkeep of the house and estate, or sell it.'

'So, she opened the gardens and started a plant nursery. Good for her.'

'Do you think your Liverpool will do the double? It looks like they've got the First Division sewn up,' Stuart asked a few minutes later.

Frank really hoped so. 'It's not over yet. It'll be tough to win the UEFA cup, Borussia are a class act, but I'll put my trust in Shankly and Kevin Keegan.'

'Ipswich aren't doing too badly and with a bit of luck Norwich will get relegated.'

'That's very small-minded of you, Stuart. You never hear me saying derogatory things about Everton.'

Stuart sniggered. 'There's the turning.' Stuart pointed to a narrow tarmac road leading off the main one. There was an eye-catching sign at its entrance:

YOXFORD MANOR GARDENS AND
PLANT NURSERY
Open 10.00 a.m. to 4.00 p.m.
Entrance 50p Children free
Woodland Walks, Maze, Stumpery and Japanese Water Garden
Children's Play Area and Treehouse
Tea room

'Will we have time for a visit to the tea room?' Stuart pondered.

'That might be possible. You haven't had your pipe out yet,' Frank said. 'Want a quick puff before we get there?'

Stuart sighed. 'I thought I'd have another go at giving it up.'

'In that case I'm sure we'll have time for a coffee and a bun. My treat. I hope you manage to give up the deadly weed. It'll be tough. I know. I still get the urge when you and Dorothy light up and the insidious fumes tickle at my former addiction.'

'Really? Well, that's another reason for trying. I don't want to be accused of starting you back on the fags.'

The well-hedged road wound its way for about a mile before

another sign, a duplicate of the first, marked the entrance to the gardens. To the left of the drive was a wooden hut with a sign saying PAY HERE. A grey-haired man stepped out.

Frank wound down his window. 'Mr Diamond and Mr Elderkin,' Frank said. 'We've an appointment to see Mrs Gage.'

The man nodded. 'Mrs Gage told me to expect you. No charge,' he said, sounding disappointed.

Frank was sorry for him, it was an isolated spot, and he felt like giving him something for his lonely post. He resisted; he didn't want to spoil his reputation. 'Thank you. Have you worked here long?' he asked. 'Lovely part of the world.'

The man pulled back his shoulders. 'I used to work in the house. Retired. I'm a volunteer now.'

His brusque but pleasant manner made Frank think he must have some military background. 'Do you always do *this* job? It must be a bit lonely.'

'No. Mrs Gage makes sure all the volunteers take turns at the different jobs. Great organiser, Mrs Gage. Known her since she was a child.' His voice was full of affection and pride.

'Are there many volunteers?'

'About twenty of us. All local. Many with former connections to Mr and Mrs Bangham, Mrs Gage's parents.'

'She must be a popular woman if so many people are willing to help her,' Stuart said.

'She's a great lady.'

'Is there a Mr Gage?' Frank asked.

'There is.' He didn't elaborate and Frank didn't ask for more details. The man's tone was enough to indicate he didn't think much of him.

'Nice to have met you. We'd better not be late for our appointment,' Frank said, winding up the window and slowly driving off.

'Do you know anything about this Mr Gage?' Frank asked.

'Not a lot, mostly gossip. Name is Keith Gage, he's a solicitor, has a practice in Saxmundham.'

'Is there much work for a solicitor there?'

15

'I really don't know. They've been married a long time. I suppose he thought he was landing in clover when he married into the Bangham family. Must have been a shock when a lot of the wealth disappeared into the Government's coffers.'

'Does the husband have anything to do with the nursery?'

'Mabel said he plays a lot of golf, and you know how much time that can consume if you're playing regularly. He's a member of Aldeburgh and Thorpeness Golf Clubs.'

'I wonder if we'll see him today?'

'Why do you want to see him? I can't see he'll be able to tell us anything Mrs Gage can't.'

Frank parked the Avenger in front of a small Georgian manor house. 'I'm always interested in the dynamics of couples.'

'Really? Is that why you've never formed one?'

Frank turned and gave him a look. He hoped it was suitably cynical.

'What about Laurel? In December, when we all went to her old school's Christmas concert, I wondered if she might want to return to teaching. You could see she loved being back there, and they all thought a lot of her, girls and staff.'

Frank remembered her face, glowing with joy. 'I wondered too, but she's still with us.'

'Do you think she's serious about this tennis coach, Carlton whatnot? Carlton – sounds like a cinema.'

Frank shrugged his shoulders. 'Who knows? He's a bit young for her.'

'Dorothy's seen him at church. Said he's good-looking.'

There was a sour taste in Frank's mouth. 'Laurel's her own woman. She'll do as she pleases.'

'Wouldn't you rather she was *your* woman, Frank? I wish it had happened for both of you. I think you'd make a great pair.'

Frank smiled and shook his head, glancing at Stuart's bulk. 'I don't think you're equipped to play Cupid.' He glanced at his watch. 'Right, enough of this gossip, at the moment we're on time. Let's make a move.'

★

16

'Welcome to Yoxford Gardens and Nursery,' said a husky-voiced, petite woman as she strode towards them, 'Thank you, Janet,' she said to the elderly woman, probably another volunteer, who'd brought them into the walled garden nursery. 'Don't forget to pick up your plant before you leave. See you on Friday?'

'I'll be here, Pamela, and thank you for the epimedium.'

'Nonsense. I know it's going to a good home.'

'Pamela Gage.' She had a hearty handshake, and it was a gardener's hand placed in his: broken nails needing a good scrub, and quick, capable fingers. She must have been a pretty girl, Frank decided; about fifty, with faded blonde hair and, despite the weather-beaten skin, she'd neat features and a slim figure. Best of all was her dimpled smile, radiating energy. He introduced himself and Stuart.

'Let's go into the potting shed and I can tell you my problem.' She set off at a brisk pace, past well-organised beds of plants grouped together into different habitats, each one laid out alphabetically. They passed woodland, subdivided into dry shade and damp areas; plants for dry sunny spots, easy-to-grow plants, climbers and roses. He was impressed; if she'd organised this, she was someone he'd like to work with. Also, Mrs Gage looked fun.

At the far end of the nursery were glasshouses and to the right a brick building with a green-painted door and a row of windows set high in the wall. Pamela waved them in. It was a long, spacious room, with a potting bench running underneath the windows, and on the opposite wall, shelves with neatly arranged rows of clay and plastic pots of different sizes, also seed trays, dibbers, plastic labels and all the other paraphernalia needed for a nursery. Frank felt at home. Perhaps this is what he should have done instead of joining the police; used his botany degree to train to be a horticulturalist. Would it have been exciting enough? Would he get tired of pricking out seedlings and trying to sell plants to Joe Public, who were happy enough to spend ten pounds on a meal out, but quibbled when a plant they wanted cost five bob, even if it had taken three years to bring it to selling size? Perhaps not, his customer relations wouldn't be good enough.

Pamela took them to the far end of the room and pulled out three stools from under a bench. She waved a hand towards an electric kettle. 'Cup of coffee? I'm dying for one, been up since six, breakfast seems a long time ago.'

How could they refuse? 'Thank you,' Frank said.

Coffee poured, she offered cold milk from a Thermos and opened a battered tin. 'Chocolate digestive?'

Stuart beamed and helped himself. Frank politely refused.

'I'll talk and sip. You two listen and drink. I'm sure you're as busy as I am.'

Frank didn't think so.

'Someone is stealing from me,' she said, her sunny nature disappearing, her voice indignant.

'What are they taking?' Frank asked.

'Plants. Can you believe it? Who would stoop so low as to steal my precious plants?'

He wasn't sure what he'd been expecting, but it wasn't this. 'Mrs Gage, I hope you don't mind me saying this, and I'm sure the thefts must be causing you a great deal of distress, but would it be right to involve us? Would the expense be worth it?'

She glared at him. 'You obviously don't know much about horticulture, young man.'

He heard Stuart snigger.

'I grow some very rare plants, especially snowdrops and erythroniums – commonly known as dog's tooth violets.'

'I do know something about plants, Mrs Gage.'

'Mr Diamond has in degree in botany,' Stuart chipped in.

'Really? Then what are you doing running a detective agency?'

Oh dear, he'd got on the wrong side of her. 'I'm sorry, Mrs Gage. I didn't realise you grew rare plants. I know they can be worth a considerable amount of money.'

She looked mollified. 'It's not uncommon for one of my snowdrop bulbs, in the green, to cost ten pounds.'

Stuart's mouth dropped open. 'Ten pounds for one bulb. But they grow in the wild. Dorothy's got them round the apple tree.'

'Dorothy?'

'Miss Dorothy Piff, the Agency administrator,' Frank said.

'I sold one bulb, of my own crossing, it has pale yellow petals, unnamed as yet, for thirty pounds last spring. I had a small group growing in the woods, in an out-of-the-way area. They were all stolen.'

'How many were there?' Stuart asked.

'Twelve, and I had a buyer for all of them. What's more, this year I'd put the price up to forty pounds a bulb.'

'Good heavens, that's four hundred and eighty quid! That's enough to buy two colour tellies,' Stuart exclaimed.

'Or half a Cortina,' Frank riposted.

'Exactly.'

'And I presume they are not the only plants taken?' Frank asked.

Pamela looked grim. 'No, far from it.'

'When did you first notice the thefts?' he asked.

'A few plants disappeared last spring, at first I thought a fox had been digging for worms and beetles. I was upset — I'm very fond of my plants and hate to lose any to diseases or insect predation. It isn't just the money, although we can't afford to lose the income — I take this personally. It must be someone who knows their plants and who also knows where they grow in the garden. They are taking the rarest and the most expensive.'

Frank's interest was whetted. He liked Pamela, her straight talk and her passion for plants. 'Have you any idea who could be doing this?'

She raised her eyebrows. 'If I had I wouldn't be asking for your help, I'd have called in the police.'

'Haven't you done that? See if they'll help?' Stuart asked.

'I did have a word with someone, not officially, you understand. A friend knew this person and I did talk to him. He was the one who suggested I contact you. I didn't want a lot of policemen questioning people. It would look bad, and I didn't want to upset my volunteers. I can't believe it could be one of them, they've been so good; I couldn't run the nursery without them.'

'Can I ask who recommended us?'

'A Nicholas Revie. He was charming.'

He exchanged glances with Stuart; he couldn't wait to get back to Greyfriars and tell Laurel. 'Yes, we do know him. Very good of him to recommend us.'

'He sang your praises.'

'Let's hope we can live up to his words if we take the case.'

'You mean you have doubts?'

'No. We always bring details of a prospective case to a full meeting of the Agency staff before we decide to take it.' He hesitated. 'I'm sure we'll be pleased to help you.'

Stuart gave him an old-fashioned look.

She was charming and he wanted to help. 'Roughly,' Frank asked, 'how much do you estimate the loss so far?'

She pursed her lips. 'Between three and a half to four thousand ponds.'

'That's half a house,' Stuart said.

She nodded. 'But it isn't just the money, in some cases all the plants of that species or variety have been stolen. I haven't got any stock left for propagation. Those plants will have to be wiped off the nursery list for next year. At this rate, my 1974 catalogue will be severely depleted, I'll lose some of my customers if I can't offer a wide variety of unusual or rare plants. I want you to find who's doing this and I want my plants back.'

For a small woman she packed a punch. He'd give quite a bit to see Pamela Gage confront the thief. His money was on her.

'Do you think the thief will have sold your plants already?' Stuart asked.

She banged her mug onto the bench. Luckily, she'd drunk all the coffee. 'Possibly. I wondered if they were stealing to order.'

'What do you mean?' Frank asked.

'If there was someone, a plantaholic, like me,' she said, with a wry grin, 'who persuaded someone who works here to steal for them, telling them which plants they wanted. They'd have to pay the thief, but that would be cheaper than buying the plants.'

'But if they had that kind of money, why wouldn't they buy them from you, rather than risk the thief being caught, and then their involvement in the crime revealed?' Frank asked.

She nodded. 'Good point, but there are some peculiar people in the world of plants. Some, not many, can be very jealous of another gardener's collection of rare plants, and you should see the scenes you get at flower shows when someone doesn't win that silver cup for the best dahlia which they've won since the year dot.' She put a hand to her face, and laughed. 'We're a queer old bunch.'

'What you've said so far is very interesting, and all ideas are useful when we try and find your thief.'

'So, you will take the case?'

'I'm sure we will. And if I'm wrong, and my partners aren't interested, I'll work on it myself in my spare time.'

Her smile was brilliant. 'Mr Diamond, I salute you!' She got up and rinsed her mug at the sink. They followed suit. 'Have you time for a tour of the gardens, so you can see the sites where the missing plants were taken from?'

Frank couldn't think of a better way to spend the next hour. 'We'd be delighted.'

'Good. Wait here, I'll fetch my head gardener, Miss Gibbs, she knows the situation, and she'll take you round.'

'You haven't got her down as a suspect?'

'No. I trust her completely. Also, she was away on leave when one theft occurred.'

'She could have come back to steal the plants.'

'She was in Jersey, visiting her parents.'

Frank cocked his head.

'I telephoned her to tell her of the theft.'

'And to possibly check if she was really there?'

'You're sharp! Living up to your name, Mr Diamond. I've learnt there are very few people whose word you can trust.' She didn't blink.

She was charming, but with a steel rod for a backbone, Frank thought; he was glad she wasn't a criminal; she'd have done very well. 'I trust you don't put me or Mr Elderkin in that category.'

21

'Time will tell.' She turned. 'I'll be back shortly with Miss Gibbs.'

Stuart let out a long breath. It sounded as though he'd been holding it in for quite a time. 'Well, she's a case and a half. Glad I'm not married to her.'

'Oh, I don't know, I like a strong-willed woman. Pity she's married.'

Stuart leant back against the bench. 'She must be in her fifties, surely you're not that desperate. Anyway, you've got a girlfriend. She seems nice.'

'She is. That's the problem.'

'So, you're not serious about her? Time you got hitched, Frank. If you don't watch it, you'll turn into a crusty old bachelor.'

'There are worse things than that.'

'Such as?'

'A husband who bores his wife, and vice versa. I don't mind being infuriated, but I'd dry up and shrivel if I was bored.'

Stuart shook his head, looking irritated. 'I don't understand you sometimes. I know where I am with Mabel.'

'It wasn't so long ago when you didn't.'

'That's true, but she'd just lost Matthew. She was beside herself. I'm not saying she's got over it, but once it was proved she was right, and he'd been murdered, she did calm down.'

'True. She's nearly back to the old Mabel.'

'Except now she's started worrying about what she should do about all the money she got from the sale of the fish and chip shop and the boat.'

When her son died, Mabel sold up to her old friend Ethel and her son, Tom. ' "Keep it in a building society," I said. Another thing, I don't think you should have told Mrs Gage we'd take the case. That's not like you, you usually stick to the rules.'

'I'm not sure why I did. She was charming and so indignant and hurt by the theft of her plants.'

'Shush, here she comes,' Stuart whispered.

With Mrs Gage was a young woman with a mass of unruly ginger hair.

'This is my head gardener, Georgina Gibbs, known as Georgie. Mr Diamond and Mr Elderkin.'

Georgie looked as though she'd just left the sixth form: fresh-faced, shy and with a tentative handshake.

'Georgie will take you on a general walk of the gardens, as well as showing you the sites of the crimes. How much time can you spare?' she asked. 'I'd like to have another word with you before you leave.'

Frank glanced at Stuart. 'Say forty-five minutes?' He didn't think Stuart could walk for longer than that.

'Good. Georgie, please bring Mr Diamond and Mr Elderkin back to the house when you've finished. I'll be in my office.'

'Yes, Mrs Gage.'

Why did a volunteer call her Pamela and Georgie didn't? Or was it just in front of them? Although she was quiet, Georgie Gibbs didn't seem intimidated by Pamela.

'Please follow me.' She led them out of the nursery garden and paused outside the wrought-iron gate. 'I'll take you past the herbaceous borders, through the stumpery and finally to the woodland walk. Do you wish to go through the maze?'

'I don't think so, unless you do, Stuart?'

Stuart shuddered. 'Can't stand them. They give me claustrophobia. I got left in one as a child and couldn't get out.'

'Weren't your parents worried? Surely they came to look for you?' Georgie sounded concerned.

'Perhaps they wanted to have a rest from him for a bit,' Frank said. 'Were you a demanding child, Stuart?'

'It's so long ago, I can't remember.'

Georgie smiled. 'I see your partner has a sense of humour, Mr Elderkin.'

'He comes from Liverpool, what do you expect?'

The exchange seemed to relax Georgie. 'Mrs Gage tells me you have a degree in botany, Mr Diamond?'

'It's quite a few years ago now, but I'm looking forward not only to seeing where the plants were stolen from, but also walking round the garden. It looks well kept.'

'Thank you.'

'Where did you train?'

'At Wisley.'

Stuart frowned.

'The Royal Horticultural Society's main garden,' she said.

They were walking between wide flower beds that wouldn't reach their zenith until July and August, but already plants were showing above the weed-free soil, and clumps of early tulips and daffodils gave colour to the borders.

'How many gardeners are under you?' Frank asked.

'Just one,' she said. 'A great deal of the work is done by volunteers.'

As they approached the end of the borders a young man was hoeing at the back of the right-hand bed. He waved. 'Hello, Georgie.'

Georgie's freckled face pinked up and she waved back.

'Is he the other gardener?' Frank asked when they'd passed him.

'He's the one,' she replied.

Frank wondered if he was the special one, he certainly looked pleased to see her. 'Good worker?'

'Very keen,' Georgie said, her colour deepening. She waved a hand to the left. 'There's the maze.'

'It must be difficult working with volunteers,' Stuart said. 'They'll need training, won't they?'

Georgie raised her eyebrows. 'I knew the situation when I was appointed, but I hadn't realised some of the volunteers would think they knew far more than me; after all, some of them have been gardening for over thirty years.'

'Does that lead to difficulties?' Frank asked.

Georgie smiled. 'I ask them to do a job a certain way, they agree and then when my back is turned, they do it their way. I can't put my foot down too heavily, or they go to Mrs Gage to complain about me.'

Was this young woman so frustrated she might decide to branch out on her own, and take some of the plants with her? She had an alibi for one theft, but nevertheless she'd go on the list.

Half an hour later they made their way back to the house.

'I'm sorry your shoes got muddy,' Georgie said.

Stuart's shoulders were drooping – walking was not his favourite pastime, and Frank was sure he'd be itching to light his pipe. In order to see some of the places where bulbs had been stolen, they'd had to leave the woodland path and tramp through ferns and brambles. Mabel would go mad when she saw Stuart's brogues.

After removing mud from their shoes using a Victorian boot-scraper, Georgie led them through the house to Mrs Gage's office, which was a spacious room with two sash windows overlooking the herbaceous borders.

'Thank you, Georgie,' she said. 'Sorry to have taken you away from your work. Could you get the contents of number three compost bin ready to go on the borders?'

Georgie nodded. 'Goodbye, I hope we'll see you again.'

It was a neat and well-organised room. What else would he expect from Pamela Gage?

'Do sit down.' She pointed to two upright chairs in front of an old, battered, wooden desk. 'I won't keep you long.'

'You have a beautiful garden, Mrs Gage, and Miss Gibbs was a very knowledgeable guide,' Frank said.

She gave him her mega-watt smile. 'Thank you. I was lucky to get Miss Gibbs, she's a very talented gardener for her age.'

'Which is?'

She pursed her lips. 'I think she's twenty-nine. Is that relevant?'

Frank ignored the reply. 'Is she good at managing the volunteers?'

She frowned. 'What's this got to do with the theft of my plants? How the nursery is run is not on your brief, Mr Diamond.'

A sensitive subject? 'I didn't know we had a brief, Mrs Gage.'

Her eyelids fluttered and her face expressed embarrassment. 'Yes, sorry, but I still can't see why you're interested in that topic.'

'It's useful to build up a picture of the dynamics of all the possible suspects.'

'But I told you, Miss Gibbs isn't a suspect.'

'If we take the case, you'll have to allow us to do as we think best. If that isn't possible, then we might have to reconsider.'

She shook her head in frustration. Clearly, she was used to having things her own way.

'Yes, I can see that. I'm so used to taking responsibility for everything, it's hard for me to take a step back. I promise I won't interfere.'

'And you won't want a de-brief every five minutes?'

This time she chuckled. 'You've summed me up well, haven't you? I'll restrain myself.'

The door of the office was flung open and a tall, dark-haired man rushed in. 'Pamela, that's where you are. You've remembered you're coming with me to have lunch with the Summers, haven't you?' he said, ignoring Frank and Stuart, who got to their feet.

Pamela's face darkened. 'Mr Diamond, Mr Elderkin, may I introduce my husband, Keith Gage.'

Gage looked at them as though they'd appeared from thin air. He shook their hands and then looked at his wife.

'They are from the detective agency. Georgie has shown then round the gardens. I'm happy to say Mr Diamond has said they will probably take the case.'

As Pamela spoke, Gage's face showed anger and frustration. His appearance was certainly satanic: dark hair, receding on either side of a widow's peak, deep-set hazel eyes, with curved black eyebrows above and a thin-lipped mouth. He only needed a forked tail and the picture would be complete.

'This is a waste of time, Pamela. I thought we'd agreed on that.'

Pamela drew herself up to a possible five foot one. 'I did not agree. I merely refused to argue with you. If the Agency takes my case, I hope they will start their investigations as soon as possible.'

Gage took a pace towards her.

Frank glanced at Stuart.

Pamela didn't step back, she looked up at her husband, her expression one of contempt. 'And I did tell you I wouldn't be able to go to the Summers, for one thing I'm too busy, and secondly, I don't like them. They drink too much and I find Mr Summers' jokes distasteful.'

Gage's nostrils flared, but he didn't move. 'I hope you realise with the fees you'll have to pay this lot,' he jerked his head in their direction, 'you could have bought as many bloody plants as you've lost. For Christ's sake, Pamela, see some sense.'

Frank felt they ought to leave, but the scene was enlightening. Gage might be bigger and stronger than his wife, but she wasn't afraid of him. Tough lady – he wasn't sure he'd like to tangle with Gage, he looked like he might have a vicious streak, but on the other hand he wasn't in the best of shape, sprouting a developing beer gut. Lunchtime drinking? Hypocrite, he thought. A pint of Adnam's would go down well after this lot.

Stuart was shuffling on the spot, looking embarrassed.

'I'm sure Mr Diamond and Mr Elderkin don't want to hear us quarrelling, Keith. I'll tell you all the details later,' she said dismissively.

Gage's upper lip curled. 'We'll discuss it now. How much do you charge?' he snarled at them, then turning to Pamela, 'Have you asked how much this will cost? Knowing you, probably not.'

Frank moved forward. 'If we decide to take the case, which I hope we will, Mrs Gage will be told our terms, and before we start investigating, she'll have to sign a form agreeing to them.'

'Got her all sewn up, haven't you?'

'Mrs Gage will be able to make a decision, and if she finds the terms too costly, she can decide not to go ahead with the investigation. The total cost will depend on how long we take to find the thief, and how many detectives work on the case.'

'Hear that, Pamela,' Gage fumed. 'They could take months, they'll rip you off.'

Frank had had enough. 'We have a reputation for quick and successful resolutions to our cases, unlike *solicitors*, whose general reputations are the opposite, so I've heard.'

Gage looked ready to kill him, Stuart looked nervous, but Pamela laughed out loud. 'That's told you, Keith.'

Gage stood there, hands clenching and unclenching. Would he gnash his teeth, Frank wondered?

'You'll be late for your lunch appointment. Aldeburgh Golf Club?' Pamela asked.

'Thorpeness,' he snarled, turned, and strode out, slamming the door behind him.

Frank wasn't sure what to say.

Pamela waved a hand. 'Don't pay any attention to him. If I had time, I'd divorce him, but he might try and get hold of part of the business. I ought to consult a solicitor!' She threw back her head, her laughter loud and genuine.

Frank joined in; Stuart looked gobsmacked.

'I think we should be leaving,' Frank said.

'I hope that's not put you off. I'll make sure he doesn't interfere if you take the case.'

'Why is your husband so against the investigation?'

Her face hardened. 'Confidentially, he doesn't do a lot of business now. At one time the practice was rolling along nicely, although a country solicitor will never make a fortune, farmers are too canny. He'd like to turn the gardens into a theme park and get rid of the nursery.'

'Really?' If Gage was short of cash, or wanted to destroy the nursery, was he a possible suspect? He didn't think Pamela had thought of that.

# Chapter Four

Laurel placed her dessert spoon onto the dish; there was a smear of custard and a few crumbs left. 'Goodness me, Mabel, that was delicious. I've eaten far too much. I'll never be able to run round the tennis court at this rate.'

'Going for another coaching session with the handsome Carlton?' Frank asked.

She smiled and shrugged her shoulders, pleased at the tone of his voice.

The partners of The Anglian Detective Agency were enjoying lunch around the dining table in Greyfriars House.

'I'm glad you liked it, Laurel. It's a bit since I've made that pudding,' Mabel said.

'What did you say it was called?' Laurel asked.

'Ipswich almond pudding, it's an old eighteenth-century recipe.'

'I can't remember you making that since I've known you,' Stuart said, rubbing his stomach. 'I hope you won't wait as long to make it again, it was lovely.'

'Is that *knowing* in the biblical sense, Stuart?' Frank asked.

Mabel threw her napkin at him.

Over lunch, Frank and Stuart told the rest of the team about the goings-on at Yoxford Manor Gardens.

'Do we need a formal meeting to agree if we should take the case?' Frank asked.

'Sounds right up your street,' Laurel said, 'you'll be able to demonstrate your vast knowledge of horticulture.'

He gave her a dark look.

'Did you meet Keith Gage?' Dorothy asked.

'Yes, don't you remember me saying?' Stuart said.

'That must have been when I went to the front door. It was only the postman with a parcel. What did you make of Mr Gage?'

'I didn't like him,' Stuart replied. 'Mrs Gage said if she'd time, she'd divorce him – fancy coming out with that.'

Dorothy tapped her nose. 'My grapevine tells me he's in trouble financially, people have stopped consulting him, he's developed a drink problem, and he's unreliable.'

'They usually go hand in hand,' Mabel said.

'So, can I have everyone's agreement?' Frank asked.

There were nods and yeses all round.

'Who's going to be involved with the case?' Laurel asked.

'I'd like to take this one on,' Frank said.

'That's cos he's got a crush on Pamela Gage,' Stuart said, chortling as he started to pack his pipe with tobacco.

'I thought you were giving that awful thing up,' Mabel said.

'I've cut down to just one pipe a day, I like a pipe after a meal, especially when it's so delicious.'

'Silver-tongued devil,' Mabel said, starting to pack up the plates.

'Pamela Gage is far too old for you, Frank, she must be nearer my age. And she's married,' Dorothy said.

'I've always been drawn to mature women, they have so much more to offer than those under forty: wisdom, experience and they're usually grateful for my attentions.'

'You can be disgusting at times, Frank Diamond,' Laurel said.

'It's better than baby-snatching. How old is Carlton? Ten years your junior, I think.'

Heat suffused her face. 'He's my tennis coach, not my lover, and there's only nine years' difference.'

'Goodness, is he that old? He doesn't look thirty.'

'I'm not thirty-nine I'm only thirty-three, and he's twenty-four. Anyway, it's irrelevant, I'm not interested in him in that way.'

'What about him, though? Word's got back he's taken a shine to you,' Dorothy said. 'He's a good-looking man, best pair of legs I've seen in a long time.'

'Dorothy Piff,' Mabel exclaimed, 'I thought you were past all that.'

'Well, you aren't. Why should I be? Nancy Whittle took me there as a guest, so I sat on the veranda and had a good gawp at all the men. Thoroughly enjoyed it. Do they have a bowling green at the Country Club? I might find a sprightly nonagenarian with a pair of reasonable pins.'

Frank rapped the table with his spoon. 'Stop! This is getting out of hand. Going back to the case of the stolen plants, I think perhaps it might be best to wait and find out what Judge Hanmer wants before we decide on who does what.' He looked at Dorothy. 'Shall we take a break, as he's not coming until three?'

She nodded. 'Yes, it'll give us time to either relax or take some exercise and work off our splendid lunch,' she said.

'I'll take Bumper for a walk. Anyone like to come with me?' Laurel asked.

'I'll keep you company,' Frank said.

'Don't forget,' Mabel said, 'there's only sandwiches for supper; Stuart and I are going into Aldeburgh, I'm going to Matt's grave, then we're off to see *The Poseidon Adventure*. After that we're meeting Ethel and Tom at The Cross Keys. We'll be late in, Dorothy.'

'*The Poseidon Adventure*? What kind of film is that?' Laurel asked.

'Disaster movie,' Stuart said, putting his dead pipe onto an ashtray. 'Ship on its way to New York capsizes.'

'There'll be some cat-calls from the fishing folk, if it's a load of bollocks,' Frank said.

'It sounds like a good night out; give my regards to Ethel and Tom. How's the chip shop doing?' Laurel asked.

'It's doing well. They haven't changed anything,' Mabel said, looking sad.

'You'd a winning formula, Mabel,' Stuart said, 'the best fish and chips I've ever eaten. Perhaps we can nip in for a bite before the film.'

31

'Stuart Elderkin, we're taking sandwiches with us and a Thermos of coffee; we can eat them in the car before the film. If you don't watch it, you'll need a new set of clothes, size ginormous.'

Frank got up from the table. 'Ready, Laurel?' His green eyes smiled at her.

'Yes, let's get some fresh air. Where shall we go? Through the woods to the heath?'

'I fancy some air directly off the North Sea.'

'We'll make for the beach and walk towards Southwold.'

A brisk easterly wind scudded white-topped waves towards the shore. Bumper plunged into the sea, chasing his blue ball. She wished Frank wouldn't throw it so far, she always worried Bumper would miss it and he'd keep swimming towards the horizon. She knew it was a groundless worry as he'd never missed a ball and was a strong swimmer, but she loved him and needed his unwavering love for her. He was one male who didn't change his mind.

Bumper turned back, the ball in his mouth, and paddled vigorously towards them. He surged out of the water, ignoring Frank and dropping the ball at Laurel's feet; she swiftly picked it up. 'Quick, get back, Frank,' she shouted, as Bumper shook his body from head to tail, spray arcing the air. They both laughed, scrambling away from him. Tail lashing, Bumper danced around them.

'God, that dog's a tonic. He should be prescribed for depression,' Frank said. He pointed to the ball. 'Shall I chuck it again?'

'No, I think he's wet enough. Let's walk and he can dry off before we go back.'

Frank glanced at his watch. 'We're OK, plenty of time.'

'I think we ought to change before Judge Hanmer arrives. Have you got any spare clothes at Greyfriars? Or will you need to go back to your cottage?'

Laurel, Stuart and Mabel all lived with Dorothy, but Frank remained at his cliff cottage overlooking Minsmere beach.

'I think I've got a spare pair of trousers somewhere, probably in Stuart's wardrobe. They'll have to do.'

Whatever Frank wore, he looked good. He was one of those infuriating people on whom even the cheapest clothes hung well. She looked at him, the wind lifting his dark hair, his green eyes glinting dangerously. What woman wouldn't be attracted to him?

It was never the right time. When she was the Senior Mistress at Blackfriars School and Frank was the detective inspector on the Susan Nicholson murder case, she was more than ready to turn their friendship into something deeper, but at that time Frank wasn't sexually attracted to her. Then, things changed. When she'd been involved with Oliver Neave, Frank seemed to find her more attractive. How serious was he about his current girlfriend? What was her name? Emma.

She'd started getting that delicious pain under her ribs again whenever she saw him. It was so frustrating. If only she knew what he really felt. He seemed reluctant to make a firm commitment to any woman. She'd seen him with his girlfriend at a pub in Aldeburgh, but he hadn't seen her. The girl was the antithesis of her, petite, with dark hair, cut like Audrey Hepburn. In fact, she looked a lot like her, with enormous brown eyes, high cheekbones and a slim, almost breastless figure. Also, she was beautifully turned out in a chic black dress, with a rope of pearls adding to the sophisticated look. Then the pain under her ribs had been sharp and unpleasant. Worse, Frank looked entranced, his eyes never leaving the girl's face as she chattered to him, pausing to smile into his eyes.

She'd have to settle for his friendship. That would have to be enough. They also had their professional relationship; they worked well together, as did all the team.

Frank had run ahead, Bumper chasing after him. They turned and raced back to her, Bumper leaping up, trying to wrest the blue ball from her hands.

'You've put him in a skittish mood. Come here, you tyke.' She waved the lead at him. He stood his ground. 'Bumper!' He gave up and slowly moved into grabbing distance.

'Time to go back? I needed that fresh air. I feel invigorated,' Frank said.

'You didn't look tired when we started.'

'You're no good at reading me, are you, Laurel?'

'I can read you're set for an argument. Don't spoil a good walk.' The pesky man always looked as fresh as a daisy, whatever time of day or night it was, even if he had had about an hour's sleep. Was he right? Didn't she understand him? He could be enigmatic at times. What did his remark mean? Or was she giving too much weight to any words he spoke?

Laurel came down the stairs at Greyfriars House and went into the dining room. Dorothy was busying herself setting out the table ready for the meeting with Judge Hanmer. 'You're obviously out to impress him,' she said, waving at the five places, each set with blotting paper, pencil, a sheet of blank A4 paper and a glass; a jug of water was in the centre. 'We don't usually have all this for an initial meeting.'

'You're a fine one to talk, dressed up to the nines. Or were you trying to impress Frank?'

She'd changed into a grey suit, twisted her hair into a chignon and added another three inches to her five foot eleven with a pair of black court shoes.

'The Judge has only seen me in shorts bashing a tennis ball. I thought I'd better show him my professional side.'

Dorothy smiled. 'You look very elegant and quite formidable.'

Was that the impression she wanted to give? Perhaps to the Judge, but would Frank compare her to his diminutive girlfriend and be happy he was going out with someone he could put his arms round, and not be afraid she'd wrestle him to the ground if he got fresh? 'Thank you, Dorothy. You don't look too shabby yourself.'

Dorothy had put on her best tweed suit and an immaculate white blouse. 'I just hope Frank comes up to scratch.'

If only, she thought.

Stuart bumbled in. 'My word, you both look . . . er, not sure how to describe you.'

'Try,' Dorothy said, 'but be very careful.'

34

Stuart blew out his cheeks. 'I never get it right. How about efficient? I would say tasty, but I'm not sure how you'd take that.'

'Efficient but tasty. I think that's a description more fitting for beans on toast,' Dorothy said.

Stuart groaned. 'Women! We men can never say the right thing.'

Mabel bustled in. 'We need to leave at four, Stuart. Do you think you'll be finished by then?'

'Goodness, I hope so,' Dorothy said. 'I can't imagine Mr Hanmer will have that much to tell us. It is only a preliminary meeting.'

'Where's Frank?' Laurel asked. 'It's five to three, the Judge will be here any minute.'

'He's sprucing himself up in our room,' Stuart said.

'Well, I wish he'd get a move on, he hasn't told us what the Judge said on the phone,' Laurel said.

'He did tell me this morning, on our way back from the gardens. Not much, as far as I can remember.'

'Talk of the devil,' Dorothy said as Frank entered the room.

'Wow! I think we can ask for top fees looking at you lot,' he said.

He'd changed his jeans for black flared trousers, and under his leather jacket he wore an open-necked shirt with an extravagant collar. 'Do I look trendy enough?' he asked, but in a tone that suggested he wasn't concerned by their replies.

'I think our dress reflects our different personalities and suggests we're not cut from the same cloth,' Dorothy said. 'Oh, I think I've made a joke!'

They all laughed. These were the moments Laurel loved, when they were a tight-knit group, different but the same.

'If everyone will take a seat, I'll go over my conversation with the Judge.'

'You'd better hurry up, he'll be here in two minutes,' Laurel said, as she sat down next to him.

'I assure you, I only need one minute. He said he'd like to talk to us about a problem he has, but wouldn't say what it was. I asked him how he'd heard of us and he said his friend, Pamela Gage, had told him she was hoping we'd help her; it seems they're old friends.

That's it. I suggested we visit him at Thorpeness, it's always good to see the environment of a client, if possible, but he said definitely not. He didn't want anyone to know he might be employing us. That suggests the problem lies in Thorpeness itself.'

'What was his tone like?' Laurel asked.

'I thought he sounded deeply worried, and uncertain if he was doing the right thing consulting us. He did say he wasn't sure if there was a problem, that he might be worrying for nothing, but he needed to check and he might want us to investigate someone.'

'Intriguing. I'm looking forward to hearing what he's got to say,' Laurel said.

'Right,' Mabel said. 'You don't need me, do you? I'm off to the kitchen. I'll set out a tea tray if he wants a cuppa, and I'll leave sandwiches on the table under a basin.' She poked Stuart in the shoulder. 'Four o'clock prompt. I'm going to have a bath and change. Looking at you lot, I think I'd better pull out all the stops tonight. You'll be bowled over when you see me, Stuart.'

He got up and hugged her. 'So, I'm in for a treat?'

'Play your cards right and it could be your lucky night!'

Stuart flushed. 'Mabel!'

'I meant I might pay for the cinema. What did you think I meant?'

'Mabel Elderkin, you are a tart of the first water. Kindly remove yourself before the Judge arrives,' Frank said.

Mabel came into the dining room in her best coat. 'It's quarter to four, Stuart. We'll have to go soon. Jim's cut me some lovely flowers for Matt's grave.' Jim McFall was the gardener and he also helped with the cooking on Mabel's days off. 'What's happened to the Judge?' she continued.

Frank looked up from doodling on his piece of blotting paper. 'I don't know, but I think I'll give him a ring.'

Stuart got up. 'Do you mind if I leave? You can tell me what he has to say, if he turns up.'

Laurel glanced at Frank, who nodded. 'No, you get off.' She turned to Frank. 'You did give him clear instructions on how to get here?'

36

Frank gave her a hard look.

'Sorry, I remember you said he knew where Greyfriars House was.'

'Correct.'

'Come on, Stuart, let's make a move. See you all later,' Mabel said.

Dorothy looked over the rim of her spectacles. 'We'll all be in bed by the time you two get back from carousing in The Cross Keys.'

'That's all right. Get your coat, Stuart. There's a nippy east wind. See you all tomorrow.'

Stuart sheepishly waved goodbye.

'Have you got his number, Dorothy? I did give you his address and telephone number,' Frank said.

'Of course.' She went to a filing cabinet and drew out a sheet of paper from a grey file and passed it to Frank.

He went to the telephone on his desk and dialled.

Laurel studied his face. There was a frown between his eyebrows. He put the phone down. 'He's not answering.'

'He could be on his way,' Laurel said.

'I can't sit here twiddling my thumbs any longer,' Dorothy said. 'I'm going to type up some invoices and I've a few letters I need to answer.'

Laurel didn't fancy sitting around. 'What should we do, Frank?'

'Let's take Bumper into the garden for fifteen minutes, get some fresh air. If he hasn't appeared by then, I'll ring again.'

'And if he doesn't answer?'

'I think I'll drive over to Thorpeness, and check if he's all right.'

'Why? Are you worried?'

'The man I talked to on the phone didn't seem like someone who wouldn't keep an appointment.'

'What will you do if he's there and he's decided he doesn't want to consult us?'

'I'll tell him his manners are appalling, he's wasted our time, so he'll be receiving a bill from our administrator.'

'Jolly good,' said Dorothy. 'Serves him right.'

Laurel looked at Frank. 'If you go to see him, I'm coming with you.'

'Why? Are you afraid I can't handle a crusty old judge?'

'I thought we could pay a visit to the Country Club, afterwards. Have a drink, perhaps.'

'Hoping to bump into the handsome Carlton?'

'It would be good to see you side by side, then I could decide who I prefer.'

Frank looked as though he wanted to strangle her. 'I'm spoken for, Laurel, so you'd be wasting your time.'

The pain below her ribs was sharp.

# Chapter Five

It was approaching six as they neared Thorpeness. Frank eased his foot off the accelerator. 'I think it would be better if we went to the public car park, rather than making for the Judge's house. If it's been a simple mistake about the time, or date, and he still wants us to take the case, he won't be impressed if we make it obvious we're in contact with him.'

'That's sensible,' Laurel replied.

The sky was darkening, grey clouds rolling in from the east and rain spattered onto the windscreen. 'Should have brought a coat,' Frank said. 'Have you got one?'

'On the back seat.'

The House in the Sky came into view. Once a disguised water tower, now turned into a place to live. 'Why don't I check on the Judge and you wait in the car?' Laurel said.

'What's the thinking behind that?'

'As I visit the Country Club frequently, if I was seen near the Judge's house, it wouldn't look as strange as the two of us being there.'

Frank turned the Avenger into the car park and chose a spot at the far end. 'No. We'll both go.'

'Why? Isn't my suggestion sensible?'

He switched off the engine. 'It is, Laurel, but I think we'll both go.' If something was wrong, he didn't want her facing it alone.

'Don't you think I can deal with him?'

'I spoke to him on the telephone, I think it would be better if

I was there. He'll probably have seen you on the tennis courts, it might be confusing for him.'

She gave him a sulky look.

'Right, let's make a move before these spots turn into a shower.'

'You'll probably get soaked,' she said, sounding pleased.

'Good for the complexion, I'm told.'

She opened the passenger door and pulled a raincoat from the back seat, struggling as she tried to put it on. He took hold of the collar and eased her into it. The heat of her body and the floral perfume she often wore made him take in a sharp breath. Her flirty remark before they left had angered him. It was always the same. Encouraging words, then the cold shoulder. He'd had enough of that.

'At least it's not far to his house,' she said, walking ahead, 'there's a path to the right of the car park that leads into The Dunes.'

'We don't want to go onto the beach.'

She laughed. 'Silly! The Dunes is a short road just before The Benthills.'

He hated all the twee names, he didn't know the village well, but he'd never been into *Peter Pan* and Never-Never Land. What could you expect from the son of a rabid trade unionist? There'd been no Enid Blyton, or Peter Rabbit books in their house; best you could expect was a copy of the *Beano*.

A row of six houses looked out over the beach and the North Sea. 'I thought he lived in a bungalow?' The house was impressive; a row of railed steps led up from the garden to the front door. To the left and below was a balcony sheltered by an overhanging roof which was supported by white pillars. He thought the many-paned windows, some set into the tiled roof, others in the weather-boarded walls, must make the interior of the house light. 'Not bad for a holiday home.'

'You should see some of the other houses in the village,' Laurel said. 'The whole place is incredible.'

'Built by the rich for the rich,' he muttered.

'Oh, come on, Frank, the village was built before the First World War.'

'I read somewhere it was meant to be exclusive. What was it? It would never be "vulgarised by a pier", or open to "nose-bag trippers".'

'That was then, this is now. We had lots of lovely family holidays here, and we're certainly not an upper-class family.'

'True, must be my father's influence, and I can't have that.'

'His house is the second one from here.'

'No lights on in the first one. Looks deserted.'

'It's early in the year, most of them are holiday lets.'

They walked up The Benthills, rain starting in earnest, driven in by the easterly wind. Waves were racing up the beach and a few lonely gulls were heading south, looking for an overnight roost.

'Sure this is it?' Frank asked.

'Yes.'

'No sign of a light on this side. What's on the other?'

'The back of the house faces westwards onto part of the Country Club. It's known as The Wilderness, just rough ground planted with pines and gorse.'

'Let's explore,' Frank said, opening the garden gate and running up the stairs to the front door, Laurel following him.

He knocked and waited. Then he tried the door handle. It was locked. He knocked louder.

'Perhaps he's at the Country Club. He sometimes eats there, I've seen him,' Laurel said.

He signalled for her to join him under the porch, which at least gave them some protection from the rain.

'Why don't you nip along to the Club and check? If he's there, don't say anything to him. Come back and we'll go home. I'll try and contact him tomorrow.'

'I can't go in there looking like this, it would look suspicious.'

'Afraid the handsome Carlton will see you looking like a drowned rat?'

She glared at him. 'You have a charming way with words. What will *you* do?'

'I'll go round the back, so people can't see me. Not that there are many around, especially in this weather.'

41

She turned on her heels, ran down the steps, and turned left towards the Club.

Frank followed, but made his way to the back of the house. A tamarisk hedge separated the back garden from The Wilderness beyond, it was as Laurel had described: pines, gorse and broom, which was already in flower, the heady smell of one bush, close to the hedge, was strong, even through the rain.

He knocked on the back door and waited, pressing close to it to try and avoid the rain, although the house was sheltering him from the worst of the weather. He pressed an ear to the door. No sounds. He tried the handle. It turned and he stepped into a scullery with butler's sink and cupboards; a pair of wellingtons sat neatly beneath a short row of hooks. An old, rubberised coat hung on one, on another a cross-over apron. Did they both belong to the Judge?

From the scullery he stepped into a small kitchen. It was well equipped with modern stove, fridge and rows of cupboards lining the walls. Everything was well organised and spotlessly clean, but the air smelt stale. On the table in the centre of the room was a Pyrex bowl covering something on a plate. Beside it was a note – 'Salad in the fridge. Mrs H.' – He lifted the bowl up. The smell of decay escaped into the air. Triangles of bread, the edges curling up, revealed dried-up cheese on one sandwich and greenish-tinged ham on the other. His stomach tightened and adrenalin surged through his body. This was not good. He looked round and took a tea towel hanging from a hook near the fridge.

The inside kitchen door was shut. He moved carefully towards it and, using the tea towel, he grasped the rounded brass handle and turned it, slowly easing the door open. Beyond was a hall. The light was dim, but he could make out, on the far side, a wooden stand, with a square, bevelled mirror; a red scarf hung from a hook, and below there was a container for umbrellas and sticks. He stepped out and nearly tripped over something at the foot of the stairs. It was soft and gave in to his foot.

He leapt back. The Judge? Who else could it be? Get a grip. He slowed down his breathing rate and, carefully circumventing the body, found the light switch. An opaque glass lampshade focused a circle of yellow light onto a grotesquely twisted body. A large, black insect – a cockroach? – scuttled from near the body and disappeared under a skirting board. He flinched. He remembered having to handle a live one in a zoology practical; its greasy smell and slippery body revolted him.

The body was lying face down, the upper part resting on a patterned, red wool runner, arms twisted above his head, as though he were trying to fend off the dragon woven into the carpet. His legs were bent, one foot in its brogue shoe caught on the first step of the stairs, the other twisted under his body. He was wearing a tweed jacket and cavalry twill trousers.

He knew it was pointless, but he placed two fingers against the Judge's neck. Not only was there no pulse, but the skin was as cold as a long-dead eel, and had the same texture, slimy with incipient putrefaction. Was this an accident? One of those many domestic deaths that occurred with such regularity throughout the nation? Or was this death caused by the person the Judge was worried about? There was only one way of finding out. Where was the telephone?

There was a tentative knock at the back door. God, Laurel. He'd momentarily forgotten all about her. He turned and went back into the kitchen. The back door was slowly opening.

'Frank?' she whispered. 'He's not at the Club.'

He put the kitchen light on.

'What are you doing? He might come back.'

He pulled the door fully open.

Eyes wide, she stared at him. 'No!'

'I'm afraid so. I'm going to ring Nick Revie when I find the phone.'

'He's dead?'

'Someone is, and I presume it's the Judge.'

'How? Please don't tell me he was murdered?'

'Come and look for yourself. Try not to touch anything. Could be an accident, looks like he fell down the stairs.'

Her eyes welled.

43

'Sorry, there's no need for you to see him.' He pulled out a kit-chen chair. 'Sit down for a bit.'

She brushed past him. 'I *am* a detective,' she muttered.

He followed her back into the hall. She stood at a distance to the body, her head moving as she took in the details. 'He fell very awk-wardly,' she said. 'He couldn't have banged the back of his skull; the way his arms are above his head suggests he tried to save himself.'

'They're well above the body, almost looks as though he dived down the stairs,' Frank said.

'Have you turned him over?'

'No, I thought it better to leave that to the pathologist.'

'Hope it's Martin Ansell,' Laurel said.

'Ah, another of your fan club.'

'This is not the time for scoring cheap points, Frank.' She was reverting to teacher mode.

'Sorry, but a bit of humour helps at a time like this. Let's find the phone.'

She pointed to a small table beyond the hall stand.

Laurel looked out of the uncurtained window in the Judge's sitting room. Frank was on the phone talking to Dorothy and explaining he and Laurel probably wouldn't be back for dinner. He sounded calm, even a little bored, although she knew that wasn't the case. He was dying to turn over the corpse, rifle through his pockets, but he wasn't a detective inspector any more, and he wouldn't want to rile Revie and whoever was the pathologist.

He came into the room. 'Laurel, keep an eye out for Revie, I don't think he'll be here for at least another half an hour, if he's pick-ing up Ansell.'

'Why? What are you going to do?'

'I thought I'd just snoop around.' He waved the tea towel at her. 'I'll make sure I don't mess up any prints, but I'm afraid I left some on the back door, and you must have done, too.'

'You'll never change, will you?'

44

'Do you want me to?'

'What does that mean?'

He shrugged. 'I'm not sure, pay no attention to me. Are you all right staying here? You could take my car and go back to Greyfriars. I'm sure I can get Revie, or whoever's driving, to give me a lift back to Minsmere.'

'No way. I want to be here when they arrive. I'm not going to spend a sleepless night wondering what you learnt, and having to wait until tomorrow to find out.'

He shrugged. 'OK. In that case give a shout when you see a car's headlight, then I can race back and look innocent.'

'I think you're asking too much of yourself, Frank. Anyway, I'm coming with you. I'm not sitting here like a wallflower at the Palais de Dance.'

'You a wallflower? I don't believe it.'

'If all the men were below five feet ten, I can tell you it's happened.'

'Come on then, let's look at the landing and the rooms upstairs.'

'They're here!' Laurel pointed out of an upstairs window. The storm had eased, just a few clouds moving slowly across the face of the moon. The lights of two slowly approaching vehicles shone through the descending night, the driver in the front vehicle no doubt looking for the right house. They ran down the staircase, making sure they kept to the side and didn't touch the walls.

'We shouldn't have done that, Frank. Revie's bound to guess. He knows you too well.'

'Especially as we didn't find anything interesting. Certainly, I couldn't see any reason for him to fall. The stair carpet is in good nick, there doesn't seem to be any objects he could have tripped over and his shoelaces were firmly tied.'

'I suppose he could have had a heart attack, or just missed his footing. It happens.'

They went to the front door. Frank slid back the Yale lock,

secured it, and opened the door. Backlit by the light of a full moon were the silhouettes of three men. One short and squat, the second tall and slim, the third in between.

'You're standing there like a pair of vultures,' Revie said as he barrelled up the wooden steps, dressed in his usual Gannex raincoat and trilby.

She was pleased to see Martin Ansell, the pathologist, behind him, carrying a large black leather bag; following them was Detective Constable Johnny Cottam, who smiled and waved. She waved back.

'Laurel, stop flirting with Cottam. I know you're used to seeing dead bodies, but show some respect. Right, where is it?'

She shuddered. *It*. Once dead, and in the hands of the police, the victim lost all individuality, and became something to look at and explore, until the cause of death had been established. It was only a few days ago she'd seen the Judge having a drink as he watched the tennis. She'd never spoken to him, but he was a tall, distinguished man, with a quiet manner. Carlton disliked him. He wouldn't say why. In fact, she thought it was more than dislike, the way he talked about him bordered on hate. She hoped the Judge's death was accidental. She didn't want to tell anyone her thoughts about Carlton. She liked him, and he was certainly attractive to look at, as well as being a good coach.

They led Revie into the hall and pointed to the body.

Revie turned his small blue eyes onto both of them. 'What have you found?'

'What do you mean?' Frank said, looking puzzled.

'Don't give me that. You wouldn't be able to help yourself. Once a cop always a cop.'

Frank raised his hands in submission. 'We were careful, didn't touch the corpse, didn't turn him over. We haven't found anything suspicious, although there is nothing obvious that caused him to fall.'

'I should hope you didn't touch it,' said Ansell, shaking his head, making his long, floppy hair sway from side to side. 'Right, I'll deal with the body. I presume, Inspector Revie, you'll want to snoop around.'

'Snoop? You mean investigate. I want the time of death and anything else you can tell us. If it's an accident, I'm wasting my time here. I've got enough on my plate without being involved in old men falling downstairs.'

Sometimes Laurel wanted to throw a brick at him.

He took off his coat and hat, hanging them on the hall stand, and smoothed back his wavy hair. 'Cottam, take statements from these two, save dragging them to Leiston Police Station.' He marched into the living room.

Cottam gave a wry smile. 'He was about to go home when you rang. He's not in the best of humours,' he whispered. 'Where do you suggest we go?'

'The kitchen?' Frank asked. 'There are a few very stale sandwiches, perhaps Inspector Revie would like one. Hopefully they'd give him food poisoning.'

Cottam laughed.

'No levity,' Revie shouted. 'The corpse might hear you.'

Ansell tut-tutted as he opened his bag and took out a thermometer.

Laurel put down her biro after signing her statement; Frank had finished his statement a few minutes earlier and was drumming his fingers on the kitchen table. Irritating man!

'Well, Dr Ansell, have you finished? Do I need to send for the photographers?' Revie said from the hall.

There was a long silence.

'Come on, man, spit it out.'

Frank jerked his head. 'Let's join in.'

Laurel's chest contracted. Was this more than a domestic accident? They crowded into the hall. Revie was sitting astride a chair taken from the sitting room, looking more interested than before. 'What do you two want?'

'Mr Hanmer was a potential client; if there is something wrong, I think we need to know,' she said. 'That is if you don't mind, Nick.' She gave him her best smile.

He scratched his chin. 'You might as well hear what he's going to say. I have some sympathy for you: another client bites the dust. What is it with you two? Were you bluebottles in a former life? If there's a corpse within five miles, one of you will find it.'

Laurel bit back the comment she wanted to make, and managed a smile.

Revie looked pleased. 'Ready to tell us?' he asked Ansell.

Ansell levered up his long frame. 'I'll need to get Judge Hanmer back to the mortuary, before I can be completely sure, but there are certain facts I'm not happy about.'

Revie's head shot up and he eyeballed Ansell. 'Do I have to get the photographers and the fingerprint wallahs out here, or not? Don't waste my time, tell us what you think.'

'I calculate the time of death to be between eight and two, on Friday night and Saturday morning.'

Soon after he phoned Frank, Laurel thought.

'The most common cause of death when someone falls down the stairs is a head injury. The only external injury to the head I can find is a broken eye socket and some bruising to the chin. These injuries are more consistent to punching or kicking. There may be broken bones and more bruising, I'll see when I get him on the slab.'

Laurel shuddered.

'However, there may have been internal haemorrhagic shock from intra-abdominal and intra-thoracic visceral injuries and injuries to the neck—'

'Stop there,' Revie said. 'Translate, please.'

'You really should have mastered some basic anatomy by now, Inspector Revie.' Ansell smiled up at Laurel. 'I'm sure Miss Bowman understands.'

'She's not in charge of this murder case – I am.'

Ansell sighed. 'Briefly, I would have expected to see more external injuries if he fell the entire length of the stairs. The way his body is . . . arranged, suggests he fell from a height. However, when I perform the autopsy, I may discover he died from internal bleeding when vital organs were injured by the fall.'

Revie grunted. 'Any more?'

48

'Yes. The parietal and temporal bones of the skull are the ones most frequently fractured in head injury cases. A superficial examination doesn't suggest that. However, there could be cerebral oedema and subdural haematoma – swelling and bleeding of the brain.' He paused.

'So, he wasn't murdered?'

'Oh, I think he was.'

Laurel's stomach contracted, and Frank grasped her arm. She glanced at him. His green eyes were concentrated on Ansell's face.

'I think he was attacked, thrown down the stairs and then finished off.'

'How?' she gasped.

'There are signs of cyanosis on the face, the skin coloured by the red blood cells, and there are haemorrhages in the eyes. I'll have to do more tests, but I think the murderer realised he hadn't killed him, and so he, or she, smothered him.'

She clasped a hand to her mouth. 'Like poor Sam Harrop!' A murder victim in their first big case.

'Exactly,' Ansell replied, 'but not as skilfully. We're not dealing with a professional killer, but nevertheless, a dangerous murderer, if I'm correct.'

She'd never known him not to be correct. If only they knew who the person was the Judge had wanted them to make enquiries about. And were they the murderer?

# Chapter Six

In Aldeburgh, Ann Pemberton glanced at the kitchen clock. Four thirty, plenty of time for her to finish everything before Adam came home from work. She needed a cup of tea; should she take David one? The nagging doubt returned. What was the matter with him? He hadn't been like this for ages; he seemed to have suddenly reverted to the boy she'd met when she came to work for the Pembertons as their housekeeper. Seated at the table, a cup of tea in front of her, she remembered how impressed she'd been when she first saw the kitchen: smart new fridge, modern electric oven, plenty of drawers and cupboards for storage, *and* a larder. She'd been pleased about that; fridges were excellent, but there was nothing like a larder for storing preserves, fruit and vegetables.

She smiled ruefully. If someone had told her that one day she would no longer be Adam's employee, but his wife, and mistress of this large and elegant house, she would have told them they were a fool.

When she started work here, Adam was married to the beautiful Carol, and David was a disturbed and silent boy. Then David ran away from home when he was thirteen, was missing for two years; then found and rescued, mainly through the bravery and ingenuity of Laurel Bowman, a member of The Anglian Detective Agency; Adam had divorced the unfaithful Carol, and David had blossomed.

She'd picked him up from their house in Thorpeness the previous afternoon. They'd bought it the year before, when a friend of Adam's had tipped him off it was coming onto the market. They'd bought it mainly because of David. He'd expressed a love of the village, and the house had a spacious front room, with a large window – ideal for his drawing and painting.

It was the second weekend they'd allowed him to have a few days there by himself. The first weekend had been a success; when he came back, he was chatty and thanked them for letting him have the time to himself.

What a strange little boy he'd been when she first came as house-keeper. He hardly talked; they didn't know he chose not to. She'd grown to love him, and was proud he'd confided in her. Then he ran away. He'd never said he loved her, but she hoped he did.

Yesterday they'd had lunch with one of Adam's solicitor friends in Ipswich.

'Can you drive over to Thorpeness and get David?' Adam asked when they got home. 'I need to sort out some papers for tomorrow. A solicitors' work is never done!'

She was pleased he'd asked, as she enjoyed driving; if they went out together, Adam always drove. She phoned David before she left to tell him she was on her way. She was surprised when he'd grunted and slammed the phone down.

When she arrived, he was sitting on the doorstep, his bag by his side. She waved and opened the passenger door. Head down, he strode to the car, threw the bag onto the back seat, and banged the door shut. What was the matter? He looked dreadful.

'I'm glad to see you, David. Did you have a good weekend?'

He didn't reply and didn't look at her, but out of the corner of her eye she saw him shaking his head. She decided to ignore his rude-ness. 'We had a lovely lunch in Ipswich. It was nice to have a break from cooking.'

'Don't you like cooking any more? Tired of us already?'

Her throat tightened. 'I love cooking for you and your father. It's the one thing I'm good at. It gives me a lot of pleasure when I see both of you have enjoyed a meal I've made. It makes me feel I'm worth something.'

He groaned.

What was the matter with the boy? What had happened to make him act like this? Perhaps he was unhappy with something he'd been working on; his art meant so much to him. Or was he beginning to resent her? He'd seemed pleased when they told him they would marry; perhaps his father should have talked to him first, made sure he was happy to have a stepmother, but Adam hadn't thought it necessary. 'The boy adores you,' he'd said. She thought that was rather strong, David adored her puddings, but did he think a middle-aged plain Jane was a suitable substitute for his mother, the beautiful Carol? But David had hated his mother for being unfaithful to his father. Did he still feel the same now, or was he missing her love and her belief in him as an artist?

David's place at the dining table was empty as they ate dinner.

'Is the boy ill?' Adam asked.

'I don't think so.'

'Did you ask him if he felt sick?'

'No, I didn't.'

Adam wiped his moustache with a napkin, and helped himself to another spoonful of fish pie. 'Well, he's missed a most delicious supper, my dear. How did you manage to produce this so quickly?'

'It's the magic of the freezer.'

Adam laughed.

She forked up her last prawn. 'I'm worried about David, Adam. He's not himself, and I don't think he's ill. I'm sure he would have told me if he was.'

Adam put down his cutlery. 'What do you think is the matter? He's been on top form lately. He's loved going to Thorpeness, and I must say – that latest painting! Well, I don't claim to know much about art, but I thought it was jolly good. Do you think this is just teenage behaviour? One reads so much about it nowadays. At least he doesn't go around with one of those dreadful transistor radios glued to his ear. The slang used nowadays! They call them "trannies" and I hear them talking about "deejays" and asking for a "mensch" on one of their deplorable shows.'

'He's only seventeen, I suppose that's possible.' She put a hand over her stomach, feeling the pain of incipient indigestion. 'I haven't seen him like this for ages; in fact I'm not sure I've ever seen him like this.'

'Ann, you're frightening me. I'd better go up and see him. I thought he was just in one of those moods when he wants to be alone. Although he wasn't like that after the first time he'd been by himself in Thorpeness. He was pleased we'd trusted him; I think he felt quite grown up.' He half-rose from the table.

She put a hand on his arm. 'No, don't go to him, Adam. I have a feeling you might make him worse.'

He frowned at her. 'I am his father, Ann.'

'Yes, and I know I'm not his mother, but . . .'

He placed his hand over hers. 'He loves you, I'm certain, and you were the one he opened up to before he ran away.'

Her chest loosened, and she grasped his hand. 'I'm not sure what's happened to him, but when I went to Thorpeness and saw his face, my heart stopped. He looked as though the bottom had dropped out of his world. He seemed in utter misery.'

'My God. What should we do?'

'I'm not sure, Adam. Let's leave him for tonight and then when you've gone to work tomorrow, I'll see if I can get him to talk to me.'

Adam went to bed with a new book from *Reader's Digest*, saying he was sure he wouldn't be able to sleep. She'd tidied up an already tidy kitchen and on her way to their bedroom she stopped outside David's door. The light was off, but she thought she heard sobbing. Her heart shrank. She wanted to go in and comfort him, but she was afraid to. He still didn't like people touching him. She must be patient and hope tomorrow he'd tell her what was wrong.

# Chapter Seven

Wednesday, 18 April, 1973

At Greyfriars, the members of the Agency were sitting round the dining-room table at a late-morning meeting, going over what had happened at Thorpeness on Monday. Laurel could see the rest of the team felt as she did; shocked by the possible murder of Judge Hanmer. 'If only he'd confided in you, Frank.'

He looked at her, his green eyes as hard as emeralds. 'That might not have prevented his death, but at least we'd be able to give more information to Nick Revie.'

Dorothy nodded. 'The timing seems to suggest the murderer knew the Judge was suspicious of him, and was afraid he was about to reveal . . .' She shook her head. 'Whatever he knew about him.'

'We'll turn you into a detective yet,' Stuart said, gazing longingly, as Dorothy lit up a cigarette. He fumbled in his jacket pocket and brought out a paper bag. 'Anyone like a Flying Saucer? They're lovely, a wafer full of sherbet.'

'No, thanks, Stuart,' Laurel said, holding back the comment she wanted to make; it wasn't her job to nag him.

Dorothy shook her head, and Laurel was surprised when Frank took one. 'Thanks, Stuart.'

Stuart beamed at him and popped one into his own mouth and proceeded to munch it.

Laurel inwardly squirmed. Since trying to give up his pipe, Stuart's consumption of various sweets had drastically increased. It was a good job Mabel was in the kitchen making coffee, or Stuart would have definitely received another tongue-lashing about increasing girth and extra weight being bad for the heart. Lungs or heart? Cancer or a stroke? Which one did he want to die from? What a conundrum.

Yesterday, Laurel and Frank had been at Leiston Police Station most of the day, going over their statements. The strong possibility the Judge had been murdered made Revie want their statements checked again. Dorothy had used the time to send Pamela Gage details of their fees and conditions, and Stuart had compiled a list of local plant nurseries. Even though it wasn't certain Pamela Gage would accept their proposal, Frank thought it was a safe bet, and it put them ahead of the game if she accepted. He thought it would be worthwhile checking the nurseries to find out if they'd had plants stolen.

The kitchen door swung open and Mabel bustled in with the coffee tray. 'My, what long faces. I thought we were all used to the shock of sudden deaths. It isn't as though any of you knew the Judge.'

Laurel bit her lip.

'Anyone who's been murdered deserves our mourning, even if we don't know them,' Frank said.

Laurel's stomach clenched. Oh, Frank, be careful.

Mabel paused as she put the tray on the table near Dorothy. 'Sorry, you're right. I expected everyone to mourn with me for Matt. I never met the Judge. I'd seen him around Aldeburgh. Never came in the chip shop. He seemed a bit of an aristocrat to me. I hope Nick can catch his killer. At least we're not involved in this murder, even if you two did find the body.'

Laurel glanced at Frank; she hoped he shared her feelings. She'd like to help in this case. Whoever did this was a coward. The Judge was frail, and lying at the bottom of the stairs, he was a husk of the elegant figure she'd seen at the Country Club, sitting on the terrace, sipping an aperitif as he watched the tennis players. Whenever Carlton saw him, his jaw tightened, nostrils flared and he looked as though he'd smelt something distasteful. After a few such incidents she'd asked him if he didn't like the Judge, and if so, why.

He'd looked at her, a scowl spoiling his handsome face. 'Why do you say that?'

'Whenever he appears you look as though you'd like to murder him.' Had she really said that?

'Chance would be a fine thing. I can't stand the man.' He leant closer. 'He's a raging poof. A dirty old faggot.'

This wasn't like Carlton. Although she didn't know him well, and they mostly talked about tennis – the best equipment to buy, tournaments Carlton was going to enter, and gossip about tennis stars – she'd never had him down as a bigot. This seemed personal. Had the Judge made a pass at him?

'I think you're being unfair to the Judge, Carlton. You shouldn't be so intolerant. I had a good friend when I was at college, Tony, he was gay. We aren't all made in the same mould.'

'Gay? What the hell does that mean?'

'You must have heard it used. It's another word for homosexuals, usually men; they prefer to be called gays rather than homos or other derogatory words. I do find your attitude offensive.'

Carlton looked shocked, but didn't reply.

She sighed. Would she have to tell Revie? Should she talk it over with Frank? Would Frank be glad to put Carlton into the deep end as a possible suspect? Surely, he wasn't that mean? After all, Frank wasn't a rival for her affections. If only!

Coffee was passed round as well as a plate of fairy cakes. Stuart gobbled one quickly and then eyed the last; it had green icing. 'Anyone want that one?' he asked, taking up the plate.

Laurel was tempted to take it, just to see the expression on his face and to help preserve his figure, but the green top looked poisonous.

'Thank you,' Frank said, snaffling the cake. Stuart looked shocked and then peeved.

Was Frank trying to save Stuart's life? He'd never shown a sweet tooth before. A Flying Saucer and now a slime-green bun?

Frank demolished the cake. 'Delicious, Mabel.'

'Thank you.' She looked puzzled.

'I hope we don't have to go back to Leiston Police Station to give our fingerprints,' Laurel said. 'It was a nuisance they couldn't do that yesterday.'

'Why was that?' Stuart asked.

'There wasn't anyone at the station who'd been trained. Revie said he'd phone today, he thought they may still have our prints from the David Pemberton case.'

'Surely they should have destroyed them – after all, you weren't the criminals?' Dorothy sounded miffed.

'You know what the police are like, they'll hang on to anything they think might be of use in the future,' Frank said. 'You never know, Laurel might take up cat-burglary – she's got the strength and nerve to scale up walls and dance across roofs.'

In the silence that followed this remark they stared at each other; Stuart gazed at the empty plate, Dorothy lit another cigarette, Frank drummed his fingers on the table and Mabel took a deep breath and then noisily expelled it.

'Laurel,' Frank said, 'can you think of anyone at the Country Club who disliked Mr Hanmer?'

Her stomach contracted and guilt suffused her brain. If she didn't say anything now, she'd have to remain silent about Carlton. Perhaps she could pretend to remember it later, if the murderer wasn't caught quickly. 'Let me think, er, no, no one comes to mind.'

'Why don't we go over to the Country Club today? We haven't anything on; we're waiting to hear from Pamela Gage and I don't fancy sitting around all day waiting for Revie to decide whether we need to be fingerprinted.'

'I don't see what we can do there. Why do you want to go?'

'I've never been in the place. Can you take me as your guest?'

'Oh, she can do that,' chipped in Dorothy. 'As I said the other day, I've been there. Nancy is a member, although she doesn't go very often. She's taken me as a guest more than once. That's where I first saw Carlton Mavor's legs.'

'You're obsessed with his legs,' Mabel said. She turned to Stuart. 'She was on about them the other day. Gave me quite a turn, talked about finding some old man with a decent pair of pins. I ask you!'

57

Dorothy glared at Mabel over the top of her blue spectacles.

Laurel and Frank burst into laughter and Stuart shook his head.

'What about it, Laurel?'

She couldn't think of a good reason for refusing. 'We can go after lunch. What do you want to do? Play tennis?'

'I'd like to prowl around a bit, have informal chats with anyone there, especially the staff.'

'Frank, this is not our case. Revie won't be pleased if he thinks we're interfering.'

'I won't mention the Judge or ask people for their alibis, I'd just like to get my bearings, meet a few people, hear what they have to say. The murder of the Judge is bound to come up, I can listen, and I won't ask questions.'

'The police may be there already,' she said.

'If they are, we'll make it a short visit, especially if Nick is on the scene. However, he's always been grateful if we've picked up something about a case he's working on. He trusts us.'

'I think it's a good idea,' Dorothy said. 'Better than sitting round here with nothing to do. I think I'll nip into Aldeburgh and visit Nancy Wintle, see what she's got to say. What about you, Stuart? Why don't you and Mabel come with me? We can have a bite to eat at The Cross Keys.'

Stuart came alive. 'What about it, Mabel? They might have some crab sandwiches.'

Mabel got up and patted his stomach. 'Only if we have a walk before we eat. Remember what I said. Ginormous!'

# Chapter Eight

Frank glanced at the Judge's house as they passed it on their way to the Country Club; two police cars were parked outside. Laurel turned her Ford Cortina left into a narrow road to the left of the Club and pulled into a parking space behind a tamarisk hedge. She was a good driver, but he didn't like being driven, however attractive the person at the wheel was. When he'd offered to drive, she'd said, 'Certainly not, there are strict rules about parking – members only.' She'd given him a cool look. 'Please remember you're *my* guest – no misbehaviour. I want to retain my membership.'

Ever the teacher. 'Yes, miss.'

'Good boy.'

'I believe the latest teaching methods advocate rewarding the pupil if they've shown improvement, either in work or behaviour. Is that true?' he said.

'Yes, you're right.'

'So, if I'm good, you'll give me a reward?'

She backed up, straightening the car, so it was neatly parked between two others, turned off the ignition, and faced him. 'Are you in need of being rewarded? I thought from past conversations all your needs are being catered for?'

What an acid remark, he thought; it went with the look on her face. She wasn't pleased with him. Why? Was it possible she was jealous? Of Emma? Or was she upset by the comment he'd made after she'd wanted to see him and Carlton side by side? What made him say he was spoken for? It certainly wasn't true. He liked Emma but he certainly didn't want a long relationship with her. 'One can never have too much praise.'

'Well, you're not getting any from me. I've brought my tennis things, so I'll see if I can get a game. That will leave you free to chat up all and sundry.' She got out, banged her door and started taking things out of the boot.

He blew out a stream of air. He'd been looking forward to some time with her, but not if they were going to have a row. They'd never had a full-blown argument; disagreements, yes. He knew he sometimes annoyed her with his motor-mouth remarks, but he'd never come across her in a mood like this. Was this a good or a bad sign? He didn't know. Better go carefully. Should he let Laurel know he wasn't serious about Emma? But, if he did, what would she read into that? Christ – women.

'I'll take you into the Club and sign you in,' she said, marching ahead, swinging a games bag, a tennis racquet head poking out of the flap. 'We'd better go in through the main entrance.'

They circled the Club until they came to the front. It was an attractive, gabled building, with black clapboard walls under a red-tiled roof. Two short flights of steps, either side of a square construction with a porthole in the centre, ran up to an enclosed balcony.

'What on earth is that?' he asked, pointing to the nautical structure.

'Storage space,' was her curt reply, as she ran up the right-hand flight of steps and pulled open a door.

On either side of twin doors leading into the enclosed balcony were pointed gables, with windows below. He remembered reading in a book about the origins of the Club, that it was one of the first buildings to be erected in the village. Then it was called the Kursaal: a German word for meeting place. Bet they dropped it like a hot brick when the First World War started.

He followed her through the door into a lobby, which opened out into a large room furnished with tables and chairs. Laurel walked to the far right to a smaller room labelled Bureau. She knocked and went in, he followed her. A small man seated at a desk got up.

'Ah, Miss Bowman. I don't think we have you booked in for a lesson with Mr Mavor, do we?' He was about five foot five, chunkily built, with wide shoulders. His dark hair was thinning, but the most distinctive feature was his nose, which resembled the end of a can opener.

'No, I haven't, I came on the off-chance I might get a game. Mr Shires, may I introduce my friend, Mr Frank Diamond?'

He grasped Frank's outstretched hand, vigorously pumping, until Frank was sure water would soon gush from his mouth if Shires didn't stop. He pulled his hand away. 'Very pleased to meet you.'

'Mr Shires is the manager,' Laurel said. 'He'll be able to answer any questions you have about the Club. Does Mr Mavor have any vacancies?' she asked him.

He looked at a chart on the wall. 'There may be a vacancy in fifteen minutes, unless he's booked something in himself.'

'Thank you. See you later,' she said to Frank, turned and left the office.

Shires raised his eyebrows. 'Miss Bowman isn't her usual sunny self. Any idea what's upset her?'

A nosy parker? Let's hope he gives as much information as he gets. 'I've really no idea. I think she's just keen to get a game.'

He shrugged. 'I take it you're interested in joining the Club, Mr Diamond?'

'Yes. Miss Bowman has told me how much she's enjoyed coming here, I thought I might like to join. Are you taking new members?'

'I'm sure we can make room for one of Miss Bowman's friends. Do take a seat and I'll give you some details you can study at your leisure.' He opened a drawer in the desk and riffled through papers.

'Miss Bowman said you've recently taken up the role of manager?'

'Yes, January this year. Since I started, we've been rather quiet, but things are picking up.'

'I expect you'll be busy soon – Easter is next weekend.' This wasn't getting him anywhere.

Shires passed him a pamphlet and some papers. 'I think you'll find most of what you want in these, including a membership form and details of the fees.' He paused as Frank glanced at the papers. 'Let me know if I can be of further assistance.'

'Would it be possible to have a wander round now? I can't leave until Miss Bowman has finished her game as she drove me here.'

Shires raised a suggestive eyebrow.

'Perhaps I could have a drink and study these.' He tapped the papers.

Shires pursed his lips. 'Very well. I'll give you a temporary pass, you must show it if you are challenged.'

'Challenged? Goodness, is that because of the police cars I saw as we came in?'

'That's got nothing to do with us, I assure you. Some of the older members are a bit snotty about who joins the Club, and they're suspicious of strangers. They'd like to have a say in who joins, and black ball anyone they didn't think came up to scratch. They're still living in the Edwardian era.'

'What percentage of the membership do *they* make up?'

'About five per cent, I'd say. Don't worry, the majority of the members won't be offended by your leather jacket, but some of the elders might raise an eyebrow.' He sniggered.

Frank decided he didn't like Shires. 'And the police cars? I hope no one is injured.' He'd promised Laurel he wouldn't bring up the murder of the Judge, but, at the moment, she couldn't hear him.

Shires leant over the desk. 'Please don't let it alarm you, but the occupant was found dead on Monday.'

Frank put on a sympathetic face. 'Really, how awful. Who was it?'

'A Mr Neville Hanmer. He liked to be called Judge Hanmer, but he didn't get that title from me.'

'Oh, why's that?'

'He was no longer a judge, just a retired old man, and an old man who was usually in a bad mood.'

This didn't sound like the man he'd talked to on the phone. He'd been the epitome of politeness and courtesy. Mr Shires didn't like the Judge. Frank nodded. 'Old people can be trying. Sometimes, as they age, they seem to develop a taste for nastiness and causing trouble.'

Shires gave him a sharp look. 'He wasn't my favourite member of the Club.'

'He was a member? Did he come here frequently?'

'Yes, quite a lot. But I shouldn't speak ill of the dead.' He stood up and handed Frank a small card. 'Show this to anyone who challenges you. It's only valid for today. If you wish to join, please give me a ring, the telephone number is in the pamphlet.' He ushered Frank from the room.

Frank thanked him and wandered back to the front entrance and stood on the balcony looking out over the North Sea. He opened the pamphlet Shires had given him and read: the Club house was built on the highest point of the sand dune facing southeast, giving unbroken views of the beach and the incoming waves. The view *was* fantastic.

He turned back to the lounge area and sat at one of the tables dotted round the room; on each one was either newspapers, magazines or notepaper. It was all very between the wars. He pretended to study the pamphlet and papers Shires had given him, glancing casually around at the same time. It was an attractive room; the double set of windows looking east over the sea and west over the playing fields made the room light and airy. The pamphlet said the room could be extended to form a dance floor, and even a theatre, and there was also a card room. If his father could see him now, his eldest son, contemplating becoming a member of a Country Club, he'd have a heart attack.

He got up and went to the balcony overlooking the playing fields, found an unoccupied table, and focused on the tennis courts, especially on an interesting mixed-doubles match. On one side were Laurel and Carlton Mavor; their opponents were a dark-haired woman and blond, rather etiolated man, whose physique belied the strength with which he walloped the tennis ball cross-court, hitting Laurel, as she tried unsuccessfully to get her racquet to it. She winced and rubbed her arm.

'Good shot, Harry,' shouted the dark-haired woman. 'Forty–thirty. Five games to four to us, I believe. My serve.'

Carlton glowered at her. 'Stop gloating, Beattie, and both of you stop bashing the ball at Laurel.'

'I'm sure when you're coaching, Carl, you always tell your pupils to play on the weaker opponent in a doubles match. I do.'

Laurel's face coloured. It looked as though she'd met *her match* in Beattie, at least on the tennis court.

Beattie was nearly Laurel's height, with a flat-faced prettiness. Wide shoulders, long legs and narrow hips completed a boyish look, especially as she was flat-chested. She seemed to have a close relationship to Carlton, almost a rivalry. She served and soon the final game of the set was over, finishing with an ace from Beattie.

Frank got up and went down the flight of steps leading to the tennis courts. 'Hello, Laurel. Good game?'

She gave him a rictus grin. 'I think the word is humiliated. Although I'm sure Beattie and Harry didn't mean to make me feel two inches tall.'

Good girl – no faffing about, tell it as it is. He looked at her enquiringly.

'Beattie, Carlton, Harry, this is one of my partners, Frank Diamond.' She waved her hand at him.

Beattie's sea-green eyes bored into his. She *was* attractive with loose dark hair tumbling round her face; Carlton had the same pale green eyes. He gesticulated with a hand, from one to the other. 'Are you related? There's certainly a resemblance.'

'Beattie's my older sister,' Carlton said. He was boyishly handsome, with the same thick dark hair as Beattie, but a characterless face, perhaps one teenage girls might swoon over, he thought. However, Dorothy was right, his six-foot-three physique *was* impressive, to say nothing of his legs. There was no way he could compete with that body. It was a good job Laurel wasn't a mind-reader; she'd be in tucks of laughter.

'We're going to have some lemon squash,' Harry said. 'Care to join us?'

'Thank you. Have we time, Laurel?'

Carlton stared at him.

64

She nodded, the corners of her mouth twitching.

'Then, thank you, we will. I'm not sure about the lemon squash, do they serve beer?'

'You can have anything you want, old man. Follow me,' Harry said.

Frank felt he was in a 1950s Ealing comedy.

Harry led the party up the steps to the balcony and commandeered a table. A waitress took his order and was soon back with a tray of drinks.

'Put it on my tab, Betty,' Harry said.

The beer was a tad too warm and tasted like the end of the barrel, but he decided not to make any derogatory remarks.

'Beattie's also a tennis coach at the Club,' Laurel said. 'So, I'm afraid Carlton's skills couldn't compensate for my poor play. Sorry, Carlton.'

Beattie drained her glass and refilled it from the jug. 'Having played against you, Laurel, I don't think racquet games are for you. Carlton said you *used to be* good at athletics?' Her voice was deep and throaty, reminding him of a smouldering fifties film star, with the proverbial cigarette dangling from her lips.

'Yes, I love field sports, the javelin was my best event.'

He had a feeling Laurel might be contemplating skewering Beattie with one.

'I disagree, Beattie. Laurel has come on leaps and bounds since I started coaching her. I think you'll make a fine player, Laurel. Don't pay any attention to Beattie,' Carlton said.

Beattie sniffed. 'You would say that. Ladies like Laurel are your bread and butter, aren't they?' She turned to Frank. 'They swoon all over him, in fact sometimes their behaviour is quite indecent.'

Laurel's lips tightened.

'Of course, I don't mean you, Laurel. It's teenagers and the young women who slaver all over him.'

Beattie was living dangerously. 'How long have you been coaching tennis?' Frank asked, afraid Laurel might throw her lemon squash in Beattie's face.

'I started this year. Carlton told me it was a cushy number so I thought I'd join him. You put in a good word for me, didn't you, Carl?'

Laurel wasn't the only one she was upsetting.

'I don't think you heard me say that,' Carlton snapped.

'What did you do before coaching tennis, Beattie?' Frank asked.

'This and that, but I've been keen on sport since school days. I'm good at most games.'

'But not quite good enough,' Carlton said.

She shot him a hard look.

How old was she, he thought? Probably about the same age as Laurel: early thirties?

'What about you, Carlton? Did you try anything else before turning to a sporting career?' Frank asked.

Beattie faced Laurel. 'Gosh, your partner doesn't switch off from detecting, does he? He'll be asking for our birth certificates next.' She laughed throatily.

Carlton ignored her. 'I've played tennis professionally, I've entered a few tournaments this year; I trained to teach PE, but couldn't stand the kids.'

Laurel frowned.

Perhaps Carlton didn't know she was a former PE teacher, and she adored children.

'It was the children who couldn't stand you, Carlton.'

'Beattie, for God's sake!'

'It's true, he couldn't control them. After one year he jacked it in.'

'Teaching isn't for everyone,' Laurel said. 'I admire you for making that decision. Some teachers stay on, even if they don't like children. They give the profession a bad name.'

Carlton blushed and looked as though he wanted to kiss her. 'Thank you, Laurel. I do like kids, but only on a one-to-one basis. I enjoy coaching them in the summer holidays. Some of them have done quite well.'

'That must be rewarding,' Laurel said.

Yuck, thought Frank.

'He especially likes coaching the teenage girls, don't you, Carlton?' Beattie said.

'Stow it, Beattie, or I'll tell them about your foibles.'

She threw back her head, laughing, showing off her strong white throat. 'We can't have that.' She offered the depleted jug of lemon squash. 'Anyone care for more?'

Harry pushed forward his glass, but the rest either shook their heads or politely refused. She poured the last inch into her glass. 'Can I call you Frank, Mr Diamond?'

He smiled at her. 'Certainly, Beattie.' He imagined waves of anger radiating from Laurel.

'Thank you, Frank.' She leant towards him, with a predatory smile.

He imagined her cornering him in a dark room and ripping his clothes off – God, the beer must have hallucinogenic qualities. He'd make sure he never found himself alone with her.

'You and Laurel have very interesting jobs. What's your latest case about?' she asked.

'We never discuss our work,' Laurel said, before he could answer.

'I wondered if you might be involved in Judge Hanmer's case?'

'Why would we be?' Frank said. 'I was told it was an accident. There were police cars outside a house near here. Is that where the Judge lived?'

Carlton moved uneasily in his chair. 'Yes, on The Benthills.'

'What was he like?' Frank asked. 'Did you ever speak to him, Laurel?'

She turned to face him, the corners of her mouth lifted in a slight smile. She approved of his line of questioning. He'd thought it rather neat himself.

'No, he'd been pointed out to me, but we never met. He often used to watch the tennis.'

Frank pulled a face. 'Ah, an eye for the ladies?' He winked at Beattie. She laughed.

'You've got to be joking,' Carlton fumed. 'He was as queer as a cuckoo.' He pointed at Laurel. 'Don't be fooled he was gawping at *your* legs, it was mine he was ogling.'

Laurel glared at him. Was she offended by his language, or upset his legs were preferred to hers? He certainly had an unhealthy attitude to homosexuals.

'You sound as though you didn't like him, Carlton?' Frank asked.

Carlton's black eyebrows knitted together. 'Can't stand poofs.'

'Have you had some bad experiences? I'm not fussed about anyone's sexual preferences, provided that excludes children and animals. Live and let live, I say,' Frank said.

Laurel nodded in agreement.

'I agree,' Harry said. 'There's too much bigotry about so many things, you'd have thought we'd have moved on by now.'

Carlton's nostrils flared, but he didn't reply.

Frank noted the spiteful look Carlton gave Harry, but he wished Beattie was right and they were involved in the case. The Judge had been a potential client, and he felt some responsibility to him. If only he'd gone to see him the day he phoned, then even if he'd still died, at least they would have known who he was worried about, and why. 'Did the Judge make a pass at you?' Frank asked him.

An angry flush seeped upwards from Carlton's neck and suffused his face. 'It would have been the last thing he did, I can tell you.'

Beattie raised her eyes to heaven. 'Carlton, if the police heard you, they'd have you behind bars in no time.'

'Why? He wasn't murdered, was he?'

'You are amongst friends here, Carlton, but I have to tell you your attitude to homosexuals is antediluvian. You should judge people on what they say and do, not on whether they're hetero or homosexual,' Laurel said.

Carlton looked crestfallen. He did care about having Laurel's good opinion. Nevertheless, he's no friend of mine, thought Frank. No one's answered my question. 'What was the Judge like? Did anyone know him?' Frank asked.

Harry nodded. 'I knew him slightly, through my parents, you know. Pa's a lawyer, knew Hanmer in London. I agree with Carlton, no doubt he was a queer, but pretty harmless, I think. Met him a few times at dinner parties, seemed a nice cove, but he hasn't been over to our place since he permanently moved here. Lovely manners, my Ma said. Pa liked him, said it was a shame he retired so early, said he was a top-rate judge. Never made a pass at me.'

Carlton laughed, his anger seemingly over. 'Not surprising, you can't keep a girlfriend, never mind arousing lust in old men.'

Beattie laughed.

Harry flinched. 'I say, that's uncalled for. At least I wasn't the object of the prefects' lust at school. Bet they came after you with their tongues hanging out, when you were a shrimp.'

Carlton's face reddened. 'You're disgusting.'

Harry looked ready to lay one on him. Instead, he got up and picked up his tennis bag. 'I'm off. You can forget the coaching sessions, Carlton, until you've learnt some manners.' He made a slight bow to the other three. 'Sorry about that. See you around.' He stalked off.

'Really, Carlton, you've upset him. Let's hope it doesn't get out that you're losing customers, and more importantly why,' Beattie said.

Frank glanced at Laurel, and tipped his head slightly towards the door. She nodded.

'I think we ought to be making tracks, Laurel. OK?'

'Yes, time we made a move,' she said, getting up.

Carlton went to Laurel, who was rummaging in her sports bag, probably for her car keys. 'I do apologise, Laurel. I don't know what came over me. I do hope this hasn't spoilt our friendship,' he muttered, obviously wishing they were alone.

Laurel patted his shoulder. 'We all have off days. Don't worry about it.'

'So, you'll be back for our next lesson?' He was like a dog begging for a bone.

'Of course, and thank you for your remarks about my tennis improving. Although I really let you down in that match.'

Beattie was glowering at them. He felt like joining her.

69

Carlton grasped Laurel's hand. 'Thank you, Laurel. Perhaps we can go for a drink after your next lesson?'

'That would be lovely, Carlton. We must go now.' She turned to Beattie and gave her a mega-watt smile. 'Nice to have met you, Beattie. Ready, Frank?' She didn't wait for a reply, turned on her heels and headed for the Cortina.

Frank raised two fingers to his forehead and saluted the brother and sister. He was tempted to turn it into a V sign.

# Chapter Nine

Thursday, 19 April, 1973

Frank drove to Greyfriars for a nine o'clock meeting; it looked as though it was going to be one of those rare, glorious spring days – the sun had risen through a shroud of light mist and the air was already warm and balmy. Why weren't his spirits in unison with the weather?

He went in through the kitchen door. There was a lingering smell of grilled bacon. Somehow his bowl of muesli and a banana seemed a long way away. 'Morning, Mabel. Any coffee going?'

'You'll be lucky, this is my day off and Jim won't be here to cook dinner until four at the earliest. You have to fend for yourself until then. Dorothy's in the office, Laurel's taken Bumper for a walk, and my Stuart's still in the bedroom.'

He pulled a sad face.

She laughed. 'I'll see what I can do. I'm not going out until the meeting's over. See if the others want a drink and I'll bring it in.'

'You're an angel, Mabel, and you also look ravishing.' She was dressed in a green two-piece suit and sported a bright pink lipstick.

'I'm not sure if angels are supposed to look ravishing, but thank you. Don't bother asking them, I know they'll say yes. I'll make a big pot of coffee!'

In the dining room Dorothy was moving a bowl of narcissi from the table to her desk. 'Hello, Frank. Will it be a long meeting? I've decided to spring clean the filing cabinets and get rid of all the unwanted paper we've generated.'

'And good morning to you, too. No, it shouldn't take too long, we need to decide who's doing what. How are you going to deal with the paper?'

'I'll have to either burn it, or put my multi-cut scissors into action, but that's going to take me ages.' She shrugged. 'It's got to be done, I can't put it into the dustbin as it is.'

'Why don't you buy a few more pairs of scissors and we can all have a go. Spend a jolly evening cutting up paper.'

She raised her eyes. 'I can just see it.'

'We could down a bottle of Scotch to keep us going.'

'What's this? Sounds like my kind of entertainment.' Laurel came in, Bumper on her heels; her flushed cheeks and Bumper's steaming red tongue showed they'd been on a brisk walk.

Dorothy shook her head. 'It's Frank fantasising again.'

Mabel appeared with a coffee tray. 'Help yourself. I'll tell Stuart you're all here.'

As Stuart walked into the room the telephone rang. Dorothy answered it. 'Greyfriars House. The Anglian Detective Agency. How can I help you?' She listened. 'I'll put him on.' She covered the mouthpiece. 'Frank, it's for you. Pamela Gage.'

'Mrs Gage, good morning.' He listened and gave them the thumbs up. 'Excellent. I'll be over this afternoon. Two o'clock?' A pause. 'Goodbye, see you then.'

As they took their seats round the mahogany table, he said, 'Mrs Gage has agreed terms and I'll collect the signed contract this afternoon. She's keen for us to start the investigation as soon as possible.'

'That's good to hear, after the awful news about the Judge,' Dorothy said. 'Shall we formally start the meeting?'

Frank nodded, and waited until everyone had settled down. 'If we can go through what everyone is doing today. Dorothy, I believe you've had a phone call from a prospective client?'

'Yes, an owner of an antique shop in Southwold wants us to investigate the theft of some valuable snuff-boxes.'

'Has he informed the police?' Laurel asked.

'No, he doesn't want to do that, but wouldn't say why over the telephone.'

Laurel sighed. 'Just like the Judge, look what happened to him.'

'Stuart, could you take this one on? Until I know exactly how we're going to tackle the plant thefts, I won't know how many of us we'll need on that case,' Frank said.

'Fine by me. I'll ring them up and try and get over today. By the way, I've rung round a few plant nurseries, but they haven't had any plants stolen. I'm dropping Mabel off in Aldeburgh, she's going to her old fish and chip shop to see Ethel, and I'll join her later. We won't be in for dinner, we're going to try the Brudenell Hotel, Ethel said she had a lovely meal there last week.'

'Fish and chips?' Frank asked.

'Ha ha! Very amusing,' Stuart said, pulling a face.

'You can't expect witty remarks before eleven o'clock,' Frank said.

'Or later,' Laurel retorted.

'What are you doing today, Miss Acid Tongue?' Frank asked. 'Going to the Club for another drubbing by the delectable Miss Mavor?'

'No fear. I think I'll get out my wet suit and have a long swim. The sea looked very tempting when Bumper and I were on the beach, as flat as a pancake. Then I'll come back and help Dorothy.'

'Right. Everyone's got something to do, so see you two at dinner tonight. Any idea what Jim's cooking?'

'He had a word with Mabel yesterday. I think he was checking what was in the larder. She might be able to tell you,' Stuart said.

As if he'd conjured her up, Mabel poked her head round the door. 'Meeting finished? Right, Stuart, let's get going.'

He got up. 'They want to know what Jim's cooking for dinner.'

Mabel smiled at them. 'I promised not to tell. You know he likes to surprise you.'

Pamela Gage led Frank to her office. She bounced along in front of him, seemingly as full of energy as the last time he'd seen her. She waved to a chair in front of her desk, and passed him a sealed envelope. 'The signed contract.'

'Thank you. I'm pleased we're taking on the case.'

'So am I. I do hope you'll be able to quickly solve who has been pinching my plants.'

'We'll do our best, but there are no guarantees, and if the thief suspects you've employed a detective agency, they may stop. That doesn't mean we can't discover who it is. It would help if they stole again.'

Pamela shuddered. 'I can see that, but I can't afford any more plants to disappear.'

'We may even be able to recover your treasures, it will depend on what they've done with them, but even if they have been sold on, whoever bought them might not realise they've received stolen property. That in itself is a criminal offence.'

'Mr Diamond, if you are able to do that . . .' she threw open her arms, 'you'll be in danger of an old lady giving you a very long hug!'

Frank laughed. 'An added incentive.'

She gave him a broad smile.

There was a rapid knocking on the door, which was immediately thrust open. Keith Gage came in. 'Good Lord, are *you* back again?'

Frank didn't bother getting up, or making a reply; he thought he'd leave this one to Pamela.

'Do you want something, Keith?'

'A private word, if I may.'

'Can't it wait?'

'No. I need to speak to you *now*.'

'If it's about money, the answer is no.'

His nostrils flared and cheeks suffused with blood. If looks could kill, he and Pamela would be hitting the floor, stiff as a pair of ironing boards.

'I'll see you later,' he snarled and slammed the door.

Frank didn't know what to say, and ran a finger over his top lip. Pamela was a brave woman, but she must know her husband and his capabilities. He hoped she was correct.

'I'm sorry about that. I really can't afford him any more. He'll have to go, I'm afraid.'

74

'I'm sorry.'

'Thank you. Are you married, Mr Diamond?'

'No.'

'Don't let Keith put you off, but make sure you choose very carefully.'

This conversation was getting too close to the mark. 'I think I'm destined for continuing bachelorhood.'

She cocked her head. 'Oh, you're far too tasty for that. Some young woman is no doubt dying to walk towards you up the aisle.'

He shuddered at mental pictures of Emma, wearing a black ensemble and veil, galloping up the aisle towards him, followed by Laurel wearing her wet suit and carrying a harpoon gun. He tried, unsuccessfully, to stop a snort of laughter.

'I'm glad you find the idea amusing, Mr Diamond.'

'Sorry.'

'So, have you any idea how you're going to tackle this?'

He moved his chair nearer to the desk. 'I have a proposal. I'd like to put it to you as I'll need you to be comfortable with it.'

She leant back. 'Go ahead.'

'I propose I act as a consultant you've brought in to look at the layout of the garden, all the activities and the commercial side of the nursery. The aim is to give you advice on improvements to raise the profile of the garden and increase income. I have a degree in botany and I think I can blag my way round. After all, *I'll* be the one asking the questions.'

She gave two slow nods. It looked like she was going for the idea.

'How would we inform the staff?'

'I suggest you call a meeting of all staff, plus volunteers and I'll address them. If you could say something on the lines of no jobs are in peril, and how you appreciate the work of the volunteers. Plus, although I'll be making recommendations, this is not a cost-cutting exercise, and you hope the nursery will expand, and possibly new staff will be recruited – something like that.'

She nodded again. 'When do you suggest we hold the meeting?'

'It's Good Friday tomorrow, and Monday is a Bank Holiday, so how about Tuesday?'

'I'll let you know.'

'I'll need to get them on my side, so that when I talk to them, hopefully they'll open up, and we may find out more about the plant thief.'

'Will you do this by yourself?'

'Possibly, but I may bring in one of the other detectives – as my assistant.' How would Laurel like that? 'It will mean more cost, but should speed up the case.'

'This is thrilling! Yes, I'll agree to that.' She wriggled on her chair like an over-excited schoolgirl who'd been promised a trip to Wimbledon to see her favourite player.

'Excellent.' Pamela was the ideal client.

'Any other ideas?'

'Just one.'

'Yes?'

'Are there any other rare plants you're worried may be stolen?'

'Yes. Why?'

'Have you thought of moving them to somewhere safe?'

She made a deep sigh. 'I have a lovely clump of very special snowdrops; it's one I bred myself. It's in the wood in some wonderful soil. It's bunched up so well, the conditions suit it to a T. I'm hoping to make it available for sale in a few years.'

'How do you think the thief found out about the other snowdrops in the wood?'

'I've racked my brains, and the only answer I can come up with is they saw me going into the wood and followed me. I don't even allow Georgie to tend my specials.'

'Tend? What do you do?'

'Not a lot. Snowdrops, if they're happy, are easy plants, unless you've got a weak variety.' She frowned. 'There are no effete plants in my garden.'

Frank could believe it; he imagined her having them all on parade and any that didn't come up to scratch would be ruthlessly exterminated.

'I keep them free of weeds, and at the right time, I dig them up and split the bulbs into singletons. You'd be surprised how quickly numbers build up.'

'You don't do any increasing by cutting up the bulbs?'

She shuddered. 'I went on a course, far too fiddly.' She opened her hands. 'Where is this getting us?'

'Sorry, I've taken you a long way round. Another possibility is, somehow, to let the thief know where these rare bulbs are. Then we could do a stake-out over several nights and try and catch them as they dig up the plants.'

'Goodness me, this is serious stuff. Can I come? I'd love to be there when you catch them – the swine.'

'Would you be able to stop yourself from attacking them?'

'Probably not.'

'I don't think you'd like hiding in a cold wood for several nights on the trot. Would you?'

She laughed. 'It's always been my weak point: unhappy to delegate. No, I'll leave night vigils to you. You won't do it on your own, will you? That wouldn't be safe.'

'I think I can manage, but I'm sure my partners will agree with you.'

'So, what next?'

'I'll put these suggestions to my partners, see if they can improve on them, or think of other ways we can tackle this. If you can decide on a suitable date for a meeting of the staff and let me know, we should get going as soon as possible. Think about us staking out the snowdrops. I presume you're involving Georgie in our plans?'

She nodded. 'Certainly. She knows about you already. I hope you don't suspect her?'

'No one is off my list. If it is her, we're wasting our time. Unless someone we talk to points us in her direction. Perhaps you could omit to tell her about a possible stake-out?'

'Agreed.'

'Does she know where these rare snowdrops are?'

Pamela frowned. 'I don't think so. I haven't told anyone. I must admit it gives me so much pleasure to know I'm the only person who knows they're there.'

'Does your husband have any idea how much some of these bulbs are worth?'

'Why, yes. I've made such a to-do about losing them. Surely you don't suspect Keith? He may be a drunk and a lazy sod, but I don't think he'd stoop that low.'

Frank wasn't sure.

'He wouldn't know what to do with them, and I can assure you by ten at night he's had it. He's either passed out on the sofa here, or he's blotto in a friend's house. That's happening less frequently – the number of friends is dwindling. Everyone is getting fed up with him.'

He felt a twinge of sympathy for Keith, but quickly suppressed it.

'I think, before I go, we ought to run this past Georgie. She may have other ideas worth considering,' he said.

'Let's go and see her.' Pamela marched out of the office and Frank followed.

'She's working in the Japanese water garden. Did you visit that last time you were here?'

'No. We glimpsed it as we walked to the woods.'

'Some plants were stolen from there as well.'

'Including?'

She strode between the herbaceous borders at a brisk pace; taking three paces to his one. 'Some choice primulas, hepaticas, fritillaria and one particular Adonis plant I was very fond of.' She gave him a piercing glance. 'Are you familiar with these plants?'

Checking up on me? Not sure if I can pull off my role as a horticultural advisor? 'Yes, I'd recognise each of them, but not a particular variety.'

'Good.'

She turned left through a red-painted moon gate into the Japanese garden.

Frank stopped. 'This is beautiful. You've managed to capture the essence of the Orient, congratulations.'

78

Pamela's face flushed and she beamed at him. 'Thank you very much indeed.'

The garden was an amphitheatre of sloping banks, covered in trees and bushes surrounding a small lake with a cascading stream feeding water into it, as it tumbled over a shallow waterfall. A red wooden bridge arced over the stream and a line of silver-grey, wooden planks zig-zagged over the lake from one bank to the other.

'It must look fabulous when everything is in flower.'

'It does. There's Georgie on the far bank. Follow me.'

She climbed some shallow steps and walked across the lake using the zig-zag path. He saw groups of irises, and below the water, koi carp silently glided, their orange and silver scales glistening in the sunlight.

'This is wonderful, Mrs Gage.'

She stopped and pointed to the iris clumps. 'If I'm unlucky and you don't catch the thief soon, you'll be able to see the irises in flower.'

'What colour are they?'

'Clumps of blue, white and mauve. Perfection.'

He didn't think she was exaggerating.

'Georgie! Can we have a word?'

Georgie was up to her thighs at the margin of the lake chopping at a clump of reeds.

'We have to keep them in check or they take over,' Pamela said.

Georgie hauled herself out of the water, making glooping sounds. She was wearing waders. Frank remembered wearing a pair when he'd helped to remove a body from one of the meres at Minsmere Bird Reserve. He thought they looked better on Georgie.

'Mr Diamond, would you tell Georgie your suggestions as to how you are going to investigate this case.'

Georgie rubbed a hand over her face, then pushed back a strand of red hair, leaving muddy smudges on her cheek.

Frank went through the proposed plan, omitting the part about staking out the gardens at night.

'Well, Georgie, what do you think? And have *you* any suggestions?' Pamela asked.

Georgie eyelids fluttered. She swallowed. 'I don't like this idea at all. I think it's dreadful. You'll be lying to all the staff. What will happen when they find out? I don't want to have anything to do with it.'

Pamela's mouth opened in surprise and shock. 'What on earth do you mean? Do you want these thefts to continue? I'm not asking for your approval. Indeed, it was Mr Diamond who thought we should inform you of the plan. I'm very disappointed in you, Georgie. I think you had better reconsider your words. See me in my office tomorrow morning at eight thirty sharp. I shall expect a change of heart and an apology.' She started to march off.

'I'm sorry if this has put you in a difficult position,' Frank said to Georgie.

Pamela turned. 'Do not mention this to any other member of staff, or volunteer,' she shouted.

Georgie bit her lip and tears trickled down her face, washing away the traces of mud.

Frank followed Pamela across the zig-zag path. The sun was hidden by clouds and the lake's surface was now grey and unfriendly. Why was Georgie against the plan? She didn't want to lie to the staff, but surely if the thief was caught, wouldn't they all be pleased? Pamela could easily explain the reason behind the deception. It would mean the garden and nursery would be in a better position financially. What was Georgie hiding?

# Chapter Ten

Outside the kitchen door at Greyfriars, Laurel rubbed down a sopping wet Bumper with an old towel; he'd spent a great deal of his walk skipping in and out of the North Sea.

'You rascal,' she said, 'you don't get any better as you get older.' He'd been in one of his defiant moods, unwilling to end his time in the briny. Now, the harder she rubbed him, the more he enjoyed it, flexing his body like an enthusiastic belly dancer, his mouth agape, pink tongue lolling over sharp white teeth. She flicked the soaking towel at him, then opened the kitchen door. 'Get in there, you fiend from hell.'

He bounded past her.

'That's no way to speak to him, he's a good old dog,' Jim McFall said, as he poked at something in a pan with a kitchen knife.

'Hello, Jim. I'll get him from under your feet.'

'Och, there's no need. We've come to an understanding, haven't we, Bumper? If I give him titbits, he won't growl at me.'

Laurel had first met Jim when he was the groundsman of Blackfriars School and she was the newly appointed Senior Mistress. During the murder investigation of the death of the headteacher's wife, Susan Nicholson, it was revealed Jim had served time for his own wife's murder. A reformed man, he'd even teamed up with Dorothy to help track a suspect.

'What are we eating tonight? Smells delicious.'

'I've got some early asparagus, and for the mains I'm branching out. Trying a French recipe from a cookbook my Ayla bought me.'

'Oh, la-la! I must thank your daughter when I next see her. Is she paying you another visit soon?'

'I hope so. I'm telephoning her this weekend.'

'Frank back yet?'

'I've not seen him. Did you know that Inspector Revie is coming for dinner?'

Laurel's diaphragm tightened. 'Really? Why? I thought he'd be too busy investigating Judge Hanmer's death. Did Dorothy tell you about that?'

'Ay, she did. Is the Inspector sure it's a murder case?'

Laurel shrugged. 'I presume so. In fact, I've been expecting him to get in touch with Frank and me. He'll need our fingerprints to eliminate us from any others the forensics found in the Judge's house.'

Jim scowled. 'Polis! I still don't trust them, and I'm not too happy cooking dinner for him. I shouldn't think he'll be too happy eating it – he'll worry in case I slip some poison into his helping.'

Laurel laughed. 'I thought you two had called a truce.'

Jim stabbed at the contents of the pan again. 'We'll see,' he said.

'Did Dorothy take his call?'

'Ay, came in to break the news and promised me a large whisky if I behaved.'

'I'll go and see her.' She looked at her watch: five to six. 'Have I got time to change?'

'Ay, I had to put dinner back a wee bit. He can't get here until about seven.'

She decided she needed to get a move on. 'Asparagus and a French dish, sounds delicious. I'm looking forward to it, Jim. I've starving.'

A damp and sandy paw grazed her leg. 'So is Bumper. All right if I feed him?'

'Ay, go ahead. We've even got a pudding. Mabel made a black-currant tart from berries she found in the freezer.'

'Scrummy!' She gave Bumper his meal, which disappeared in seconds, and they left Jim muttering into the saucepan. Incantations?

As she opened the sitting-room door, there was the sweet smell of burning wood. Dorothy was reading in front of the dancing flames. Bumper bounded up to her, and pushed his nose under the book, which shot out of her hands.

'Bumper! Bad boy,' Laurel said, restraining a laugh.

'Just when I'd got to a critical point,' Dorothy said, retrieving the book from the floor, then patting Bumper. 'He's a bit pongy, Laurel.'

Laurel bent down and sniffed. 'Smells wonderful to me, but I'll give him a bath tomorrow. Shall I put him in another room?'

'No, don't be silly. He can stay here when we eat.'

'Jim tells me Nick Revie is coming to dinner. Is this a social call?'

Dorothy patted the sofa next to her, and Laurel sat down; Bumper stretched out in front of the fire, head closest to the flames. 'He phoned and said he needed to speak to all of us, but especially to you. I invited him to dinner, and explained Stuart and Mabel wouldn't be here. He said he needed to see us before tomorrow.'

'Did he say why?'

'I did ask him, but no, he wouldn't say.'

'What did he sound like?'

'Grim.'

Laurel felt confused. What could he possibly want with her? Had she done something wrong? 'Do you think it's something to do with the Judge? I hope we didn't mess something up on Monday and he's come to give us a wigging.'

A door opened and shut. Frank and Jim's voices came from the kitchen.

Laurel shot up. 'Sorry, I must change, these clothes have got rather damp when I was drying Bumper.' She ran from the room, and took the stairs two at a time. What should she wear for dinner?

Frank dipped an asparagus spear into the mayonnaise; he loved the contrast between the bite of the asparagus, and the richness of the mayonnaise. 'First of the season, Jim. A real treat.'

Jim grunted. Somehow, he'd managed to seat himself next to Nick Revie, with Dorothy at the head of the table and Frank and Laurel opposite to him.

Revie had turned up at five past seven, and had only managed a few gulps of Adnams bitter, before Jim announced dinner was served and if they waited any longer it would be spoiled.

'Are you going to tell us why you're here, Nick?' Frank asked.

'Not until we've eaten. Why spoil a good meal? I'm afraid I'll have to ask Mr McFall to leave. What I have to say is only for the Agency's ears.'

Frank wished he hadn't asked.

Jim glared at Revie. 'I'll be only too pleased to get on with the washing-up.'

'Boys!' Laurel said. 'Please, no squabbling. This is a lovely meal, Jim. Isn't it, Nick?'

This girl had bottle. What's more she was looking very sexy. She was wearing a dark blue wool jumper dress, which had a deep V neckline, giving intriguing glimpses of the tops of her breasts, blue eyeshadow and red lipstick. Who was this for? Revie? Jim? Or dare he hope . . .

Nick swallowed his last asparagus spear. 'I'm very fond of asparagus. What's next, Jim?' He sounded genuinely pleased.

Jim raised his head. 'It's Porc Robert,' he said, rolling the words round his mouth.

'You'll be rivalling Mabel in my affections soon,' Revie said, winking at Laurel.

Laurel smiled on both of them, as though they were schoolboys who'd shaken hands after a bundle. Dorothy looked sharply at Laurel, then she looked at Frank.

He gave a slight shrug. Not only was the meal good, but was Laurel's attitude towards him a tad warmer? Let's see. 'You're looking very glamorous tonight, Laurel,' he said.

Dorothy smirked.

'Thank you. I felt like making an effort. Sometimes it's fun to dress up a bit.'

'You always look fine to me,' Revie said. 'If I were younger . . .'

Cheeky bastard, Frank thought.

'Thank you, Nick.'

'Ay, Miss Bowman always looks fine,' Jim said.

This was beginning to get monotonous, but there was something about her tonight that was different. A challenging look in her eye? The way, as she leant forward, helping herself to mashed potatoes, her thigh pressed slightly against his? Deliberate? This wasn't like her usual behaviour.

Jim was in the kitchen, washing up, and in the sitting room, glasses in hands, Frank watched as Revie took a deep swallow of whisky, then put his glass on a side table.

'I've said this before, but I need to repeat it. What I have to say mustn't go any further than this room. If it got out I'd told you what is going to happen tomorrow, I'd be lucky to only get demoted. But I felt I must, especially you, Laurel. I know everyone will be upset, I am, but you,' he looked at her, her face pale and worried, 'will be horrified.'

'For God's sake, Nick, what is it? You're scaring me to death,' she said.

Frank couldn't imagine what he was going to say.

Nick Revie took a deep breath and then audibly expelled it. He looked as though he was dreading their reactions to his words. 'I don't want any interruptions until I've finished. And I have to tell you nothing you say can change what has to happen tomorrow. I'll be very sorry I have to do it, but there's no alternative. Understood?'

Frank had never seen him like this. 'Understood.'

Revie nodded. 'I dare say you've been wondering why we haven't asked you two,' he indicated Frank and Laurel, 'to come into the station and give us your fingerprints?'

'Yes,' Frank said. 'I presume you still had them on file from the Pemberton case, as you said on Monday.'

He nodded at Frank. 'I contacted forensics and they'd still got them on file. Save the buggers making a trip and getting their fingers inky, I thought.'

'Were there other prints at Mr Hanmer's house?' Frank asked.

Revie nodded. 'The Judge's, and also Mrs Hegarty's, the woman who looked after him, and one other set, person unknown.'

'That's lucky,' Frank said. 'Criminals are usually savvy nowadays and wear gloves. Shouldn't be allowed. Any idea whose?'

'Not only an idea, a definite identification.'

'A known criminal?' Laurel asked, looking relieved.

Why? What had she got to be relieved about?

'No, not a criminal. Along with your prints, in the Pemberton file, are the prints of the two dead men, Tucker and Hager, and one other set.'

Frank's brain went into overdrive. No!

'The fingerprint man ran them through the system – why, I don't know. They match those we found in Judge Hanmer's house. Several of them had yours or Laurel's fingerprints superimposed over them.' He paused, biting his lip. 'They were David Pemberton's fingerprints.'

Laurel gasped. 'No. I can't believe it. What was he doing there?'

'I'm afraid, Laurel, it looks as though he was murdering Judge Hanmer.'

'No, I refuse to believe it. Why would he want to kill the Judge?' She turned to Frank. 'You don't believe it, do you?'

What could he say? Agree with her, in the hope it would make her feel better? 'We'll have to hope there's some rational explanation for David being in the Judge's house. If he's got an alibi for the time of the murder, then he'll be eliminated.'

Laurel gasped. 'Of course, how stupid of me. He was probably with his parents.'

'Why did you feel you needed to tell us this, Nick?' Dorothy asked.

The tone of her voice seemed to bring a much-needed calm to the febrile atmosphere. Both Laurel and Nick were looking strained, and Frank was sure he didn't look too relaxed.

'I know how we all felt when David was rescued from the clutches of Tucker. It was one of the best feelings I've ever had to see that boy back with his dad. I learnt how you,' Revie nodded his head towards Laurel, 'managed to keep him alive, to thwart Hager, and at the risk of your own life, you attacked a professional killer.'

Laurel's eyes were swimming with tears. All Frank wanted to do was to take her in his arms and comfort her. He didn't move.

'If it hadn't been for Frank, both David and I would have died,' Laurel said.

'Tomorrow, I'll be interviewing David. His fingerprints will be taken again. If they match those found in Judge Hanmer's house and he hasn't an alibi for the time the Judge was murdered, I'll be charging him. I couldn't bear the thought you might hear about this from someone else. I must ask you not to do anything stupid. I do genuinely pray he has a cast-iron alibi and he can explain why he was in the Judge's house. The boy has suffered enough.' Revie's words were moving. Frank could see how much Revie was hating what he had to do.

'Nick, I believe you saw the list of the men who'd taken part in Tucker's paedophile ring. Was Hanmer's name there?'

'No. But I've made enquiries and he was a friend of one whose name was on the list. We know while David was incarcerated in Tucker's house, Hager talked to him about the men involved and taunted him with what they did to young boys. Hager may have said Neville Hanmer's name to David.'

'Do you think he was involved?' Frank asked.

'No. I'm sure he was a homosexual, but that doesn't make you a paedophile. There's no evidence he's ever been involved with boys, or indeed with any boy or man at any time,' Revie said.

'So why would David kill him?' Laurel asked.

'We know he felt deeply about the death of his friend, Peter. Perhaps he saw this as a way of retribution, that he owed it to Peter,' Revie said.

Laurel was biting her lip, trying to keep back the tears. 'What will happen to him if the worse happens and he goes to trial and is found guilty?'

'He's seventeen, at the moment he'd be sent to Borstal, or a Detention Centre, as they're now called. God knows what the sentence would be.'

Laurel cupped her face with her hands. 'He'd never survive in a place like that. It would be the end of him.'

# Chapter Eleven

Tuesday, 24 April, 1973

Frank and Pamela Gage waited as the people who worked at the gardens and nursery filed into the room. Although spring sunshine poured through three long windows, the room felt damp and smelt musty, as though it hadn't been heated during the winter. Everything was in a state of neglect: the cream and gold striped wallpaper was peeling from the walls in several places, and dusty outlines of spaces, once occupied by pictures, added to the uncared-for look.

The staff stood in small groups, as there were no chairs. Pamela stepped up onto a wooden box to address them. He hoped she didn't expect him to use it; he might be tempted to do a rant as if he was at Speakers' Corner in Hyde Park. Several people shuffled away from the door as Keith Gage pushed his way in; he leant against a wall, his arms folded, looking in a dark mood. If he gave the game away, he thought Pamela would do him some serious harm.

'Thank you for coming today, especially my volunteers,' she said. 'Although the nursery and garden have been successful over the past few years, I decided we shouldn't sit on our laurels, but try to make improvements to the garden and nursery to increase our visitor numbers, and hopefully our income. Extra money would enable us to employ more paid gardeners, make improvements to the gardens and increase plant sales. I can assure you this is not a cost-cutting exercise and no paid jobs are under threat – as I said before, we may be able to increase our staff.'

There were mutterings.

Pamela smiled at them. 'I hope you won't think if we are able to employ more people, you, my volunteers, won't be needed. I can't thank you enough for the unpaid work you do, and the gardens would not exist without your help, and indeed, will not exist in the future, if you do not continue to volunteer.'

More mutterings, but of a positive nature.

'I'd like to introduce Mr Diamond, who will be looking at the garden, the nursery, and talking to all of you. I'm pleased to say he is carrying out this work for a most modest fee.'

That was the first he'd heard about that.

'Mr Diamond.' She stepped off her box and waved a hand, inviting him to ascend.

He shook his head. 'Thank you, Mrs Gage. I'm very pleased you've asked me to take on this survey. I'd like to make it clear, when I talk to you individually, I'll be interested to hear your views about the garden and nursery. If you have any suggestions for improvement, or if you can see anything you feel is deleterious, I would value your contributions. Any comments you make will be in confidence, and although they may be passed on to Mrs Gage, I will not be revealing who said them. So, I hope to chat to all of you in the next few days. Thank you. Are there any questions for myself or Mrs Gage before I start on my work?'

'I hope you don't mind me asking, but what are your qualifications for doing this job?' Someone tittered. Asking the question was the man at the gate, who'd spoken to him when he and Stuart made their first visit to the garden.

'Thank you. I'm sorry, I don't know your name?'

'I'm Bill, one of the volunteers.'

'Well, Bill, I have a degree in botany.' True so far. 'And now I run my own agency.' Also true, though it had nothing to do with plants.

Bill nodded as though satisfied.

'Any other questions?'

He hoped Keith Gage wouldn't ask how his detective agency was doing. He was glowering at him, so he smiled back. Gage curled his lip, wheeled round and stalked out of the room.

A woman raised her hand. He'd seen her before on his first visit. Pamela had given her a plant.

'I'm Janet Lamb, a volunteer. I'm very pleased to hear you have a botany degree, but have you ever worked in a garden, Mr Diamond?'

'Yes, I have, specifically in the gardens of Mr John Coltman, the owner of several holiday camps.' There were nods of approval. He wasn't going to tell them he was an undercover gardener at one of the holiday camps near Orford, working on the disappearance of two members of staff.

As there were no more questions, Pamela thanked them for coming, and said she would be in her office for the next thirty minutes following the meeting, if anyone wanted to have a chat.

The last person leaving was Georgina Gibbs. 'Georgie,' Pamela shouted. 'Please come back.'

Georgie had a pinched and unhappy face as she walked towards them. 'Yes, Mrs Gage?'

'Mr Diamond would like to start his questioning with you. I suggest you go to the potting shed and have a chat there. I'm sure Mr Diamond is ready for a cup of coffee?' She cocked her head, like a blackbird eyeing up the waving tip of a juicy earthworm.

Georgie nodded, turned, and silently led the way out of the house.

Frank sipped the weak drink Georgie had made and refused a digestive biscuit. 'I realise you aren't happy with what I'm doing, but it's a good way of learning about people's feelings and ideas. If everyone knew the real reason for me being here, I don't think I'd get much information. I believe they'd be upset and resentful if they thought they were suspected of stealing plants.'

She flushed. 'If someone finds out, and tells everyone who you really are, they'll be very upset. They'll think Pamela didn't trust them. Some of them might leave. We can't do without their help.'

Frank studied her face. The flush deepened. 'But if we don't find out who's stealing the plants, the nursery could be in danger of losing so much income from the rare plants its future might be in jeopardy.'

She bit her lip, frowning. 'I know, but . . . I don't like deceiving them.'

He didn't want to waste any more time helping with her soul-searching. 'I think we ought to get on with the job. I've a number of people I need to see in the next few days.'

She nodded and glumly sipped her coffee.

'Can I start by asking you a few questions, Georgie? Is it all right if I call you Georgie?'

'I suppose so, but I'll have to call you Mr Diamond, won't I?'

Definitely prickly. 'In that case, I'll revert to Miss Gibbs.'

Her hazel eyes widened. He wasn't sure what her expression was telling him. Annoyed? Worried? 'Would you briefly outline your gardening career so far, please.'

She took a deep breath. 'I took biology, geography and chemistry A levels and then went to a horticultural college and from there to RHS Wisley.'

'Which college was that?'

'Does it matter?'

He shrugged. 'Why did you choose gardening as a career?'

'What on earth has that got to do with stolen plants? This is ridiculous.'

'Bear with me, Miss Gibbs. I need to know everyone's background. This information will help me.'

She raised her eyebrows. 'But you're looking for the thief. You know it's not me, so why waste your time?'

Although she'd an alibi for one theft, he wasn't sure she was in the clear. He didn't want her to know she was still a suspect, with every-one else, including the smouldering Keith Gage.

She threw the dregs of her mug into the sink. 'I've always loved gardening. We have a large garden at home, and as a child I was given my own plot, where I could grow what I liked. I love being outdoors, I didn't want an office job, or teaching, but I didn't want to go into agriculture. I may look rather slim, but I'm strong enough to do most of the jobs needed in a garden, and I can operate any machine.'

'I'm sure you must be an excellent gardener, or Mrs Gage wouldn't have employed you.'

She pushed back the mass of red hair away from her face. 'She got a good bargain, she doesn't pay top wages.'

'Really? But this job will be good experience for you. You are a head gardener, even if it's only in charge of one other full-time gardener. What's his name?'

'Owen Albrighton, and he's not completely full-time.'

'Was he the chap we saw working in the herbaceous border on our first visit?'

'Yes.'

'How many days does he work here?'

'Usually four days a week, but it depends.'

'On what?'

'I don't know, you'll have to ask him.'

He didn't believe her.

He rinsed out his mug. 'Thanks for your time, Miss Gibbs. I'll leave now and talk to some other people.'

She sprang up from her stool. 'I'll take you round and introduce you to everyone. I'll stay while you talk to them.'

Oh, no, you won't. 'Completely unnecessary. I can manage by myself. No need to take up any more of your valuable time.'

Her lips trembled. 'But . . .'

'Goodbye, see you later.' He marched out before she could say anything else. It was good to get into the spring sunshine, away from the airless potting shed. Her attitude was different to when they'd first met. Before she'd seemed worried, but now she was antagonistic to the strategy. Surely she wanted the thief caught?

He decided he'd take pot luck on who he met, and strolled into the nursery. There were no volunteers tending the plants, but in a wooden building, acting as a sales point, Bill, who'd asked the first question at the meeting, was talking to a customer, who was buying several potted plants. Frank waited until Bill had put the pots into a cardboard box, taken a cheque and escorted the lady to the nursery entrance, chatting all the while.

'Hello, Mr Diamond. Have you come to interrogate me?'

This sounded ominous. Had Bill sussed him out already? 'Just a few questions, if that's OK?'

'Certainly. Come into the shed. Like a cup of something?'

'No, thanks, just had a coffee with Miss Gibbs.'

'She's a sweet little girl, isn't she? A real hard worker. Only a slip of a thing, but my, what energy.'

'You don't mind being given your orders by a woman? Some men find it difficult.'

Bill laughed. 'I've been trained by the best – my wife. If I like and respect the person, I'm not worried if they're male or female. I don't have qualms about them telling me what to do. Look at Mrs Gage, she's a right bossy boots, but we all love her.'

He hoped Bill wasn't the thief.

'Have a seat.' Bill waved to a stool. 'Fire away, I'll be free until another customer comes along. Mind you, they usually take their time pottering around before they make up their minds.' He turned his hands palms upwards, and moved them as though weighing something in each one. 'Which is the better plant? Does this one have more buds than the other? Drives me crazy. I usually have to choose for them.' He said this as though it amused him.

'The last time I saw you, you were taking money at the entrance to the gardens,' Frank said.

Bill nodded. 'That chap who was with you, is he also an expert in assessing gardens?'

Frank shook his head. 'He usually assesses supermarkets, especially the display of foods. Making sure they are attractively displayed and maximising their sales.' Stuart would like that.

Bill raised his eyebrows. 'Really? I'd never have guessed that. He must know a great deal about food.'

'Oh, he does, especially confectionery.' He managed to keep a straight face. 'How long have you been a volunteer here?' he asked, switching the direction of the conversation.

93

'Seven years. Soon after I retired.'

'Was there any reason you chose to work here?'

'My wife's a keen gardener, she's been friendly with Pamela, Mrs Gage, for a number of years. She'd volunteer herself, but she's tied up with other charities, so she volunteered me.'

'How often do you come?'

'I do one day a week, sometimes as two half-days. It depends. If it's a busy time, as it's going to be soon, I'll do a bit more, and then not so much in winter.'

'Do you do any gardening at home?'

Bill laughed again. 'I'm a mow the lawn and cut the hedge man. My wife won't let me in the borders and neither will Pamela. She gave me a few gardening jobs to do when I first volunteered, but when she realised I didn't know a dandelion from a tulip, she pulled me out of the borders pretty quick.'

'Do you do any other jobs apart from this one, and taking money at the entrance?'

'I have delivered plants, not often. I'm also good at sweeping the paths and removing leaves from the lawns in autumn. I don't mind what I do. I like a bit of physical activity.'

'You must be a great asset. Is there anything you think could be improved in the running of the garden or nursery, that would either help things to run more efficiently, or would increase sales?'

Bill's face became serious and his brow creased in concentration. 'I can think of one thing, but it might not be legal.'

'I hope it isn't growing cannabis?'

Bill roared with laughter. 'No, and I shouldn't have said that. It could get me into trouble.'

Frank thought he knew where this was going. 'Would it be the removal of a certain person?'

Bill grimaced and nodded. 'She'd be a lot happier if he wasn't around, and the money he wastes would help her to make the improvements needed.'

So, Pamela's problems with dear Keith were well known. 'Apart from your fantasy solution, have you any other ideas?'

'Since you talked to us this morning, I've been thinking of ways to help. I was wondering if it might be worth considering a scheme people could sign up to, become Friends of the Garden. They'd pay a one-off sum that would entitle them to as many visits to the garden in a year as they like. I thought it might bring in some capital, encourage them to visit regularly and hopefully buy more plants. Shouldn't be too dear to set up.'

'That sounds like a first-rate idea, Bill. Staff would be needed to administrate it.'

'A volunteer, or two, could run it. I wouldn't mind setting it up.'

'What did you do before you retired?'

'Bank manager.'

Frank laughed. 'You're the first bank manager I've met who looks like he'd be fun to spend a night at the pub with.'

'I might take you up on that, Mr Diamond.'

Frank nodded. But not yet. 'That's all the questions I've got for you at the moment, Bill. I may be back to ask more. I'll certainly include your suggestions, apart from one, for Mrs Gage.' He got up.

Bill pointed out of the window to a stout woman rummaging amongst some plants. 'There's Mrs Crossley, looking for a bargain. She always finds a plant that looks a bit tatty and tries to push the price down.'

'Is she successful?'

He shook his head. 'Oh, no. If we started reducing plant prices for one customer, they'd all be at it. News spreads like wildfire round here.'

Frank thanked him and left the nursery, heading for the Japanese garden. He decided it was his favourite part, and he especially loved the zig-zag path over the lake. As he walked through the herbaceous borders, the man Georgie had named as Owen Albrighton was clipping one of the topiary yews that stood sentinel at the ends of each border. Not a good time to clip hedges; birds might be nesting, but he supposed with such a meagre workforce, they had to do jobs when they had the time. He waved to Owen. 'Will you be there in half an hour?' he shouted.

Owen paused, shears dangling from his right hand. 'Yes, sir. I'll be in the maze later on.'

Frank wondered why he didn't pull at his forelock. Sounded sub-servient. Why?

The Japanese garden was as impressive as the last time he'd seen it, sun glinting off the waters of the lake, and a slight breeze ruffling the surface, scintillas of light dancing around the zig-zag path. Walking over the lake, the air smelt different, as if cleansed by the rippling water. Really peaceful. He headed for the pavilion on the far side. It wouldn't hurt to spend a few minutes there, looking at the lake and the pair of exotic ducks who were gliding towards him, probably hoping for some food.

He must bring Laurel here; she would love it. Quite a romantic spot; perhaps if they sat in the pavilion together, who knew what might happen? His mother's voice rang in his brain. 'Francis Xavier Diamond, you have a girlfriend. What are you playing at?' He pushed her away. Perhaps he should just do it, take Laurel in his arms and kiss her. He shuddered. Supposing she reacted negatively? Slapped his face – punched him senseless – kicked him in the balls. He laughed.

'Mr Diamond? Do you want to talk to me?' He flinched. The voice came from behind a clump of brown ferns to the right of the pavilion. A tall woman appeared; she had dark, tightly bunched hair, streaked with white, reminding him of a badger. 'Mrs Lamb?'

'Miss Lamb, but please call me Janet.'

She looked in her mid-sixties and had a plain, but not unpleasant face. It was the woman he'd seen on their first visit, a volunteer who'd been given a plant by Pamela, and who'd asked a question at the meeting.

Frank shook her hand, which she'd wrenched from a leather gardening glove. It was a strong, long-fingered hand, and her grip was firm. 'You gave me quite a shock, Miss Lamb. What were you doing behind the fern?'

She gave him a hard look. 'Nothing I'm ashamed off. I was weeding and preparing to cut down last year's fronds. They should have been done before now.' She sounded disapproving.

'Really?'

She gave him another hard look. 'As an expert, you surely know that.'

Oh dear. A slip-up. 'Sometimes, depending on the delicacy of the fern, they are best left with their old foliage until all danger of frost has passed. But on closer inspection, I can see this is a tough old dryopteris.' He was pleased with his get-out-of-trouble answer; so apparently was Janet, as her face softened.

'Very true, Mr Diamond. Do you want to have a chat? I can spare half an hour.'

He'd have liked to spend some time contemplating the beauty of the garden, but not if Janet was going to be there, testing his horti-cultural knowledge.

'Yes, shall we sit in the pavilion?' He waved a hand, ushering her towards it.

She was wearing corduroy trousers and a green gilet over a brown polo-necked jumper. She would have passed for a professional gar-dener any day.

'I think this is the most beautiful part of the gardens,' he said.

She beamed at him. 'I'm pleased to hear you say that, it's mine too. It's a privilege to work in it.'

'How long have you been a volunteer?'

'Six years, from when I retired. We've always loved the garden and Pamela is a close friend.'

We? She said she was Miss Lamb. A sister? A lover? 'What did you do before you retired? I hope you don't mind me asking.'

'Not at all. I was a geography teacher.'

Probably retired at sixty, makes her sixty-six. 'A local school?'

'St Mary's at Southwold. We lived at Southwold, but moved to Yoxford when I finished.'

'You don't miss the sea?'

'I do, but here we were able to buy a house with a large garden. Prices on the coast were not affordable. It was our dream to make a garden.'

He looked at her enquiringly. 'I live with my dear friend Muriel, she taught French at St Mary's. She retired a year before me. We're very happy here, near Yoxford.'

'Don't you have enough work in your own garden without doing voluntary work?'

'Too true, Mr Diamond, but I don't mind sparing some time to work here. I've learnt a great deal from Pamela, and she's very generous, she often gives me plants, or sells them to me for a reduced price, so I'm sure I get back as much as I give.'

A plant fanatic? Her own garden? A possible suspect? Pity, she seemed a nice woman, if a bit uptight. What was the relationship with Muriel? Not that it mattered, but it was interesting.

He asked her if she had any suggestions or criticisms of the way the gardens were run.

'I think some of the other volunteers spend too much time gossiping instead of getting on with their work.'

He wondered if she gave them a hundred lines to write: *More digging, less chatter.* 'Is that all of the other volunteers?'

She pursed her lips. 'Quite a few.'

'Any other comments?'

'I think it would be a good idea if more of the plants we grow in the garden could be propagated for sale; sometimes the plants bought in are not of the top quality.'

'Any reason why this isn't happening?'

She sighed. 'Lack of staff, I suppose. It's a pity because visitors often ask me about a certain plant they've seen in the garden, and want to buy one.'

'Thank you, a valuable suggestion. I'll pass it on to Mrs Gage.'

She waved a hand. 'No need. I've told her myself several times.' She stared at him. 'Is there any other reason you are asking us questions, Mr Diamond?'

His spine tightened. 'I don't follow.'

'I wondered if it might be to do with . . .' She paused. 'Sorry, ignore what I've said.'

He didn't reply, he thought it safer not to.

'What kind of garden have you made for yourself?'

She beamed, obviously pleased to have been asked. 'We were very lucky, the previous owners weren't gardeners; they kept two ponies in a half-acre field attached to the house, so we had a blank canvas to play with.'

'Wasn't that intimidating? Must have been a lot of hard work?'

'Very true, but we were sensible and mapped out the main paths, a pond, and planted hedges before we started the exciting bit – planting the borders. We paid a firm to do the landscaping.'

'Have you built a Japanese garden?'

'We have, and we managed to buy some woodland on the edge of our land as well.'

'Put in any snowdrops?'

She eyed him knowingly. 'Are you a galanthophile?'

He shook his head. 'I prefer the ordinary snowdrop in large masses to the specials. I must admit I can't see some of the differences between the various varieties.'

She shook her head. 'I suppose it's like any collector, you catch the bug. We're both passionate about our snowdrop collection.'

'That can be an expensive hobby?'

'I know, but Pamela has been very generous and I've bought several varieties from her at very reasonable prices.'

Would she be telling me all this if she was the thief? Or was she trying to allay my suspicions? he wondered.

'You must come over and see the garden someday if you have time. We love showing people who are interested in gardens round it.'

Frank got up. 'Thank you, Janet, that's very kind of you. I'd better continue my tour, see who else is able to help me. Thank you for your suggestions.'

She pushed herself up from the bench, groaning slightly. 'I'll have to do a few exercises when I get home. I shouldn't have sat down – fatal. I do hope you'll be able to help Pamela, she deserves to have success, she's had a lot to put up with.'

'Really?'

She gave him an old-fashioned look. 'I presume you've met Keith?'

'I have.'

'Need I say more?'

He shook his head. 'Goodbye, Janet. No doubt we'll talk again.'

She walked jerkily back to the clump of ferns, holding the small of her back; a moment later there was a groan and the sound of secateurs.

He reluctantly left the Japanese garden and wandered off towards the maze, making diversions to talk to two other volunteers, both women, one a timid creature tackling a patch of celandines and the other a large lady, who told him all about her medical history including two breech births and a hysterectomy. Frank promised himself he'd avoid her in future; if she gave such intimate details on their first meeting, what horrors would she reveal if they talked again?

From the maze there was the sound of clipping; he hesitated – if he went in, he might never find Albrighton, and get lost in the process, facing the humiliating prospect of having to shout for a rescue. He decided to call out. 'Hello, Mr Albrighton, could you come out and speak to me, please? It's Mr Diamond.'

The clipping stopped and a man emerged from the maze entrance, a pair of shears in his right hand. It was Owen Albrighton, the other professional gardener, who strode towards him with an easy gait. About the same height as Frank, but a more muscular build, with thick dark hair down to the collar of his check shirt, he was gauntly handsome with sharp cheekbones, but a sour face.

'Mr Albrighton?'

He nodded.

Frank inwardly sighed. One moment it was a lady who wouldn't shut up, now a man who didn't want to part his lips. 'I'd like to talk with you for a few minutes. Is now a good time?'

Albrighton scowled. 'It's never a good time. I've got the whole bloody maze to clip.' He shook the shears in front of Frank's face. 'And all I've got is these.'

Better than nail clippers, Frank thought. 'It must take a while to complete that job.'

100

'She won't let me use any machines. Says she doesn't like the noise they make. Everything must be done in the old ways.'

'So, one of your suggestions for improving the efficiency of the gardens would be to bring in more mechanisation?'

Albrighton blew out a stream of air. 'Too right, but she won't do it. I've told her I could do these jobs in no time at all if she'd buy some up-to-date equipment, but she's as stubborn as a mule.'

'By she, I presume you mean Mrs Gage?'

He nodded. 'You won't tell her I said she's like a mule, will you?'

'As I said at the meeting, whatever you say to me is confidential. Shall we sit over there?' He pointed to a weathered wooden bench, looking in need of a sand-down and a coat of varnish.

Albrighton turned and marched ahead of him and slumped down. 'You'd better tell Mrs Gage you've kept me from my work, or else she'll be complaining I've taken too long finishing off the job.'

Frank bit his lip. 'I thought Mrs Gage seemed to be a fair woman. Is she a good employer?'

Albrighton glanced at him slyly. 'She's not bad, bit old-fashioned, as I've said. Pays as much as she can afford. As long as I do a good day's work, she doesn't bother me too much.'

He seemed to have changed his tone. 'You're part-time, aren't you? How many days do you work a week?'

'Four.' A pause. 'It depends.'

'On what?'

He moved uncomfortably on the bench. 'That's my business, not yours.'

Frank didn't say anything.

Albrighton sighed. 'I suppose I'd better tell you. If I don't, some-one else will. I just don't like talking about it. I don't want anyone's pity.'

Frank remained silent.

'I look after my mother. She's widowed, has been for a long time. Dad died when I was a toddler. It was all right until she got arthritis. Some days she's real bad, especially in the winter. I have to stay with her then. She can't manage by herself.'

Frank felt a heel. 'I'm sorry.'

Albrighton glowered at him.

'I'm sorry your mother is in pain. I know arthritis can be a devil, I've an aunt who suffers with it. It's no joke.'

Albrighton pushed out his bottom lip and nodded.

'Mrs Gage is flexible when you can't make it to work?'

Once again, he nodded. 'Yes, can't fault her there. I make up the days when Ma is better.'

'Do you have any other work?'

'On her good days, when I've done my four days here, I see if I can get work at some people's gardens.'

'You mean private gardens. Or other nurseries?'

'Private. It's mostly cutting the lawn or hedge work. I can't give any of them a regular slot, and sometimes they find someone else.'

It was a precarious way to make a living. 'Do you live near here?'

'Near Darsham. We live a bit out of the village, that's another problem; Ma can't walk to the shop, so I have to do all the shopping.'

He sounded resentful, but who could blame him. 'I don't suppose you have your own garden to look after?'

'Why do you say that?'

Frank shrugged. 'It always seems to be the case, whatever work you do, you never want to do that work at home. Like a carpenter will never get round to putting up shelves in his own house. I was thinking if you had a garden the last thing you'd want to do is plant vegetables in your time off.'

'You're wrong there. I'd rather be working on my garden than other people's. I'm proud of my garden. It keeps us in veg all year, not to mention apples, raspberries and strawberries. I raise plants and sell them when I can. There's money to be made from plants.'

'You mustn't have much time for hobbies, or for chasing girls, from what you've said.'

Albrighton smirked, and brushed back a lock of hair that had fallen over his forehead. 'I don't need to go chasing after girls – they chase after me.'

He wondered if Georgie Gibbs had been in pursuit of him. She'd blushed nicely when they met Albrighton on his first visit.

'Lucky dog,' he said. Owen's chest expanded and he smiled lasciviously.

'What does your mother think of all these girls after you?'

'She wishes I'd settle down and marry one of them.'

'Really? Isn't she afraid of losing you?'

'I'd never leave Ma. I'll only get married when I've made some money, and my wife would have to agree to Ma living with us.'

'You're a good son.'

Albrighton gave him a friendly smile, transforming his face. Now he saw why the girls chased him.

'Who gives you your orders, Mrs Gage or Miss Gibbs?'

Albrighton cast a swift glance. 'Why do you want to know that? Does it make any difference?'

'Remember, I'm trying to find out how the business works. If I can find better ways for things to happen, it will benefit everybody. Can you answer the question, please?'

'It depends. It's who I see when I come in first thing. Sometimes I see Georgie and she doesn't know what Mrs Gage wants me to do. Many's the time she's set me on something, so not to waste time, and then Mrs Gage comes along and wants me to do something else. I don't like that, being ordered from pillar to post.'

Frank nodded. 'That's very helpful. If I can persuade Mrs Gage it would be better for decisions to be made in advance, preferably for the whole week, then you wouldn't have to chop and change your jobs.'

Albrighton nodded. 'That's a good idea.'

'Georgie's a nice girl. Do you mind taking orders from her?'

Albrighton's tongue darted from his mouth and flicked over his top lip like an adder testing the air for prey. 'She's all right.'

More than all right, as far as Albrighton was concerned, he thought; if that wasn't a look of lust, he was losing his touch. 'You get on well?'

'She's a clever girl. Smart. She always asks me nice, and she's taught me a lot about plants. I don't mind her giving me orders.' The tongue flickered again.

Frank wondered if any of the orders were zoological, rather than botanical.

'How do you get on with the volunteers? Do you have much to do with them?'

Albrighton rolled his eyes. 'I sometimes have to have some of them with me, say if we're clearing a border. Half the time they don't know a bindweed from a clematis. I have to check they're not pulling up the good plants instead of the weeds.'

'Really? I wouldn't have thought Mrs Gage would let anyone on her borders who wasn't capable.'

'They suck up to her, tell her she's marvellous.'

'I certainly met one volunteer who knows her plants. Miss Lamb. Have you worked with her?'

Albrighton sniffed. 'Miss Know-it-all. Thinks she knows everything, her being a teacher. They're all the same, teachers.'

'You have to admit she seems to be a good gardener.'

'I don't have to admit anything.'

'Why don't you like her?'

'I've told you – she's bossy, and nosy, thinks she's a cut above the rest of us.'

Frank decided to leave it at that. Albrighton, despite being a good son, was getting on his nerves, and he didn't like the look on his face when they talked about Georgie Gibbs.

# Chapter Twelve

As Laurel approached the outskirts of Aldeburgh, she remembered the first time she'd met Adam Pemberton. Then, the Agency was involved in the search for his missing son, David. Now, she was unsure why he wanted to see her, but it *must* be something to do with David. But how could she help? He'd been arrested for the murder of Judge Hanmer, and held at Ipswich Police Station.

That morning, after Frank had left for Yoxford Gardens, Dorothy had taken a phone call. 'It's for you,' she'd hissed, covering the mouthpiece with her hand. 'It's Mr Pemberton.'

'Hello, Mr Pemberton. How can I help you?'

'Miss Bowman, I'm so glad I've caught you in. Ann and I urgently need to talk to you. Could you come over to Aldeburgh today?'

His voice was desperate, cracking with emotion. How could she refuse? 'Yes, I can come over this afternoon. Say, two?'

'Thank you. Thank you. We'll see you then.'

'Can you tell me what it's about?'

'NO, NO. Not over the phone. I need to talk with you face to face. You will come, won't you?'

He sounded at the end of his tether. 'Of course. I'll be with you at two.'

She'd come to Aldeburgh by the Thorpe Road, passing the fishermen's huts and the Moot Hall, such a dear building, the last remnant of Aldeburgh's Elizabethan past. The town was quietly busy, but the fishermen's huts were closed after selling their morning's catch. She turned the Cortina up the steep Victoria Road, then left into the quiet street where the Pembertons lived. It was nearly two years ago when she'd last been in this house. Then Adam was married to the beautiful, but unfaithful, Carol. Two years. It was the Agency's first big case and she'd been disturbed and surprised by Frank putting his professional conduct at risk by nearly having an affair with Carol. Luckily, he'd discovered her propensities in time and had backed off, and confessed his involvement to the team. Then she was half in love with him herself. Was it a reaction to his conduct that made her take up with Oliver Neave? In the end, she realised she was longing for a relationship, with all that meant, but not with Oliver. What did she want now? She sighed as she pulled into the gravel driveway of the Pemberton's home.

The house was imposing, if sombre. Built before the First World War, its three stories were topped by tall mock-Tudor chimneys, but the former high hedge had been lowered, letting light into the front garden which was full of bright yellow daffodils and pools of early tulips. Ann's doing?

She answered the front doorbell. There were deep shadows under her eyes, but she seemed calm and contained. She grasped Laurel's outstretched hand.

'Laurel. I can't say how glad I am that you've come.' She ushered her into the spacious hall with its wide staircase leading up to a double minstrel gallery. This area was more welcoming than on her last visit: two cosy chairs near a low table, with a vase of spring flowers, had replaced the upright hall chairs, and there was a red Turkish rug spread out over the wooden floor.

'Adam's in the library.' She opened the door into a room filled with tiers of books on the walls, a library table and three leather chairs grouped round a fireplace, logs crackling and yellow flames licking the backplate.

'Laurel.' Adam Pemberton got up from one of the chairs. 'So good of you to come.' He waved to the seat opposite his, then drew another close for Ann.

She remembered she'd seen signs of affection between them when Ann was the housekeeper; how she'd blushed with pleasure when Adam had praised some cakes she'd brought in with the coffee; he'd said he and Carol couldn't manage without her. Who'd have thought that two years later they'd be husband and wife?

'Would you like some tea, Laurel?' Ann asked.

'Perhaps afterwards when I know what you want to see me about.'

Adam looked relieved. 'Yes, much better to get the business done.'

She wasn't so sure. How would she be able to help them? This wasn't the Agency's case and it looked as though, much as she didn't want to believe it, David had murdered Neville Hanmer. She looked from one to the other and nodded.

Adam took a deep breath. 'You know what's happened?'

'Yes. I'm truly sorry and very upset, for both of you, and for David. It's only two years since he came back to you and I know he's made great progress, both with his art and as a person.' Perhaps she shouldn't say this, but she felt she must. 'I find it hard to believe that David killed the Judge.'

Adam gulped, looking close to tears. 'Thank you, my dear, for saying that. It means a great deal to me.'

'Thank you,' Ann said. 'I don't believe for a minute David would kill anyone.'

She remained silent, but nodded at Adam, trying to encourage him to continue.

'As you can imagine, Inspector Revie was also upset, and he talked to us before he arrested David, and said it was a sad day, and the boy had been through so much suffering and anguish, and he was sorry. But the evidence was against David because his fingerprints were found in the Judge's house, and he'd no alibi for the time of the murder.'

'Do you know what David has said to Inspector Revie?'

Adam mopped his forehead with a handkerchief. 'That's the crux of the problem. He hasn't said a word to anyone. He won't speak. The Inspector even asked me and Ann if we would talk to him, at least get him to say *something*, but all he did was to hide his head in his hands – he wouldn't even look at us.'

Laurel's heart sank. He'd regressed. Gone back to the boy who'd often refused to communicate. They'd learnt, after he was rescued, he could talk fluently, indeed he had a good vocabulary, but he chose not to do so. Along with his dislike of being touched it was difficult for anyone, never mind a stranger, to forge a relationship with him. But before he ran away, he'd formed a warm friendship with Ann who, because of her calm nature and instinctive understanding, had built a close bond with him. 'Did you see him by yourself, Ann?' Laurel asked.

Ann nodded. 'We tried talking to him together, and then separately, but he didn't respond.'

'You did say he looked at you, Ann,' Adam said.

'Yes, he peeped at me from behind a hand. He looked frightened, so young and vulnerable. He seemed to move his lips, as though he wanted to say something, but no words came out. I foolishly stretched out a hand and he instantly retreated.'

Laurel smiled at them. 'But that's encouraging. He does realise how serious the situation is?'

'We presume so,' Adam said. 'He's been formally arrested. I tried to explain to him how grave the charge is, and if he won't tell them why he was in Judge Hanmer's house, the police have nothing to go on, and his silence will be taken as the silence of guilt.'

Laurel thought she knew where this was going. She waited, not wanting to volunteer if she was wrong.

'Laurel, we have a big favour to ask. When you were both imprisoned in that room at Tucker's house, you inspired David to help you come out of that room alive. He's often spoken of how he admires you, in fact I do believe he adores you. To him you were a goddess. Righting wrong. The person who fought to save his life,' Adam said.

She knew this was true, but she also knew David was disillusioned when the men involved in the case, many in important roles in government, the judiciary and the Church, were never brought to book for their crimes. Some disappeared, or had unfortunate accidents, a few committed suicide, but no one was brought to the dock to face charges, and the three Pembertons and all members of the Agency were made to sign the Official Secrets Act. She thought a change came over David when he realised his murdered friend, Peter, would never have justice. His attitude to her changed, and he seemed puzzled by her silence. To him she was no longer the super-woman he'd drawn, hair flowing, a stiletto in her hand, Diana the huntress, ready to fight the foe. He felt she'd failed him, and she had to agree.

'Laurel, would you talk to David, see if he'll tell you why he was in Neville Hanmer's house, and hopefully say he didn't kill him?' Adam asked. Ann was leaning towards her; a pleading look on her face.

How could she say no? 'Will Inspector Revie agree to me seeing him? He's bending the rules already.'

A smile split Adam's face. 'Yes, yes. I've asked him. He's willing to try anything. They, the police, have brought in different experts; a child psychologist, even a negotiator, someone who can talk down a person about to commit suicide, or persuade a kidnapper to release his hostage. He's tried everything he can. He's agreed. You could see him today, if you've time.'

Everything was happening too fast. 'Yes, of course I'll try to get him to talk to me.'

Adam got up and took both her hands in his. 'God bless you, my dear. I've prayed as I've never prayed before for someone to help us. That someone is you.'

'Thank you, Laurel,' Ann said. 'I know you'll try your best.'

She realises, Laurel thought. Adam is sure I can once more break through the barriers David builds around himself, but Ann realises this is a different scenario. Before we were fighting for our lives, he was full of hate for the men who'd stolen two years of his life and who'd taken the life of his friend, and possibly other boys as well. Now, she wasn't sure how he felt. Had he hated the Judge? Did he know the Judge was a homosexual? Did he believe the Judge had been part of the cabal of paedophiles? Had he sought justice for Peter? Or was he innocent? Caught up in the real murderer's web of deceit? Lured to the Judge's home and used to set a false trail away from the real murderer?

'Does it have to be today?'

'We need to move quickly, Laurel. I'll drive you to Ipswich this evening. I'll ring Inspector Revie and ask him what time we should come,' Adam said, obviously fired up by her acceptance.

Would she have enough time to think about how she would tackle this? She needed space to think. She'd only have a few hours, if that.

'Please ring Inspector Revie now, but I'd rather go alone, if you don't mind.'

Adam frowned.

'I can understand that,' Ann said. 'Please do as Laurel asks, Adam.'

He left the room.

'Time for a cup of tea?' Ann asked.

'Thank you.' She also left the room.

Laurel didn't want Adam's nervous worrying getting to her as they drove to Ipswich. She would have to be calm. Go through the different things that might happen, have a strategy for each one. She'd need to bottle up her emotions, not let David see how upset she was, let him know she thought he was innocent, and she had faith in him. She must try and re-establish the special relationship they'd built up in the room they'd shared as they waited to die. Would Frank drive her to Ipswich? It would be ideal. She'd have more time to think, to role play in her head, before they got there. If Frank was driving, he'd be calm, quiet, and a sounding board if she wanted to try out an idea to make David talk to her.

Ann was back first. There was a plate of scones besides the teapot. They looked and smelt delicious, but she wasn't sure she was capable of swallowing anything but tea at the moment.

Adam strode back into the room. 'It's all fixed. Can you be there by half six? Inspector Revie will be there to take you to him.'

She glanced at her watch. There was little time to prepare. She needed to get back to Greyfriars. God, she hoped Frank was back from Yoxford. Should she ask Stuart to drive her if he wasn't? Or

Dorothy? No, with Dorothy it would be a bumpy journey; a fatal combination of Dorothy's driving and her old Morris Traveller. If Frank wasn't there, she'd go by herself. She gulped down the tea, scalding her mouth. 'I must go. I'll phone you when I get back to Greyfriars tonight. Please don't expect too much. If experts have tried and failed, I'm not sure I'll be any more successful.'

Adam's face showed disappointment and despair. He nodded. 'I know you'll do your best.'

'I will.' She tried to think of something positive to give them. 'It may take more than one visit. I'll go on trying as long as Inspector Revie lets me.'

There were tears in Adam's eyes; one slid down a cheek. 'God bless you, Laurel. Give David all our love and tell him we believe he is innocent, and we'll do everything in our power to prove it.'

# Chapter Thirteen

Frank followed the instructions the man at the pub in Yoxford had given him; he found Badger Lane, a narrow but thankfully tarmacked road, on the outskirts of the town and drove slowly down it looking for Pear Tree Cottage, the home of Janet Lamb and her friend Muriel. He was acting on impulse. He'd been given access to the staff files and after his chat with Owen Albrighton, he had gone to Pamela Gage's office and found Janet's home address. She was the ideal candidate for the plant thief: knowledgeable about plants in general, knew Yoxford Gardens well, a plant collector, possessed a large garden, possibly unable to afford some of the rare plants she desired, and a confessed galanthophile. Against this was her openness, her friendship with Pamela Gage and she had been a teacher. They were mostly good, law-abiding citizens, or so Laurel said.

He knew Janet was working late, and hoped her friend, Muriel, would also be out, but if not, he'd do a bit of blagging. The main thing was to get a look at the gardens and see if he could see any suspicious plants; Pamela had lent him books that contained relevant illustrations. If he did see any, this wouldn't be proof, as Janet could say she'd bought them from another plant nursery, but she'd have to prove she'd done that.

A white-washed cottage, set back a short way from the lane, appeared on his right. He slowed the car down to a crawl. On the wooden gate was a sign – Pear Tree Cottage – and in the small front garden there it was, a gnarled pear tree, covered in blossom; it looked so old, it might even be the original tree the cottage was named after. Where to park? There was a rutted lane to the right of the cottage; he backed up and tucked the Avenger just inside it; the lane's surface was rough, full of large pebbles.

Walking back to the gate, with its low picket fence, the front garden was also covered in gravel; it was alive with the buzz of honeybees feeding on botanical tulips that must have seeded themselves, clumps of miniature daffodils, wild violas and dwarf daphne shrubs, their sweet scent heady in the sunshine.

He opened the gate; the middle part of the house looked older than the rest, probably once a farm labourer's cottage. On each side of it, extensions made a sprawling and attractive house with its blue door and window frames; a gleaming brass knocker in the shape of a wheat sheaf added the final touch.

He gave several raps, hoping there would be no answer. He waited a few minutes and repeated the action. He was in luck. He might be able to have a prowl round the garden before anyone came back and then Janet would never know he'd been.

He followed a brick path to the left of the front door, and peered in through a window; luckily there were no net curtains. Although the small window didn't let in much light, he was able to see it was the sitting room; there was an old, but comfortable-looking, three-piece suite, upholstered in brown corduroy, a couple of floor-to-ceiling shelves bulging with books, a TV and a small, ornate cast-iron stove, with a pile of logs beside it. He sighed. It looked a friendly, comfortable room. Sometimes it was difficult not to become biased, one way or the other.

At the back of the house the garden stretched away to a small copse of oaks. This must be the wood Janet said they'd bought. Would he find some suspicions snowdrops in there? Attached to the house was a stone terrace with a wooden table and two chairs. Birds chattered overhead, and a small flock of jackdaws wheeled round the chimneys, calling, as some settled on the rims and others on a nearby cherry tree.

The lawn had wide borders on each side, with ornamental bushes, the rosy heads of emerging peonies and other perennials. A yew hedge cut off this part of the garden from whatever lay beyond. As he walked towards the hedge a slender figure appeared round the side, stopped abruptly, stepped back, her hand holding a trowel, clutched to her chest.

He stopped where he was. 'Muriel?' he said, hoping for the best, and almost as unnerved as she obviously was.

'Yes?' She approached slowly and cautiously. She was about five foot three, with soft brown hair tied back. At a distance she appeared young, but as she neared, he saw fine lines at the corners of her mouth and eyes, and her skin, though soft, sagged round her chin. Sixty?

He held out his hand. 'Hello. Sorry if I startled you, I'm Frank Diamond. I've just been talking to your friend, Janet Lamb. She was telling me about your garden and invited me to drop by and see it if I was ever nearby. I had to come this way, and I hoped you might be here. Would it be possible for you to show me round, if you have the time, that is?' His words sounded genuine, even to his ears. Silver-tongued devil, Laurel would say.

Her eyes flitted from side to side. 'Oh, really? Perhaps it would be better to wait until Janet comes back. I'm not sure. Who are you? Why were you talking to Janet?'

A nervy one. What was she worried about? Or did he really represent a threatening figure? He could hear Laurel. 'Frank! She's a woman on her own, in an isolated cottage. A strange man has wandered into her garden. He's got long hair and a leather jacket. And although he's madly handsome –' she wouldn't have said that – 'she's scared.'

He explained about his role at Yoxford Hall Gardens, and how he'd been talking to Janet only a few hours ago. 'She's such an enthusiast, and talked about the garden you've both made with such interest and passion, as I was passing I couldn't resist coming to have a look.'

The hand with the trowel slowly moved down to her side.

'I'm sorry, I did knock, but as no one answered, I thought I'd see if you were in the garden.'

114

Still no reply, but her shoulders dropped and she seemed more relaxed.

'Perhaps I'd better go, and come back another time?'

She smiled. 'No, of course not. You gave me a fright, that's all. I'm not the brave one, that's Janet. She'd have had you in an arm lock first, and then questioned you.' They both laughed.

'Would you like to see the rest of the garden?'

'If you're sure it's no trouble.'

She walked towards him, holding out her hand. 'I'm Muriel, as you know. I'm sorry, I didn't catch your name, I was in a blue funk.' She gave a slight smile.

Easy to see who was the dominant partner in this relationship. 'Frank Diamond. You've made a wonderful job of the front garden; a gravel bed isn't easy to establish.'

Her eyes sparkled with enthusiasm. 'Do you know, since we planted the bed, we've never watered it, and any weeds are easy to pull out of the gravel. You just need to keep on top of it, not let them grow too big.'

Frank could see he'd need to do a lot of nodding his head, and making congratulatory noises. He hoped he would get more out of this dodgy episode than horticultural tips. Pretending to be an expert in a field he had only superficial knowledge of was beginning to become tedious; he'd be glad to get back to proper detective mode.

Behind the hedge was a small Japanese garden, quite different to the one at Yoxford; fewer plants, some areas of gravel raked in concentric circles, a formal pond surrounded by small trees.

He pointed. 'Acers?'

She gave him a broad smile and nodded. She seemed a nice woman. 'I believe you and Janet worked at the same school?'

'Yes, that's right. St Mary's, at Southwold. I taught languages, mainly French.'

'Did you enjoy teaching?'

She pulled a face. 'It depended on who was in my class.'

'Really? At a private school I didn't think you'd have any problems with the pupils.'

She glanced at him. 'Children are children, whether their parents live in council houses or mansions. The accents may be different, but you'll find troublemakers at every school.'

He thought Laurel would agree with that. 'But a private school has an advantage, it can tell the parents of the naughty ones they need to find another educational establishment.'

They'd moved from the Japanese garden, down a slope to a dew pond, with wild planting on its edges, the oak copse beyond.

She sniffed. 'You'd think so, wouldn't you? But if the parents are influential and have made a substantial donation to the building, say towards a new theatre, it's more likely *the teacher* will be asked to move on, if there's a problem.'

As they neared the pond, a blackbird, with a beak full of mud, flew back to the yew hedge. 'You must have a lot of wildlife in the garden,' Frank said, hoping to soften her up for his next question.

'You saw the bird feeders in the front garden?'

'Yes, and the birdbath. Obviously, you don't deprive the animals of water even if you're tough on the plants.'

She laughed.

'St Mary's School? Gosh, I think I met a former pupil a few days ago. I was at Thorpeness Country Club. She's a tennis coach there. What was her name? You might know her? Perhaps *she* was one of the naughty ones.'

She looked at him enquiringly.

He pretended to be racking his brains. He clicked his fingers. 'Yes, that's it. Beatrice Mavor. Tall woman, jolly good tennis player.'

Muriel's face whitened. 'Beattie Mavor. So that's where she's ended up.'

'How interesting. Did you teach her?'

'Unfortunately, yes.'

'Not your favourite pupil?'

She raised her eyebrow. The look said it all.

'She was with her brother, Carlton, he's also a tennis coach. I must say their relationship seemed a bit stormy.'

'Beattie couldn't stand being second best – in anything. Languages

116

were not her strong point, but she hated to not be top of the class, even though she excelled in many other subjects and of course in anything physical.'

'She certainly took a delight in helping to wallop a friend of mine at tennis who was playing with her brother.'

'Typical. I found her difficult to deal with, as I refused to give her good marks for a subject she was not good at. I'm not saying she didn't try, but she didn't have a facility for languages. Good enough to get a GCE pass, but no more than that.'

She jumped as a jay shot out of the wood, its blue-black plumage shining in the sunlight.

'It was probably looking for the last of the acorns,' Frank said. He thought he'd better not ask any more questions about Beattie; he was supposed to be interested in the garden.

'I'm afraid you've missed the best of the snowdrops, the flowers are mostly over. We've got several varieties planted on the edge of the wood. They seem to do well under the oaks.'

Were there any clumps hidden away in secret places? Finding a new home after being dug up from Yoxford Gardens? 'Will there be bluebells soon?'

She shook her head. 'No, we decided not to plant any, as they can spread rapidly and smother some of our smaller bulbs. We enjoy looking at them in the woods near here.'

'Pity, such a wonderful perfume en masse.'

'True. Well, Mr Diamond, I think you've seen most of the garden. You must come back in the summer, when more of the flowers are out. Shall we go back?'

That was him told, but he hadn't had enough time on his own to look for suspicious plants.

As they walked up the incline towards the yew hedge, Janet Lamb strode round it, her face angry. 'What idiot has left his car in the lane? I can't get in,' she shouted, then abruptly stopped. 'Mr Diamond. What on earth are you doing here?' She was surprised as well as angry.

Muriel flinched. 'Mr Diamond came to look at the garden. He

said you'd invited him.' Her voice wavered. This didn't seem like a relationship of equals.

Janet strode towards them, then ground to a halt a few feet from Frank. 'Why have you come here?' she demanded.

Frank ignored her red face and breath coming from her nostrils like an aggressive bull. 'Hello, Miss Lamb, I was hoping you'd be here when I came by, but I've met your delightful friend, Muriel, who's shown me round your garden.'

'You knew I was at Yoxford Gardens.'

'I wasn't sure what time you finished. As I said to Muriel, I was passing, and you'd invited me to see your garden. I'm sorry if I've made a mistake.'

She stood her ground. 'The invitation was to see the garden with me, not Muriel.'

'Does it matter?'

The colour had subsided in her cheeks, but there was a mulish look on her face. She wasn't happy with his story.

'I'm sorry if I've offended you, but I'm impressed with your garden, it has so many different areas, and seems full of wildlife.'

'Mr Diamond especially liked the Japanese garden,' Muriel squeaked.

Janet's face softened. Good old Muriel, or should it be poor old Muriel? She was certainly in a lather about Janet's attitude towards him. Did she dread a scene after he'd left? 'You mustn't blame Muriel, Janet. I came into the garden looking for you. She didn't invite me in.'

Definitely a softening now. Janet turned to Muriel. 'Sorry I lost my temper, Mue. I don't like to think of you alone with a strange man.'

'But Mr Diamond is working at Yoxford Gardens, isn't he? I thought it was all right to show him round.'

'I think I'd better be on my way,' Frank said, realising this conversation would be going round in circles for the foreseeable future.

'*I'll* show you out,' Janet said. 'Muriel, perhaps you could start the dinner?'

'Yes, Janet. Goodbye, Mr Diamond.' She scurried back to the house.

There was silence as they made their way to the front garden. Janet's car was parked in the road. Frank waved to his Avenger. 'Sorry about that, I didn't know you put your car up there.'

Janet grabbed his arm. Through his leather jacket the pressure of her fingers bit into his flesh. He gave her a hard look, and glanced down at her claw-like hand. She released her grip. 'Thank you.'

'You've upset Muriel. Please don't call again unless you're sure I'm with her. She's been in a fragile state lately.'

'Really? She seemed fine when we were going round the garden.'

'Did she take you into the wood?'

'No, just to the edge. She didn't think there was too much to see, although I caught glimpses of wood anemones and patches of celandine. She tells me you've several varieties of rare snowdrops.'

'Rare? I wouldn't say that. Those are beyond our means, even some of the more popular sorts are expensive, and you have to wait several years for them to bulk up and make a show.'

She'd calmed down. Perhaps he could risk it. 'We also talked about your old school.' He told her about Muriel's assessment of Beatrice Mavor.

'Did you teach her as well?'

'Yes, she took geography O level with me. I never had any trouble with her.'

Frank could believe it.

'She could have gone on and taken A level geography, but she took physics, chemistry and mathematics. That's unusual in a girl's school, most of them go for the arts, or humanities. Not many do science.'

'I don't think Muriel liked her.'

'She nearly had a nervous breakdown, you know. Retired before me. She's much better now, but we have to be careful.' She pushed out her bottom lip. 'That's why I lost my rag. She gets agitated if someone she doesn't know comes to the house when I'm not here, especially if it's a man. Although you seem harmless.' She gave a throaty laugh.

Harmless? He hoped Laurel didn't think so. He'd have to up his

119

image. 'I'm sorry if I upset her. Was Beattie Mavor part of the reason for her leaving teaching early?'

She gave him a swift look. 'Why so interested in Beatrice Mavor? It's several years since she was at St Mary's.'

He'd better drop it. 'Oh, no reason. It's just I met her the other day and she mentioned she was at St Mary's. I found her rather aggressive and wondered what she was like as a schoolgirl.'

'Your interests seem to spread far and wide, Mr Diamond. Do you only specialise in gardens or have you other areas of expertise?'

This was tricky. She was a sharp and intelligent woman, Janet Lamb, but she didn't live up to her surname; Janet Wolf would be more appropriate. 'There are a few other areas I've worked in, but horticulture is my main forte. Garden centres and nurseries are a growing business.'

He put out a hand. 'Goodbye, no doubt I'll see you at Yoxford Gardens in the near future.'

She shook his hand with a steel-like grip. 'Goodbye, Mr Diamond.'

He decided she'd make a good baddy for the next James Bond film. 007 would have his work cut out with Janet Lamb.

# Chapter Fourteen

Laurel drove into Ipswich, and eventually found Elm Street and the monolithic building that was the police station. Built a few years ago in the late sixties, it was a slab-sided erection consisting mostly of glass and plastic. She shuddered. Like many newly built schools, the rooms would be too hot in the summer, and freezing in the winter. Oh, for the days of brick and stone. She found a parking slot in front of it, and made for the main entrance. Frank hadn't got back before she left, and she'd decided not to ask Stuart if he'd drive her; she didn't think she'd be able to concentrate on thinking how she was going to tackle getting David to talk if he was crunching gobstoppers all the way to Ipswich.

The desk sergeant asked her to wait, pointing to a scuffed plastic seat. It looked as though someone had danced on it with rubber-soled shoes. Why did the front offices of police stations always look so unwelcoming? Not everyone was a criminal and if you came for help it was very off-putting.

'Hello, Miss Bowman.' A smiling Johnny Cottam came dancing down a flight of stairs. 'Inspector Revie is waiting for you. Stairs or lift?'

She didn't fancy the lift, possibly smelling of urine. Frank had told her absolved criminals took it out on the police by having a sly pee on the way out. 'The stairs, I need the exercise.'

In an impressive but stuffy office on the second floor, a tired and morose-looking Revie waved her to another plastic chair, this time scuff-free. 'Well, I hope you can get him to say something; we've failed to get a squeak out of him. I'm sorry for the boy, but he's trying my patience, and that of those "upstairs".' He pointed to the ceiling. She presumed he meant the Chief Constable.

'Is he eating?' she asked.

Revie looked at Cottam.

'Not much. He's only drinking water, won't touch the tea or coffee.'

Laurel didn't blame him if it was anything like the stuff she'd got in Leiston Police Station. 'Have you seen him, Nick?'

'Cottam thinks I frighten him, make matters worse. Cheeky devil.' He gave Cottam a diabolical grin.

'I think that was good advice, Sergeant Cottam.'

'I thought you were my friend, Miss Bowman,' Revie said.

'I am, and I'm very grateful you're letting me see him. I've warned the Pembertons I may not be successful. After all, you've had specialists trying to break his silence, the Pembertons tell me.'

Revie sighed. 'I hope you can crack this one. I don't like to see him in that cell. It's worse than the room he was kept in for two years. It must bring it all back. Want to ask me anything before Cottam takes you to him?'

'Has he been allowed to have anything to draw with? Paper, pencils?'

Revie tightened his chin. 'Can't allow that, I'm afraid. Might poke himself in the eye with an HB, or try and penetrate his brain via a lughole.' He laughed. Laurel and Cottam didn't join in.

'You think it would help?' he asked.

Laurel eye-balled him. 'It's possible. That's how he managed to survive before, sketching and painting. He didn't do any self-harm then. Can I ask him if he'd like some paper and pencils?'

Revie pursed his lips and nodded.

'Thank you, Nick.'

'Right, Cottam, off you go, and you,' he pointed to her, 'come back to me when you've finished. You've got forty-five minutes.'

She shouldn't feel cross with him; she knew his brusque manner often hid kindness. She followed Johnny down a corridor. 'Risk the lift going down?' he asked, smiling.

'Frank told me it sometimes doesn't smell too good.'

'True, but I've used it in the last hour. It was all right then.'

'I'll risk it.'

He raised an eyebrow. 'It's not like you to be put off by a possible stink.'

'I must be turning into a sensitive soul.'

'I shouldn't think so.'

They waited for the lift to arrive.

Was this how people saw her? Was it how Frank saw her? A toughie, unafraid of anything? As brave as most men? Did he see her as a rival? No wonder Frank was attracted to the feminine, petite woman in Aldeburgh. She believed small, delicate females usually made men feel strong and powerful. When was the last time a man had offered to carry her suitcase? Unfortunately, she couldn't be like Alice in Wonderland, and drink a potion that would shrink her, so she'd have to accept there weren't many men who'd be attracted to a woman who might square up to them if they got out of hand. But some men desired her: her former fiancé, Simon, who'd dropped her after she persisted in searching for her sister's murderer, he'd desired her; then there was Oliver Neave, and Carlton seemed keen to take their relationship to another level. But Frank? She'd seen a certain gleam in his eyes, but not lately.

'Penny for them?' Johnny said.

She sighed. 'I was thinking it would have been better if I was several inches shorter, and a touch more feminine.'

Johnny looked horrified. 'No! You're unique. We've got enough tiny women. Also, you wouldn't be much use to Frank if you weren't the build you are.'

She laughed. 'I'm not sure how to take that.'

'You must know he's mad about you?'

'You mean mad with me.' Could it be true? What about Emma? The lift door slid open; she sniffed, only the smell of dust.

'Come on, Laurel, even old Nick fancies you. Swears if he was twenty years younger, he'd break a habit of a lifetime and seriously think of marriage again.'

'Again?'

'Didn't you know? I suppose not, he doesn't like to talk about it. He married young, but the pressures of police work, getting promotion, took its toll. His wife left him.'

Poor Nick. 'Were there any children?'

'No. He says I'll have to do as a surrogate son. We've got really close; you wouldn't think so at work, but we see each other occasionally out of hours, not often, the job doesn't allow it. I'm fond of the old bastard.'

Laurel's heart softened towards both of them. 'I'm glad he's got you to talk to. I'd better not mention his marriage, had I?'

'Better not.'

'Can I tell the others?'

'Only if you're sure they won't bring it up when they're talking to him.'

'I'll just tell Frank.'

'Good idea. Here we are.'

The lift door slid open to reveal another corridor, wider than those on the upper floors and with several cell doors on either side. She shivered, but not with cold.

'I need to find the duty officer. He'll be in the room at the end of the corridor. Wait here.' He marched off.

How many of the cells were occupied? There was no sound from any of them. The air was chilly, carrying a faint smell of disinfectant. She walked slowly up the corridor. In the top half of each door there was a sliding metal rectangle, so the occupant of the cell could be easily and safely checked. She imagined sitting in the cell and suddenly hearing a metallic sound, and a face appearing, unsmiling, with hard eyes. Then the metal slammed back, and you were once more alone. She shivered again. David would hate it. She wanted to help him, but she wasn't looking forward to seeing him miserable, uncommunicative, turned in on himself, and even worse, looking guilty. Dear God, she hoped she could help him.

Johnny came back with a burly officer, who nodded to her, selected a key from a large steel ring, and put it into the lock of the middle cell on the right-hand side. He didn't turn it. 'You have forty-five minutes. Do you want me or Detective Cottam to come in with you?'

'No, thank you. I think it's better if I see David by myself.'

The officer glanced at Johnny. 'Inspector Revie did say it would be OK for Miss Bowman to go in alone. Can you wait outside? I'll bring you a chair.'

Johnny nodded. 'If you have any trouble, Miss Bowman, give me a shout. The cell door won't be locked.'

'Wait there,' the officer said, striding down the corridor to return with a plastic chair. He turned the key and pushed open the door. It squeaked. 'Hinges need an oil,' he said, as he walked away.

'Good luck,' Johnny said, putting the chair inside the cell.

She stood on the threshold; it was a small space, stark and unwelcoming, with cream-coloured distempered concrete walls, a bed at the far end, and high above was a barred window, letting in slots of sunshine. A chair and table were riveted to the floor, and a lavatory, without a seat or cover, completed the furniture. Lying on the bed, with his face to the wall, was David.

This was worse than she'd imagined. It was soul destroying. Bile rose in her throat, her nostrils tightened. How disgusting. She put the plastic chair near the bed and sat down.

His shoulders flinched.

'It's me, David, Laurel. This is awful. I'm angry you're here. You must be so upset. We must get you out as soon as possible. I know I couldn't bear to be shut up in a place like this. When you think what you had to put up with when you were kidnapped, and now this.' She stopped herself, putting her hands over her mouth. She'd lost it. This wasn't how she'd planned to speak to him.

She gripped her knees, squeezing tight, trying to bring herself back to earth. 'I'm sorry, David, I didn't mean to lose my temper. I'm horrified to see the conditions you're in. I didn't mean to shout. Do you want me to go?'

There was no reply, but a slight shake of his head.

She put a hand to her chest. He wanted her to stay. 'Frank and

Stuart send their regards. No one believes you're responsible for Mr Hanmer's death.' Not strictly true, but so what? 'I certainly don't.'

No reply and no movement.

'I suppose you're wondering why I'm here today, and how I've been allowed to see you.'

She shuffled the chair a bit nearer to him. 'Your father and Ann asked me if I'd come. They are frantic with worry for you.'

His shoulders twitched.

'They told me you wouldn't talk to anyone.'

No reply.

'I said I would help in any way I could.'

Silence.

'They asked Inspector Revie if I could come.'

As she mentioned Revie's name, his shoulders hunched as though expecting to be attacked.

'I know you don't like Inspector Revie, but he doesn't want to keep you here. He knows what you went through before. He may seem uncaring, but like a lot of people he hides his true feelings behind a brusque exterior.'

She bit her lip. She was getting hardly any response. How could she make him remember their former closeness?

'He wants you to be found innocent, but he's got nothing to work with.'

She was frustrated, and a feeling of helplessness overwhelmed her. She glanced at her watch; she hadn't looked at it when she came in, but she thought about ten minutes had passed. Thirty-five more to go. She decided to risk remaining silent for five minutes. Give him time to think. How was she to know which way his feelings might go? Would he, in five minutes, decide to continue with his silence, or would he slowly warm to her presence and want her to talk again?

She closed her eyes, concentrated on taking long, slow breaths. Would her calmness somehow seep across the space between them? Would he pick up the waves of concern and, yes, love, coming from her? Her muscles relaxed, her breathing softened, and her resolve returned. She slowly opened her eyes.

He was looking at her, his deep blue eyes staring as though he couldn't believe what he saw. Their eyes met. He swiftly turned and once more his back faced her.

She didn't know how to respond. She decided to carry on as before.

'Goodness, that reminds me of when I opened my eyes after being drugged in Tucker's house, and found you wiping my face with a damp towel. I thought it was a dog's tongue licking me.' She laughed. 'We made a good team, didn't we? All those jars and pots we filled with pee to throw on Hager. And do you remember I showed you how to throw an LP record like a discus? How on earth we thought that would stop him, I can't imagine. But we were desperate, weren't we?'

No response. Reminiscing didn't seem to be working. What to say now?

'I've not seen you lately, but I've heard how well the painting is going. Would you like me to arrange for some paper and pencils to be brought to you, so you can do some sketching while you wait to be released? I've asked Inspector Revie and he's agreed. Perhaps you could sketch him. I'd like to see that.'

She waited a few minutes, but there was no response of any kind. Looking at her watch she saw there were only ten more minutes left.

'David. I'm not sure if you want me to go, or if you'd like me to stay for a bit longer. I don't know how to make you see I want to help you. I know you've never liked talking to people, but after you came back to your father, you were able to and seemed to want to talk more. You mustn't let what's happened take that away from you.'

Her calmness was seeping away. How could she get through to him? Had something she said touched a chord? Or was it hopeless? Five minutes left. There was a movement behind the door. Please don't come in yet.

'David, my time is nearly up, please help me. I don't know what you want me to do.'

There was a slight movement of his body. Was he turning?

'David, do you want me to come back?' She leant forward. Almost touching him.

'Yes.' Said so softly, she wasn't sure she hadn't imagined it.

'Thank you. I'll be back tomorrow.' She wanted to take him in her arms and comfort him, to kiss his cheek and tell him it would all be all right. One little word. *Yes*. She, Adam and Ann would have to cling to that, and hope tomorrow David would talk to her.

# Chapter Fifteen

Wednesday, 25 April, 1973

In his cottage overlooking the sea, Frank poured himself another mug of coffee from the percolator on the stove; he glanced out of the window. Another fine spring day, but with more of a breeze and a lower temperature than yesterday, even the sea was blue. He rubbed a finger over his top lip; he must stop dreaming about Laurel – he needed to concentrate on the case. Was he imagining she fancied him? She was a flirt – nothing wrong with that, flirting helped the world go round. But at the dinner with Revie last week, if it had been any other woman, he'd have sworn she was encouraging him to . . . what? He placed the mug on the kitchen table, next to an A4 pad and several coloured biros. Time to gather his thoughts about the thefts from Yoxford Gardens.

He picked up a biro and wrote: *possible motives*.

Why would you steal rare plants? Simply for gain? If so, you'd have to know how to make money from them. Although there had been a number of thefts, no great numbers of each variety had been stolen, apart from snowdrops. The thief was not going to make much money by selling them individually. Was he or she stealing them to order? Or were they using them as mother plants for reproduction until they'd enough to be commercially viable? He made some notes on the pad.

Suppose you were stealing because you lusted after them, but couldn't or wouldn't buy them from the nursery? Was this a jealous

129

thief, who couldn't bear not to possess a plant they'd seen in the garden? Some of the snowdrops, not yet for sale, were hidden in the wood. How had they known about them? He made further notes, spreading the jottings over the page, trying to see a connection.

He'd spoken to most of the volunteers, except for a few on holiday; he'd have to hope they weren't involved. From the notes Pamela kept on the volunteers, those absent didn't seem likely. He'd have to work with what he'd got.

Now for some of the main suspects. Georgina Gibbs. She knew which were rare plants and their worth. She had the opportunity, and it was possible she knew where the snowdrops were hidden in the wood. She'd been antagonistic towards his investigation. But what could be her motive? If she was the thief, and she was discovered, her career would be over. No garden or nursery would want to employ a plant thief with a criminal record. He drank a mouthful of coffee, then made further notes.

If she was the thief, what did she do with the plants? He shook his head. Couldn't answer that one. She lived in a rented cottage in Yoxford, he'd checked it out. It was a terraced house with only a back yard. She certainly couldn't hide any stolen plants there. Unless . . . he made further notes.

Janet Lamb. Originally, he'd thought she was a pleasant woman, but after that outburst at her home and her relationship with Muriel, he wasn't so sure. Her knowledge of plants was deep, she'd worked in the gardens for several years and knew where rare plants were sited. Her own garden was her pride and joy. He imagined her arriving at night, trowel in one hand, and in the other, a plastic bag; her face greedy. She'd carefully, and even lovingly, dig it up and retreat, clutching her prized possession to her bosom. He laughed at himself. Get back to reality, he thought.

Several plants had been taken from the Japanese garden and she'd created one in her own. Were any of the stolen plants there? He hadn't had time to have a good look. Could he risk another visit when he knew she was at Yoxford Gardens?

Owen Albrighton. Why was he on his list? He wasn't sure. Possibly because he didn't like how he'd talked about Georgina. Let's see. He worked at the gardens, so he'd know where the rare plants were, but from his staff notes, he wasn't a highly educated man. Did that matter? Many gardeners didn't have formal training, so much was learnt on the job. Why would he steal plants? To sell them? To whom? He lived in an isolated house, miles from anywhere. Frank couldn't imagine Owen would have the kind of contacts he'd need to make the risk worthwhile. But he'd a garden at home. Was he thieving because he lusted after the rarities? Wanted them for his own? To be able to look at them whenever he wanted? Frank frowned. He didn't think Owen was a plant collector. They'd have to have a use, for food, or for sale to make some money. He wasn't able to work full-time because of his crippled mother. But stealing rare plants for sale? He couldn't see it. If he was desperate for money, he'd be better off raiding a post office. He scribbled down a few notes.

Keith Gage. He'd be really happy if Keith was the thief. What a disgusting human specimen. However, just because someone is a drunken idiot, doesn't make them a thief. Pity. Why on earth did Pamela marry him?

He loosened his shoulders. Nevertheless, he must consider him. There were two motives for Keith. One, he wanted the nursery to fail. Why? So they'd have to sell up and he was hoping for half of the money? Or was he flogging the plants for ready cash? The former motive was more likely, he couldn't see Keith expending much energy on the returns he'd make, and he was sure possible buyers might be suspicious of a seedy solicitor trying to flog them rare snowdrops. He wouldn't even know their botanical names. No, if it was him, it would be because he peevishly wanted the gardens to go down the tube.

There was no one else he felt could be the thief, but he wasn't convinced by any of the subjects he'd made notes on. There was no prime suspect for this crime.

Laurel threw the blue ball along Dunwich beach and Bumper chased after it, sending up a spray of fine pebbles and sand at the sea's edge. He skidded as he scooped it up in his mouth, turned, and ran back, skeins of drool hanging from his chin. He dropped it at her feet and, grimacing, she picked it up and washed it in an incoming wave. 'That's enough. Let's go to the café and have a drink.'

He cocked his head, as if to say, 'Why don't you throw it again?' She put him on the lead and made for the beach café. Opening the door, she went inside, keeping Bumper back with her foot. 'Do you mind if I bring Bumper in? He's not wet, only sandy.'

The girl behind the counter laughed. 'No, of course not, he's always welcome. What can I get you?'

'A coffee, please, white, and one of your Chelsea buns if you've got one.'

'Coming up. What would Bumper like? A bowl of water?'

'Thanks, and I suppose another bun wouldn't go amiss.'

Bumper, having had a drink and devoured his bun in two bites, settled under the table. Laurel sipped her coffee thinking of David, and how his days, and nights, must seem interminable. How could she get him to open up? She tried to remember how she'd got him onside when they were imprisoned, waiting to be killed. Then she'd involved him in their survival. Could she involve him in trying to find the murderer of Judge Hanmer? She had to assume he was innocent. Yes, she'd try that. She needed to get the help of the team, and especially Frank. She needed his brains. There were other parts of his body she was interested in, but that would have to wait. Possibly, she might never get her hands on any part of his anatomy. Stop it, she thought – keep your mind on David.

It seemed likely that the murderer was someone who lived in Thorpeness, or someone who'd visited regularly. Possibly a member of the Country Club? She shook her head; it seemed unlikely it was anyone she knew. She frowned. She mustn't let her personal feelings about people stop her from thinking of them as possible suspects. She was a detective. She must follow Frank's example and analyse the people she'd met.

First Carlton. He disliked the Judge; in fact, she'd been shocked by the violence of his feelings and his hatred of homosexuals. Was it something he'd learnt from his parents? Did Beattie feel the same way? She'd made an enemy of Beattie, no, Beattie had made an enemy of her. Why? Was she possessive of Carlton? But she'd made him angry with her vituperative remarks. Somehow, she'd have to get Beattie's cooperation if she was to find the murderer. She was an intelligent woman, she knew people at the Club, and she wouldn't be worried about dishing the dirt on anyone.

Why did Carlton hate homosexuals, and the Judge in particular? Had he been assaulted by someone when he was a child, as Harry suggested? He would have been a pretty boy. Or had the Judge tried it on with him? She shook her head. She'd never seen the Judge make much contact with anyone; he had seemed happy to sit alone, sipping a drink on the terrace. Could she get Carlton to open up? Was that fair? But who was most important, Carlton or David? No competition there.

Was there anyone else who'd shown a dislike of the Judge? Frank mentioned Mr Shires had made derogatory remarks about him. But why would he want to do him harm? Perhaps he'd come up before the Judge for a crime. But if so, and the Judge had recognised him, wouldn't he have reported him to the police, or to the owners of the Club? Nothing like that had happened. She wasn't keen on Teddy Shires; she wasn't sure why. There was something about him. She pulled a face. Was he trustworthy?

What about Beattie Mavor? She hadn't expressed any feelings about the Judge. Why would she want to kill him? She smiled to herself. Perhaps she'd lusted after the Judge and he'd repulsed her advances; she certainly gave Frank the eye. She smiled again. She must ask Frank if he was attracted to Beattie. She thought she knew the answer. This was not helping her analysis. She couldn't think of one reason for Beattie murdering the Judge.

'Come on, Bumper, time to go home.' She thanked the girl behind the counter and waved goodbye. She hoped she could get David to tell her why he was in the Judge's house. She'd try involving him in finding the real murderer, and hope that worked.

★

133

Frank felt bloated after the lunch Mabel cooked. She'd decided, as Laurel was going to Ipswich for six, she must have one proper meal today. She, Stuart and Dorothy would make do with sandwiches for their evening meal. After cottage pie, buttered cabbage and apple dumpling, Frank was sure he wouldn't want to eat until tomorrow.

'Ready to begin the meeting?' he asked, looking at their sleepy faces.

Dorothy blew out her cheeks and slowly picked up her biro and notepad. 'Please don't talk too fast, I won't be able to keep up with you today. My shorthand is feeling drowsy.'

'Did I overdo the carbohydrates?' Mabel asked.

'It was delicious, and a nice change to have a proper lunch in the middle of the day,' Laurel said. 'It was good of you to think of me, Mabel.'

'Can't have you going to prison on an empty stomach,' Mabel replied.

Frank couldn't be bothered putting her right. The poor boy wasn't in gaol yet.

Stuart looked as though he would fall asleep at any moment, his chin resting on his chest, and his eyelids flickering.

Mabel dug him in the ribs. 'Stuart. You're dozing off.'

He jerked up. 'No, I wasn't, just resting my eyes until the meeting starts.'

'It's starting now, Stuart, so concentrate,' Frank said.

Stuart glared at him.

'There's no formal business today. I want to tell you my thoughts about possible suspects for the theft of the plants from Yoxford Gardens, so we can discuss them and see if any new ideas come up. Then Laurel would like to tell you about her visit to David Pemberton last night, and how she proposes to structure tonight's visit. Has anyone any other business they'd like to bring up? Stuart, have you anything to report on the stolen snuff boxes?'

He jerked upright and shook his shoulders like an old dog who'd been lying in front of a fire, dreaming of chasing cats, or possibly bowls of food. 'I've not much to report, but I'll tell you what's happened so far.'

'Excellent,' Frank said. 'I'll start.' He told them about his interviews at Yoxford, and then his analysis from the morning's work.

'Gosh, Janet Lamb seems like a Jekyll and Hyde character,' Laurel said.

'Are she and Muriel lesbians?' Dorothy asked.

'Really, Dorothy, what has that got to do with anything?' Laurel asked.

'I'm not asking out of idle curiosity,' Dorothy snapped, 'it sounded to me as though she didn't like Frank being alone with Muriel. She could be jealous, as from Frank's description Muriel is the more feminine of the two. I've got nothing against lesbians, as long as they don't try it on with me.'

Stuart chortled. 'That's woken me up. You sound as though you've had a nasty experience. Have you?'

She grimaced. 'It only happened once, I was a young girl, at a secretarial college, and the shorthand tutor said I was the star pupil and asked if I wanted a few advanced lessons. Of course, I was delighted, and my head must have blown up out of all proportion. I soon found out what kind of advanced lessons she wanted to give me. I was horrified, I didn't know such people existed. It wasn't like today, men wearing make-up, and women dressed as men, smoking cigars.'

'But it must have been a long time ago,' Frank said. 'The Edwardian era?'

Dorothy threw a pencil at him as the rest laughed.

Frank tossed it back to Dorothy, who caught it neatly. 'Any more thoughts? No? In that case, Stuart, would you go next?'

Stuart pushed himself upright. Mabel looked at him as though he was going to give a speech to the House of Commons.

'The owner of the antique shop, a Mr Hargreaves, suspects one of his best customers, a titled lady; he's noticed changes in her behaviour over the past year. I suggested it may be to do with old age, her brain isn't working as it should. When I asked him if he'd thought about talking to other members of her family, he was shocked. Felt he couldn't do that, he's afraid of offending them. I asked if he'd like me to take that on. I suggested I might be able to visit her son, who she lives with – he's inherited the title. I could take photos of the snuff boxes with me, and pretend I was enquiring if he'd had any stolen, or if he'd been offered any of the boxes for sale. Mr Hargreaves is thinking that over.'

'Excellent, Stuart. Very diplomatic. Let's hope he says yes,' Frank said.

Mabel beamed with pride.

'Right, Laurel. Tell us about David. How is he?'

She described his cell, and how she'd tried to persuade him to talk, about anything, never mind what he was doing in the Judge's house, but the only word he'd uttered was 'Yes', when she'd asked him if he'd like her to see him again.

'Excellent, Laurel,' Frank said. 'That's more than anyone else has managed.'

She smiled at him, and his heart flipped. He swallowed hard; she was such a caring woman.

'And tonight? I bet you've thought of a way that might get him to open up. I'm putting my money on you,' he said.

An even more dazzling smile. 'Yes, I have. What does everyone think about this?' She explained she was going to try and involve David in helping her to find the murderer.

'How can you do that, Laurel? The poor boy's incarcerated,' Dorothy said.

'David spent a lot of time at Thorpeness, mostly drawing and painting. He'd be seated in the front room of their house; he'd observe people walking by. Remember, he has this extraordinary facility to recall detail, and to be able to draw a perfect likeness. The portraits he drew of the teachers and pupils at his school, and how he captured not only their likeness, but by a few touches, also showed their character.'

Frank mentally shuddered, remembering the drawing David had done of his mother, Carol, as she had sex with one of David's tutors; he wondered if the others were also thinking of that portrait.

'He walked every day. He may have seen something. He's very observant. At the time he may not have thought much about what he saw, but if I can motivate him tonight, give him some paper and pencils and say I'll return and we can talk about what he's remembered, I hope he'll also tell me why he was in the Judge's house.'

'When are you going?' Frank asked.

She looked at her watch. 'Revie said I could see him at six for an hour, so I'll leave about four thirty, to make sure I'm not late. I'll need all of the sixty minutes.'

'Would you like me to drive you?' Frank asked.

'Would you? I'd be very grateful.'

'My pleasure, Laurel.'

'What will you do while I'm with him?'

'I'll see if I can have a word with Revie, and persuade him to let me into the cell with you, towards the end of your session.'

Laurel looked startled.

'Only if David agrees. It might be good if he feels all members of the Agency believe in him. After all, I was the one who dealt the fatal blow to the man wanting to kill him.'

'And you saved me from a fate worse than death,' Laurel said, beaming at him.

'I need to go back to the cottage; I'll be back for four fifteen,' Frank said.

'Plenty of time for me to get changed. I must look nice for David, mustn't I?'

And possibly me? Frank thought.

# Chapter Sixteen

Laurel was more optimistic than last night; it was the combination of having a plan to involve David in helping to free himself, and Frank driving her to Ipswich, offering to get involved – if Revie would allow it. She glanced at Frank, who was concentrating on getting past a lorry on the dual part of the A12. Her feelings for him had changed. Why? She'd always found him attractive, the combination of green eyes, long hair and handsome features was sexy – or, as he'd told her Pamela had described him – tasty. It was also his quick mind, sense of humour, bravery and his humanity; all these qualities drew her to him. He'd infuriate her at times with his glib motor-mouth comments, but he'd never bore her. She sighed. Unfortunately, she'd missed the boat as far as Frank was concerned. How could she compete with the delicate creature from Aldeburgh?

Was it fair to try and get him interested in her again? But wasn't that just what she was doing tonight? She'd changed into an aqua–blue woollen tube dress with a cowl collar, which clung to her curves and emphasised the colour of her eyes; she'd added a touch of blue eye-shadow for good luck, plus pink lipstick and low–heeled shoes.

When he'd picked her up, he'd said, 'Wow! David will be pleased.'

'Aren't you?'

'Should I be?'

'Of course.' Infuriating man.

'In that case, fancy a drink afterwards?'

She swallowed. 'Is that a date, or a working drink?'

'What do you want it to be?'

'I'd like a date, please.' She'd committed herself.

He'd stared at her, his emerald-green eyes unblinking. 'You're living dangerously.'

'So are you.' She internally shivered. What would happen after the drink?

As Frank parked in front of the Elm Street Police Station, he said, 'It's three years since I worked here, but it seems a lifetime ago.'

'You may see some of your old pals. They might even be pleased to see you.'

'Or not. If anyone calls me Danger Man, they'll regret it.'

Johnny Cottam was waiting for them.

'Any chance of a word with Inspector Revie?' Frank asked.

'He's in his office. Go up, you know where it is. I'm to take Miss Bowman directly to the cells.'

'I've got paper and pencils for David; Ann Pemberton brought them over to Greyfriars this morning. Do you want to check them? Make sure I'm not smuggling something in?'

Cottam laughed. 'Wouldn't put it past you. I'll go through them when we get down there. Or the duty officer better do it.' He stopped by the lift. 'Want to go up, Frank? We're going down.'

'No, I'll take the stairs. But I may be down later.'

'Really?'

'It depends on Revie.'

'He's in quite a good mood today, so you might be lucky.'

The duty officer opened the door of David's cell and passed her a plastic chair. David was lying on the bed as before, his back to her. The rank smell of urine and faeces was barely masked by the chemical smell of Harpic. She wanted to gag, but suppressed the urge. The last thing she needed was for him to hear sounds of heaving, which he'd translate into disgust. She moved the chair close to his bed.

'Hello, David, it's Laurel. I'm afraid you can't get rid of me. I hope we'll be able to talk, but that's up to you. I very much want to hear your thoughts, but I know you may not want to talk to me.' She placed the paper and pencils on the bed, where he could see them.

She waited. Did he want her to go away? 'Ann brought paper and pencils for you this morning. I was out with Bumper so I didn't see her, but Miss Piff did. She sends all her love, as does your father. I hope you'll want to start drawing again. I'm sure you could capture Inspector Revie's likeness.' She thought a chuckle came from him.

She paused again. This was it. Either he'd decide to help himself or he'd reject her idea. If he took the latter course, his future looked black. Revie couldn't afford to let her come to see him indefinitely if her visits weren't productive.

'David, I'm not sure if they'll let me come and talk to you again. I want to, and I would keep coming back, even if you won't speak to me. My hope would be that eventually you would trust me enough to tell me why you went to the Judge's house. Unfortunately, we haven't got that luxury. I've been thinking how we could work together to try and find out who did kill the Judge. I think you could play an important role.' She waited, hoping her words would sink in. 'Do you want me to tell you what you could do? I think you may not realise, but you might hold vital clues in your head. Shall I tell you?'

If he didn't reply she wasn't sure if she should go on. Would it be better to leave it like that, and hope Revie would give her another shot? Or, should she tell him anyway?

He levered himself up, and swung round so he was sitting upright, facing her. His deep blue eyes looked enormous in his thin, pale face, staring at her with the look of a frightened child, who cannot understand what has happened to him. His shoulders were hunched forward, hands clasping his knees. He looked broken. Imprisonment must have brought back those two long years when he was locked in a room in Tucker's house. Then he was surrounded with everything a teenager could want – except freedom. He'd kept himself sane by drawing, painting, television, music and the hope that one day he'd be free. Also, the motivation he'd be able to get justice for his murdered friend, Peter.

Probably all he could see, stretching before him, was imprisonment in harsh surroundings, the only companions, men who he'd despise and fear. And if he'd killed the Judge, he would know there was no way out. She prayed he wouldn't admit his guilt. She needed him to be innocent. She couldn't believe he would kill anyone. But did she really know him? Did anyone truly know the workings of another person's mind, even if they were your parents? Your best friend? Your lover?

'Thank you, David. Shall I tell you how we can work together?' She must get him to talk. Once those first words were uttered, it would break his inner silence.

'Yes, please.'

She stopped herself from breaking into a smile. 'Good. You've spent a lot of time recently at Thorpeness?' She raised her eyebrows.

He scowled. 'Yes, I wish they'd never bought the house.'

'That's water under the bridge, David. When you're working, you sit at the window in the front room?'

He scuffled back against the rough blanket on the bed. 'I can't see how this is going to help.'

'Please, be patient. You have phenomenal powers of recall, and your portraits of people catch remarkable likenesses and also reveal their characters. A true gift.'

'It's very nice of you to say so, Laurel, but I can't see how flattery is going to help me.'

Excellent, as Frank would say – he's being sarcastic. She risked a smile. 'I was reminding you. Did you go out much when you were at Thorpeness?'

'I used to walk round. I liked the Mere, the swans, ducks, and the boats. I'd come back and draw them sometimes.'

'And the people? Did you draw them?'

His shoulders slumped. 'Yes,' he whispered.

Laurel's stomach dropped. He looked afraid, guilty. 'Did you draw the Judge?'

'Yes.'

'Have the police found it?'

'Yes.'

'I presume it was a good likeness?' She tried to keep her voice

141

light. Unsurprised. She remembered his other portraits of people he disliked. They were often sinister.

He nodded. She decided not to take this any further.

'I'm pleased you're still able to capture likenesses. This is what I want you to do.'

He looked up at her, a gleam of hope in his eyes. 'I'll try and do whatever you want, Laurel. You saved me before. Please help me.' He tentatively put out a hand. She grasped it. His hand recoiled at her touch, but she held on tight. Slowly his hand relaxed.

'David, I don't know if anyone has told you, but the Judge contacted the Agency just before he was killed. He was worried about someone. We think that someone lived in Thorpeness.'

He pulled his hand away, his eyes wide, shocked. 'But that someone could have been me. I met him when I was out walking.'

'When?'

'Friday morning, before he was killed. He said hello to me, but I didn't say anything.'

'You didn't like him?'

He shook his head. 'No, I hated him.'

She knew, but she needed to ask. 'Why did you hate him?'

'He was like those others. The men who hurt young boys. The men who killed Peter.'

'You told me that Hager, when you were locked up, used to tell you the names of the men who came to Tucker's house. Did he ever say the Judge's name?'

David stared at the floor. 'No.'

'Neville Hanmer was a homosexual, but, as far as we know, he wasn't active. No one can help how they are born. Homosexuality is not a crime, as long as it's between consenting adults, and no one is hurt.'

'It's wrong. The Church teaches us it's wrong.'

'I've got friends who are homosexuals. Everyone has the right to be loved, and to love. It's wrong to make everyone try to conform to the norm. *You* must know that better than anyone.' This was not how she'd wanted the meeting to go. They were getting deep into his beliefs. She should have tried to steer it back to how he was going to be involved in helping to free himself.

'You really believe that?'

'Yes, I do. And I believe in justice and that the right person should be punished for the crime they've committed. You may have drawn a cruel portrait of the Judge, but I don't believe you murdered him.'

'You haven't asked me if I'm guilty.'

'I don't think I have to.'

His face collapsed and his eyes were clouded with tears.

She took a handkerchief from her pocket and leant forward to wipe his face, then pressed it into his hand.

'I'm sorry, Laurel.'

What was he sorry about? She tensed, dreading to hear those words from his lips. 'What have you got to be sorry about? Doing a sketch of the Judge? That's just bad luck, it doesn't prove a thing.'

'I didn't kill him, but if I hadn't hated him, I wouldn't be here.'

'I'm sorry, I don't understand.'

'*You* may believe me when I tell you, but no one else will.'

'You're wrong, there's another person, probably outside the door, who believes in you, and wants to help.'

'Who? My father? He must . . . how does he feel? If I hadn't been so stupid . . . all I've ever given him is grief . . . I was happy . . . he was happy . . . it was the best it's ever been . . . I love Ann, as well . . . Dad was happy . . . happier than I've ever known him . . . and now I've spoilt it all again.' His shoulders heaved.

This was no good. He was wallowing in self-pity. 'Mr Diamond is waiting outside. I don't think you want *him* to hear you acting like this, do you?'

He raised a shocked face and quickly wiped his cheeks with her handkerchief. 'Mr Diamond? He believes in me?'

'He certainly does. Would you like him to come in? Then you can tell both of us why you went to the Judge's house.'

'I'd like to see him. He saved us, didn't he?'

'He came in the nick of time. Shall I ask him to come in?'

David nodded, scrubbing his face with the handkerchief and pushing his hands through his dark hair.

Masculine pride. It was all right to blub over her, but Frank mustn't see he'd been crying. Never mind. If it made David tell them why his fingerprints were all over Hanmer's house, she didn't care. She hoped Frank *was* outside. What could she say if he wasn't?

She knocked on the door. She knocked again, louder. 'He's probably having a quick drink with the duty officer,' she said, turning to look at David, pulling a face.

He laughed nervously.

The door opened. 'Ready to leave?' the duty officer asked.

'No. Is Mr Diamond about?'

'Yes, he's in my office. I'm telling him he shouldn't keep on supporting a rubbish football team.'

'And you're still alive?'

The man grinned. 'Want to see him?'

'Yes. Mr Pemberton would like to talk to him.'

He looked shocked. 'What did you give him to drink?' He jerked his thumb towards David.

'Just get Mr Diamond.'

'If you say so, Miss Bowman.'

He walked down the corridor. 'Frank, you're wanted,' he shouted.

Frank walked briskly towards her. He looked at her enquiringly. She nodded. 'Excellent,' he whispered, as they went into the cell.

The duty officer came back, carrying a chair. 'Here, you'll need this, pal. Knock when you want to come out.' He looked at his watch. 'You've got twenty minutes left.'

Frank took the chair. 'Thanks, Bob. Isn't your watch a bit fast? Don't you mean thirty minutes?'

'Could be,' Bob said. 'I'll check it.'

'In about thirty minutes?'

'You've not changed, have you? Danger—'

'Don't say it,' Frank interrupted. 'See you soon, and we'll fix up a date for that drink.'

144

Bob grinned, the door closed on them, and the key turned in the lock.

David was sitting up straight, trying to look composed.

'David, good to see you, but not in a place like this.' Frank walked up to him, holding out his hand. Laurel held her breath.

David, his face white, lurched up and tentatively took Frank's hand. Laurel kept hold of her breath and sat down on her chair. After a brief shake, Frank released David's hand and took his seat. For a moment David seemed to be frozen, as though shaking hands had numbed his body. Then, he sat on the bed, back erect, looking like a schoolboy ready for a wigging by the beak.

Frank glanced at her, obviously waiting for a lead.

'David was pleased you believed in him, and didn't think he killed the Judge. He agreed to you joining us, so he could tell both of us why he was in the Judge's house.' She wasn't sure that was what Frank thought, but it was important David believed it.

'Excellent,' Frank said. 'You've made a good decision, David.'

David's shoulders straightened. He gulped and then nodded. Frank had hit the right note. She wanted to hug him – perhaps later.

'Is there anything you want to say or ask, before you tell us,' Laurel asked.

David bit his lip, the edges red and sore. 'My father? How is he? Is he cross with me? I said I'd never leave him again, but I may have to. If you can't find the murderer I may go to prison for a long time. That's true, isn't it?'

Frank leant forward, and waved dismissively. 'That's not a scenario we're going to contemplate. Laurel, you've seen Mr Pemberton. Do you think he's cross with David?'

'Certainly not. He asked me to help. He believes in you, and so does Ann. They won't be the only ones, all Aldeburgh will be behind you.'

Frank raised an eyebrow.

David looked between them. 'I think Laurel's exaggerating, don't you, Mr Diamond?'

'Just a tad.'

'Are you ready to tell us, David?' Laurel asked.

He nodded.

'In your own time. If we need to, we'll ask questions as you go along,' Frank said.

David gulped, looking as though he wished the concrete floor would gape open and he could slip down into the underworld. 'It was sometime on Saturday, in the afternoon. The phone rang. I thought it must be Ann ringing again. She'd phoned in the morning and we'd arranged what time she'd pick me up on Sunday. I was happy, I love being on my own, drawing or painting. I'd started a new painting. It was a beautiful sunrise over the sea, the sky shimmering with red light turning the foam rose-pink, then the colours had gone, the sky pale blue, the sea green. I'd captured the moment, and I'd the rest of the day to work on it.

'But the voice wasn't Ann's. I didn't recognise it. It was a man's voice. I asked him who he was.'

'Are you sure it was a man speaking?' Frank interrupted.

David looked puzzled. 'I think so, it was a deep voice.' He bit his lip. 'He said, "I'm Judge Neville Hanmer. Please don't ring off. I've something important to tell you."'

'Did you recognise it as the Judge's voice?' Laurel asked.

He frowned. 'He has spoken to me, but we've never had a conversation . . . now you've asked me, I'm not sure.'

'Has Inspector Revie told you when the Judge died?' Frank asked.

David shook his head.

'Please continue, sorry to have interrupted you.'

'I was disgusted to be talking with him, but his tone was so urgent. I didn't put the phone down.

'"Yes," I said.

'"I want you to know, David, I had nothing to do with what happened to your friend. I want to help you to get justice for him. I can give you the names of the men who killed him."

'I said, "Why me? Why now? Why don't you go to the police?"

146

'"They won't do anything, you know that."

'I didn't know whether to believe him, but if he did know the names, I wanted to know them too. "Who are they?"

'"I can't say over the phone. It's too dangerous. I shouldn't even be speaking to you like this, but I knew you'd never talk to me if we met by chance."

'"So, when are you going to tell me?"

'"Come to my house, tonight. Wait until after dark, so no one will see you. Come in through the back door, into the kitchen. I'll be waiting for you in the hall."

'I wasn't sure what to do. Was he going to attack me? Try and rape me? I started to feel angry.

'"Will you come, David?"

'"Yes."

'"I'm thankful. I need to get these names off my conscience. Have you a torch?"

'"Yes."

'"Bring it with you. All the lights will be off."

'"Why?"

'"It's to make sure anyone passing will think I'm out. I don't want anyone knocking on my door and disturbing us. No one must know we're meeting. Please don't tell anyone, will you? I'm afraid they might harm me."

'"Who might harm you?"

'"The establishment. If they knew I had the names, they might kill me."

'I believed him, the way they shut us all up after you'd rescued me.

'"Come about eight o'clock, David. I'll be waiting for you." He rang off.'

It was an incredible story, Laurel thought. This person obviously wasn't the Judge, he was already dead. How did this man know about David, and his knowledge of the paedophile ring, and his hatred of the men who'd taken part?

David took a deep breath. 'Do you believe me?' he asked.

'I do,' Frank said. He looked at Laurel.

'Implicitly,' she said. 'What happened when you went to the Judge's house?'

'I decided to take a weapon in case it was a hoax, and he attacked me.'

Laurel didn't want to know, but Frank asked, 'What did you choose?'

David grinned sheepishly. 'A rolling pin. A good solid one. Ann sometimes does some baking when we're all here at Thorpeness.'

Frank laughed. 'Do you think you'd have used it?'

David pulled a face. 'I'm not sure. I thought of you, Laurel. How you didn't want to use a stiletto on Hager, but you made yourself do it as you knew if you didn't, he'd have killed us.'

She wanted to hug him. Fancy him remembering that when he was under such stress. She smiled and nodded encouragingly.

'I went round the back of his house; it was five past eight. There was no one around. I'd tucked the rolling pin into my belt, held the torch in my left hand, and turned the kitchen door handle. Everywhere was dark and quiet. I shone the torch round making sure he wasn't hiding, ready to leap on me. I went through a scullery and into the kitchen. It seemed colder than outside. I didn't like it.

'"Judge Hanmer," I called. Not loudly, but enough for someone in the hall to hear. The kitchen door was closed. I thought perhaps he was a bit deaf. I opened the door to the hall quickly and then leapt backwards in case he was waiting behind it ready to strike me. But there was no one. "Judge Hanmer," I called again. There was no movement. I didn't know what to think. Had he had to go out? Had someone overheard our phone conversation and he'd been attacked?

'I took the rolling pin from my belt. That was a relief as it was hurting; I held it raised in my right hand, so I could strike. I shone the torch into the hall. I moved slowly forwards, playing the beam over the walls. Then I tripped, and went flying. The torch and rolling pin shot from my hands and I landed on something lying in the hall. It gave under my weight. My hand touched material and then flesh. Flesh as cold as pebbles on a winter shore. I think I screamed, then I scrambled away. I was shaking. It was horrible.' Tears welled up and he was trembling from the dreadful memory.

She put out her hand to him, but Frank seized it, and shook his head. 'Go on, David,' he said. He didn't let go.

David shivered. 'I crawled back to the kitchen. I'm not sure how long I stayed there in a huddle, not knowing what to do. I knew there was a dead body, but was it the Judge? Slowly, I calmed down, enough to realise I must find out. Then I must phone for help. I wanted to phone Dad. He would know what to do. I couldn't bear the thought of searching for the torch. It had gone out, so I didn't know where it had landed. I stood up and found the kitchen light switch. That was better. I found the hall switch, and I saw it was the Judge. He looked as though he'd fallen down the stairs. I picked up the torch and the rolling pin, I switched the torch on and put out the lights.

'I didn't know what to do, my mind was a whirl of confusion. The police might think I'd killed him. If the establishment knew the Judge was going to talk . . . perhaps his telephone line was bugged. If I rang from there, they'd know about it. Would it be better to just leave and not tell anyone? Then he'd be found, and they'd think it was an accident. I was afraid I'd be blamed. Dad would be horrified if he got caught up in this mess. I knew he'd help me, but he'd hate the publicity. He'd been horrified the last time, when the press bothered him.

'I decided to go back to our house and not say anything. So, that's what I did. I didn't think about leaving my fingerprints. That was stupid of me. I could have wiped down everything I'd touched. Then, even if the police were suspicious, as all the prints would have disappeared, at least they wouldn't have found mine.'

He exhaled a great breath of relief. 'I'm glad I've told you. I feel better.'

'David, have you any idea how this person knew how you felt about the Judge, and that you wanted justice for your friend, Peter?' Frank asked.

He shook his head. 'I can't imagine. I racked my brains the next day, and it's been something I've been wrestling with ever since.

Will the police believe me? Or will they say I've made the whole thing up?'

'We won't know until you tell them,' Frank said.

David looked horrified. 'I can't talk to them. Can't you tell them?'

She knew it would come to this, but there was no escaping it. 'David, we can tell Inspector Revie what you've said, but he'll need to get a statement from you, it must be an official statement that can be used in court, if it's needed. We hope we'll never get as far as that, and the true murderer will be found.'

He shook his head rapidly. 'No. I won't do it.'

She glanced at Frank. By a slight movement of his head, he was telling her not to push it too far. 'That's all right, David. You've done very well today, and you've shown a lot of bottle telling us your story. That's a great step forward,' Frank said.

There was a knock on the cell door. 'Five minutes left. Time to wrap it up.'

David reached out towards Laurel. 'Do you have to go? Can't you stay a bit longer? I can tell you about my paintings.'

Laurel took his hand and squeezed it. 'I would love to, but Frank persuaded the officer in charge to give us extra time. Have you remembered what I asked you to do? We've got to work together on this one. I hope I can persuade Inspector Revie to allow us to come and see you again. Promise me you'll try and think about anyone you've seen at Thorpeness, and what they were doing. Please, David.'

He sighed, and withdrew his hand. 'I promise.'

The key turned in the lock and Bob appeared. 'Time's up. Could you bring out the extra chairs?'

Laurel and Frank stood up; David remained sitting on his bed.

'Goodbye, David,' Frank said, picking up the chairs and leaving Laurel with the boy. She blessed him, and sat by David's side. 'Remember, we're all with you. You've lots of love on your side.'

He blushed.

'Just sit down and draw. See what appears. You can do it, you're a genius.' She stood up again.

He looked at her, his blue eyes full of pain. 'You won't let me down, like last time, will you?'

She didn't understand. How had she let him down? Was it because no one had been brought to justice for the murder of his friend, Peter? Now was not the time for an inquest. 'No, I won't let you down. Goodbye, David. I hope to see you soon.' She turned, her mind in a turmoil.

Frank was waiting at the end of the corridor. He looked concerned. 'All right?'

'I think so. Something he said at the end confused me. I'll tell you later.'

'We're off, Bob. Looking forward to that drink.'

In the lift she turned to him. 'I hope *you're* still up for a drink with me, never mind the one with Bob.'

He pulled a face. 'I don't think you're going to like this.'

'What?'

'I'm afraid our date has turned into a threesome.'

'Not Bob!'

He laughed. 'Even I wouldn't do that to you; it's Revie. We're meeting him in his local, he wants to know what we've found out. I couldn't say no, could I?'

She quelled what she wanted to say – she wanted to be alone with him. Why? So, she could do what? Seduce him? See if he was at all interested in her, as a woman, and not just a partner? 'No, I can see that. I'm glad you're driving as I'll be hitting the Scotch.'

The lift door opened. 'Do you think he'll go for David's story?' she asked.

'Do you?' he asked.

She wasn't sure. 'Yes. Of course, I do.'

He smiled and took her arm. 'Let's hit Ipswich's hot spot.'

Frank steered the Avenger into a space at The Seahorse's car park. They'd first visited this pub last September, when Revie, in the middle of a difficult case, had wanted to talk it over with them.

151

Frank was looking forward to some good draft beer; but he wasn't so sure about how the conversation would go.

Although it wasn't his kind of pub, a large 1930s brick building, last time he'd been pleasantly surprised by the jolly atmosphere, but that was a Saturday night; what would it be like midweek? The main bar wasn't so smoky, and only a few people were present, mostly men of a certain age leaning on the bar. One of them was Nick, but this time still suited and booted, no Saturday-night casuals as before.

'Hello, Nick,' he said, remembering he didn't like being addressed as inspector in his local pub.

Nick wearily turned. 'What's your poison?' He raised his eyebrows as he saw Laurel. 'Who's the glamour puss?' Frank tried not to laugh as Laurel coloured up and glared at Nick.

'Oh, sorry, Laurel. Didn't recognise you. Are you undercover as a film star?' He nodded to a group of men, their eyes on stalks. 'They'll be over for your autograph soon.'

'And good evening to you. I'll have a double malt whisky, thank you.'

Nick pulled a face.

'It serves you right. No ice or water, thank you,' she said to the barmaid.

With his pint of Tolly bitter in his hand, Frank followed Nick and Laurel to a back room the landlord allowed them for their sole use. It hadn't changed since they'd last used it for an intimate discussion. It was cosy with two tables and chairs to match; but the redundant fruit machine had disappeared.

Nick took a long pull on his pint. 'Ah, that's better. I'm looking forward to hearing what he said. Well done, both of you, for getting young Pemberton to talk.'

'It was Laurel's doing, not mine. I came in when she'd persuaded him to tell us why he went to the Judge's house.'

Nick grinned. 'Laurel, you can use your mouth better than a fifty-dollar whore.'

Frank choked on his beer.

Laurel banged down her glass. 'Nick Revie, you are disgusting!'

Nick dissolved with laughter, covering his mouth to keep the beer in.

The expression on Laurel's face was incredible; if Nick had exposed himself, she couldn't have looked more offended.

'I'm sorry, Laurel,' Nick spluttered. 'Forgot I wasn't with my police buddies.'

She looked mollified. 'I'll take that as a compliment.' Her expression became worried.

She'd probably remembered she needed Nick on her and David Pemberton's side.

Nick wiped his face with a handkerchief. 'God, I haven't had such a good laugh since . . . I can't remember.' He put on a serious face. 'Right, let's hear what the boy said. You did tell him he'll need to make a statement? Hearsay is not good enough.'

'Yes, we told him that,' Frank said.

'How did he react?'

'We'll need to do a bit more work to make that happen.'

Nick raised his eyebrows. 'I may need to sign you up to the force, Laurel.'

'She's tall enough, but I'm sorry, Nick, she belongs to me,' he said.

Laurel turned sharply. Now *he* was for it. But she smiled at him. His stomach knotted.

Nick glanced between them.

Please don't say anything stupid, Frank prayed.

'Shall I start?' Laurel asked.

'Go ahead,' Nick said.

She slowly repeated every word David had said, glancing at him when she needed help. When she came to the end of David's story, she took a drink of Scotch, waiting for Revie's reply.

He sat there, like a puzzled buddha. Then he shook his head. 'I don't think that story would stand up in court. Do you believe him, Laurel? Now be truthful, we'd all like the boy to be innocent, but that's a hell of a tale.'

She tilted back her head, looking anguished. 'I realise that. The

153

prosecution counsel would shoot holes in it if he ever came to face the court. I want to believe in him, and I think he's telling me the truth. I don't think he'd lie to me. We've been through so much together. He's an intelligent boy, he knows how feeble his explanation must seem. I think that was why he ran away from the scene of the crime. He knew he wouldn't be believed. He was hoping it was an accident, and he wouldn't be involved.'

Nick pushed out his lower lip. 'What do you think?' he asked Frank.

'I watched him carefully as he talked; he was concentrating telling Laurel, rather than me. I believe he is telling the truth.'

Laurel leant over and squeezed his hand.

'Whew!' Revie emptied his glass. 'Now what am I going to do?'

Frank stood up. 'I'll get these. Same again?'

Revie nodded.

'A single this time,' Laurel said.

'Malt?'

'Do you mind?'

'Not for you.'

She blushed.

He went to the bar and ordered. He wondered what Laurel and Nick were talking about. Was Nick asking her if their partnership was blossoming into something that might bear fruit? If he was, he wished he could hear Laurel's answer. On his return, he was disappointed to hear Nick asking how Mabel was, and when was he going to be invited for dinner again, preferably not when Jim was cooking, as he didn't like being glowered at as he ate.

When they'd clinked each other's glasses, Revie said, 'I think I'll have to have a conversation with the Chief Constable.'

Frank looked at him. This sounded hopeful.

'Do you think David was telling the truth?' Laurel asked Nick.

'What I think is immaterial, Laurel. It's possible he is. That means, the murderer of Judge Hanmer is at large. We can't afford to overlook that. As far as upstairs are concerned this is a solved case, but I'll put it to him that we'll look right nanas if we're wrong, and we haven't even looked at other possible suspects. Though who to God they might be, I don't know.' He paused, his small blue eyes searching their faces. 'Unless you two have got any ideas?'

Laurel looked down, her eyes blinking. Did she know something? Something she hadn't told him? Why wasn't she mentioning Carlton Mavor? He hadn't been complimentary about the Judge when they'd met him at the Country Club. Was she protecting him? Why? Was she in love with him?

'I think it must be someone who lives in Thorpeness, from the little the Judge said to me over the telephone. If we presume David is innocent, I think the big hole in David's statement is how on earth did the murderer know about David's involvement with Tucker, and his hatred of the men who were responsible for his friend, Peter's, death?' Frank said.

Laurel sighed. 'I don't think a jury would believe him. It seems fantastic. Why would the murderer involve David the day after he'd murdered the Judge?'

'I suppose when the murder wasn't discovered on the Saturday, he decided, in case the police were suspicious, and suspected foul play, which I presume he was not hoping for, he went for a belt and braces exercise, pointing to David as the murderer,' Frank said.

'But how did he know about David?' Laurel said.

'It again points to someone living in Thorpeness,' Frank said.

'I'm enjoying this,' Revie said. 'You're doing my thinking for me.'

'It must be someone who lives near the Judge, who'd be on the lookout for police cars outside his house,' Frank said.

'Not necessarily,' Laurel said. 'Plenty of people come and go, especially if they're visiting the Country Club.'

Nick shifted in his chair. 'Laurel, you're a member, aren't you? Is there anyone there who you think is a likely customer?'

She bit her lip.

'Well? Is there or isn't there?'

Laurel glanced at Frank. 'I should have said this sooner.'

'You've been keeping a secret? I think young Frank must be as shocked as me,' Revie said, looking questioningly at Frank.

'I'm made of sterner stuff, Nick. Has this anything to do with the handsome Carlton?' he asked Laurel.

Laurel's face suffused with colour. So, she was in love with him. He'd been misinterpreting the signs she was changing her mind about him. He'd obviously misread her. Disappointment and jealousy washed over him. Women!

'You'd better tell us about this Carlton. Who is he?' Revie snapped.

'He's a tennis coach at the Club.'

'Good–looking, is he?'

'Yes, he is, but I'm not interested in him in that way. He's several years younger than me.'

'That doesn't stop some women,' Revie said, a bitter tone to his voice.

'Well, I'm not one of them,' Laurel said angrily. 'He's a good coach and I like him, but I don't fancy him.' She addressed the last words to Frank.

Suddenly he felt a whole lot better. He didn't care she hadn't told him of her suspicions, but he was delighted Carlton was toast as far as romance was concerned. Was Laurel really serious about him? How could he find out? What should he do about Emma?

Revie was shaking his head. 'OK, I can see where this is going.'

'I wish I did,' Frank said, smiling at Laurel.

'Right, Laurel, tell us about Carlton.'

She explained about Carlton's hatred of homosexuals and especially the Judge as he thought he was eyeing him up when he was playing tennis.

Frank nodded. 'Yes, when I was with you at the Club, he reacted badly when a chap called Harry implied he'd been a favourite of the older pupils when he was at school. He'd said the Judge wasn't eyeing up Laurel, but was giving him the glad-eye.'

'What's his full name?'

'Carlton Mavor, I don't know if he's got a middle name,' Laurel said.

Revie searched in his jacket and brought out a tattered notebook. 'Anyone got a biro? I didn't think I'd be taking notes tonight.'

Laurel searched in her handbag and passed him a pencil. 'Will this do?'

'Thanks. Any more suspects from the Club?'

Laurel shook her head.

'It might be worth looking at the manager, Mr Shires,' Frank said.

Laurel looked astonished. 'Really? I don't particularly like him, but I don't see him as a murderer.'

Frank cocked an eyebrow. 'Remember going off to have lunch with Tucker? Can we trust your judgement?'

'Don't remind me.'

'Cut the banter and tell me about this man. Shires, you say? Full name?'

'Teddy, short for Edward, I presume,' Laurel said.

Frank explained when he'd been talking to Shires he'd made derogatory remarks about the Judge, and this hadn't fitted in with his impressions of him.

'Bit thin,' Revie said. 'Still, it's a beginning. Anyone else?'

They both shook their heads.

'What about Beattie?' Frank asked Laurel. 'Have you heard her say anything about the Judge that might implicate her in his death?'

'I wish I could say yes. She's not my favourite person, and I hate the way she treats Carlton.'

'Can't the man stand up for himself?' Revie asked.

'You should see Beattie, she'd frighten anyone. She did me. On meeting her I immediately decided never to be alone with her in a dark room, or even a well-lit one,' Frank said.

Laurel laughed. 'She looked as though she wanted to swallow you whole, I saw the look on your face.' She turned to Nick. 'She's Carlton's older sister, there seems to be a great rivalry between them.'

Nick pulled a face. 'Usually, older sisters look after their little brothers.'

'I don't think she can be involved, she's only recently come on the scene, the end of March, I think. She's also a tennis coach,' Laurel said.

Revie downed the last of his pint. 'Right, I'll see the Chief and if

157

he buys it, I'll renew our investigations. I'll start with the two you've mentioned.'

'Looks like your coaching sessions might come to an end, Laurel. I suppose you could ask Beattie to take you on.' Frank looked at Revie and they both laughed.

'I was going to offer to buy a round, but—'

'I'll join you in a Scotch,' Revie said. 'You,' he pointed at Frank, 'can't have any more alcohol as you'll be driving me back home before you take the lovely Miss Bowman back to her, or your, place and tuck her up in bed.'

Laurel glared at him and stalked off to the bar.

'And don't spit in my drink,' Revie shouted.

# Chapter Seventeen

Thursday, 26 April, 1973

Frank waited for the explosion. It came.

'You did what?' Pamela Gage shrieked, rising from behind her desk, leaning towards him, her hands splayed out on the desk's surface.

'I don't think I need repeat it,' he said. He'd thought he'd better tell her before Janet Lamb did.

Pamela blew out her cheeks. No wonder Keith was frightened of her, she was formidable when angry.

'I presume she's been to you to complain about me?'

'No, she hasn't.'

'That's interesting.'

'Is it?'

'She was very upset when she found me looking round her garden with her friend Muriel. Don't you think that's interesting?'

Pamela sat back in her chair, her expression less angry. 'You're not suggesting she's the plant thief?'

'Look, Pamela, I know you don't want the thief to be one of your volunteers, or gardeners, but I think you must face the strong possibility it's going to be one of them. It's much more likely than a complete stranger.'

She blew out her cheeks again, but much more slowly, sounding like a shrivelling party balloon letting out the last of its air. 'I suppose you're right. I need to have the thief caught, but the thought it's someone I trust, or even worse, I'm fond of, is too dreadful. It makes me wish I hadn't started this witch-hunt.'

She cut a sad figure, and he was sympathetic to her. 'You can call us off, if you want.'

She smiled at him. 'Thank you, very gentlemanly, but no, we must go on. It's just me being silly. What with this and Keith cutting up, I'm afraid I'm not myself.'

Keith? He didn't want to know about him at the moment. 'I've a hunch about Janet. She's knowledgeable about plants, has a large garden, and she's a plant collector. I thought I'd like to see what she's got in her garden. What's more, she did give me an invitation to visit her garden; what she didn't expect was to see me there so soon.'

Pamela frowned. 'Did you see any plants that might have come from here?'

'No. She came back before I'd had a chance to make a detailed study. She was furious, and poor old Muriel got it in the neck.'

'Hmm. I've met Muriel. Janet brought her over to a couple of open days. Obviously enjoyed showing her over *her* Japanese garden. You'd think she'd designed and planted it herself.'

So, Pamela did have at least one negative thought about Janet. 'Yes, when I spoke to her the other day when she was working there, she did seem proprietorial.'

'Very well, I suppose she must go down as a suspect.'

'Now I've fessed up, I'd like to put the next stage of my plan to you.'

She nodded her head.

'Somehow, and here you may have suggestions, I want you to drop hints about the position of the rare snowdrops to the following people: Janet Lamb, Georgina Gibbs and Owen Albrighton.'

'Really? All of them?'

'Yes. I could pick them off one by one, and either eliminate them, or discover they're the criminal, but that would take time, and we need to press on.'

'Why not do it that way? I'd be much happier then telling them where the snowdrops are.'

'The snowdrops, are they're still in the green?'

'Yes. Oh, I see what you mean. Soon their foliage will have withered, the thief wouldn't be able to find them, therefore they wouldn't try.'

'Correct – unless you've labelled them.'

'*No*, I haven't.'

'Today is Thursday. I want you to drop hints, or you could take Georgie to see them. I don't think you can do that with the other two, it would look obvious. But you could chat to them, and give them the opportunity to follow you. I'd like you to do this on Friday.'

'You're going to do a stake-out?'

'Yes, I had a meeting with my partners this morning. Mr Elderkin will be with me on Friday and Saturday nights, and Miss Bowman on Sunday night.'

'Goodness, I didn't realise there was a woman on your staff. Will she be of much use if there's a fight?'

Frank laughed. 'You've not met her. She's five eleven and built like an Amazon. I'm not sure I'd come off best if we had a set-to.'

Pamela laughed with him. 'Gracious. She sounds very handy. Would she like to be a volunteer?'

'I don't think gardening is Laurel's bag.'

'What is?'

'Running, sea-swimming, throwing the odd javelin, and recently she's taken up tennis.'

'Where does she play?'

'The Country Club, Thorpeness.'

Pamela's face clouded. 'Did you hear about poor Neville Hanmer? I couldn't believe it.'

'You knew him?'

'Yes, he was a dear friend of mine. We shared a passion for gardening. Used to go to the RHS flower shows together, more so when he lived in London.'

He didn't want to discuss the Judge at the moment, but when they'd sorted out the details of the stake-out, it would be useful to find out if she'd any interesting information about the Judge. 'Are you happy with us starting on Friday night?'

'Yes, I suppose so.'

'I must ask you not to come into the woods after dusk on stake-out nights, but I will need you to take me to the site today. We'd better do that when everyone else has gone home. Mustn't alert them too soon to the position of the snowdrops.'

'What will you do in the meantime?'

'There are a few volunteers I haven't spoken to yet. From the details Georgie has given me, they should be in today. I'll also familiarise myself with the general layout of the gardens, get it fixed in my head in case we have to chase anyone from the wood, onto the herbaceous border through the maze and into the stumpery.' He grinned at her, hoping to lighten her mood.

'Don't you dare. I don't want my garden damaged.'

'Haven't you heard about eggs and omelettes?'

She sniffed. 'Supposing something goes wrong? The thief might be violent. Have you thought they might have someone with them? Then it would be two against two.'

'Yes, there is that possibility, but I'm sure we'll be able to manage. We'll have the element of surprise and Mr Elderkin can blow his old police whistle and they'll think there's an army of bluebottles about to nab them.'

'You're looking forward to this, aren't you?'

'Nothing like a touch of violence to warm you up on a cold night.'

'I heard you once killed a man. Is that true?'

Frank inwardly groaned, and regretted his last words. 'He was not only threatening my life, but one of my partners, and a young boy. He was a professional killer.'

'Crikey! I'll stop worrying about you.'

'Good. I'll see you at the end of the day, and you can take me to the snowdrops. I hope we'll be able to solve this shortly and then you can get back to normality.'

'Amen, to that,' she said.

As he walked into the garden, he decided he'd ask her about the Judge after they'd visited the snowdrops.

As he walked past the maze, again there was the sound of clippers being used on the yew hedges. He imagined Owen Albrighton muttering to himself, wishing he had a hedge-cutter with a long lead. Was Owen a strong suspect? He was short of money, no doubt about that, but he was sorry for him, having to look after his mother. It meant he couldn't have a full-time job, and therefore no chance of building a career. The only bright spot seemed he was fond of his mother, and didn't seem resentful towards her. He didn't seem fond of Mrs Gage, as most of the other workers were. Was he clever enough to make much of a profit if he was the thief? Would he have the connections for selling them on? Would he take the risk of losing his job, and possibly serving a prison sentence if he was caught? What would happen to his mother, if he wasn't around to care for her? He decided Owen didn't fit the profile of the plant thief. But there was something about him he didn't like. A touch of lasciviousness? He shook his head. You can't be sent to gaol for that. Otherwise, the prison system wouldn't be able to cope. And he might be one of its inmates.

He decided to visit the Japanese garden again; hopefully he might be able to sit quietly and watch the koi carp swimming through the waterweed. He could do with some thinking time in peaceful surroundings. He went through the moon gate, saying hello to two visitors who were just leaving, talking excitedly about creating something similar in their own garden.

He was determined to bring Laurel here. Perhaps they could come over in the next two days, before they started their stake-out. She needed to familiarise herself with the surroundings. That would be the excuse he'd make. Although he hoped he and Stuart would nab the thief in the first two nights of the stake-out, he imagined he and Laurel lying side by side on Sunday night, waiting for the thief to emerge. God, he hoped it didn't rain. Was a bed of forest soil erotic enough to send Laurel's hormones into overdrive? He laughed to himself. He wished they were intimate enough to share such a silly idea. But he wasn't sure how she'd take it. She seemed to be warmer towards him, but he'd thought that before.

Oh no! On the far bank was Janet Lamb talking to Georgie Gibbs, who was once more up to her thighs in the water, no doubt having another go at the reeds. He was tempted to turn back. Janet was hammering away, gesticulating with her hands. Then she saw him, and pointed, her face hard and cross. Georgie looked his way and said something to Janet, who stomped off towards a nearby border, where a kneeling pad and gardening tools were scattered on the path.

He sighed. He couldn't disappear now; it would look as though he was frightened of her. He was sure Janet had been complaining to Georgie about him. He'd better try and smooth her down. He grimaced. Not a pretty thought.

'Hello, Georgie. Still battling with the reeds?'

She raised her head. 'Yes. Not my favourite job, but it has to be done.'

'The compensation must be the view all around you. I couldn't resist coming to have another look.'

She continued to slash at the plants. 'Yes, it is lovely,' she muttered, obviously not keen to talk to him. He couldn't blame her; first Janet going on at her and she must be embarrassed if he'd been the topic of their conversation. He decided to bite the bullet and tackle the formidable Janet Lamb. What with her and Pamela he'd had enough of strong women.

Janet was head down in a border, wielding a narrow alpine trowel as she carefully extracted weeds from between primula plants, tossing them into a plastic container.

'Miss Lamb, could I have a few words with you, please?'

She shot round, pointing the trowel at him as though she would like to do him a mischief. 'I have nothing more to say to you, Mr Diamond, except you haven't fooled me,' she shouted.

'I came to apologise for my behaviour the other day. I should have made an appointment to see your garden. I hope I didn't upset Muriel?'

She pushed herself up, grimacing, until she faced him. 'You did. It took a good few hours before she recovered.'

Not helped by your attitude, he thought. 'I'm sorry to hear that.'

'Your weasel words aren't cutting any ice with me,' she snapped. 'I know why you're here, and if I didn't dislike you so much, I might have been able to help you,' she hissed. 'I know what's been happening, I'm not stupid. And I've got a good idea who's behind it. Why should I help you? All I need is proof. Then I'll be the one who solves this problem, and I won't be asking for an enormous fee.' She was livid, and flecks of saliva shot from her mouth as she spat her words at him.

This was not good. Did she really know about the plant thefts? Or was this a double bluff? He needed to think this one over. It was no good talking to her when she was in this mood; he was definitely off her Christmas card list.

'I'm not sure I understand you, Miss Lamb. Perhaps we can talk again tomorrow. Please remember, I'm here to help Mrs Gage. I know you respect and like her, and I'm sure those feelings are mutual. Please put aside the unfortunate events of yesterday for her sake, not for mine.'

'Your words don't butter any parsnips with me,' she said. 'All you're doing is taking money away from the garden. I can sort this out without your or anybody else's help.'

She must be stopped from whatever mad-cap scheme she was planning. She could ruin everything with her meddling; the thief might catch on, and decide to call a halt to his activities.

'Please, Miss Lamb, don't do anything rash. I'll ask Mrs Gage if the three of us can have a talk together,' he said. They might have to take her into their confidence. But supposing she was the thief? And this was a ruse to divert their attention from her?

She sniffed. 'I need to finish my work. I can't waste any time talking to you. The garden closes in half an hour.'

He decided to say no more and make his way back to the house and Pamela. He took the zig-zag path over the lake; ahead of him was Georgie. She was hurrying towards the moon gate, her waders squeaking.

★

Frank and Pamela walked between the herbaceous borders towards the wood. It was after eight, the sun was setting and the garden deserted.

'I wonder how Janet discovered the plant thefts?' she asked.

'You said some plants had been taken from the Japanese gardens. Did she notice they'd gone?' he asked.

Pamela walked in silence. 'Yes, I remember. She came to see me, she was agitated. She said some of her favourite plants had disappeared. Perhaps I should have been straight with her, but I didn't want everyone to know plants were being nicked. It would have created bad feelings between the volunteers. Some of them are rather jealous of each other, it's only a minority, but it's surprising how vibes can spread. I told her I'd dug them up as I had buyers for them, and I couldn't afford to not make the sales.'

'Do you think she believed you?'

'Yes, but she wasn't pleased, she's quite obsessed with the Japanese garden. Sometimes she's resentful if I ask her to work in a different part and let another volunteer work in there. Afterwards she always complains they haven't done things right. She can be a pain, but she's a good gardener, and doesn't cost me a penny.'

'She told me you often gave her plants, or sold them to her at cost. Is that true?'

They were approaching the wood. A fox darted out from behind a shrub, slithered between the oaks, and disappeared.

Pamela laughed. 'There she goes. That vixen has cubs, she's got a den near where we're going. I recognise her by the black tips of her ears.'

'You don't mind her being part of the garden?'

'No, she catches those pesky rabbits, helps to keep their population in check. They do so much damage.'

'You haven't answered my question. Do you help Janet out with plants?'

'What if I do? She's a hard worker and I like her.'

'I'm wondering if she's trying to bluff us. To make us think someone else is the thief, when it's really her.'

'Mr Diamond, you have a circuitous mind!'

'That's a new description. I've been called many things, but not circuitous.'

'You'd better concentrate on remembering the way to the snow-drops. It's dark in the woods, so I'll use my torch and lead the way, going slowly so you can take it all in.'

'I've brought a piece of chalk with me. If I make marks on the trees, it should help me on Friday.'

'Trying to catch the Minotaur? Won't the marks possibly help the thief?'

'I'll put them in inconspicuous places. Otherwise, they might wonder who's making the marks – the chalk fairy, perhaps?'

'You're a clever man, Mr Diamond. You enjoy your job, don't you?'

'Some parts are better than others. I always like a bit of improvisation.'

The path between the soaring oaks was narrow, the leaf mould soft beneath his feet, earthy smells wafting up from the woodland floor as they scuffed up the soil. He shone his own torch onto the ground, careful not to trip up over the many exposed roots, thick and gnarled as the legs of aged weightlifters. A slight breeze soughed through the leafless branches, moaning as if the birth of spring was painful.

Every few yards he bent down to make a discreet chalk mark. If he hadn't done that there was no way he'd have been able to find his way on Friday night. He hoped it didn't pour with rain before then, for although the trees would give some protection, the marks might be washed away.

Pamela turned back towards him. 'Do you really need to make so many marks? We'll never get there at this rate.'

'Patience, Pamela. Don't rush me.'

The undergrowth thickened, bramble shoots arcing over the path and forming thickets on either side of it, interlacing with the russet fronds of last year's ferns. Pamela muttered as she battled through a particular spiny patch, and one whipped back into his face as she pushed forwards.

'Ouch!'

'Sorry. Pesky things. I didn't want to cut them back; it would have made it obvious someone had been this way.'

'Perhaps tomorrow it might be a good idea to do just that. Give the thief a head start.'

'And help you that night?' she replied. 'Kill two birds with one stone?'

'Correct.'

'Here we are.' She'd stopped in front of a small glade. Looking up there was a circle of black sky, sprinkled with stars. The beam of her torch shone on the central space. The earth was clear of weeds, and the glaucous leaves of snowdrops, their edges beginning to brown and flag, covered the area; the only sign of flowers, swollen seed heads. In a few weeks they would have disappeared beneath the woodland soil.

'How many are there?' he asked.

'About two hundred.'

'As many as that?'

'I think so, it's surprising when you separate them. I must admit I'm always amazed. But some of them, the smaller bulbs, won't be of a saleable size. They'll need to be grown on for another two years.'

'Even so, if they are worth ten pounds a bulb, that's two thousand pounds.'

'Oh, they'll be worth much more than that. They'll have rarity value. I would hope to get at least forty pounds a bulb in the first few years. Later on, as their numbers increase, the price will go down.'

'So that little lot could be worth eight thousand pounds; if it were me, I'd put them in a safe.'

Pamela laughed. 'Do you a lot of good there. Shall we go back? Sure you'll be able to find your way here without my help?'

'Hold on a minute. I'll take a reccy, see where the best place is for me and my partner to hide. We must presume they'll be coming in on this path.' He skirted the snowdrops and moved to the other side of the glade. There was a large oak, with brambles clawing their way up its great trunk. He used the torch to push them back. Behind the tree would be a good place to hide. He'd bring some secateurs to cut down the brambles, and then they could place them back to give them cover. He went back to her. 'Would you mind if I cut down a few brambles to give us access to the space behind the tree?'

'Not at all. Right, ready to go? I'm starving and I don't suppose Keith will be waiting with a ready meal for me.'

'Does he do any cooking?'

'You must be joking. Do you know any men who cook?'

'I know two, and I'm one of them.'

'Goodness, Mr Diamond, you are a most eligible bachelor.'

He thought she must have been reading too much Georgette Heyer. Although he quite fancied himself in a tight-fitting coat, breeches and shiny boots. Would Laurel go for that?

'And who's the other male chef?'

'He's a wife–murderer, who does occasional meals for the Agency. Very good cook. And before you ask, he didn't poison his wife.'

She laughed, and slapped her thigh, as they emerged from the wood.

Was this a good time to ask about the Judge? 'Mrs Gage, you mentioned you were friends with Neville Hanmer?'

'Yes. How he could have been so careless as to trip up and fall down the stairs, I don't know. He was always good on his feet, but I suppose old age catches up with all of us, sooner or later.'

He thought old age would have to move fast to catch Pamela.

'It does matter, Pamela. The Judge contacted us, and we'd arranged a meeting for the Monday after he died.' He played the beam of his torch so he could see her face.

She shook her head. 'I can't see that makes any difference.'

He placed a hand on her arm and they stopped at the entrance to the herbaceous borders. 'I must tell you he was murdered, it was not an accident.'

Her eyes widened, her expression was one of horror, then anger. 'Who did it? Do the police know?'

This was awkward. 'There is a suspect, but I and the other members of the Agency don't believe he is the murderer.'

'You never talked to the Judge?'

'No. He phoned me on the Friday afternoon, and was murdered that night. Why I'm telling you this is I wondered if Judge Hanmer had talked to you about why he needed to contact the Agency?'

'Come back to the house. We can talk there. I'll try and remember what he said.'

She didn't wait for his reply but marched ahead of him, her shoulders hunched, expletives drifting back to him as she fumed her way to the house.

She led him to her office. 'Better not go into the sitting room, Keith will probably be in there demolishing any alcohol he can find.' She opened the office door. 'Take a seat.' She went to a cupboard, took a key from her pocket and opened the door. 'Gin or whisky? My secret stash. Nothing special, I'm afraid, can't afford top-quality booze. But sometimes, I do need a pick-me-up, especially after I've had a row with Keith.'

'Does he know you keep alcohol in here?'

'I certainly hope not. That's a good old cupboard, eighteenth century. If he breaks into that to get at my drinks, it will be him who's found dead, and you'll know who the murderer is. So, what's it to be?'

He wasn't keen on cheap whisky, but he didn't want to seem snobbish. 'Whisky, just a small one. I've got to drive home.'

'Water?'

'Just a tad.' It might cut through the roughness.

She passed him a tumbler with an inch of brown liquid glinting in the bottom. 'Say when.'

He lifted a finger and she sploshed water into his glass.

She sat behind her desk, a large measure of what he presumed was gin in her glass and a small bottle of nearly full tonic beside it. 'Cheers.'

He raised his glass. 'Bottoms up.' He took a careful sip. It wasn't that bad, and it warmed his throat and belly. 'I'm sorry if I shocked you about Mr Hanmer's death. Did he tell you in any detail what he was worried about?'

170

Pamela took a deep swallow of the colourless liquid. 'He came over, let me see, when was it? About a fortnight ago. He liked to look round the garden at different seasons, and this was his spring visit. I told him about the plant thefts and how I was going to make contact with you. I said I'd checked up on the Agency and I was satisfied you'd do a good job. I needed to make sure I had the money to pay for your services. At that point I hadn't quite made up my mind. It was a big step to take, and I did worry about how you would investigate the thefts without upsetting the staff, both paid and voluntary.' She leant back in her chair. 'I could see what I'd said had intrigued him and later, over a cup of tea, he said he also had a problem, and didn't know what to do about it.'

'Can you remember exactly what he said?'

'I'll try. We were in the sitting room; it was about three in the afternoon. The light was fading, but it had been a good day, weatherwise, and we'd enjoyed walking round the garden, seeing the late snowdrops, the narcissi and the camellias, those in bloom. It's always good to walk a garden with someone who knows what you're talking about, and doesn't ask the name of every plant they don't know. Such a waste of time telling them, as you know they'll immediately forget it. I believe they ask just to see if you know the name. Very irritating.'

He needed to steer her back to the Judge.

'It's all right, I haven't forgotten. I was setting the scene.'

'And beautifully described.'

She frowned, knitting her brows so tightly deep furrows appeared, like the lines in a ploughed field. 'I can't swear these were the exact words, but my memory is good, so here goes.

'"Pamela," he said, "I've also got a problem, and I'm not sure what to do about it. I wonder if it might be a good idea if I contacted your detective agency."

'I was surprised. "Goodness, Neville, why would you do that? You don't suspect Mrs Hegarty is stealing your boiled ham?"

'He laughed. "Dear Mrs Hegarty. No, indeed, she often brings me treats, last week it was a very nice ginger cake."

'He looked at me and smiled. He was such a gentle man, although he was strict when he was a judge. I do miss him.

'"So, what's the problem?"

'"There's someone I've seen recently I met in the past. I don't like to think of them being in this part of the world and I'm worried as to why they are here."

'"Why? What do you think they'll do?"

'"Forgive me, Pamela, if I don't reveal their name at this point. Their presence here could be innocent. It may be they've changed, it's several years since I saw them. I don't want to blacken someone's name without more proof. That's why I'm thinking of contacting your agency. They could make discreet enquiries without alerting the person, or their employers."'

Frank's back straightened. They were in work. That was something.

'"Why don't you wait until I've decided if The Anglian Detective Agency comes up to scratch? I'll let you know how good I think they are, then you can make up your mind."

'"When will that be? I don't want to wait too long."

'"Say, a week?"

'"Very well, I'll do that."

'"Do you think this person has recognised you?"

'"I'm not sure. I don't think so."

'"I presume it has something to do with a case you were involved with?"

'"Yes, it does."

'"As a lawyer, or as a judge?"

'"As a judge, but please don't ask me any more questions. I know what you're like once you start."

'"Like a dog with a bone?"

'"Precisely. Now tell me more about the plants that have been stolen. Do you have any suspects?" he asked.'

She took another swallow, then coughed as the spirit hit her throat. 'That's it. If I remember anything else, I'll let you know.'

'Pamela. I think you must talk to the police and tell them what you've told me. There are some important points you've brought up that are new to me, and will be to the detective in charge of the case.'

'Really? What points?'

'That someone is in employment, and were involved in a case the Judge presided over.'

She shook her head. 'I don't want the police here.'

'No need for that. If you like I can contact Detective Inspector Revie, the man who recommended us to you, he's in charge of the case. He'll phone you and make arrangements for you to go to Leiston Police Station. Would that be all right?'

She didn't look happy. 'I suppose so.' Then she slapped her hand. 'Of course it's all right. What am I thinking about? If I can help to catch the swine who did Neville in, I'll be happy to visit the police station as many times as necessary.'

'Thank you. Can you think of anyone who'd want to harm Mr Hanmer? Are you sure he never mentioned a name?'

'No. I would have told you if I knew that.' She hesitated, then wagged a raised finger at him. 'Was there anything in his diary?'

'Diary? I'm not sure. I didn't see one.'

'You were there?'

He inwardly winced. 'Yes, with Miss Bowman, my partner.'

'Dead?'

'Three days' dead. I'll ask Inspector Revie if he found a diary. Why do you think there might be something in there?'

She gulped down another mouthful of gin. 'How awful to find him like that, but I suppose you're used to it,' she said, shuddering.

'The diary?'

'Oh, as long as I've known him, he's kept a dairy. Usually a beautiful leather-bound book, with one page for each day. He didn't just write about the weather, or what was flowering in the garden, he also wrote about his thoughts, his impressions of people. There might be something in there that would be useful. I hope so.'

Revie hadn't mentioned a dairy, not that he told them everything that was going on with the case, but surely if there was one, and the

Judge had written anything derogatory about David, he would have mentioned it on the night he came to see them to tell them it was likely he'd be arresting David the next day. He'd phone Revie as soon as he got back to Greyfriars.

'Like a drop more?' she asked, waving the bottle.

'Just another inch.' Why shouldn't he celebrate a little? This had been a productive day.

174

# Chapter Eighteen

Friday, 27 April, 1973

Laurel doodled on the blotting paper in front of her, as she waited for Frank to arrive for their early-morning meeting.

Dorothy came into the dining room/office and put five glasses near the five pieces of blotting paper and pencils. 'Laurel – that was a fresh piece of blotting paper. If I tried to analyse your drawing, I wonder what it would tell me?'

Laurel looked at the jumble of lines. 'I really don't know. I wouldn't like a psychologist to see it, it might reveal a character flaw.'

Dorothy leant over her shoulder to have a look. 'I think you're constipated.'

Laurel laughed.

Dorothy sniffed. 'Nice perfume. Who's it for? Or needn't I ask?'

'It's for Bumper. He appreciates a good smell.'

'Really? I wouldn't say you smelt of dog poo. I think perhaps it's for another male of a different species.'

'Dorothy Piff, you're becoming a nosy old maid. And what if I am wearing something rather seductive?'

Dorothy looked at her watch. 'At nine in the morning . . . and by the way, where is Frank?'

Laurel bristled. 'I don't know.'

'Perhaps he had a late night in Aldeburgh,' Dorothy said, moving swiftly out of Laurel's reach.

Laurel felt anger rising, and gave Dorothy a hard look.

'I'm sorry, Laurel, but he's got a girlfriend, and they seem happy together from what I've heard. Do you think it's right to come between them? I may have read it wrong, but I don't think so.'

Laurel bit her lip, feeling tears building up. Was it so obvious? Was she being cheap? What did Frank think? She'd dressed carefully for the meeting, putting on a clinging moss-green sweater, and black ski pants, her hair washed and shiny. Did the others think like Dorothy? Were they embarrassed by her appearance and behaviour? She decided to go upstairs and change, and to wash away the mascara and blusher. Too late. Frank and Stuart's voices were in the hall, and growing louder. She inwardly shrank.

Dorothy squeezed her shoulder. 'I'm sorry, Laurel. You look and smell lovely.'

'Good morning,' Frank said. 'Sorry I'm late, had a heavy session last night.'

She surreptitiously glanced at him. He, as usual, looked full of beans. Perhaps Dorothy was right. She kept her head down.

'Morning, Laurel. Not speaking to me today? What have I done now?' Frank said, sitting down beside her.

'Oh, sorry. I was thinking about something else,' she whispered.

'Are you all right? You're not feeling ill, are you?'

The caring tone of his voice made her eyes well again. This was ridiculous. Stop it, Laurel, she told herself. She looked at him and smiled. 'I'm fine, just a few sad thoughts, that's all, and I'm not cross with you. Far from it.'

He leant back, looking relieved. 'That's good. You're looking especially charming, by the way, that colour suits you.'

She felt herself blushing. 'Thank you.' She didn't dare look at Dorothy.

Stuart and Mabel came in and took their places.

'Right, let's make a start,' Frank said. 'My heavy session last night was with Mrs Gage, sorting out how we'd stake-out these snowdrops.'

The tension in Laurel's shoulders eased; he hadn't been in Aldeburgh with the lovely Emma.

'Heavy session?' Stuart chortled. 'Was that a heavy petting session?'

'Stuart!' Mabel said, rapping him on the knuckles.

Frank laughed. 'No, attractive and lively as I find Mrs Gage, I have learnt not to mix business with pleasure.'

'Surely you don't fancy her, Frank?' Mabel said, her eyes as round as pennies. 'She must be my age?'

Frank shook his head. 'Get a grip, Mabel. The heavy session was downing a great deal of Scotch. Mind you, Pamela demolished her share of gin. But it was worth it.' He told them about the new facts he'd learnt about the Judge. 'When I got back to the cottage, I phoned Revie, and he's making arrangements to see Mrs Gage. He says they didn't find any diary. He's getting Cottam to have another look. He says there's a mountain of paperwork at Hanmer's house that needs looking into.'

The phone on Dorothy's desk rang. She got up.

'The Anglian Detective Agency. Miss Piff, the administrator, speaking. How may I help?'

Laurel smiled; Dorothy did love saying that.

'I see. Please hold.' She covered the mouthpiece with her hand. 'It's Mr Pemberton. He wants to come over now to see us. What shall I say?'

Laurel's chest tightened. Had something happened to David?

Frank looked at the others. 'By the time he gets here, we should have wrapped up the meeting. Tell him to come over?' He looked enquiringly at them. Yeses and nods.

'Hello, Mr Pemberton. We're having a meeting at the moment, but that should be finished by the time you arrive.'

She listened. 'We look forward to seeing you soon.' She put the phone down and took her seat. 'He sounded determined. About what, I'm not sure.'

'We'll find out soon enough,' Frank said. 'What I want to discuss is the equipment and supplies we'll need for our stake-outs. Dorothy, could you make a list, please.'

She waved her biro at him. 'Don't I always?'

'You never know, you might get sloppy.'

'You're living dangerously,' Laurel whispered.

His green eyes glinted. 'Like to join me?'

She wanted to say yes, please, but she didn't reply.

'Coward,' he whispered.

'Will you two stop whispering, we need to get a move on, or Mr Pemberton will be here before we've finished the meeting,' Dorothy said.

Frank suggested what they might need on their stake-outs: waterproof clothing, including hats and warm clothes underneath, a tarpaulin to lie on, torches, spare batteries.

'Stuart, could you bring your police whistle? I presume you've still got it?'

Stuart grinned. 'I have, and I'll have my truncheon handy.'

'Stuart Elderkin, you're not in the police now, they'll have you if you biff people up,' Mabel said.

Stuart shrugged and popped a sweet into his mouth.

'Mabel, could you do us some food supplies, please?' Frank said.

She nodded. 'Lots of sandwiches, pork pies, flasks of tea and coffee. Stuart, we'd better go into Leiston and get another flask. I can borrow a tarpaulin from Tom in Aldeburgh, no point in buying something like that.'

'What about a bottle of brandy?' Dorothy said. 'I know if you're cold, alcohol is not the best thing to drink, but it does make you feel warmer.'

'I'll go for that,' Frank said. 'Only make it Scotch.'

'Didn't you have enough with Mrs Gage?' Laurel asked.

'I wouldn't mind sharing a bottle with you, on Sunday night,' Frank said.

Somehow spending a night in a damp wood with him seemed madly attractive.

The doorbell rang.

'I'll bring him straight in, shall I?' Dorothy asked.

'Stuart, get another chair,' Mabel said. 'Shall I make some coffee?'

'Let's wait until we know what he wants,' Frank said. 'Perhaps afterwards.'

178

Dorothy led Adam Pemberton into the room, and after saying hello to everyone, he sat in the chair Dorothy indicated.

'What can we do for you, Mr Pemberton?' Frank asked.

'First, thank you again, Laurel, for seeing David and getting him to open up. It's made the world of difference to Ann and me, and to David himself. Now we know why he went to Mr Hanmer's house. I hope Inspector Revie believes David's story, but I don't think he does, and he won't until the real murderer is discovered. That's why I came today. I'm asking you to work for me again, this time not to find David, but to find the man who murdered Judge Hanmer. Until he's found, David will be thought guilty of this heinous crime. Will you do that? Please, I beg you. I never thought I'd see David alive after he ran away, but you found him, and you, Miss Bowman, and Mr Diamond, you saved his life at the risk of your own. Will you do this? Please.'

Laurel wanted to shout out *Yes, we will!* – but she held back.

Frank leant towards Mr Pemberton. 'I must tell you, Mr Pemberton, that Inspector Revie has not stopped searching for evidence of another person's guilt. Also, we couldn't do this while the police are still investigating the case. It isn't all over for David, not by any means.'

'But supposing the police don't find anything incriminating about anyone else. I don't want to wait for that. Time will be lost.'

He turned to Mabel. 'I believe you were not happy when you heard the verdict of your son's death and you asked Laurel to investigate? That's what they say in the town. Is that right?'

Mabel nodded. 'Yes, that's true. And she did a marvellous job, and so did Frank.'

'Inspector Revie knew then you were investigating that case, didn't he?' he asked Laurel.

She bit her lip. 'Yes, but then the coroner's verdict was accidental death; here we're dealing with a murder case.'

'You could ask him. See if he agrees to your helping. Surely it's worth a try?' He sounded desperate.

'I'll talk to him,' Frank said. 'We've worked together before. I

179

know he's sympathetic towards David. I don't think he wants him to be the murderer.'

Pemberton looked relieved.

'Leave it with me,' Frank said, 'but please don't tell anyone I'm talking to him about this. If he agrees, it mustn't get out. It would put him in a difficult situation.'

Pemberton nodded. 'I won't say anything. But can I tell Ann?'

Frank looked at the rest of the team. They all nodded. 'Yes. But don't either of you say anything to David. He might let it slip to one of the other policemen at Ipswich. Not likely, but you never know.'

'I agree. Thank you so much. I can't bear the thought of David going on trial; you know how badly he reacts to strangers. Imagine him in a full court room, it would be useless to let him take the stand, he wouldn't reply to the cross-examination. He'd look guilty.' He buried his head in his hands. 'Dear God, please save him,' he muttered.

Laurel went to him. 'Please bear up, Mr Pemberton, David needs you to be strong and positive. Let him know you believe the true killer will be found. Can you do that?'

He looked up at her, straightened his back and shoulders. 'Yes, I can. Thank you for reminding me what I must do. If only they would let us see him more often.'

'David is a strong person, remember how he survived by himself when the only company he had were two dreadful men. Now, he's broken his silence and he knows you believe in him, he'll come through this.'

Mr Pemberton got up. 'Thank you, Laurel. Thank you, all. I'll wait to hear from you, Mr Diamond.'

'Would you like a drink before you go?' Mabel asked. Her face was white and drawn.

'No, thank you.'

'I'll show you out,' Dorothy said, and escorted him from the room.

Stuart blew out his cheeks. 'I'm having a pipe after that. Poor bloke. I hope you're right, Frank, and Revie does find the killer.'

'I'm with you there,' Frank replied. He turned to Laurel. 'How about a walk after we've had some coffee? I need a breath of fresh air. We can take Bumper to the beach.'

She was glad Dorothy was out of the room. 'Great idea. Shall I help you get coffee, Mabel?'

Frank watched as Laurel threw the blue ball for Bumper to chase over Dunwich beach. It was a game the dog never got tired of. What a simple life he had. All you needed was a good owner who fed you regularly, played with you and provided a comfy bed, preferably in front of a roaring fire in the winter. Bumper was happy with the same food, day after day, playing the same games, going on the same walks. What an uncomplicated life. Would he be happy doing that? No, but possibly doing different things, eating different foods with the same person, would make him happy. Would she feel the same?

'Laurel?'

She turned, her back to the sea, blonde hair whipping around her in the strong wind. 'Yes?'

'Would you like to visit Yoxford Gardens before Sunday night, have a look round? Perhaps we could go out for a meal afterwards? The garden is lovely, especially the Japanese garden.'

Her eyes widened and she smiled – a lovely smile. 'I'd like that very much. Thank you.'

Relief flooded through him. She looked pleased, no funny comments, just pure acceptance.

'When would we go?' she asked.

'I thought sometime on Saturday.'

'If you and Stuart catch the thief tonight, will you still want to go?'

A leading question. 'Yes, I think you'd like the garden, but I'll be surprised if our stake-out works on the first night.'

'So, what time on Saturday? You'll be going back there Saturday night. You won't want to go out for a meal and then go straight to the gardens, will you?'

He moved towards her, wanting to put his arm round her shoulders. 'I talked to Mrs Gage last night, and asked if I could bring you to see the gardens at a time when there aren't many people about. She suggested early Saturday or Sunday mornings, before the gardens open and the first volunteers arrive. How about Saturday, then we could have lunch afterwards?'

'That sounds great. Any idea where?'

'How about driving to Orford and going to the Oysterage?'

'Lovely. But you've got another night in the woods with Stuart, shouldn't you be catching up on some sleep after tonight?'

He shrugged. 'I can't think of anything more relaxing than spending most of the day with you.' Had he overcooked it?

Her cheeks flamed. 'Then it's a date? Is it a date?'

'Looks like it, doesn't it?'

She put a hand to her cheek. 'Goodness, Frank, you've made me feel all missish. This won't do. I'll give Bumper a few more throws and then we'd better get back.'

What was he waiting for? Why didn't he get hold of her now? Afraid of rejection? He wasn't sure where this was leading. She hadn't put him off. She looked pleased at the thought of *a date*. This was ridiculous, he was acting like a teenager daring to ask the most popular girl in the sixth form to the Christmas disco. But what about Emma? He thanked God their relationship hadn't yet gone beyond the kissing and heavy snogging stage; he'd been tempted to take it further, especially when she pressed her body close to his when they kissed, but he hadn't. She'd asked if she could see his cottage; he'd given a vague reply. What did Laurel want? Would history repeat itself? Would she back off if he made advances?

Laurel and Bumper were dancing round each other, he trying to get the ball, she trying to attach the lead to his collar. He ached for her. Was this love? After all they'd been through? What did she feel? He didn't like the uncertainty. What was going to happen? He had to know. One way or the other.

# Chapter Nineteen

Saturday, 28 April, 1973

Laurel opened the passenger door of Frank's Avenger, and stepped out into the car park at Yoxford Gardens. The air was sharp; the overnight temperature had been near to freezing, but now the sun was shining brightly from a cloudless sky. Frank had picked her up from Greyfriars at seven, looking for once a little bleary-eyed, but freshly shaved and immaculate in a cream polo-necked jumper under his leather jacket. Had he had any sleep?

On the way over he'd told her about their night vigil. Stuart had demolished most of the food before midnight, and the only excitement were a couple of brown owls furiously hooting nearby, and a sighting of the resident vixen.

'Let's hope you have more luck tonight,' she said.

'I'm not sure I want to catch him tonight, then I wouldn't be able to spend a night with you in the woods,' he'd replied, giving her a quizzical look.

She'd wanted to say: nothing to stop us spending it somewhere else – but she didn't dare. She wasn't sure what was going to happen. She decided to enjoy the day, and not waste it worrying if she was saying or doing the right thing. For once it would be just them, Frank and Laurel.

'Pamela Gage has invited us to have coffee with her after we've had a look around,' Frank said.

She was looking forward to meeting her, this older woman, who, according to Stuart, Frank had a crush on.

'Let's start with the herbaceous border,' Frank said. 'Not much out at the moment, but you can use your vivid imagination, and conjure up their summer magnificence.'

He was full of enthusiasm; she imagined him as a botany student, head bent over a microscope, studying some primitive algae. Certainly, his knowledge of plants had been vital in the case at the holiday camp; his recognition of poisonous plants had opened up a new angle. Somehow, studious Frank didn't go with the man she knew – a man of action. But he was good at analysing the multitude of facts a case threw up; the discipline of studying for a science degree must hone your ability to sort through a plethora of details and find the vital connections. There was so much she didn't know about him.

'Well?' he said. 'Impressions so far?'

'Sorry, my mind had drifted away.'

'You certainly looked deep in thought. Penny for them?'

She looked into his eyes. 'I was thinking there's so much I don't know about you.'

He looked shocked. 'You want to know more about me? I should think you know a great deal.'

Bugger! Had she crossed a forbidden boundary? 'Don't you want to know more about me?'

'I know enough.'

What did that mean? She decided she was getting into dangerous territory; she'd better go onto a different tack. 'I can see why you're impressed with the garden, it looks well tended.' She couldn't see any weeds and the borders had been mulched, the dark layers setting off the yellow and the whites of the narcissi and the vivid colours of the tulips. 'I think Dorothy would like it here.'

He made a non-committal noise. Had she blown it? Gone too far, too fast? Misread the whole thing?

'Would you like to see the maze?'

'I love mazes. Yes, let's see if we can get lost.'

184

He groaned. Obviously, he didn't like mazes.

'Gosh, it must take ages to trim the hedges. It's well clipped.'

'The gardener, Owen Albrighton, was working on this during the week. He wasn't happy – Pamela, Mrs Gage, doesn't like mechanised devices so he has to cut it by hand.'

'Does he karate chop it?'

'Very funny.' He took hold of her arm, and pulled her in the opposite direction. 'Don't think it's that way.'

'It's no fun if you find your way out of the maze straight away. You have to get lost a couple of times or it's a very poor maze.'

He didn't reply. She could tell by his body language he was irritated. If she wanted to be his girlfriend, not just his working partner, should she play up to him, and ask him to find the way out? If she did, would she have to keep on doing that? Letting him be the dominant partner, taking on the usual male role mantle. What she'd enjoyed about the partnership was they were equals, she never gave it a thought if she disagreed with him, or any of the other members of the Agency. If they were going to take their relationship to a different plane, she'd have to be herself, just as she would want him to be himself.

But perhaps, until she knew where they were going, she might let him have this one tiny victory. 'Are we in the centre? Do you know the way out?'

'I think we are, and I can lead you out if you can stop darting down blind alleys.'

'Right, lead on, Macduff. I want to see the rest of the garden.'

'Thank God for that.'

'Don't you like mazes, Frank?'

'I do not, they're a waste of gardening space. Now you know another fact about me. Satisfied?'

She laughed, put an arm round his shoulder and kissed him on the cheek.

For a millisecond his body was rigid, then he took her in his arms and kissed her, a very long and hard kiss. Nothing gentle. It spoke of frustration and longing.

They parted.

'I'm beginning to like mazes,' he said.

'Frank, you'd better show me the rest of the garden.'

'I'm not sure I can remember the way out.'

She punched him in the arm. 'Onward.'

He pulled her to him and they swayed clumsily out of the maze, laughing.

He looked at his wristwatch. 'Let's go to the Japanese garden, and then I think we'd better see Mrs Gage before the volunteers arrive.'

Happiness was bubbling inside her. His arm was round her waist and hers around his. Desire was flooding her body. Did he feel the same? Should they be doing this? What about Emma?

They came to a red gate. 'This is lovely, what an unusual shape.'

'It's called a moon gate,' he said, kissing her on the cheek.

Her body was reacting like a teenage girl on her first date. Was this love? Or was it so long since she'd had sex, she was just desperate?

'Oh, Frank. I can see why you wanted me to see it. It's quite wonderful.' The lake stretched out, with a wooden pathway over it that seemed to float on the water; a stream fed into the lake with a red-painted bridge over it and there was a little house on the far side. She turned to him. He was looking at her, his green eyes scanning her face, fixing on her lips.

'I think it's beautiful. I wanted you to see it. Glad you came?'

'Very glad.' He kissed her again, this time slowly, his mouth lingering over her lips. She gently pushed him away. 'Steady the buffs.'

He laughed. 'That's a new way of saying back off.'

'I can't cope with the sudden change. Give me time.'

'You can have all the time you want.' He looked at his watch again. 'Say half an hour?'

'Oh, Frank, you're a fool. Take me to that dear little house on the other side of the lake.'

'Your word is my command.'

If only, she thought.

His hand was on the small of her back and he moved her towards the zig-zag path. The sky had darkened, slate-grey clouds reflected

186

in the still waters. His pulled his hand away. 'Stay there.' He started to run towards the path.

'Frank, what is it?' She ran after him, up a shallow flight of steps, slowing down to negotiate the changing angles of the wooden planks. Frank had reached the opposite bank. She stopped. What was he doing?

He was running to the right, along the bank. Then she saw it. Something in the water, at the edge of the lake. A body. Someone had fallen in. Frank leapt into the water and grappled with the person. Was it a man or a woman? She couldn't tell. She started running again. He was struggling to hoist them onto the bank. Were they alive?

She slid into the lake, wincing as the icy water seeped through her clothing, weighing her down. She slowly moved towards them. The body was face down, but he'd managed to get the head and upper chest above the water. It was a woman. She clumsily moved to the other side of them.

'Get hold of her under the arm, Laurel, and heave when I say three.'

She nodded.

'One, two, THREE.'

She grimaced, pulling hard, helping to tow the woman to the bank.

'Again. One, two, THREE.'

One hand under the woman's arm, the other clawing at the bank, trying to find a hold, she heaved at the well-built body, heavy with sodden clothing. They dragged her and themselves up the steep bank until she was flat on the ground; both lying beside her, panting.

'Help me turn her over,' he commanded.

The woman's face was blue. Frank pressed two fingers against her neck, then bent down and put an ear to her mouth. He looked at her and shook his head.

'Who is she?'

'Janet Lamb, the volunteer I told you about.'

'Phone for an ambulance. I'll try mouth-to-mouth. She isn't breath-ing, is she?'

'I think she's well dead, Laurel.'

'Just go.'

He scrambled up, water pouring from him, his dark curls plastered to his scalp. 'You're sure? I don't like leaving you.'

'Come on, Frank, let me get on with it.'

She pinched the woman's nose, opened her mouth, tilting back the head, took a deep breath and then closed her lips around the woman's and breathed out. Janet's chest didn't rise.

'Right, I'm off.' He bounded across the zig-zag path. She watched him between breaths, praying he didn't fall into the lake, but he was as sure-footed as a mountain goat. Water sprayed from him, joining the drops of water falling from the sky. It had started to rain.

# Chapter Twenty

Sunday, 29 April, 1973

Frank drove away from Greyfriars, Laurel by his side.

'Are you surprised Janet Lamb turned out to be the plant thief?' she asked.

'Yes and no,' he said, as he turned left from the Dunwich Road into the village of Westleton. 'She fitted the thief's profile: rare plantaholic, especially snowdrops, own garden, very knowledgeable about plants in general, admitted she couldn't afford some of the plants she wanted. On the other hand . . . I'm not sure.'

Laurel sighed. 'But to meet your death trying to dig up plants, on a slippery bank in the dark, it doesn't bear thinking about. It seems crazy to me.' She sighed again. 'There's no doubt she was the thief, is there?'

Frank slowed down as they approached Scarlett's Garage. 'I'm a bit low on petrol. They may be open. Yes, they are.' He pulled up in front of the garage and got out. He chatted to the owner as he filled the tank, and glanced at Laurel, who looked deep in thought. It had been a shock to find Janet Lamb, her body submerged in the water of the lake. Laurel had acted coolly, quickly; she was dependable in any difficult or dangerous situation. She'd been upset, but that didn't stop her from being level-headed and unflappable. He paid the owner and got back in the car.

'Didn't want to run out of petrol on the way home,' he said.

'Not one of your usual ploys then?'

'I don't know what you mean.' He didn't think she'd go for making love in the back of his Avenger. Yesterday his plans for a romantic interlude in the Japanese Garden's pavilion had crumbled to dust.

'You haven't answered my question. Do you have doubts Janet Lamb was the thief?'

As they passed the road leading to Eastbridge, and The Eel's Foot, he glanced at her profile, then tried to remove romantic thoughts from his mind and concentrate on an answer. 'There was a dirty trowel on the bank, and two rare primula plants in a plastic bag nearby, pointing to her digging up the plants ready to take home. But, no, I'm not happy. Why was there no torch at the scene? Surely she'd have needed one to see what she was doing?'

'It was a clear night, but the moon was waning. She knew the garden well. I suppose she didn't want anyone to see a light,' she said.

'Where was her car?'

Laurel shrugged. 'I suppose the police will find that. Why did you phone Revie? I bet he wasn't pleased.'

Frank laughed. 'He wasn't. Said he'd have to have us transported, he couldn't deal with any more dead bodies.'

'Will they do a post-mortem?'

'They'll have to, and I managed to persuade him to get Ansell.'

'Frank, you're beginning to see a murder in every death. Who would want to kill Janet Lamb?'

'The real plant thief?'

'It looked as though she'd slipped and banged the front of her head on one of the boulders buried in the bank.'

'It's a good explanation, and it may turn out to be correct, but I'd rather Ansell did the post-mortem; if there's anything fishy, he'll root it out.'

'I bet you had a word with him, didn't you?'

He nodded. 'And I made sure Revie wasn't around when I rang him.'

He turned onto the road leading to Thorpeness; they were heading for the Country Club.

'What did we decide was our reason for this visit?' Laurel asked.

'I'm still dithering about whether to join the Club, and you wanted to see the handsome Carlton, also I want another chance to chat to the dynamic Beattie. We want to form a friendly foursome, but not on the tennis court.'

'I checked and they've both got bookings up to lunchtime, but are free this afternoon. When I rang Carlton and said I might be over about two-ish, he was very pleased.' She wriggled her body saucily. 'Who wouldn't be pleased.'

'Don't expect me to say anything.'

'All your sudden friendliness doesn't mean a thing?'

'I wouldn't say that.'

'Let's get back to the plot. What are we trying to find out?'

'I'd like to know more about Carlton's early sexual experiences. That chap, Harry, implied Carlton was a pretty young boy and may have been on the prefects' hit list.'

'Why is that important?'

'It may not be, but it could be a reason for his hatred of homosexuals – if his school days' experiences were awful. Can't imagine anything worse than being buggered by some toffee-nosed sixth-form yob.'

'That's an awful image, Frank. Poor Carlton, I hope it didn't happen. He isn't likely to tell us, is he?'

'No, but Beattie might. There's a lot of animosity between them, especially Beattie towards Carlton.'

'That's true. You'd think as the older sister she'd feel motherly towards him. I know I did towards Angela.'

Frank squeezed her thigh with his left hand. 'I thought you'd stopped blaming yourself for her death.'

She didn't knock his hand away. 'I'm afraid I'll carry some guilt for the rest of my life.'

He removed his hand back to the steering wheel. 'You didn't kill her, Laurel, you loved her, and still do, I expect.'

'I still do.'

'Try and remember the good times, when you were both young, before it all happened.'

'Thanks, Frank. At least now I can come to Thorpeness and not get upset. We had some great family holidays there.'

They were in sight of the House in the Sky, its tower bright against the blue; now they were driving past the Mere, a few rowing boats on its waters, swans and ducks gathered round the boathouse. It was a peaceful scene.

'Remember not to react when I start chatting up Beattie. It's all pretence, I assure you,' Frank said.

'Likewise, when I melt into Carlton's arms.'

'There's no need to go that far,' Frank said, trying to make his voice reek with disapproval.

Laurel laughed. 'You know I'll make any sacrifice to further our investigations.'

'Remember what Revie said, he didn't mind if we tried to find out anything that would help him solve the Judge's death, proving David Pemberton didn't do it, but no direct questions — be subtle. You do understand the meaning of that word, Laurel?'

She kicked his left leg.

'Careful, I'll go off the road.'

'It was only a tap.'

'Really? It felt like a tackle by Norman Hunter.'

'Who?'

'Plays for Leeds. One of our more cultured footballers.'

He pulled into the Club's car park and switched off the ignition.

'I'll need to sign you in. Carlton said he'd meet me on the terrace.'

'Do you know what he had in mind?'

'He mentioned I might like to have tea in his rooms. I think he might be a tad upset when he sees you.'

'I should hope so. Was he planning to seduce you over a cup of Earl Grey tea?'

'If he was, he's not got a hope, unless he's also offering me a delicious slice of chocolate cake as well.'

They made their way to the Bureau. Laurel went in without knocking. Teddy Shires was seated at his desk. He looked startled and thrust some papers into the top drawer. His face reddened, and he didn't look pleased to see them.

'Sorry, Mr Shires,' Laurel said. 'I didn't mean to startle you.'

He plastered a false smile on his face. 'Goodness, I need to take something for my nerves. I don't know what's the matter with me.' He frowned. 'Mr Diamond. Have you made up your mind whether you want to join the Club or not?'

'That's why we've come,' Laurel quickly said, as though she didn't trust what his answer would be. Very wise of her.

'Frank is full of indecision. I suggested he should pay another visit and then make up his mind. Could you give him a day pass, just one more time?' She added a seductive smile to her wheedling words. This woman couldn't be trusted.

Shires' face softened, and his gaze travelled from her face, downwards. 'Anything for you, Miss Bowman, and may I say you look charming. I don't usually see you with your clothes on.' He tittered.

Frank felt like laying one on him. But Shires was right in one respect – she looked lovely in that dark blue woollen dress, her hair loosely gathered at her neck.

'Mr Shires! You're a naughty man!' she said, giving him a come-hither look.

This was going too far. He didn't know whether to laugh or tell her to behave.

Shires wrote out the pass and grudgingly gave it to Frank. 'Remember, Mr Diamond, this is the last day pass I can give you. We have a waiting list, you know. I'm only doing this as a favour to Miss Bowman.' He gave her another lascivious look.

'I'm meeting Carlton,' she said.

'He's a lucky man,' Shires said. 'What are you going to do, Mr Diamond? Play gooseberry?'

Frank forced a smile. 'I'm sure Miss Bowman can look after herself. I'll have another look round. I may see Miss Mavor, is she here? I thought I might book some lessons with her, if I join.'

Shires sniffed. 'I'd better get back to my paperwork.'

They left his office and made for the terrace. 'Don't you desert me,' Laurel whispered to Frank. 'I don't want to be alone with Carlton.'

'Do not worry, fair maiden, I will protect your honour.'

'What about later?'

'Then it's all change. You'll have to do the protecting.'

'I think I'll be far too tired to do that.'

'Goodness, but not too tired, I hope?'

'Frank, stop it. There's Carlton.'

Carlton's face was a picture as he saw Frank behind Laurel. He went red, then the colour faded to be replaced by a disappointed and angry look.

'Hello, Carlton, lovely to see you. Frank brought me over as my car has a problem, hope you don't mind. He's still trying to make up his mind whether to join the Club or not.'

Carlton was having difficulty in forming his words. 'Oh, no . . . of course not.'

'Do you mind if I join you for tea?' Frank asked. 'Is Beattie around? I thought I'd have a chat with her.' Carlton looked astonished. 'About possible tennis lessons.'

'Why her? I could do that?'

Frank winked at him. 'I'm sure you could, but I don't fancy you, Carlton. I'm not the Judge, you know.'

Carlton looked ready to explode, and Laurel's eyebrows nearly disappeared into her hair.

'There's Beattie,' she said. 'Hi, Beattie,' she shouted, as the woman in question strode towards them from the tennis courts. She bounded up the terrace steps, her gaze locked on Frank.

'Well, Mr Diamond, this is a pleasure, I didn't think we'd see you again.'

'I'm sure Carlton told you he'd invited me for tea, perhaps we can have it together?' Laurel said.

Beattie pulled a face. 'I'm afraid my little brother forgot to mention that. But what a good idea. Have you got something tasty for us, Carl? Is there enough for four? I can see if the kitchens have got anything we could nibble.' She bared small white teeth; she reminded

Frank of one of those scary dolls, who looked as though they'd like to take a chunk out of your face.

'I'm sure I've got enough for everyone,' Carlton said in a stiff manner. He was one unhappy chappie. 'Follow me.'

'You have digs here?' Frank asked Carlton.

'Yes, the two wings of the Club were built for staff accommodation. At the moment Mr Shires and I are the only people in the south wing, Beattie is the only one in the north wing. Male and female accommodation, you know. There used to be quite a few residential members of staff, but most live out nowadays. Can't say I blame them. When everyone's gone home, it isn't too lively.'

He led them out of the front entrance and went to a door in the right-hand wing, taking a Yale key from his pocket. 'Come on in.' He led them down a short corridor and opened a door on the right. It was a medium-sized room, furnished with a sofa and two armchairs, a small table with four dining chairs round it, and in the corner, under a window, a single bed, which looked freshly made up, with crisp white sheets poking above a chenille bedspread. Cosy. He gave Laurel a quizzical look, she pulled a face and shrugged her shoulders.

'Have a seat,' Carlton said. 'I'll make some tea.' He disappeared out of the door.

Beattie sat down on a dining chair and patted the one next to her. 'Come and sit next to me, Frank.'

He hoped Laurel might rush ahead of him and they could have a game of musical chairs, but she was studying a painting on the wall next to the bed.

'Where's the kitchen?' Frank asked Beattie.

'It's a communal one, at the end of the corridor. Mr Shires' room is next to it. The bathroom is at the other end.'

'Do you like living on the job?' Frank asked her.

'It's cheap and handy, but boring. I've lived in better places.'

'What did you say you did before this job?'

'I said this and that. I'm a rolling stone, easily bored, I like to try new things.'

'Are you a local girl? I think you said, or someone said, you went to a school in Southwold.'

She moved an inch closer to him. 'Fancy you remembering that. I didn't know you were interested in me, Frank,' she said, her already deep voice, deepening.

He inwardly recoiled, but managed to smile at her with his eyes. 'It's good to meet someone who can beat up my partner.' If Laurel had heard that remark, he'd pay for it later.

'It wasn't that difficult,' she sneered.

'Did you stay on and do A levels?'

She moved away slightly. 'Yes.'

'What did you take?'

She hesitated, and glanced round before answering. 'Oh, art, English and history.'

These weren't the subjects he remembered the late Janet Lamb telling him, he was sure she'd said maths, chemistry and physics. Was Beattie lying, or had Janet confused her with another pupil? And if Beattie was lying, why? He decided not to take it further. At the moment.

Carlton came back carrying an overloaded tray, the cups and saucers clinking furiously as he strode across the room.

'Where did you get the china, Carl?' Beattie asked. 'My, you've put on a spread.'

Laurel sat down at the table. 'This is splendid, Carlton,' she said. 'Thank you.'

'He must think you've got an enormous appetite, Laurel, if all this food was for just the two of you. It's a good job we're here to help you eat it, isn't it, Frank?' Beattie said.

'It's certainly a magnificent tea,' he replied.

Carlton put plates of sausage rolls, sandwiches, jam tarts and slices of Battenburg cake onto the table.

'Laurel, why don't you be mother,' Beattie said. 'I think you must be the oldest one here.'

Frank grasped the teapot. 'In that case, I should pour.'

'You're older than Laurel? I am surprised,' Beattie said, her voice as sweet as saccharine.

'Frank has a portrait in his attic – there his face is terribly wrinkled,' Laurel said, helping herself to a sausage roll. 'Lovely, Carlton,' she said, sprinkling shards of puff pastry down her sweater dress. 'As good as Smiths, the bakery in Aldeburgh.'

Carlton smiled. 'That's where I got them from, and the cakes.'

Frank took a sandwich, though he didn't feel hungry. 'I was asking Beattie about her school days, Carlton, while you were in the kitchen. Did you live locally?'

'Yes, not too far away. Our mum and dad lived in Stowmarket, they still do.'

Frank nodded.

'You didn't tell me where you got the crockery from, Carl. It certainly isn't from your kitchen,' Beattie said.

She was keen to turn the conversation away from their home life. Why?

Carlton blushed. 'I borrowed it from the Club; Teddy arranged it.'

'Does Teddy like you? I didn't know he'd turned into a queer,' Beattie said, smiling at him, but not with her eyes.

Frank was surprised but pleased that Laurel didn't spring to Carlton's defence. Like him, she was waiting to see what developed.

Carlton's nostrils flared. 'Teddy Shires likes women. You only have to see him gazing at Laurel to know that.'

'He's not made a pass at me,' Beattie said.

'The man has no taste,' Frank said. That would be another kick in the shins from Laurel.

Beattie smiled at him and made back the lost inch.

'Did you go to boarding school as well, Carlton?' Laurel asked.

'Yes, Mum and Dad made a lot of sacrifices to send both of us to good schools,' Carlton said.

'So did we,' Beattie replied. 'No foreign holidays, and an old banger for a car.'

'How did you two get on in the holidays, after being apart all term,' Frank asked.

'You have to remember Beattie is much older than me,' Carlton said. 'We've never had much to do with each other.'

'What is the age gap?' Frank asked.

'Six years,' Beattie snapped.

'It's seven,' Carlton said, smirking.

'You must have been a lovely surprise for your parents, Carlton. I bet you were a beautiful baby,' Laurel said, smiling at him.

He smiled back; his pale eyes fixed on her.

Beattie got up. 'Oh, you can say that again, my parents doted on him, still do. Dear Carlton can't do anything wrong, can you, Carl?' Her tone was venomous. 'Excuse me a minute. There's something I must show you.' She left the room.

'God, what's she up to now?' Carlton said. 'She's in one of her moods.'

'Can I have another cup of tea, please,' Laurel asked.

'Shall I make some more?' Carlton asked. 'Would you like another cup, Frank?'

'No, thanks.' One cup of tea a day was one too many.

Beattie burst into the room holding what looked like a photograph album.

'Beattie, no. Where did you get that from?'

'I brought it from home the last time I was there.'

'Do Mum and Dad know you took it?'

'Yes, of course.'

Carlton's sullen face spoke of disbelief.

Beattie put the album on the table, pushing aside everything else.

'Shall I clear this away, Carlton?' Laurel asked.

'No, I'll do it,' he said, looking resentfully at his sister.

'It was a lovely tea,' Laurel said. 'Thank you.'

'Yes, excellent,' Frank added.

Looking mollified, Carlton piled everything onto the tray and went to the kitchen.

'Quick,' Beattie said, 'while he's not here. He doesn't like anyone seeing some of these photos.'

She flicked page after page; most of the photos were presumably of Carlton, from snaps of a bonny baby being bathed, then going through the ages of toddling, first short pants, to those of a young boy. In some photos he was wearing fancy dress, perhaps for a school play, or a party. Frank caught his breath at one coloured photo. Carlton looked thirteen or fourteen, his dark hair curling round his face, his skin as smooth as a peach, his lips carmine, slightly parted. He was dressed in something resembling a toga, one shoulder was bare. Frank glanced at Laurel. She'd seen it too, and looked shocked.

'Aren't there any of you, Beattie?' Frank asked.

She sniffed. 'After Carlton was born, I didn't feature much in the family albums.'

'Poor you,' Laurel said. 'It was the same when my younger sister was born. Your nose gets put out of joint.'

Beattie glared at her. 'But *she* wasn't *a boy*, was she?'

Frank decided he'd had enough, and also, he wanted to see if Laurel would agree to his suggestion. 'I think we need to make tracks, Laurel.' He got up and tapped his wristwatch. 'I promised Stuart I'd help him with his report.'

'Oh, yes, I remember. I'll say goodbye to Carlton.' She quickly left the room.

Beattie closed the album, got up and advanced towards Frank. 'It's been nice to see you again, Frank. How about going for a drink sometime next week? Do you fancy doing that?' She slid an arm round his neck, and twirled a lock of his hair round her finger.

Frank steeled himself, then put an arm round her waist. For God's sake, Laurel, where are you? Beattie moved in for the kill.

'Ready, Frank? Oh, sorry!'

Frank broke away. 'I'll give you a ring, Beattie. Lovely to have met you again.'

Beattie gave Laurel a murderous look.

'Bye, Beattie,' Laurel said as she followed Frank from the room.

Frank held back his laughter until they were safely in his car, driving away from the Club.

'You should have seen your face, it was an absolute picture. I'll never forget it,' Laurel said, wiping her eyes with a handkerchief.

'She's more frightening than some of the villains I've met over the past three years,' Frank said. 'I don't know what I'd have done if you hadn't come back from snogging Carlton.'

'All he got was a chaste peck on the cheek. I'm no baby-snatcher.'

He let out a stream of air. 'What about the photo?' he said, his voice now serious.

'I nearly said something. Can it be a connection? It's so like that picture in Tucker's house. Do you think he could have been involved with Tucker, when he was a young boy?'

'It doesn't seem likely. But he was away at boarding school. It might explain his hatred of homosexuals, and the Judge in particular.'

'Will you tell Revie?'

He glanced at her. 'I think I must. He'll remember that picture on Tucker's wall, and he did see the photos secretly taken by Hager of the men, and the boys they had sex with. We need a copy of the photo Beattie showed us.'

'If Revie is serious, he would be able to get hold of it, but then Carlton would know we'd told Revie, and our links with the police would be discovered,' she said.

'Better the murderer to be Carlton, than to have an innocent David locked up for a crime he didn't commit,' he said.

'That's true.'

'I'll phone him tomorrow.'

'Why not tonight?'

'I have other plans for tonight.'

'Really. Do they involve me?'

'They do, if you're willing.'

Different emotions played over her face: surprise, delight, and hopefully a frisson of desire. He was going to disappoint her.

'I'm willing – possibly.'

'Always a caveat.'

She shook with what was probably impatience. 'Are you going to tell me, or not?'

Frank tried not to laugh, but didn't quite succeed. 'How would you like to spend the night with me . . .' He hesitated as her eyes widened and cheeks coloured. She really was a darling. 'In a wood.'

'Frank Diamond. No, I would not.'

'In that case, I'll go by myself.'

She glared at him. 'I presume you mean the wood at Yoxford Gardens?'

He nodded.

'Why? The thief has been caught, true, in most unfortunate circumstances. Please explain.'

He pulled into a parking spot on the left-hand side of the Dunwich Road. He remembered it from when he and Carol Pemberton had parked there; Carol had come on to him, and he'd rejected her; they'd been in her car, and he'd had to walk back to his cottage through driving rain. He didn't think he'd tell Laurel about that. Thank goodness he was driving this time.

'I'm not totally convinced Janet Lamb is the thief, and if I'm right, I think the real thief might be tempted to make one last sortie into the wood to steal the rare snowdrops. The thefts will have to stop, or it will be obvious Janet was not the thief.'

'But won't they have already stopped, if what you think is true?'

'The gardens were closed yesterday and will be for the next few days. I think they might risk one last heist. It would be difficult for Pamela to know when the plants were taken.'

'You make it sound like they're stealing gold bullion.'

'Almost as valuable, weight for weight.'

'Are you going to tell Revie?'

'No.'

'Why not?'

'I don't want to risk him saying no. Anyway, at the moment he's not that interested. He will be if it turns out Janet was murdered.'

'Why me? Why not ask Stuart? After all, you didn't stake-out the snowdrops last night.'

Frank slid an arm along the back of her seat. 'Do you really have to ask why?'

She looked at him, put a hand over her mouth and giggled. 'This is not the most romantic proposition I've had.'

'I realise that. But we could keep each other warm.'

'I'll be wearing at least three jumpers and a waterproof.'

He sighed. 'What a turn-on. So, it's a yes?'

She smiled at him. 'You'd better make up for this, Frank Diamond.'

'I'll try.'

'What time should we get there? Are you going to tell the others, and also Pamela Gage?'

'Between six and seven, and no and no.'

She shook her head. 'I can't agree to no one knowing. I think we ought to tell Stuart, and then if we're not back by a certain time, he can raise the alarm.'

'Completely unnecessary, but if you insist.'

'I do.'

'You drive to me, and we'll take it from there. I've got the torches and all the other equipment.'

'If we don't tell Mabel, we won't have any food.'

'Greedy girl. Don't worry, I'll supply the eats and drinks.'

'You'd got it all planned, hadn't you?'

'I like to be ready for any emergency. You'd better spin a tale to Dorothy, about why you won't be in tonight.'

Her brow wrinkled. 'That's a tall order. Shall I say I'm spending a night of passion with Carlton?'

'Will she believe you?'

She shook her head. 'It'll have to be I'm going to see my parents in Felixstowe.'

He started the engine. 'I hope I can catch Stuart alone. Right. Let's get going.'

'You love situations like this, don't you? Does it remind you of your time in the police?'

He turned the Avenger onto the road to Dunwich and Greyfriars. 'It's even better, I never had such a beautiful companion before.'

'If your sidekick was Stuart, that wouldn't be difficult.'

'Come on, he's not that bad, a bit big round the middle, but those eyes!'

She gave him another punch.

# Chapter Twenty-One

The tarpaulin crackled beneath Laurel as she wriggled, trying to stave off stiffness; it wasn't as uncomfortable as she'd imagined it would be, as the woodland floor was soft. Under a clear sky, the temperature had dropped, but layers of clothing and a woollen beanie meant she was warm. Also, lying side by side with Frank, his arm around her, and their faces within kissing distance, it was, if not quite how she'd imagined their first night together, romantic and innocent.

'Are you warm enough?' he asked, squeezing her shoulder.

'Quite toasty, thank you. And you?'

'I'm getting overheated. Like some more coffee?'

They were face to face; starlight and the rays from a waning gibbous moon lit his cheekbones and played shadows over his mouth. 'I'd like some, but the thought of a trip behind some bushes, and being nettled, puts me off.'

He laughed. 'It wouldn't do if the thief caught you in that position.'

'It might frighten them to death. What time is it, Frank?'

He turned his torch on, guarding the light with a curved hand, and looked at his wristwatch. 'Ten past eleven.' He quickly switched the light off.

'When are we giving up?'

'Oh, ye of little faith. Let's give it until two, at least. I can't see them waiting later than that, if I'm right, and the thief is going to dig up the snowdrops.'

'Frank?'

'Yes.'

'Can we talk seriously for a bit?'

'What about?'

'I think you must know what I want to talk about.'

'Us?'

'Yes, us.'

'Laurel, nothing much has happened yet.'

'I know, but I'm worried.'

'Why?'

'I don't know what you're thinking.'

He laughed. 'That's just as well. If you knew, you might either flee into the night or give me a good pasting.'

She sighed. 'For once, Frank, I'd like you to be serious.'

He groaned.

'I know you don't like everything being neat and tidy, and I don't want to spoil how we feel about each other, but I need to know if this is serious or not.'

He stroked the side of her face. 'Lovely Laurel. How will we know how we feel until . . . ?'

'You've never committed yourself to any other woman before, have you?'

He moved away from her, moonlight catching his green eyes. She'd gone too far. Why had she started on this conversation?

'No. I haven't.'

'Had I better stop, Frank? I'm sorry if I've spoilt everything.'

'No, go on, I can see this is important to you.'

'But is it important to *you*?'

'I suppose it is. I think, Laurel, you'll either have to accept me as I am, take the risk that this time I'll feel differently, or you'll have to decide you don't want to take that risk, and we'll try and revert to our old relationship.'

'That's very analytical and cold.'

'I'm afraid that's part of my nature.'

'But it's not the whole of you.'

205

'Ever the optimist.'

Her mind was whirling. She desperately wanted him, longed to feel the touch of his skin against hers. What was the risk? Didn't she mean risks? If their relationship ended like all his others with women had, she'd be dreadfully hurt, she'd also possibly lose his friendship, and they'd no longer be able to work together. She was jealous of Emma, and hated the thought they'd made love; she'd tortured herself imagining his hands caressing Emma's skin, their naked bodies entwined. How would she feel if she and Frank became lovers, then they split up, and Frank went with another woman? She didn't think she could bear it.

'Come on, Laurel. We're here together. We've both too many clothes on for anything to happen, and what's more it's too bloody cold. I'm loving being close to you. Why don't you go with the flow? See what happens? You know I'm mad about you. I never thought we'd get this far. Don't overthink things. Let's enjoy tonight.' He laughed. 'What am I saying? Our first date, lying in a freezing wood, waiting for a possible murderer to appear. That's enough to turn any girl on.'

She laughed and snuggled up to him. He was right. She'd enjoy the feel of the length of his body against hers, even if it was through several layers of clothes, the erotic touches of his fingers against her cheek and brow, his breath caressing her face. Live for the moment, she told herself.

They lay in silence, her head on his shoulder, the wind moving the branches of the oak trees, the musty smell of the woodland earth, a mixture of last year's rotting leaves and the sharp smell of spring, and above, the starlit sky.

She caught her breath, and at the same time, Frank gripped her arm. Sounds of someone moving towards them. The rip of brambles on clothing, a muttered curse as a foot caught in a tree root, the beam of a torch or lamp, focused on the ground.

Frank pulled himself up into a crouching position, and she did the same. 'Wait until they start digging,' he whispered, his lips caressing her ear. She shivered, half with excitement and half with desire.

206

A figure entered the glade, a dark outline. From the height – a man? The light from the lamp, held low in his left hand, glinted off the tines of a fork. He threw it on the ground, making a dull metallic clang. Something else joined it, something soft and shapeless. He knelt down in front of a clump of snowdrops with a grunt of satisfaction. He placed the lamp so its light illuminated the plants, then passed his hands over them, caressing their leaves, now browning at the edges.

He stood up and took hold of the fork, and pulled the soft object – a sack – towards him. He seemed to weigh up where he should start digging. Then he carefully pushed the fork vertically deep into the earth under the nearest clump, put his foot on the shoulder of the fork, and levered up the bulbs. He bent down and pushed his hand underneath the clump and placed them in the sack.

She glanced at Frank. He was upright, the police truncheon in his right hand. She hoped he didn't have to use it. The man dug up another clump, sounds of satisfaction coming from him; no doubt thinking about the amount of money he was extracting from the earth.

Frank squeezed her arm. She nodded. Her chest was tight, every muscle taut. She'd never been in a situation like this before. Cold bloodedly waiting to pounce on someone and prepared to fight if needed. The nearest situation had been waiting for Hager to come into the room and kill her and David. Then she'd been scared to death.

'Wait until I blow the whistle. Then I'm going to tackle him. Back me up if needed. Get the fork away from him,' Frank whispered. He waited until the man started digging up another clump. He put the police whistle to his lips, gave a shrill blast, sprang out, diving at the man's legs, bringing him to earth with a heavy thud.

'Fucking hell,' shouted the man. Frank climbed onto him and forced his knees into the small of the man's back. Laurel darted out, grabbed the fork, which had been knocked out of the man's hands. She threw it into the clump of brambles they'd been hiding behind. The man was fighting back, and managed to turn over. They were wrestling. Frank's hands round the man's throat, bashing his head against the ground. The man's hands clawing at Frank's face. She grabbed the man's legs and pulled. He shrieked with pain. She sat on them, pressing her full weight down, her hands gripping his calves, hoping she wouldn't break his legs. He was kicking furiously. She winced as a sharp knee banged into her spine. There was a smack and the man's body went limp.

She turned her head. 'Frank, did you hit him?'

'Yes, my skill with the truncheon has not waned.' He sounded cheerful. 'Could you get the lamp?'

It had been thrown or kicked a few yards from the snowdrops, its beam of light shining upwards, into the branches of the oak. The man lay with his face in the woodland soil. 'Get the handcuffs.' Frank climbed off the prone body, and pulled the man's arms behind him, took the handcuffs and secured him.

'Let's see who you are,' he said, as he turned him over.

'Who is it? Do you know him?' Laurel asked, as she played the beam of the lamp on the man's face. He had sharp cheekbones, and looked in his mid-twenties.

'I certainly do. He's Owen Albrighton, the gardener.'

'Gosh. Do you think he killed Janet Lamb?'

'I do, and I hope the post-mortem confirms she was killed. Better get him into the recovery position.'

They heaved him up onto his side. Frank leant down so his ear was close to his mouth. 'He's breathing.'

'Thank God for that. I don't want you up on a murder charge.'

Frank smiled, the lamplight showing his glinting eyes, some cuts and blossoming bruises, and a wicked smile on his lips. 'I'd be no good to you in gaol, would I?'

Cheeky devil. 'What now?'

'Could you get the rope we brought and I'll tie his legs up. I don't want him kicking out when he comes to. Then make for the house, get Pamela up. Tell her what has happened, then ring up Revie.'

'Frank, it's well gone midnight.'

'So what? She won't mind, and he'll be pleased with us. We've caught a thief, and probably a murderer. Revie should stand pints all round.'

Frank tied up Albrighton like a trussed chicken as Laurel walked away towards the house, the light from her torch gradually fading. Frank walked back behind the brambles and poured himself a cup of coffee, and bit into a ham sandwich. Now he felt hungry. He thought of their conversation. She was not only physically brave, but she'd risked asking questions she must have known might scupper any budding romance. She didn't believe in playing games. He stood over Albrighton, who'd started to moan and wriggle. Frank felt like kicking him as he thought of Janet Lamb's body, face down in the waters of the lake. To kill someone over a few snowdrops. Why had he killed her? He thought he knew. He poked at Albrighton's body with the toe of his boot and shone the light onto him. 'Awake yet? Hope you've got a headache.'

Albrighton raised his head, squinting. 'You bastard,' he said, spitting out soil. 'You bloody bastard.'

'Charming,' Frank said. 'Anything else you'd like to get off your chest?'

'You didn't fool me. I knew what you were up to.'

'Really? I hadn't credited you with so much brain power, Mr Albrighton.'

'*She* told you, didn't she?'

Frank's body stiffened. He must be careful. 'Yes, I'm afraid she did.'

'Stupid bitch. If she'd kept her mouth shut, you'd never have known. She's ruined everything. I'll take her down with me. I suppose she thinks if she told you about that old hag, Lamb, she'd get off, her being a woman. My God, I'd like to get my hands round her throat.' His voice was brimming with frustration and hate.

He had to make sure. Pity there was no one here to be a corroborating witness, but hopefully he could get Albrighton to spout it all out again. He took the risk; he didn't think it was much of one. 'Yes, I'm afraid your girlfriend, Miss Gibbs, has let you down.'

Frank hadn't believed people really gnashed their teeth. He was wrong. Owen Albrighton was grinding away.

'I'll tell them how she helped me. She can't prove she didn't. I'll tell them what an easy lay she was. Couldn't get her knickers off quick enough.'

Frank had to hold on to his right leg to stop his boot penetrating Albrighton's chest.

# Chapter Twenty-Two

Tuesday, 1 May, 1973

In the sitting room at Greyfriars, Frank passed round drinks: Scotch for Laurel and Dorothy, a Tia Maria for Mabel, a light ale for Stuart and a brandy for Nicholas Revie. Revie had phoned in the morning and asked if he could come to dinner. He had news for them. Dorothy, who'd taken the call, asked him if it was good news. He'd been non-committal, but she'd told the others he didn't sound gloomy. As always, he wouldn't talk until the meal was over.

Over dinner the conversation had been about Nixon taking the rap for the Watergate scandal.

'He's denying any personal involvement. Do you believe that?' Dorothy asked.

'I wouldn't trust him to top and tail gooseberries,' Mabel said.

Stuart rolled his eyes. 'I don't think we're much better off with Heath. Look at the chaos yesterday, millions on strike.'

'That's your dad's fault,' Laurel said, smiling at Frank.

He held up his hands. 'Nothing to do with me, you can't choose your parents.'

'Heath doesn't understand people. They don't like being dictated to,' Laurel said.

'I'll vote for you as prime minister,' he said. She didn't look pleased.

The air was filled with the lingering smells of a roast chicken dinner, and Bumper, despite the fireplace being filled with a vase full of red tulips, lay down with his head nearest to the flowers, no doubt hoping they'd give off some heat. Frank took his Scotch and sat next to Laurel on the settee. Revie was on her other side. Cosy. Frank's thigh was touching Laurel's; she didn't move away when he deliberately pressed his against hers. But she didn't reciprocate.

Revie put his glass on a side table. 'You've been very patient, and as you two,' he looked at Laurel and Frank, 'did most of the work for me, I thought it only fair to tell you what's happened.'

'I thought you might have news about David,' Laurel said.

'Hold your horses, Laurel. One story at a time,' Revie said, sounding pleased with himself.

Frank glanced at him, and Revie winked. A bubble of hope formed in Frank's chest.

'When I arrived at Yoxford Manor, well, you two know what I was confronted with, but I'll go through it for the rest of you.' He paused, then took a deep breath. 'You'd dragged Albrighton up to the house and isolated him. Mrs Gage was jumping between anger and sorrow, flabbergasted the thief was a member of staff, and Mr Gage was three sheets to the wind, and not making any sense at all. You two made your statements and Albrighton was taken to the nick. I went with Cottam to see Miss Gibbs who lives in Yoxford, knocked her up and took her to Ipswich for questioning. She cried all the way there.'

'So, what was her story?' Dorothy asked.

Inspector Revie entered the interview room with Johnny Cottam and sat down in front of Georgina Gibbs, a legal representative by her side. A WPC stood at the door. Revie read out all the usual warnings.

'Do you understand what I've said, Miss Gibbs?' he asked.

She nodded.

'Please speak your answer.'

'Yes,' she whispered.

Revie glanced at the lawyer. He nodded.

'When did you and Owen Albrighton become lovers?'

She flinched, glanced at the lawyer, who nodded encouragingly.

'Last summer.'

'Did anyone else know about this?'

She shook her head.

He pointed to the recording machine.

'No, but perhaps his mother guessed,' she said.

'Why do you think that?'

'Owen took me back home to meet her, and she saw us kissing. I went back a few times when I . . .'

'When you what?'

'When I went to see the plants in his garden.'

'To check they were being looked after properly?'

'Yes,' she said, in the depths of misery.

'These are the plants Albrighton stole from the gardens?'

'Yes.'

'Which you identified for him?'

'Yes.'

'Do you still love Albrighton?'

She raised her head and looked for the first time directly at him, her face woebegone, her eyes red with crying. 'I don't know. After what he did.' She burst into tears. 'How could he? Poor Miss Lamb.'

'You're saying you didn't know he was going to kill her?'

'I didn't, but it's my fault. I told him what I'd overheard when Mr Diamond was talking to Miss Lamb in the Japanese garden. She said she knew who the thief was. I told Owen we must stop taking the plants. I knew he was afraid we'd be found out, and he was beside himself at the thought he might go to prison, and his mother would be by herself. She can't manage at all on some days. He was distraught, but I didn't think he'd do that.'

Revie made no comment, and gave her a few minutes so she could bring herself under control. 'Could you explain why you stole the plants?'

'We were in love. We wanted to be together. I talked to Owen about us saving up so we could start our own nursery; how we could buy land, build up the business gradually. I could continue working, while he tackled the work needed: cultivating the land, building greenhouses, sheds, compost heaps, an office. I had it all planned.'

'Why did you start stealing?'

'I'm not sure how it happened, but one day Owen showed me a plant he'd taken from the garden, and had planted in his own. The idea grew. When I told him the prices some plants could make, especially the rare snowdrops, he was amazed. We worked out if we could build up stocks of different plants, especially snowdrops, we could start up on our own sooner than we'd planned.'

'Didn't you realise you were stealing? Hadn't Mrs Gage been a good employer?'

Georgina's face took on a stubborn look. She pushed out her chin. 'She took all the credit for the garden. All the praise from the volunteers and the customers. She never seemed to give *me* any credit.'

It was Pamela Gage's garden, Revie thought, and she'd been working on it for years before you appeared. But he didn't put his thoughts into words. Let's keep the confession flowing.

'I have to tell you Mr Albrighton has confessed to the murder of Miss Lamb.'

She rocked in her seat. 'How could he have done that? It's too terrible to think about.'

'Also, he's saying you knew he was going to murder her. In fact, he says you told him to do it. If it hadn't been for you, he wouldn't have killed her.'

She looked stunned, her mouth open, eyes wide. The tears had stopped. 'NO! How can he say that? I thought he loved me. I wouldn't have deserted him, even if he goes to prison.'

'You do realise, Miss Gibbs, if found guilty as an accessory to stealing the plants, you could be given a gaol sentence?'

She shook her head wildly. 'I didn't take them. He did. You can't send me to prison for that. We didn't hurt anyone.' Her face went red, realising what she'd said.

How stupid can you get, thought Revie? 'I won't be the one handing down a prison sentence, it will be trial by judge and jury.' And if he knew anything about it, women only had to shed a few tears, look pathetic and say they were forced to carry out the crime, for the judge, or jury, or both, to believe them, as they were one of the weaker sex, hadn't the brains to realise what they were doing, and they usually got a suspended sentence.

'If you're found guilty of murder, then you'll certainly receive a long sentence.'

'But I didn't kill her,' she wailed.

It was Lady Macbeth all over again.

Frank couldn't feel sorry for Georgina Gibbs; she'd abused the trust of Pamela Gage, and he was sure she could have kept Albrighton on the right path, if she'd wanted to. 'It's a sorry tale, petty greed leading to the loss of life. How will Muriel, Janet's friend, cope by herself? Why didn't she raise the alarm when Janet didn't come home?' he asked Revie.

'She'd gone to see another friend for a few days. She only got back this morning. We left a note with a neighbour asking her to contact the station; I hadn't the manpower to leave someone at their house. I haven't seen her yet, I'll be doing that tomorrow, but the WPC who broke the news said she was devastated. Muriel thinks Janet's death was an accident, when she finds out she was murdered and how, it'll be even worse for her.'

'Poor woman,' Laurel said. 'From what you said, Frank, they were happy together.'

Frank nodded. He didn't think he'd go into details of a possibly one-sided relationship. Perhaps, with time, Muriel would find peace.

'How did Albrighton manage to get Miss Lamb into the Japanese garden? Has he said how he murdered her?' Stuart asked.

Frank glanced at their solemn faces. They were all moved and intrigued by the stories of the women, the passion of the seemingly shy Miss Gibbs for the lascivious gardener. Human nature is always incredibly fascinating, he thought.

'Albrighton hasn't been forthcoming on how he murdered Miss Lamb, but Ansell's autopsy report shows she was hit on the front of the head, possibly with a large stone, and then drowned. He says if

215

Albrighton hadn't confessed it might be difficult to persuade a jury it hadn't been an accident, that she'd slipped while trying to dig out a primula, hit her forehead on a protruding rock, and slipped unconscious into the water. How he got her into the garden and what happened, we haven't found out, yet.' By the look on Revie's face, he was determined he'd get it out of Albrighton.

'Anyone for a refill?' Frank asked.

Revie shook his head. 'This brandy is good, I'm savouring it. Got a drop left, thank you.'

Mabel refused and glared at Stuart, who was holding out his glass. He glanced at her. 'I'd better not, thanks.' He put his glass back onto the table.

Frank topped up the Scotch drinkers. He looked enquiringly at Revie. 'And?'

'Sit back, my children, I have another tale to tell.'

'Is it about David?' Laurel said eagerly.

'Patience.' Revie rolled his shoulders, pushing Laurel against Frank. The warmth of her thigh was erotic; he shouldn't have had another drink; it was lowering his resistance.

'I think you'll be pleased with what I've got to tell you.' He raised his glass to his lips and slowly sipped the last of his brandy.

God, he's an old fart, Frank thought. He's enjoying his moment of triumph.

'Ah, that was excellent,' Revie said, grinning at them.

'Oh, Nick, do get on. Stop being a tease,' Laurel said.

Laurel had found *le mot juste*. He was like a stripper in a burlesque show flashing interesting bits of his anatomy between twirls of his feather fan. Frank grinned at the thought.

Revie glared at him. 'After your visits to David Pemberton, Laurel, I started gathering information about Mr Shires, the manager of the Country Club, and also Carlton Mavor. Nothing to report on Carlton so far, but interesting news about Mr Shires, or should I say, Mr Leach.'

'What?' Laurel said. 'He isn't who he said he was?'

'Correct. There didn't seem to be any records of a Mr Edward Shires before 1971. He was fingerprinted, and lo and behold, he turns into a Mr Edward Leach who'd served three years at Her Majesty's pleasure for embezzlement. He was formerly in catering and rose to be the manager of a top hotel in London. He'd been over-egging the staff overtime and skimming off the money. He'd got a very good set of forged papers. One of his cell mates while he was in prison was a forger, he got out before our Teddy, and I suspect that's who he got his forged papers from.'

'But that doesn't mean he is the murderer,' Frank said.

Revie nodded. 'Correct, but he hasn't got an alibi for the time the Judge was murdered, and if we can find a connection between him and the Judge, we could have a motive. Perhaps he thought the Judge recognised him, and he decided to permanently shut him up. We're working on that now.'

Laurel looked delighted. 'That is good news, Nick. Thank you for listening to us.'

Everyone echoed Laurel's thanks.

'Have you told Mr Pemberton?' Frank asked.

'No. Didn't want to raise his hopes.'

'Have you interviewed .... what did you say his name was?' Stuart asked.

'Leach. Fitting name for a crook,' Revie said. 'Yes, I have.'

'What's your gut feeling, Nick,' Frank asked. 'Do you think he's capable of murder?'

Revie frowned. 'I don't like him. Nasty little man. I'm not sure, but you can't just go on gut feelings. We'll work on him.'

Laurel's eyes widened. 'I want him to be guilty, but if he didn't do it, I don't want him fitted up.'

Revie looked scandalised. 'Laurel Bowman, what kind of policeman do you think I am?'

She flushed. 'Sorry, Nick. It was when you said you'd work on him.'

'Questioning, questioning. I don't beat up suspects with a cosh.'

'Certainly not,' Frank said. 'We only used our policemen's truncheon to soften up suspects, didn't we, Stuart?'

Laurel turned on him, her eyes blazing. 'I've told you about saying stupid things when it's a serious conversation.'

There was a stunned silence.

Laurel put a hand to her mouth, her face turned white. 'I'm sorry, Frank. That was rude.'

He didn't know what to do. Whether to laugh, or tell her she sounded like a shrew-wife of the first water. He didn't do either. 'Accepted, Laurel. Let's put it down to you caring so much about David, you just lost it for a moment. No harm done.'

The look she gave him melted his heart.

The atmosphere lightened.

'A coffee before you go, Nick,' Mabel asked.

'No, thanks. Great meal, Mabel. I'll be off. I'll let you know if there are any more developments.'

Laurel offered to wash up as she was eager to get out of the room after Nick left. She refused offers of help. She'd washed and dried the glasses when the kitchen door opened and Frank came in. He took a tea towel from the rail and without saying anything started to dry the dinner plates. She busied herself, adding more hot water to the bowl, and an extra shot of Fairy Liquid, swishing it about, making a mountain of foam, tiny bubbles escaping into the air.

The work went on in silence, until all the dishes and cutlery had been put away. Frank draped the tea towel back on the rail. She sat down on a kitchen chair and looked at him.

'I've blown it, haven't I?'

'You certainly have, that was the best mound of suds I've seen for a long time.' He laughed. 'There I go again, making light of everything. You can't change me, Laurel. Do you want to?'

This time the question was serious. He'd cleverly twisted the conversation, now she had to answer a fundamental question. Did she want him to change? If she did, he wasn't having it. She'd have to take him as he was, faults and all.

'Do you want me to change?' she asked.

'You must be joking. I want you to stay my Laurel, brave, clever, impetuous and sometimes very silly.'

She didn't know where to look.

# Chapter Twenty-Three

Wednesday, 2 May, 1973

In the ladies' changing room at the Thorpeness Country Club, Laurel wriggled into her new pair of shorts; her old pair were looking grey, despite Mabel advocating her latest washing powder; she'd recently swapped Rinso for Tide. Yesterday, Laurel booked a late-afternoon coaching lesson with Carlton. She wanted some exercise and the thought of walloping a tennis ball around the court seemed exactly what she needed. Also, she wanted to see Carlton again; to try and see if she could get him to open up about the Judge. How could she get hold of the photo of him when he was a teenager? Could she persuade him to let her borrow it? She couldn't think of a suitable reason for wanting it. Perhaps something would come up, and give her the opportunity. But what good would that do? Was it likely Carlton had been one of the young boys, paid to have sex with the men Tucker invited to his house? The connection was tenuous. And Carlton had an alibi for the time of the Judge's death, he was with Beattie that evening until late, according to Inspector Revie.

She shook herself, grabbed her racquet and headed for the tennis courts. There were several games going on, and on a far court she saw Beattie with a girl.

'Hello, Laurel.'

It was Harry, coming off the courts, wearing tennis whites.

'I hope you've forgiven Carlton? Have you had a lesson with him?'

He shrugged. 'No, had a match with a friend.' He smiled ruefully.

'I lost, so perhaps I'd better make it up with him. There's no doubt he's a good coach.'

She smiled at him. 'I'm glad. It wasn't all his fault. He's rather sensitive about his looks.'

Harry pulled a face. 'I wish I had them, I might have more luck when I'm chatting up girls.'

'Really. Who have you got your eye on?' She inwardly laughed. 'Beattie?'

He looked horrified. 'She's a damn good tennis player, but I'd be terrified to have a date with her.'

This time her laughter rang free.

'Wouldn't mind chatting you up, Laurel,' he said hopefully.

'Thank you, Harry, but I'm busy sleuthing at the moment.'

He waved his tennis racquet around. 'You call this sleuthing? Who've you got under surveillance?'

Harry was too clever. 'It might be you.' She fluttered her eyelids.

He roared. 'Go and get your lesson from the handsome Carlton and tell him I'll give him a ring next week.'

She blew him a kiss from the palm of her hand. She liked Harry; pity he wasn't physically her type. How shallow was that? Her lustful thoughts needed a certain degree of attractiveness to be aroused; especially a pair of good legs. Harry didn't come up to scratch. She'd have to give up flirting if she and Frank . . .

Carlton was waiting for her, bouncing a ball up and down with his racquet. He didn't look well, skin sallow, face tired and drawn, as though he hadn't had a good night's sleep.

'Hello, Carlton. Ready to do battle?' She picked up two tennis balls, and prepared to move to the other end of the court.

'Laurel?'

She walked back to him. 'Yes. Is something the matter?'

'What did Harry say to you? I saw you laughing. Were you talking about me?'

She felt her temper shorten. 'Why do you say that?'

His eyes were huge in his face, his mouth downturned. 'I'm sorry. I'm being stupid.'

She silently agreed. 'Harry asked me to tell you he'll phone you for a lesson next week.'

'Why didn't he tell me himself? He shouldn't use you as a go-between. Hadn't he the guts to talk to me face to face?'

She wished she hadn't told him, and left him stewing in his own juice. 'I came for a lesson, Carlton. Shall we get on? If you don't feel up to it, please say so, and I'll see if I can get a game with another member.'

He looked stricken, his expression reminding her of a little boy who'd seriously offended his mother. This was all she needed. 'Come on, Carlton, forget what I said. Shall we concentrate on my backhand volley? That certainly needs to improve, especially for doubles.'

He blinked rapidly. 'Yes, of course, if that's what you'd like to do. We'll warm up for five minutes, then you can take up position at the net, and I'll feed you balls.'

'Good.' She ran to the other end of the court before he could say anything more. On the adjoining court Beattie was coaching a teen-age girl, but she was also watching them.

Back in the changing rooms Laurel showered, dressed, then combed her hair in front of the mirror. She was relaxed and happier than at the beginning of her lesson. Her backhand had improved over the course of the hour, and Carlton seemed to be in a better mood when they'd finished. He kept his comments to praising her progress and outlining which area of her game they should concentrate on next. She'd agreed to meet him for a drink before she went back to Greyfriars, but on the terrace, not in his room.

He was sitting at a table, moodily tracing circles with his finger over the table's surface. She wished she'd gone straight home, but she fixed a smile on her face and decided this would be a quick drink.

He got up as she approached. 'What would you like? Lemonade?'

'I'll have a pot of tea, if that's all right. Join me?'

'Yes. OK. Anything to eat?'

She shook her head.

They sat down – there was an awkward silence. Carlton placed the order with a waitress.

'I can't stay long, Carlton. We're having a team meeting this evening.' A lie, but she didn't fancy sitting with a glum Carlton for half an hour.

His face dropped.

She wasn't going to soften; she was going to follow Frank's example and not get too involved with people. The waitress placed the order on the table and Laurel poured the tea.

Carlton glanced at the tennis courts, where Beattie was still coaching. He leant towards her. 'Laurel, I must talk to you.'

'That's what we're doing at the moment, or haven't you noticed?'

'Laurel, please. I need your help. I can't talk here. I need to see you alone. Please, say you'll meet me.'

She was puzzled. He looked and sounded desperate. Was this a ploy to get her by herself? But he wasn't coming over as though romance was on his mind. He seemed genuinely frantic with worry. 'Give me one good reason why I should do that.'

His body jerked with wound-up anxiety. 'I can't talk here.'

'Carlton, why are you acting in this way? For goodness' sake, tell me what the problem is?'

His face paled and she was afraid he'd be sick, but she wasn't going to agree to meet him until he gave her a good reason. 'Well?'

He licked his lips, then gnawed at the bottom one. He glanced round again, and leant even closer.

She jerked back; his breath was fetid.

'It's about the Judge,' he whispered, having difficulty getting the words out.

'The Judge!'

'For God's sake, be quiet.'

She was stunned. Was he about to confess? If she did agree to meet him, it would be in a public place.

'Will you meet me tonight? Please, Laurel. I don't know what to do. I need your help.'

She tried to keep calm, but what she wanted to do was to get hold

222

of him, give him a good shake and tell him to cough up. If the meeting turned out to be a waste of her time that's what she'd do.

'Yes, I'll meet you. Where?' She wanted to know what he'd planned.

He swallowed. 'You know the public pavilion, near the Moot Hall, in Aldeburgh?'

'Yes.'

'There, at eight tonight.'

'No, I don't think so. I'll meet you in a pub. The Cross Keys shouldn't be too busy on a Wednesday night. I'll be there at eight thirty, I can't make it any sooner.'

'Someone might see us.'

'Does that matter?'

He looked frustrated and anxious. 'I'm not sure.'

'It's that or nothing, Carlton. I'm not meeting you unless it's somewhere where there are other people.' She drank the last of her tea; Carlton hadn't touched his.

He looked at her despairingly. 'Don't you trust me?'

Did she? She'd been tricked before, and got herself into dangerous situations. 'It's not a matter of trust, I just don't like meeting in mysterious places.'

'I'd hardly call the seafront a mysterious place.'

'Can you make up your mind? I need to get back home.' Yes, Greyfriars was home. She hoped Frank would be there. She'd tell him about Carlton wanting to meet her, to tell her something about the Judge. She was sure he'd find some way to shadow her, in case there was a problem.

'Well?'

He nodded. 'Yes, thank you. Please don't be cross with me, Laurel. I'm just so confused. I'm not sure if I'm doing the right thing.'

It was annoying. He was whetting her curiosity, but she wasn't looking forward to having to drive back to Aldeburgh after dinner, when all she felt like was getting back for a decent meal with her friends, seeing Bumper and, more importantly, Frank. She was hoping he might invite her for a pint at The Ship in Dunwich after

223

dinner. An evening with Carlton was not enticing. She wanted a few hours of relaxation, and then possibly a few hours of . . .

'I'll see you at eight thirty in The Cross Keys, I'm sure we'll be able to find a quiet spot.'

He didn't look so sure.

'Goodbye, Carlton. See you later.'

As she rose from the table, Beattie's voice came from behind her.

'Hello, Laurel. My, what have you said to my baby brother? He's looking down in the mouth.'

'Hello, Beattie. I think Carlton may be developing a cold. You'd better minister to him.'

Carlton looked from one to the other, his expression guarded. 'I'm fine.'

'Must go. See you . . . next week for another lesson,' she said. She'd nearly said tonight. Somehow, she didn't think Carlton would want Beattie to know they were meeting later.

She was greeted at the kitchen door by Bumper. His welcome was, as always, enthusiastic, and made her feel one hundred per cent better than a few minutes ago.

'There you are, Laurel,' Mabel said, her face red and the kitchen hot from all the lit gas rings, each one with a pan bubbling on it. 'I fed Bumper, I hope you don't mind, but he kept looking at his bowl with such a pathetic face, you'd swear he hadn't been fed for a week.'

Laurel bent down and rubbed noses with him. 'You old fake.' She glanced up at Mabel. 'Thanks for doing that. Is Frank about?'

'No, and he's not coming for dinner. Says he's got an important appointment. He won't be in until tomorrow.'

She pulled Bumper close to her, and hid her face in his fur. She'd been sure she'd see him tonight. She'd have to go to Aldeburgh alone.

'Anything the matter?' Mabel asked.

She got up. 'No. When are we eating?'

'You're as bad as Bumper. Why, does it matter?'

Her own words were coming back to bite her. 'I've got to go to Aldeburgh later, that's all.'

'Going to the cinema? There's a good film on, *High Plains Drifter*, so Stuart says. We might go on Saturday.'

She'd avoided telling a lie. Should she say something? She didn't want any of the others going with her to Aldeburgh. She'd go alone. After all, she'd be safe in The Cross Keys and she'd make sure she parked in the High Street if possible. 'I'll go and get changed. Smells good,' she said as she left the kitchen. She no longer felt hungry. Where had Frank gone to?

# Chapter Twenty-Four

Laurel managed to find a parking space in the High Street, close to the Midland Bank, so she hadn't far to walk to The Cross Keys. Was she being over-cautious? Carlton had never been pushy, and she didn't find him, despite his build, a dominant male. She couldn't stand men who assumed, because they were the stronger sex, they should have the upper hand in a relationship, from choosing what their better half wore, to demanding a detailed breakdown of the housekeeping bills. She smiled. Frank always treated her as an equal, although at the moment, she wouldn't mind him being a tad more dominant and sweeping her off her feet. How many men were strong enough to carry her over the threshold? Did she want that? Did she even want to get married? She certainly wanted Frank. Over the last few weeks her desire for him was taking over her life.

Under a street lamp she glanced at her watch. Eight forty, she was ten minutes late. Do Carlton good to be kept waiting. What was he going to say? Perhaps she should have left a note for Frank, then he might have turned up. Was this the breakthrough? Would Carlton reveal the killer of Judge Hanmer? She thought of the joy on the Pembertons' faces if David was proved innocent. She hoped with all her heart that would be the case.

These thoughts made her speed up; as she walked down Crag's Path, the sea hissing over pebbles, the night air full of the scents of salt and tar, she felt the first warmth of approaching summer. There were a few people sitting outside at the back of The Cross Keys. She didn't think it was warm enough for that, although she was warmly dressed. She'd deliberately chosen serviceable clothes for her meeting with Carlton, just in case he had any libidinous thoughts. A clean, but old, pair of jeans, her fisherman's navy-blue jumper, no makeup and her hair tightly drawn back in a ponytail. Enough to damp anyone's ardour. She looked in through the window, but couldn't see him, and decided to cut back through the car park and go in through the Crabbe Street entrance.

She pushed the door open. There was no one in this part of the pub. It was where she'd expected him to be, sitting at one of the tables. She made her way to the bar; but he wasn't there either. She inwardly fumed.

'What would you like, Miss Bowman?' the barman asked.

She wanted a large Scotch. 'I'll have a half of Adnam's ordinary, please.'

The barman carefully pulled the beer, held it up to the light, and nodded. 'Nice drop, tonight. Is Mr Diamond coming in? Even he'd approve of this barrel.'

'No, I'm meeting someone else.'

He winked. 'Not here yet?'

'No.' For God's sake go and serve someone else.

'You can give him hell when he turns up.'

She picked up her drink, managed to smile at him and retreated to a table near the window looking out onto Crabbe Street. She looked at her watch. Ten to nine. Had he got cold feet? But he'd seemed desperate to talk to her.

She turned and gazed out into the street, hoping to see Carlton approaching.

'Hello, Laurel. We don't often see you in here at this time of night.'

It was Tom Blower, a fisherman, and part-owner of the Aldeburgh Fish and Chip Shop, which he ran with his mother, Ethel. They'd bought it from Mabel the previous year.

'Hello, Tom, good to see you. How is everyone?'

He sat down, placed his pint on a beer mat and proceeded to tell

227

her. The business was thriving and young Lily was doing well, and had fitted into the family as if she'd always been a part of it.

Lily Varley had lost both her parents the previous year, her mother to cancer and her father to the sea. A dreadful man who'd killed several women, and tried to kill Lily herself.

'I'm glad about that. Give her my love and say I'll be in touch soon.'

'She'll be pleased.' He took a pull of his drink. 'Waiting for Frank?'

'No, someone else. And before you start getting ideas, it's a business meeting. Mind you, he's late.'

'Want me to disappear? You're welcome to join us at the bar – Patsy's with me. You didn't see us when you ordered, but we saw you.'

'It would be better if I was on my own. But if he doesn't come soon, I might join you.'

'In that case, let's hope he doesn't turn up. See you later, maybe.' He got up and disappeared round the corner.

Another check on the time showed Carlton was now thirty-five minutes late. What could have kept him? Had something happened? Her annoyance was replaced by anxiety. This didn't seem right. He'd been so anxious to talk to her. What should she do? She decided to give him until half nine, then she'd drive to Thorpeness and see if he was there. She knew his car, it was a white Fiat station wagon, she'd keep an eye open for it on the road to the Country Club. There was probably some simple explanation, something as mundane as a flat tyre.

The door opened and a breeze shot into the room. Two people, a man and a woman, walked past her. She shrank back into her chair. It was Frank and his girlfriend, Emma. They hadn't seen her. Thank God. Frank had his hand on the small of Emma's back. They walked towards the bar. They looked good together; beautiful, exotic. She was looking impossibly glamorous in a white coat with a white fur shawl collar, with white trousers to match. Frank was wearing a black Nehru jacket, his dark curls caressing the collar. She wished the floor would open up so she could disappear into the cellar.

What was Frank playing at? She thought of the words he'd spoken to her, how he'd touched and kissed her. Did it mean nothing? Jealousy and anger welled up, her mouth sour with bitterness. She tried to calm herself, but she couldn't. Thank God, he hadn't seen her. What would he have thought if he had? That she was spying on him? She shuddered. She wouldn't wait for Carlton any longer; she needed to get out of the pub. She pushed aside her half-full glass, and carefully moved her chair away from the table.

Frank came round the corner, looking worried. 'Laurel! What are you doing here?'

She wanted to say 'And what are *you* doing here?' but she didn't.

They stood toe to toe. 'Laurel, I need to explain. Please sit down.'

'Explain? I don't see why.'

His face hardened. 'I'd like to talk to you, please.'

'I'm sorry, I need to get to the Country Club.'

'Why?'

Before she could reply, Emma walked towards them, a glass of what looked like white wine in her hand. She looked even more beautiful from the front, the white fur a stunning contrast to her dark hair and eyes. Her face was pale, the only colour, bright red lipstick. She held out her other hand. 'Hello, you must be Laurel. I'm Emma.'

Laurel tried to smile, but couldn't; deeply aware of her dowdy appearance.

There was a hissing as air escaped from between Frank's lips. He was not pleased. Who with?

She shook the tiny hand with its red-painted nails; her own seemed to belong to a navvy. She'd never felt so huge and clumsy in all of her life. 'Good to meet you, Emma.' She couldn't say 'Frank's told me all about you', because he'd never talked about her. How could she have possibly thought their relationship had changed? How could he have been so cruel to her? Or was it her fault, imagining he wanted her?

Emma sat down. She and Frank remained standing.

'Sorry, I must go. Nice to have met you.'

'Laurel, I need to talk to you—' Frank said.

'I'll see you tomorrow. Goodbye. Have a good night.' She managed not to run out of the door.

Outside she stopped, and put a hand to her chest, tried to take some deep breaths. Her heart was pounding. Humiliation, then anguish poured through her. She couldn't bear it. She walked slowly to her car. She'd go home, back to Greyfriars. No, she couldn't do that. They'd still be up watching the television. They'd see her face, be concerned, ask her what had happened. How could she tell them she was heartbroken?

Running footsteps. 'Laurel. Wait.'

Frank! She started to run towards her car.

He caught hold of her arm. 'Laurel. Please stop.' He pulled her round to face him.

She couldn't look at him, and started to cry. This was terrible.

He put his arms round her and pulled her close, kissing her forehead and murmuring.

She tried to push him away, but for once she didn't have the strength.

'Laurel. I love you. Please listen.'

He loves me? She went rigid. What does he mean? He loves me? What about Emma? He loves me? Like a sister? He wants to tell me he's in love with Emma, but he loves me as well? She raised her head. Under the streetlight his eyes were hunter's green, so dark his pupils had disappeared. He still held her tight.

'Laurel, I was meeting Emma tonight to tell her I couldn't see her again. She knew that when we came into the pub, she asked if we could have one last drink together. I don't think she was surprised. I haven't seen much of her lately. I've also told her why. I said I was in love with you. This isn't the way, the place or the time I wanted to say those words to you. I just hope you feel as I do, if not, I've completely blown it and put you in an awful position. If I've made a mistake, I'm truly sorry, but I love you, Laurel.'

The trickle of tears became a cascade, she flung her arms round him, burying her head against his shoulder. His arms tightened, and they were locked together.

'Have you frozen, mate?' a raucous male voice shouted. There was group laughter as feet tramped by.

'I think we'd better move. Your car or mine?' he asked.

'Mine,' she whispered, not sure whether to laugh or cry. She fumbled in her handbag for the car keys, he took them from her and unlocked her Cortina, and guided her into the driver's seat, then hurried round and sat down beside her.

'It's a bit too public to get into the back seat,' he said.

She hiccupped and laughed. Oh, Frank, she thought, you'll never change.

'Laurel, do I take it from your actions, you aren't averse to my words?'

'You sound like a nineteenth-century hero from a romantic novel.'

'I didn't know you read them?'

'Not since my teens.' She felt shy, very girlish. She didn't like the feeling. She didn't know what to do. But she was supremely happy.

'Do you want time to think it over?'

'No!' she replied hotly. 'I don't. I feel the same, but it's a shock, and I'm a mess.'

'Will this make you feel better?' He pulled her towards him, and kissed her, his lips strong and smooth against hers. He drew back. 'Better?'

She looked at him and smiled. 'I'm not sure. Can we try it again?'

He laughed. 'I think you've recovered, but just in case.'

What seemed a great deal later, he said, 'Now are you sure?'

She shook her head. 'It's in the balance.'

'Fibber. Can you tell me why you were in the pub? I'm intrigued, but hopefully not jealous.'

She was tempted to play up, but decided not to. She was so happy she was no longer cross with Carlton, she felt she'd never be cross with anyone again. She explained to him what Carlton had said at

231

the Club, and how they'd planned to meet. And he was nearly an hour late.

'He did seem in fear of something. I agreed to meet him in the pub, as I wasn't sure if he was having me on, and it was a ploy to get me on my own.'

He brushed a hand through her hair, and pulled off the rubber band holding it back, then he mussed her hair up, pulled her towards him and kissed her again. Her insides melted.

'I don't believe you. You're obviously dressed to seduce him,' he whispered in her ear.

She pushed him away. 'Frank Diamond, you fool.' Her words were as soft as the first raindrop falling on dry ground.

'I think we'd better go and find him, don't you?'

'Yes. That's what I was thinking, just as you and Emma walked in.'

'I think I'd better go back to the pub and see her, if she hasn't already left.'

She tried to feel sorry for Emma, but she couldn't. The searing jealousy she'd felt was too close. But what did Frank want? Sex? She did. His touch, his kisses, were exciting. She desperately wanted him.

'Wait here, I won't be long.'

She nodded.

He gave her a stern look. 'No buzzing off to the Country Club by yourself.' He reached over and took the key out of the ignition. 'That's cooked your goose. Be back soon.' He kissed her again, opened the door and ran up the High Street.

Why had she let him do that? Was he going to take over her life? Would she care if he did? He seemed a different person, the same but different. More dominant, more male. Wasn't that what she wanted? She wanted him, but she didn't want to be controlled. Although she was living with Dorothy, Mabel and Stuart, she was used to pleasing herself, making her own decisions about her life. At the Agency, they made collective decisions, after discussing the different cases.

What was she getting into? Was he thinking about marriage? She knew he hated being committed, he'd talked about how he couldn't bring himself to make that final step. Did *she* want to marry? She had once, when she'd been engaged to Simon. They'd planned their future life, how she'd continue to work for a few more years until they were financially stable, then they'd have a family. She hoped she would return to teaching when the children reached school age, but he hadn't been keen. Then their beautiful, planned world collapsed when Angela was murdered; his family were appalled at the scandal of her death, and the rumours she'd had it coming to her. Laurel's obsession with finding Angela's murderer had been the last straw; he'd asked her to let it go, but when she refused, he'd slandered Angela. It was the end. She'd nearly ruined her own career by her reckless behaviour, and if it hadn't been for Frank, she'd have ended in prison. Despite rough patches, she and Frank were close friends.

Can a friendship turn into a lasting love? They'd known each other for four years, they'd first met in the mortuary, when she identified her sister's dead body. Friendship, respect and enjoyment of each other's company had grown when she was the newly appointed Senior Mistress at Blackfriars School, and Frank was the detective inspector in charge of the murder case.

If they were lovers as well as partners, how would this affect the Agency? Would their changing relationship make any difference? It was bound to. She was torn apart. Longing for Frank, but unsure what would happen in the future. Stop it. Stop it, she told herself. Go with the flow. All she was sure of was she loved him, wanted him and he felt the same.

A car drew up in front of hers. It was Frank in his Avenger. Her passenger door opened, and Frank threw the car keys to her. 'Follow me. We'll make for the municipal car park at Thorpeness as we did last time.'

'Look what we found then,' she said.

'Got a torch?'

She checked in the glove compartment. 'Yes, have you?'

'No, but I wasn't in the Scouts and I'm never prepared.'

'Dib, dib, dib. You'll never believe it, but neither was I,' she muttered.

'Bet you looked sexy in your guide uniform. See if you can find it.'

'If you think I'm dressing up in any kind of uniform you are going to be dreadfully disappointed.'

'Right, Miss Bowman, stop holding me up with your suggestive remarks, let's go and find Carlton.'

What a gloriously infuriating man he was. She switched on the engine, backed out of the parking space and followed his tail lights out onto the Thorpe Road. She sizzled with excitement, anticipation, and the hope they found Carlton quickly.

# Chapter Twenty-Five

Frank glanced in his rear-view mirror; Laurel's car lights were close behind. What a night. It wasn't what he'd planned. Well, he hadn't planned anything, but he hadn't expected it to happen like this. He'd wanted to clear the air with Emma before he told Laurel he loved her. He'd met Emma in her office at the cinema. By the way she was dressed, she was expecting to go out with him for the evening, although when he telephoned her, all he'd said was he needed to speak to her. She looked very attractive in a new outfit, although he thought the fur collar was a bit hot for May; but he realised she'd gone to a great deal of trouble to look nice for him. It didn't help.

'Frank, you've been avoiding me,' she said, getting up from behind her desk, holding up her face for a kiss. 'I'm so glad you rang.'

He kissed her cheek.

She looked up at him, her large brown eyes wide with disappointment. 'That's not very encouraging.'

'Can we sit down a minute, please.'

She slid behind her desk, her face pale.

He sat on the edge of the desk. 'I'm sorry, Emma, but I can't see you after tonight.'

She edged back in her chair. 'Why? I thought you liked me.'

'I do like you, but it wouldn't be fair to you if I let you think I was serious.'

'Is there someone else?'

He hesitated, he could pretend, but he owed her honesty, even if it was more hurtful than a lie. 'Yes. There is. She's a close friend, who's become something more. I'm sorry if I've hurt you.'

'It's your partner, isn't it? Laurel. You're always talking about her. Does she know about us?'

'Yes, she does.'

'Why did you let her come between us?'

'It's not like that, she doesn't know how I feel.'

'What will you do if she turns you down? Will you want to come back to me?'

This was crucifying him, but worse for her. 'I had to tell you first. I couldn't play you false.'

She sniffed. 'I think you have already. Why did you ask me out, if you were in love with her? I think you're cruel.'

He didn't want to talk about Laurel. 'I hadn't made any promises, Emma. I did tell you at the beginning I wasn't good at committing myself.'

'I thought I could change you.'

'I'm sorry.'

'I was half expecting this. Don't worry about me, I won't be alone for long.'

He could believe it.

'Shall we have one last drink? I'm certainly not going home this early, they'll think I've been stood up.'

*They* were her parents, and two younger sisters.

At the bar in The Cross Keys, they'd been greeted by Tom Blower. 'Hello, Frank. Did you see Laurel when you came in?'

'Laurel!'

'Near the door. She was waiting for someone, but he hasn't turned up. Didn't she say anything to you? Perhaps she's left.'

'Tom, please buy Emma a drink, will you? I'll be right back.'

Laurel was about to leave, her face was pale, shattered. He'd tried to talk to her, to explain, but then Emma appeared, and a terrible situation got even worse. He couldn't bear the emotions playing over Laurel's face. When she left, he needed to go after her. He must tell her he'd finished with Emma.

'I'm going after Laurel. I'm sorry, Emma, I can't let her think . . .'

'You can't leave me here,' she hissed. 'You'll see her tomorrow, you heard what she said.'

'I need to go. I'll come back.'

And then. He felt his chest would burst. When he'd kissed Laurel, she'd passionately kissed him back. He'd never told anyone he loved them, apart from his mother, and a girl he'd had a teenage crush on when he was seventeen. But the words came from the heart, and he meant them.

He turned the car left into the Thorpeness car park. Damn Carlton. He hoped they didn't find him. But should he think that way? If it hadn't been for Carlton, he and Laurel wouldn't have met tonight. He didn't have time to over-think. She'd been hurt, but if he'd planned to tell her after a lovely meal, it might not have worked. In the past, neither of them had been able to tell the other how they felt. He hadn't been sure of her feelings and, probably, she hadn't been sure of his. Was this a taste of things to come? Would they be able to keep their minds on the complexities of a case when all they wanted to do was make love?

She parked her Cortina next to his.

He couldn't help it. They immediately went into a clinch. 'Sod Carlton,' he muttered into her hair. She kissed his ear. He pulled her closer; longing for her coursed through his body.

She leant back. 'Let's get it over with. I expect we'll find him quietly fuming somewhere,' she said. She switched on the torch and they made their way past the darkened Judge's house. The next house showed lights behind drawn curtains. As they approached the Country Club a car came towards them, headlights dimmed. They stepped back to let it past. Laurel gripped his arm. 'I'm sure that's Leach's car. Did you see who was driving it?'

'It was a man; it could have been him. Perhaps he's out on bail.'

'What was he doing here at this time of night?'

'Presumably collecting his car.'

'I think we ought to check with Nick Revie.'

He nodded. 'I'll ring him when we get back.'

'Get back to where?'

'I thought we might go to my cottage.'

She kissed his cheek. 'Good thinking.'

He groaned. He wouldn't be able to keep his hands off her.

The Country Club was completely dark.

'Look, there's Carlton's car. He's probably in bed. Serve him right if we wake him up,' she said.

'What does Beattie drive? There isn't another car at the front.'

'She owns a VW camper van. I quite envy her that. I wouldn't mind going round Europe in it – it would be fun.'

'Count me out on that one, Laurel. Camping is not my scene.'

'Dib, dib, dib.'

They made their way to the wing Carlton lived in; Frank knocked on the door. It moved; the door was unlocked. Someone had left in a hurry. 'I think we ought to go in, and hope he doesn't die of fright, if he's safely tucked up in bed.'

'I don't like this, Frank.'

Neither did he, but this was a safe area, there wasn't much crime, and sometimes people didn't bother locking their doors. 'Where's the light switch?'

'I can't remember. I've only been here once, and that was with you, remember?'

'The fatal tea party.' He pushed the door open and Laurel shone the torch's beam until she found the switch. Light flooded the corridor.

'Perhaps it was Mr Leach who left the door open, he may have come back for some of his things,' Laurel said.

'If it was him, and he was in a hurry, he may have left the door open when he dashed off. Either he's skipped bail, or he didn't want to bump into anyone he knew. Too embarrassing.' Frank knocked on the door of Carlton's room. They waited.

'Go on in, Frank,' Laurel said.

'Have the torch ready in case there's someone behind the door and they overpower me.'

'Oh, do get on with it.'

'I hope you'll repeat that sentence a bit later.'

She pummelled him round the ribs. 'Be serious.'

He knocked again, then opened the door. She flashed the light around the room. There was no one there. Frank switched on the light. The room was cold, it felt damp. Everywhere looked neat and tidy; no unwashed mugs, or scattered books and newspapers, the bed was made, the red chenille bedspread tightly tucked over the pillows and down the sides.

'We'd better check the kitchen and the bathroom,' she said.

They turned left and went into the bathroom; it was in need of an update, the enamel of the cast-iron bath scratched and discoloured; some tiles around the porcelain basin and lavatory were cracked, and the yellow grouting streaked with black.

Laurel wrinkled her nose. 'I wouldn't like to take a bath in here.'

The kitchen, at the other end of the corridor, was also empty.

'Where can he be? His car's still here,' Laurel said.

'Does he know anyone who lives nearby? Could he have gone round to them, say for a drink?'

Laurel bit her lip. 'I don't know. That could be the case, but why didn't he meet me in The Cross Keys? He was desperate, I'm not making it up.'

He put an arm round her shoulders and gave a squeeze. 'I know you're not. Did you see his car keys in his room?'

'I wasn't looking for them.'

They went back. 'Here they are.' Frank picked them up from a bowl on the central table. 'Let's see if the car starts. Then we'll know something.'

'What?'

'If it doesn't start, that explains why he didn't meet you, and he's probably gone out. He might even be at the local pub.'

'Yes. We should have thought about that sooner, and gone there straight away. Shall we do that now?'

'Hold on a minute. If the car starts, it means he either decided he didn't want to talk to you, or . . .'

'Or?'

'He was prevented from talking to you.'

Laurel shivered. 'I hope it doesn't start.'

'Do you want to wait here while I try it out?'

'I'll wait, unless you want me to come with you for protection?'

'I'll scream if I'm in trouble. Won't be long.'

'You'd better take the torch.'

'Thanks.'

The wind was getting up from the east, bringing with it the smell of the sea, a cleansing, bracing odour of salt and iodine. He breathed deeply, there was something about the smell in Carlton's room he didn't like — a slight meaty smell. The car wasn't locked. He slipped into the driver's seat and grimaced; he had to pull the seat forward. The key went into the ignition lock and the engine started first time. He let out a deep breath of frustrated air. Where was he?

He switched off the torch as he entered the south wing. Laurel was standing by Carlton's bed, her face white, the chenille bedspread pulled back.

'What is it?'

She pointed to the pillow. 'It's damp, so are the sheets, and the floor.'

He moved swiftly towards her. Was that the source of the smell? He bent down and sniffed at the pillow.

'Frank. What are you doing?'

He stood up. 'I think I can smell blood.'

'No.'

He ripped the bedspread and blankets off the bed. 'Someone's washed, possibly only rinsed these. I'm afraid this may explain why Carlton didn't turn up.'

'You think someone's attacked him?'

'That, or Carlton attacked someone and has made off, but it looks to me that possibly the person who did this might have been hoping to come back and make a better job of it.'

'I think we ought to ring the police.'

'Is there a phone in this block?'

'I haven't seen one. No, I remember Carlton saying if he wanted to phone me, he had to go to the office, or go to a public phone box.'

'Do you know where that is?'

'No. There might be one by the Mere.'

'Right. Go to the house that had a light in it.'

'Near the Judge's house?'

'Yes. Hopefully they'll have a phone. Get the police and an ambulance.'

'Let's hope we need both,' Laurel said. She'd recovered some of her colour and was in her determined mood.

'While you do that, I'll take the torch and start searching the area. Any idea where it would be best to start?'

'Not really. He could be anywhere. After I phone, shall I check the pub just in case?'

'Good thinking. Go straight there, forget about the house. You can phone from there if there's no sign of him.'

'I'll come back as soon as I've phoned.'

'No, stay at the pub. You won't know where to find me, and I don't want you here on your own.'

She kissed his cheek. 'I'll get someone from the pub to come with me. They can help to search until the police come.'

'I always said two brains were better than one.'

This time she kissed him on the lips. 'It depends on the brains. I'm off, be careful.'

'Cheeky.'

He shook himself down; conflicting emotions were confusing his brain. Total happiness, and concern for Carlton, were mixing together like a potent cocktail, stopping his analytical mind from functioning properly.

Where should he start? If it was Carlton's blood on the sheets, then either he'd staggered out by himself, or someone had removed him and put him somewhere else. Could he have been in the car they'd seen being driven by Teddy Leach? Why would he attack Carlton? It was no good overthinking this, better to start searching, then if he hadn't found him by the time the police arrived, at least he could tell them where he'd looked.

He decided to start by walking round the building, then searching the tennis courts and the grounds at the back. He hoped the battery in Laurel's torch lasted, otherwise he'd have to give up. Was it worth searching the rooms for another one? For God's sake, get on with it, he told himself.

He circled the Club, pointing the beam of light under bushes, the sweet smell of broom heady in the night air. He scoured the tennis courts, rabbits scooting back to their burrows as the beam hit them, their white tails bobbing as they zig-zagged across the ground. He went to the back of the building and shone the light inside, moving it slowly, covering as great an area as possible. It wasn't likely he was here, but you never knew with this job, always expect the unexpected.

The place was eerie, no one on the site, the only signs of life the rabbits, and some disturbed pigeons, flapping away from their night roosts. He moved to the front and shone the torch through windows, but there was no sign of anything, everywhere was ghostly quiet. Where to next? Should he search up The Benthills, and the beginnings of the beach? Seemed as good an idea as any. He went down the steps from the front door of the Club and walked directly to the road in front. He decided he'd start searching the stretch of road to his left, flashing torchlight onto the beach as well; he'd go on until the bend in the road, where it became Church Road; then he'd move onto the beach to approximately where the light had reached, and inspect the lower part of the beach. If that didn't yield anything, he'd search The Benthills to the right of the Club. By that time he thought Laurel would be back with a search party from the pub. He was sure she'd whip them into shape. At times of crisis, she was a dominant figure; please God, don't let her turn into my mother, he thought.

He turned left and walked slowly along the right-hand side of the road, exploring every inch with the beam of the torch. He hadn't gone more than two yards when he stopped. He bent down, then crouched. Was he imagining it? In a patch of sand that had been blown from the beach, were two grooves, as though something had been dragged through it. He got up and followed the grooves towards the beach, where they disappeared when the patch of sand ended. He walked onto the beach, squinting, as he tried to make out any disturbances in the pebbles. He couldn't see anything. He walked towards the sea, the pebbles becoming progressively smaller. There! Two more grooves in a patch of glistening sand and pebbles. He followed the trail, increasing his pace, the sound of the waves becoming stronger, the waning moon a glowing crescent, shining in a starlit sky.

The grooves stopped at the edge of the sea, waves surging in, with each new wave the twin grooves were disappearing. The tide was coming in. He ran back several yards, threw off his jacket, pulled off shoes, socks and trousers, and holding the torch above his head, ran down the beach and waded into the sea.

It was icy. He gritted his teeth and walked slowly forward; a large wave caught him and he almost stumbled. He knew there would be a steep drop soon. If he reached that, it would be hopeless. The torch's light bounced off the water; it was useless, he couldn't see anything. Perhaps he'd be better searching by moonlight. He turned it off.

The sea was above his knees, splashing halfway up his thighs. A few inches further, and he'd be no good to Laurel tonight. Good job she wasn't a long-distance mind-reader. He needed her here. She'd be diving around searching with her hands. His right foot hit something solid. He stumbled. Solid, but giving. Not a rock. A body. He turned and threw the torch onto the beach. It bounced metallically on the stones and went out. He plunged his arms into the water and grabbed at the body, searching for the arms or legs, something he could get hold of and drag free of the sea. Another incoming wave surged over him, he spluttered, but kept contact. There was the head. He inched his hands down. Shoulders. Arms. A wave hit him in the back and his face smacked into cold flesh. He got his hands under the armpits. He twisted, facing the sea. The body was heavy – it must be Carlton. He dug his heels into gravel and hauled. Carlton's head appeared, his dark hair plastered against his scalp. Inch by inch, swearing and grimacing, Frank hauled him nearer to the beach. Where are you, Laurel? I need your strength. His body was screaming with pain, his joints protesting, as first Carlton's torso, and then the tops of his legs, emerged. Striped pyjamas clung to his body. Frank stooped, took a deep breath, then heaved again; Carlton's feet, long and white, were bare. He needed to get him some distance from the incoming tide.

He couldn't feel his own feet, and stumbled as he inched Carlton over the pebbles. Finally, when he thought he'd reached a safe distance, he slowly lowered Carlton to the ground, and tried to find a pulse. His hands were shaking so much he couldn't keep them still; there could be a pulse, but he couldn't find it. He bent down and put his ear to Carlton's mouth. This was useless, he was useless. His hands were sticky, dark – he lifted them, palm upwards. They were streaked with something black. Thick, congealed blood. His? Carlton's?

He raised his head. Moving lights near the Club.

He tried to shout, but his throat was raw with sea water. All that came out was a pathetic sound.

'Frank. Frank. Where are you?' It was Laurel, panic in her voice.

'Here,' he croaked. He cleared his throat and spat onto the beach. 'Laurel. Over here on the beach.'

The lights turned his way. Clattering as they ran over the pebbles towards him.

'My God, it's Carlton Mavor,' said a man.

'Right. You get some blankets. The south wing of the Club is open. Get some from the far bedroom, they're dry, as many as possible. You, go to the road and wait for the ambulance, direct them here. Leave me your torch.' There was no argument. Feet clattered back to the road. She crouched down beside him. 'Any pulse?'

'Can't feel a thing, my body's numb with cold. I tried but he was in the water, under the waves. There's blood on my hands. I think he's injured as well.'

'Move over. I'll try. Get back to the Club. You'll make yourself ill if you don't get dry and warm up. Get someone to make you a hot drink.'

He didn't move.

'In that case, hold the torch. Play it over him.'

He gripped it tightly, moving the light over Carlton's body.

'There.' She grabbed his hand, directing the beam onto Carlton's head. 'A nasty head wound. Can't do anything about that now. I'll try and find a pulse.' She pressed the first two fingers of her right hand against Carlton's neck, her face intense, stern in the light of the torch. 'There may be something.' She put an ear to his mouth. 'I'll start mouth to mouth.'

'You're getting addicted to it,' he said. The words came out like the ratatat of machine-gun fire, as the whole of his body rippled with shivers.

She'd pinched Carlton's nose, tipped his head back and blew the first breath into him, resting her other hand on his chest and nodding.

She took a deep breath and bent down again.

Those lips were meant for him, not Carlton. Francis Xavier, his mother whispered, how could you, the poor boy may be dead.

He wasn't able to keep the beam steady.

'Frank, for God's sake, put your clothes on,' she snapped between breaths.

'Don't say things like that to me, Laurel,' he spluttered.

She shook her head and kept breathing into Carlton.

The blaring of the ambulance siren and the flashing blue lights of police cars were the best sounds and sight ever. Powerful torches lit up the beach, and several men rushed to their sides.

'You get that one into the ambulance, and warm him up. We'll take over, lady. Can you tell us anything?'

'Frank, Mr Diamond, went into the sea looking for him. He said he was under the waves. I've felt a very weak pulse. I started resuscitation.'

Someone pulled Frank up from the beach, put a blanket round him, and started walking him to the ambulance.

245

'My clothes, I need to get them.'

'Where are they, sir?'

He pointed to the sea.

'Show me.'

His feet were so cold, he couldn't feel the pebbles beneath them. He stumbled, the man held him tight with one arm, flashing the beam of his torch in front of them with the other.

The tide had come in and washed away everything, dragged out to sea by the greedy waves. Thank God he hadn't been wearing his leather jacket. 'Nothing left,' he said, his teeth chattering.

'Let's get you into the ambulance.'

As they staggered up the beach, every step an effort, two people were working on Carlton, a stretcher by their side. Laurel had disappeared. He couldn't stop shakes racking his body. There were two ambulances. The man helped him into the nearest. Laurel was inside wrapped in a blanket, her face white, eyes enormous.

'Frank.' She reached out for him and pulled him next to her, took him in her arms and hugged him tight.

'If I take my clothes off, miss, will I get a hug?' said the man who'd helped Frank, as he closed the ambulance door.

'Less of your cheek, and get working on his legs while I rub his body.' She turned to Frank. 'Where are your clothes?'

'Washed away.'

'Pity, that was a nice jacket.'

He couldn't reply as his teeth wouldn't stop chattering. They were both rubbing his body; it was exquisitely painful.

'I'll get you both a hot drink,' the man said, putting down the towel.

Someone banged on the ambulance door. The man opened it.

'What's happened? Someone told me Carlton's hurt? Where is he?' a woman shouted.

It was Beattie Mavor.

'What are you two doing here?' she said accusingly. 'What have you done to Carlton?'

'Young lady, calm down, please. Who are you?' the ambulance man said.

'I'm Carl's sister.'

The man turned back to them. 'The man on the beach, is he this Carlton?'

'Yes, he is. Beattie, he's alive. The ambulance crew are working on him,' Laurel said.

'Oh my God,' she shouted, and ran down the beach.

# Chapter Twenty-Six

Thursday, 3 May, 1973

Laurel carried the suitcase holding Frank's clothes down one of the corridors of the Heath Road Wing of Ipswich Hospital, where he'd been kept in overnight. The doctor who'd turned up shortly after Beattie appeared had insisted, against Frank's protestations, that he needed to be kept under observation for at least twelve hours. She'd wanted to go back in the ambulance to the hospital with him, but the doctor had refused. 'You are not in need of medical attention. Go home and have a hot bath.'

Last night she'd waited until the two ambulances left. Before Beattie went off in the ambulance with Carlton, she'd accosted Laurel. 'What was he doing? Why was he in the sea?' she said accusingly. She was white with worry and concern.

'We don't know,' she'd replied, not wanting to give any details.

After they'd left, she went back to the pub with the two policemen who'd turned up; she asked them to contact Inspector Revie immediately.

'I'll tell them to let you go home. I'll see you tomorrow,' Revie said.

'I'll be at the hospital in the morning, hoping they'll let Frank out.'

'Give me a bell when you're leaving Greyfriars and I'll meet you there and you can both give me all the details.'

'Thanks. They wouldn't let me go to the hospital with Frank.'

'Just as well. Carlton Mavor's alive, you say?'

'Barely, but it wasn't an accident, Nick. He had a nasty head wound, and he was dragged into the sea.'

'I'll go over with a team to the Country Club immediately.'

'Look at the bed in Carlton's room. It's in the south wing. The bed clothes smell of blood. That's what alerted us.'

'Right, get off home. See you tomorrow.'

'Goodnight, Nick.'

'You must be joking.'

'Sorry.'

She knocked on the door of the ward. A tall, prune-faced woman opened it. She wore a dark dress with a sparkling white collar.

'Matron?'

'Yes?'

She explained the reason for her visit.

'He's been a most difficult patient. Doctor's seen him and you can take him home. There's another *gentleman* with him at the moment.' She curled her lip as she said the word gentleman.

'Detective Inspector Revie?'

'So he says.' She opened the door wide. 'They're at the far end on the right, behind the curtain. He said they needed privacy.' She sniffed and walked back to an office.

Laurel rattled the curtain. 'It's me. Are you decent? Can I come in?'

There was a throaty laugh. 'Not one of the adjectives usually used to describe me, Miss Bowman, but please enter, Frank is wearing a fetching pair of hospital pyjamas.'

She pushed the plastic curtain open. Frank was sitting up in a high metal bed, obviously freshly washed and shaved, his hair a mass of dark curls, looking as fresh as a newly opened daisy, his green eyes crinkling in a warm smile. 'Laurel!' He held his arms wide. She pushed past Nick and buried her head against his shoulder. He smelt delicious: Lifebuoy soap.

'What's going on here?' Nick said. 'Remember this is a public hospital.'

'Don't say anything,' Frank whispered.

'Why? Are you ashamed of me?' she whispered back.

He squeezed her tight. 'Just want to keep it between us, until . . .'

'Beast.' She released him, and turned to Revie, opening her arms. 'Would you like a hug too?'

'Laurel Bowman. Control yourself. Later, perhaps, but I'm not sure Mr Diamond would approve.'

She wrinkled her nose at him, not caring, just glad to see Frank looking himself once more. She passed him the suitcase. She blinked, suddenly feeling tired. She hadn't slept well. When she got back to Greyfriars the rest of the team had been in bed. First Dorothy got up when she heard bathwater running, then Mabel and Stuart followed, and by the time she'd had a bath, a couple of whiskies and told them what had happened, it was nearly two.

'Any news of Carlton?' she asked Revie.

He wrinkled his nose. 'Still alive half an hour ago, but it doesn't look good. There's a policeman by his bedside, just in case he recovers consciousness, and another sitting outside his room, guarding him. The doctor I spoke to doesn't hold out much hope. They operated last night on the head wound. They think there's been brain damage.'

She thought of the night Mabel had been attacked, struck on the head with a large stone from Minsmere beach. She'd ended up in this same hospital, a metal plate inserted into her skull. She'd nearly died, but she'd pulled through.

'There must be a chance. He's too young to die. Look how Mabel made a fantastic recovery from a similar attack.'

'True,' Revie said. 'Let's hope the doctor is wrong.'

'If the person who attacked him knows he's alive and may recover, they must be sweating blood,' Frank said.

If only she'd taken Carlton's worries more seriously and persuaded him to tell her immediately, instead of agreeing to meet him later, would that have made a difference? Poor Beattie, she'd looked distraught last night. It was terrible to lose a sister or brother, even if you spent most of your time arguing with them. She knew what such a loss felt like.

'Is Beattie Mavor here?' she asked.

'She was waiting outside the intensive care ward. She wanted to be with him, but wasn't allowed. Matron said she couldn't have more people cluttering up the ward, it was bad enough with the constable.'

'I'd like to get dressed,' Frank said. 'Would you mind?'

Laurel and Nick stood outside the curtains while Frank dressed. He poked his head out. 'Glad you brought my leather jacket.'

'He's got a fetish about that jacket,' Nick said. 'Still can't fault him for stripping and getting into the sea. He's told me all about it. You can both go into Leiston Police Station today and give full statements. I'll get Cottam to give you a ring, and arrange a time.'

The curtain parted and Frank appeared. A young nurse, smart in her uniform and white cap, with a belt with a large silver buckle emphasising her slim waist, came up. 'Going home, Mr Diamond?' She eyed Laurel. 'Are *you* his sister?'

Revie sniggered.

'Sometimes it feels like that,' Laurel said.

'Let's go,' Frank said. 'Goodbye.' He waved to the nurse and to two others who were making their way towards them.

As they pushed the ward door open Revie said, 'They've been all over him this morning, wanting to take his pulse and temperature. The old matron will be glad to get rid of him.'

'I hope you didn't enjoy being handled by these young girls,' Laurel said.

'It was a great hardship,' Frank replied.

'We can go to the Club and you can pick up your car on the way back,' she said.

Frank banged his forehead with an open palm. 'My car keys. They'll be in the briny.'

'I got into your cottage with the spare key you left at Greyfriars to get your clothes. I found the spare set of car keys.'

'Angel.'

'Frank, are you doing anything tomorrow?' Revie asked, as they walked towards the car park.

Frank stopped and turned. 'Who knows what tomorrow brings, but not at the moment. Why?'

'I was thinking you might like to help young Cottam, unofficially of course, he'll tell you about it when you go into Leiston to make your statements.'

'Can I come as well?' Laurel asked.

Revie pursed his lips, but before he could answer Frank butted in.

'I need you to do something else tomorrow, Laurel. If you don't mind.'

'What?' Was he making something up, so he could have all the fun?

'I'll tell you as we drive home.'

'As *I* drive you home.'

'I thought it was too good to last,' Revie said. 'Back to bickering again.'

Laurel glanced at Frank as she came off the A12, after passing through Farnham, onto the A1094 for Aldeburgh. His head was back, eyes closed, lips slightly parted. She was tempted to stop the car and kiss him. Control yourself, she thought. Let him rest. Her mind wandered, thinking about what might have happened if they hadn't gone back to look for Carlton.

She wished they could be transported on a magic carpet to some desert island where they would be gloriously isolated, with no one interested in their relationship. She'd seen the look in Dorothy's eyes last night when she'd talked about Frank going into the sea half-naked. She'd been proud of him, and she'd glared at Stuart when he'd made a silly quip. It must be obvious to the three of them that something had changed between her and Frank.

He'd said he loved her. She hadn't said she loved him. Why hadn't she? She'd been bereft when she'd seen him with Emma, and then the wonderful shock when he'd said he loved her, but she hadn't been able to form those words.

There was a movement from the passenger seat. Frank was yawning, his hand over his mouth. 'Sorry about that, Laurel. I didn't get much sleep last night.'

'Wouldn't those nurses leave you alone?'

'Jealous?'

'Have I reason to be?'

He put a hand over her thigh, and slowly caressed it.

'Stop it, Frank, you'll have us off the road.'

He laughed, and moved his hand away. 'Later,' he said enigmatically.

'Much later. Now you've come to, can you tell me what you want me to do tomorrow? Or haven't you made it up yet?'

'Laurel Bowman, are you going to treat me this way for the rest of my life?'

She tried to keep calm. 'I certainly am. Don't expect my standards to be lowered.'

'I just love it when you talk tough, you remind me of that sexy matron who got her rocks off ordering the nurses, not to mention the patients, about.'

'I am not wearing a nurse's uniform.'

'That's a shame. First no Girl Guide uniform, now no dressing up as a nurse. What about your Brownie gear? Still got it? You'll look delicious in the colour sludge.'

'I think that cold sea water penetrated your brain, you're more silly than usual.'

'But you do love me?'

She stretched out her left hand and rumpled his already dishevelled hair. 'Don't doubt it.'

He grasped her hand and kissed it. 'This is what I want you to do tomorrow.'

She reluctantly pulled her hand free.

'Do you remember what subjects Beatrice Mavor told us she did at A level?'

She frowned. 'What on earth has this got to do with anything?'

'Bear with me. Do you remember?'

She wrinkled her nose. 'I'm not sure of the subjects, but they were on the arts side. English? Geography? Something like that.'

'Correct. I've talked to two of her former teachers, one was the

253

late Janet Lamb, and the other her friend, Muriel. Either they'd got the wrong pupil, or Beattie was lying about the subjects she took. I want to know who's telling the truth.'

'So, what do you want me to do?'

'I want you to try and speak to someone at the school who'd definitely know. I'll see what I can dig up today, and we'll talk about it later.'

'Does it have to be tomorrow? I could come with you when you and Johnny Cottam are together. That sounds more interesting.'

'I think you should do it tomorrow, if you can. It isn't that I don't want you with me. I'm intrigued by this inconsistency.'

She drove through Aldeburgh and headed for Thorpeness, and Frank's car. In the municipal car park, they stood together, arms round each other.

'I'm going back to the cottage to have a shower. I had to have a bath last night, but I hate baths, you end up in a soup of soap and your body cells,' Frank said.

'You smell deliciously of Lifebuoy soap,' she said, nuzzling his neck. 'I'm finding it a strong aphrodisiac.'

'I can't wait to see what will happen when I use Imperial Leather,' he said.

'Will you be coming to dinner? The others will be glad to see you.'

'I'm looking forward to it. I'll do some telephoning and hopefully be able to give you some contacts tonight.' He pulled her close and kissed her. 'Laurel, I can't wait for this case to be over.'

'Me too.'

He climbed into his Avenger; the engine started first time. He gave her a thumbs up and pulled out of the car park.

She stood there for a few minutes. It was unreal. Was she meant to be this happy?

# Chapter Twenty-Seven

Friday, 4 May, 1973

Frank waited in his car outside Judge Hanmer's house; Johnny Cottam was ten minutes late, probably Revie had given him a final lecture before allowing him to leave. 'Don't let Diamond take over, you know what he's like. Assert your authority, you're the detective, he's been graciously asked to be a second pair of eyes.' Or something like that.

When he and Laurel went to give their statements at Leiston Police Station, Revie had invited Frank to help Cottam go through the contents of the Judge's house again, to see if they could find any connection between the Judge and Teddy Leach, the Country Club's ex-manager, and to have a look for the Judge's diary. He'd been delighted to accept.

Cottam's car, an old Ford, drew up and parked next to him. Cottam shouted, 'Sorry I'm late. Inspector Revie wanted a final debrief.' He waved some keys at him. 'Shall we get started?'

He followed Cottam up the flight of stairs to the front door. As Johnny opened it, he was hit by stale, damp air; already the house smelt of neglect. It was only three weeks since the Judge had been murdered, but already it felt as though it was a long time since anyone had lived here.

Outside was a sunny spring day, with a nip in the air, and a brisk easterly sea breeze added to the chill factor. He was glad he'd put on plenty of warm clothes; his dip in the sea had given him a chill – he felt shivery. Or he was getting old? Irritated, he told himself to get a grip.

Cottam went into the front room, and he followed.

'I thought we'd start in this room, then search the rest of the ground floor. By then it'll probably be lunchtime. Fancy a bite to eat at the local pub?'

Frank nodded.

'We can do the upstairs this afternoon. Agreed?'

'You're in charge, Johnny, or would you prefer I called you Detective Cottam?'

Johnny's face reddened. 'For God's sake, Frank. I'm pleased to be working with you again. Revie isn't here, so let's just be ourselves.'

'OK. I used to prefer starting from the top of a house, and working my way down when doing a search, but let's do it your way.'

'Thank you. What we're looking for is any connection between the Judge and our friend Leach.'

'You heard Laurel and I thought we saw him driving away from the Country Club, the night Carlton Mavor was attacked?'

'Yes. He's jumped bail, disappeared, so he's our number one suspect for the murder of Mr Mavor.'

'Murder?'

Cottam frowned. 'I'm sorry, I thought you'd have heard, Mr Mavor died last night. It's now a murder case.'

Bile filled Frank's throat. He hadn't liked Carlton, but that was probably partly, or mostly, because he was jealous of his friendship with Laurel. But to have his life taken. It was deliberate murder, they'd dragged him down to the sea, hoping his body would be washed away by the tide, probably thinking the verdict would be accidental death, or even suicide. Were the two killings connected? The elderly judge and the young sportsman? He couldn't see the connection. If Leach killed the Judge to prevent him revealing his criminal past, why, after jumping bail, had he risked coming back to the Club to kill Carlton? It didn't make sense.

Cottam set up his workplace on the round mahogany table in the front room. 'I'll go through the bureau, could you examine all the books in the bookcase? I can't see the Judge would hide anything in books, but you never know.'

He'd got the boring job, but it was always interesting looking at another person's taste in literature, it told you something, sometimes a great deal, about them. The painting the Judge had presumably been working on was still on its easel. It was a beach scene, looked like Aldeburgh, there were three fishing boats, and the pebbles and sand looked wet, as though it had rained. Quite accomplished, but it could have done with a few spots of bright colour, it was muted, something was lacking. Did this say anything about the Judge? Afraid to take risks?

Cottam handed him a pair of cotton gloves. 'Like old times?'

Frank thanked him and nodded. He glanced at his watch. 'It's just gone nine. Break for lunch at twelve?'

'I've brought a flask of coffee, we can have a short break at ten thirty,' Cottam said.

Frank started on the top shelf, removing and stacking books, then one by one flicking them open, waiting for a piece of paper, a photograph, a ten-pound note, to flutter to the floor. Before returning them to the shelf, he looked to see if anything was written on the fly leaf. Whoever was his housekeeper was thorough, there was no dust on the top of the books.

The first two rows were law books, some dating back several decades, which looked supremely boring. Then there were rows of magazines carefully stored in holders specially made for them; mostly copies of the Royal Horticultural Society's magazine, *The Garden*. They stretched back years. He liked plants, but what was the point of keeping all these? Did he ever read them again?

'Anything interesting, Johnny?'

There was a sigh. 'No. Usual stuff, household bills and receipts, copies of letters sent and replies. None of them relevant to the case.'

'Soon be coffee time.'

'Thank God.'

After coffee Frank started on the last two shelves. Mostly gardening books, some autobiographies of famous legal figures, but also of actors, and several books on art, including some on watercolour techniques.

They decided to walk to the pub and get some fresh air. He'd given Laurel the long straw; at least she would be talking to a live person, not sifting through a dead man's belongings.

# Chapter Twenty-Eight

Laurel was looking forward to driving to Walberswick, where the former headmistress of St Mary's School, Winifred Underwood, lived. She didn't know the village well, but the few times she'd visited it she'd thought it was charming, tucked away at the end of the B1387, isolated and surrounded by the sea on one side, and heath and marshland on the other.

After dinner at Greyfriars the previous evening, Frank had passed her a slip of paper. 'Here are the details of Beattie's former headmistress, including her telephone number. Give her a ring tomorrow morning and see if you can see her as soon as possible. You were a teacher, she'll relate to you. Find out anything you can about Beattie, but especially what A levels she took.'

When she'd rung Miss Underwood a thin, high voice informed her she'd be pleased to see her at three that afternoon. 'I live on the road which leads down to the ferry, it's surrounded by trees. Drive slowly, or you'll miss it.'

Laurel imagined she might resemble a reed, bone thin, with a long neck, and elongated fingers floating over a piano keyboard as she played hymns for school assemblies. She'd left Greyfriars with plenty of time to spare, hoping to have lunch at one of the two pubs in the village, followed by a walk before seeing Miss Underwood.

Leaving her Cortina in the Cliff Field car park, she'd lunched well at The Anchor, a pretty pub close to the village hall; then wandered down to the river to watch a ferry boat taking passengers to Southwold. She walked back to her car over the sandy, shingle

259

beach. She was so relaxed and incredibly happy, she almost felt like breaking into song, but decided she'd better get into detective mode, and find Miss Underwood's house.

A short drive, overhung with tree branches, led to an attractive tiled and gabled house; at the back ditched fields stretched out into the distance. There was a bellpull by the side of the front door, and in a few minutes the door opened, and a tall, thin woman, with silver hair pulled back in a bun, smiled at her.

'You must be Miss Bowman, please come in.'

She *was* reed-thin, her appearance complementing the high voice; she was dressed in a wafty, olive-green garment, and beckoned with graceful motions of her hand for Laurel to follow her into a spacious room overlooking fields striped with reeds, showing the lines of ditches.

'Please sit.' She pointed to a chair facing the window. Laurel imagined her using the same tone and words to hundreds of girls marshalled into the school hall for morning assembly. She couldn't help smiling.

'You seem amused, Miss Bowman?' The words were questioning, not offended.

'I was imagining you taking an assembly.'

Tinkling laughter showed she was also amused. 'A part of my responsibilities I found extremely boring. Assemblies are necessary, as one must give out the same message to all the girls, whatever their age, modifying it of course for the different age groups. But listening to them singing hymns was painful.' She sat down with her back to the window.

She'd not lost her touch, making sure the light was in Laurel's face, not hers. Her keen grey eyes scanned Laurel, who was sure she'd been categorised and placed in an appropriate box.

'You said you are a member of The Anglian Detective Agency, and want to find out more about one of my former pupils, is that right?'

'Yes, and I'm grateful you've seen me so quickly.'

'Oh, I'm the one who's grateful. This is the most exciting thing that has happened to me for a long time. A female detective! I don't think that was a career we subscribed to at St Mary's.' The tinkling laughter again. 'Have you always been a detective, Miss Bowman?'

'No, I was a teacher. My previous job was Senior Mistress at Blackfriars School, Dunwich.'

Miss Underwood threw up her arms with delight. 'Now I know why your name is familiar. You fought off that dreadful headmaster, the sex manic. Bravo for you. Now how can I help you?'

Her eyes sparkled with interest. She may have imagined her physical appearance correctly, but her character didn't fit the mould of the retired spinster headmistress. She seemed full of fun.

'Do you remember a girl called Beatrice Mavor? I think she's in her early thirties now.'

Miss Underwood leant back, closing her eyes, pursing her mouth. Her eyes snapped open. 'Yes, dreadful girl. I didn't like her.'

She certainly didn't mince her words. 'Why was that?'

'Let's see. I must get this right. She was a good-looking girl, I should think she's an attractive woman.'

'Yes, she is. Tall, strong, athletic.'

'Like yourself, Miss Bowman.'

Laurel pulled a face.

'She was an aggressive girl, she always wanted to be first whatever the situation. At games and sports, she could often achieve her ambition, but although she was academically good in some subjects, she found it difficult to accept she was not the best in all of them.'

'Did she do art subjects at A level?'

'Oh, dear me, no. Her best subjects were the sciences. I believe she did mathematics, physics and chemistry at A level.'

So, Muriel had been right and so had Frank – Beattie had lied about which subjects she took at A level. Why?

'Why this interest in Beatrice Mavor? Can you tell me?'

Laurel bit her lip. If she told her, she might get more out of Miss Underwood, but she didn't want this getting back to Beattie. 'If I do, could I ask you to treat everything I say in confidence?'

Miss Underwood stared at her. She slowly nodded. 'Yes, of course. Has she done something terrible?'

'Thank you. Why do you ask that?'

'It wouldn't surprise me. She was a passionate girl, I don't mean sexually, although possibly that too. What I mean is she would get upset if she wasn't first, but she didn't just fume about it, she would follow through with some action against the person who'd bettered her.'

'What did she do? Can you give me some examples?'

Miss Underwood nodded. 'We always put on an annual Shakespearean play, and the roles were always hotly contested. I remember, she was in her first year, and the play was *A Midsummer Night's Dream*. We wanted a number of first-year girls to be Titania's fairies, not the named fairies, Mustard Seed, etc., just ten girls with a suitable build, graceful on their feet, as the teacher directing the play wanted them to dance around, holding lit torches, when the light was dimmed. It looked quite magical on the actual nights. I was pleased with that production.' She shuddered. 'I cannot say the same for our *Romeo and Juliet*. Why she chose that girl for Juliet I cannot imagine. She was as graceful as a warthog.'

Laurel waited for her to get back on track.

'As you can imagine, all the first years wanted to be fairies. The teacher auditioned them by getting them to dance round the gym in their PE kit, and she weeded out those she thought unsuitable. Beatrice was the last one to be eliminated. It was a dance-off with another girl in her class. What was her name?' She paused, closing her eyes, and pursed her lips, once more into thinking mode. The eyes snapped open. 'Valerie Hoffman – bright little thing. Made a good marriage, some son of the minor nobility. When the teacher decided Valerie would be the better fairy, we were shown Beatrice's temper and spite for the first time.'

'What did she do?'

Miss Underwood pulled a sour face. 'She was devious. Waited until the play was about to be staged, then she *accidentally* tripped Valerie up in a games lesson, netball I think, and the poor girl broke her wrist. Of course, we couldn't prove it was intentional, but I was sure it was. Beatrice went to the teacher directing the play and offered herself as a substitute fairy. When the teacher consulted me, I forbade her to do that. In fact, I got her to accept Valerie wearing a sling. Not the usual attire of fairies, but I wasn't going to let Beattie win.'

'Did you talk to Beattie?'

'I did, but for a girl of her age, she was hard to break. In fact, I couldn't get her to confess, which is unusual for me.'

Laurel could well believe it.

'Were there any other incidents while she was with you?'

'There were skirmishes, but once she got to the sixth form and she was studying the subjects she was best at, also she was an all-round excellent games player, she wasn't put in the position of being bettered. She played tennis at junior level for Suffolk.' She paused. 'There was an incident at the end of her sixth-form career.'

'Did it involve another girl?'

'No. It involved me.'

'Goodness, what happened?'

'Beatrice was determined to go to either Oxford or Cambridge to read chemistry. She was good, but she wasn't that good. When she wasn't offered a place at either of those universities, she asked to see me.'

Laurel decided she was glad Beattie had beaten her at tennis. Although it might have been interesting to see what she'd have done if it had been the other way round. 'What happened?'

'She asked to see the reference I'd written for her. Of course, I refused. Actually, it was quite a good reference, making much of her academic achievements and her undoubted excellence in sports. I assure you I wanted as many of my girls to get into Oxbridge as possible. It's such a good advertisement for the school, and when parents are paying hefty fees for their daughters' education, a high percentage of girls going on to the best universities is always impressive, and therefore lucrative.'

'Was there anything in the reference that mentioned Beatrice's faults?'

'There was never any proof of her character defects. But I think I may have made a reference to her over-competitive nature, but that might be seen as a plus rather than a minus for those universities.'

'What happened?'

'I have no proof, but on the last day of term, when all the girls had left, either by the school bus we hired to take them to Ipswich railway station, or picked up by their parents, I left to have a few days' holiday before returning to school, to tidy up any administration, before leaving for my long holiday. As I drove away in my car, it skidded and I ended up in a ditch.'

'Were you hurt?'

'A few cuts and bruises, it could have been worse. The man from the local garage who hauled the car from the ditch – he had to use a crane, he didn't do it himself.' She laughed. 'I'm such a pedant! He said a tyre had been slashed. I hadn't noticed as I drove off.'

'You think Beattie did that?'

'I am sure of it.'

'But no proof?'

'No, and I didn't take it any further. I decided as she'd left, she could do no more harm at St Mary's, and the publicity would have harmed the school, if I asked the police to investigate.'

Laurel wasn't sure Miss Underwood had made the right decision. She'd always believed in finding the culprit for any crime or misdemeanour at her school, however minor. If a child got away with stealing, or bullying, if they weren't found out and punished, they'd every encouragement to commit further crimes, and to continue doing so for the rest of their lives.

'I can see from your face you think I should have acted?'

'It's dangerous to let a pupil get away with anything.'

'You're probably right. You would have made a good headmistress. A pity you left the profession.'

Laurel didn't want to go down that road. 'Did Beattie go to university?'

'Yes, Liverpool. They have an excellent chemistry department there. At least they used to; I've lost touch since I retired.'

'Do you know what she did after that?'

'We have an Old Girls' Letter, which we send out to all the girls who have left St Mary's. We rely on them sending us information about themselves, their degrees, their jobs, marriages and births of their children. I still receive it. I'm proud many of the girls have achieved important positions in society. Beattie got a second-class degree and went to work for Portman's in Felixstowe. They make agricultural chemical products.'

'My home town,' Laurel said.

Miss Underwood didn't look impressed. 'I believe she moved to the firm's establishment in Cheshire. I don't know any more about her. In fact, I hadn't heard her name for ages, until you came today.'

'I presume you must have talked to her parents when she was at school?'

'Yes, on several occasions. I was worried about her, and one always hopes that with help, childish faults can be remedied.'

'Were there any clues to her behaviour from talking to them, did they know why Beattie was so aggressively competitive?'

'They were reluctant to talk about her faults, but they did say they thought her younger brother's birth was a turning point. What was his name?' she mused.

'Carlton. He's also a tennis coach at the Thorpeness Country Club.' She hoped he was still alive and would recover.

'Ah, yes, Carlton. It seems his birth put her nose out of joint; she was used to having all her parents' attention.'

'When I've seen them together, they do seem to rub each other up the wrong way. Beattie is especially unkind to Carlton.'

'Siblings! There always seem to be problems between brothers and sisters, but usually they are loyal to one another. If one is in trouble, the other forgets their squabbles and helps them out.'

It was true; she still blamed herself for not realising her sister, Angela, was in trouble. The only help she could give was to get just-ice for her.

Miss Underwood rose. 'I don't think I can be of any further help . . . at the moment.'

Laurel looked at her enquiringly.

'If you agree, I could tap some sources – I have an extensive network – I may be able to find out more details of Beatrice's life. Would you like me to do that?'

Laurel got up and shook her hand. 'I certainly would, and thank you for the help you've given me today.'

'I hope it has been useful.' She led her to the door.

'You've given me an insight into aspects of Beattie's character.'

'I hope you don't find she's done something dreadful. I don't want to see headlines in the tabloids – former St Mary's pupil robs bank, or some such thing.'

Laurel smiled. Still thinking of her old school's reputation.

# Chapter Twenty-Nine

Frank felt a tad better after a pint of Breakspear's Bitter and egg, ham and chips at the Dolphin Inn, but wasn't looking forward to spending an afternoon rooting through the Judge's old clothing and checking medicine chests.

'We'll start with his bedroom,' Johnny said. 'There isn't much in the other bedrooms apart from furniture; he didn't seem to have many visitors.'

'The more I learn about him, the sadder his life seems,' Frank said as they climbed the stairs.

Neville Hanmer's bedroom was spacious, with a large window giving a good view of the beach and the rolling sea.

'All right in the summer,' Johnny said, 'but in winter? You can't keep that east wind out when it's blowing straight in from Russia.'

Frank waited for his instructions.

'Could you check the wardrobe, go through the pockets of all the clothes. I'll tackle the dressing table, then whoever's finished first can search the chest of drawers.'

The furniture looked as though it had been in the house since the Judge was a child: dark, heavy and Victorian. The men who moved it in must have worried the floor might collapse under its weight. When he opened the wardrobe there was a strong smell of moth balls; he decided he could get addicted to camphor. There was a row of suits, and at the end a judge's gown, trimmed with fur. He took out each one in turn, laying it on the double bed with its crimson counterpane, going through the pockets. His only findings at the end of the search of the suits and jackets, were a crumpled handkerchief and a silver sixpence. Small pickings.

In the wardrobe, on a row of shelves to the right, were woollen jumpers and a few cardigans, all in dark or muted colours. Like the painting there was a lack of colour in the Judge's life. On a shelf, above the row of suits, were hat boxes, mostly made of leather. It was like looking back on the history of men's clothing. One by one, he took them down and inspected the contents. A top hat, a trilby, which didn't look as though it had been used, a homburg, and in the last one, a wig the colour of bleached rope. He imagined the Judge robing before processing into court, the wig the final touch; now he became the arbiter of the defendant's fate, able by his summing-up to influence the jury, and finally to cast sentence. A powerful position. They say power corrupts. What had Neville Hanmer been like as a judge? According to people like Pamela Gage, he'd been a good judge, firm but fair. If only they'd been able to talk before he was murdered. What was the secret the Judge carried to his grave? Could he find it?

'Any luck?' Cottam asked.

'Sorry, not a bean.'

'I'll start on the chest of drawers.'

When Frank had finished with the wardrobe, he went to help Johnny. It was depressing looking at the piles of shirts, underwear and nightwear, piled on the bed, with socks and handkerchiefs. Who wore separate collars nowadays? It was bad enough wearing a collar and tie, but imagine encasing your neck in one of those starched monstrosities.

They moved to the other bedrooms on that floor. Frank was beginning to lose the will to live, Cottam looked equally bored. Frank looked at his watch. Nearly four. 'How many rooms are there on the top floor?'

'Not sure, I've not been up there.'

'Right, bite the bullet, let's get this over with.'

'I'm sorry we've wasted your time, Frank.'

'That's all right, it's reminded me why I left the force. Too much routine stuff has got to be done, you can't cut corners.'

'Can *you*?' Cottam said, as they went up the narrow stairs leading to the attic rooms.

'Cut them? I can ignore them completely.' It wasn't true, Stuart wouldn't let him, but he wasn't going to tell Johnny that.

'Bloody hell,' Cottam said as they went into the room facing the stairs.

It was filled with childhood toys: a teddy bear, one eye missing, a three-wheeled bike, a kite, toy lead soldiers in a box, children's books on a painted set of shelves, all covered in a film of dust; the housekeeper obviously didn't get, or wasn't allowed, up here.

They looked at each other. 'Let's see what's in the other room,' Johnny said.

The room to the right was the smallest they'd seen. Its walls were covered with rows of wide shelves, and on them were what looked like photograph albums. Frank wiped his finger over the top of one of them. No dust. He held the finger up to Johnny Cottam. 'Can you see the Judge wielding a duster?'

Cottam pursed his lips. 'Must have done.' He pulled down a volume and placed it on a small central table, the only other furniture in the room, except for a single chair. There was no dust on these either. He flicked it open. Pasted to the pages were newspaper cuttings, invitations to formal dinners of various societies, articles from magazines, and also photographs of obviously important occasions.

'What's on the spine?' Frank asked.

'Dates. 1964 to 1965.'

'Bingo,' Frank said, 'at last something interesting. What shall we do? No good going too far back. I'll get another chair and we can split them up between us.'

'We could be here until midnight,' Johnny groaned.

'Nonsense. We know what we're looking for, any photo or reference to Leach, or any other name we recognise. What year was Teddy Leach convicted?'

Cottam frowned. '1964, I think.'

'Right. Let's get the volumes for 1964 onwards, split them into two and see how far we get. I need to finish by six, I've got a hot date.'

'Really? Then I'll have to carry on by myself.'

'My heart bleeds for you.'

'Thanks, Frank.'

'My pleasure. Here, you have 1964 to 1966, I'll take 1967 to 1969. When did the Judge retire?'

'1971.'

Frank scoured the shelves. 'Here's 1970, I'll take 1971. Let's hope we find something. Did you bring up that mugshot of Leach?'

Cottam placed it on the table between them. 'You should recognise him.'

'I've only seen him a couple of times before, but he might look very different in the past, different hairstyle, fatter, thinner, but there is that distinctive nose. He's easily recognisable from the shot taken when he was arrested recently. Check with me if you're not sure,' Frank said.

Heads down they worked their way slowly and methodically through the volumes.

'He certainly kept a full record of his cases, achievements and failures,' Frank muttered, as he placed the 1968 volume on top of the 1967 volume on the floor.

'He must have died a rich man, I wonder who he's left his money to?' Johnny mused. 'We didn't dig up any close relatives.'

Frank was a third of the way through the 1969 volume, ready to turn to the next page, when his hand froze. It wasn't who'd they'd been looking for. He stared at the newspaper cutting. In the grainy photograph were three people. To the right an official-looking man holding a piece of paper had his mouth open, presumably proclaiming to the press. Next to him was a shorter man, with long dark wavy hair, a self-satisfied smile on his handsome face. Close to him, their bodies touching, possibly with her arm through his, was a dark-haired, attractive woman.

'What is it?' Cottam asked. 'Have you found something?'

Frank looked up. 'I believe I have, but it isn't Leach. Come and have a look.'

Cottam came round the table and peered over Frank's shoulder.

Frank pointed to the text. 'It says the solicitor is reading a statement about the acquittal of Frederick Saltash, who was found not guilty to being a member of the Retribution Group who detonated a bomb in a John Lewis store in Ipswich. His fiancée gave him an alibi for the time of the blast.' He tapped several times on the face of the woman. 'I know her. She's Beatrice Mavor, Carlton's sister.'

Johnny sat down. 'Does this help us?'

'I don't know, but it certainly raises questions. This is a link with the Judge. I presume Neville Hanmer presided over this case. It doesn't state that in the article. That needs to be checked. Then I think you'd better find out as much as you can about Miss Mavor.'

'Are you suggesting she killed the Judge? Why? In the article she hadn't committed a crime, she was a witness.'

'Yes, but it's the only link we've found so far with anyone who lives in Thorpeness with the Judge. I think it's worth looking into her background. I can tell you a few things about her.' And I may have more after I talk to Laurel tonight, he thought. He decided not to tell him Laurel was making enquiries about Beattie.

Johnny pulled the album towards him and stared at the article.

'Johnny, I think you ought to ring Revie now, and tell him you think this is urgent.'

Cottam looked up, gnawing his lip. 'I will. You always had a good nose for trouble. I wish you were still with us.'

'At the moment, I'm having the same thoughts.'

'Do you know this Miss Mavor well?'

'I've met her a couple of times, so, no, I can't say I know her well.'

'Can you see her murdering the Judge?'

'I always find it difficult to imagine anyone killing anyone else. No, that's not true. There have been a few characters Laurel and I have come across since we started the Agency who I can well imagine bumping people off. Anyone is capable of murder in the right circumstances. To answer your question – I don't know.'

Cottam frowned. 'Supposing, just supposing, she killed the Judge, although I can't see it myself; who killed Carlton?'

'The million-dollar question.'

'You can't possibly suspect Miss Mavor of killing her own brother? I saw her at the hospital, she was in pieces. She never left, even though she had to wait outside the ward when he came back from the operation. I thought it was a bit mean, not to let her be by his side.'

'There are lots of questions to be asked, Johnny. I certainly don't know any of the answers. I think you should make that phone call immediately. Tell Revie I think it's urgent.'

Cottam nodded, got up and ran down the stairs.

Frank unlocked the door of his cottage and went in, followed by Laurel. As soon as dinner was finished at Greyfriars they'd made their excuses. Dorothy had smiled as she looked over her blue spectacles, and Stuart had shouted, 'Don't do anything I wouldn't do.' Mabel told him to behave.

He pulled the kitchen curtains to, grabbed the coffee percolator, filled it and put it on the stove.

'I'm sorry about Carlton, he was so young. It doesn't seem possible, one day running round the tennis court, the next dead . . .' Laurel said.

'But you're not surprised.'

'No. He'd been too long under the water, his pulse was very weak. It's dreadful, such a strong man – physically.'

'I know you liked him,' Frank said.

She smiled, a sad smile. 'Great body, but in many ways, he was still a little boy, certainly Beattie treated him like a troublesome younger brother. She didn't let him grow up.'

'Talking of Beattie, did you see the old headmistress?'

'Do we have to talk about her? What's the hurry? You certainly created a stir rushing me out of the dining room saying we needed to talk. What's happened?'

'You tell me your news, then I'll tell you mine,' he said, with a cheeky grin.

'If I'm not mistaken, you're feeling very pleased with yourself.'

'I am, the woman I desire is sitting next to me, and if I'm not mistaken, the coffee is ready.'

She laughed. 'You infuriate me at times, but I don't think you'll ever bore me.'

He poured her a cup of coffee, placed it by her side and kissed her cheek. 'What I've got in mind is not what I'd originally planned for tonight.'

'Oh, dear. Sounds ominous.'

'Come on, Laurel, spill the beans.'

She told him all she had learnt from Winifred Underwood about Beatrice Mavor. 'Frank, what is it? You look grim.'

'So, she did lie about the A levels she took, and she specialised in chemistry at university?'

'Yes. Also, she seemed to have a vicious streak.'

'It all fits.' He told her about the newspaper cutting.

'Retribution. Our own home-grown terrorist group. Do you think she belongs to it?'

'Who knows? I need time and more facts to try and tie all the loose ends waving at me, together, but time is one thing we haven't got.'

'What should we do? We ought to tell Revie about what I've found out about her.'

'Yes. We must do that. But . . .'

'What are you thinking?'

'How would you like a ride in my car?' He put a hand round her waist.

'Now? Tonight?'

'Yes, tonight.'

'One of those kinds of rides?'

'You've guessed it?'

'I give up, you'd better tell me.'

'I think we should pay Miss Mavor a visit.'

'Really? What excuse do we give?'

'We're checking she's all right. We're calling to see if there's anything we can do for her.'

'I don't think that will wash, she knows I can't stand her, but she's just lost her brother, so I suppose I should feel sympathy towards her,' Laurel said.

'I'd hold the sympathy if I were you.'

'Supposing she's not there? She might have gone home, wherever that is.'

'Stowmarket. In that case, I think we should put one of our practised skills to good use.'

'Not another break-in? You know what we usually find when we do that. I don't like Beattie but I don't want to find her dead body.'

'Neither do I, it would ruin my theory.'

'Revie will be furious if he finds out. This is not our case, Frank.'

'When did that ever bother us?'

'I think you mean *me*, not *us*,' she said, turning towards him and kissing his cheek.

'He won't be mad if we find something helpful; after all, I spotted Beattie in the newspaper article. Johnny Cottam wouldn't have known her from Eve. I deserve some Brownie points for that.'

'Do I need to change?'

'Into what, a pumpkin?'

'Stupid! Clothes.'

'I don't think it would look good if she's in and you turned up looking like a burglar. Hopefully by the end of the night, you'll have changed into a pair of my pyjamas.' He pulled her a little closer.

'Frank Diamond, wash your mouth out. Such erotic language before nine o'clock isn't seemly.'

He looked at his watch. 'It's nearly eight, we can get there by half past if we leave soon. I'll get a few tools.' He looked at her. 'Will you be warm enough?'

She nodded.

'Right. Let's go.' They untangled themselves and got up from the table.

Her eyes were shining with excitement. Suddenly he wasn't sure if she should come with him. It might turn dangerous. He stopped.

'What is it, Frank?'

He bit his lip. 'Perhaps it would be better for you to go back to Greyfriars and phone Revie, tell him what you found out today.'

She stared at him, then her mouth curved in a smile. 'You'll have

274

to get used to it, Frank. Whatever happens between us, I'm not stopping what I love doing. That's working with you and the rest of the team.'

He hadn't thought this through. Would he be able to carry on working with her, if he was perpetually worried about what might happen? It wouldn't work. Would she allow him to steer her away when danger approached? He didn't think so.

'Frank, it's time we went.'

He didn't move.

'Frank Diamond, you'll never get me in your pyjamas if you stand there dithering. I can look after myself as well as you can. All right, there were times when I needed a bit of help, but let's get on with it. We can argue about this later.'

He hugged her hard. 'Much later. Let's go.'

# Chapter Thirty

Frank passed Laurel a pair of cotton gloves as they stood outside the north wing of the Country Club. It was deserted, no sign of life, and Beattie's VW wasn't there.

'Where did you get these?' she asked.

'Johnny Cottam got them for me.'

'Did you tell him what you wanted them for?'

'I said I'd run out, which we have, and I didn't have time to go and buy some, which I hadn't.'

'Did he ask you what you needed them for?'

'No, he's more sense.' He tried the door, but it was locked.

'I hope we're not going to have to break a window, I am a member here.'

'Which comes first, your job, or your hobby?'

'Only one answer to that.'

'Don't worry, I may be able to make a neater entry.' He pulled a key ring from his jacket pocket; on it were several slender keys.

'I hope you didn't get *them* from Cottam. We don't want to get him into trouble.'

He put a finger to his lips, looked at the Yale lock and selected a key. After a few turns, he grimaced, pulled it out of the lock, and selected another one. 'I'm a bit rusty. Found these in the back of a drawer a few weeks ago. I've been practising.'

'What on earth made you do that?'

He shook his head and frowned at her; his ear was to the door as he gently wriggled the key. 'Nearly.' He took a deep breath and concentrated. There was a definite click. He smiled, and the door opened. He waved his gloved hand at her. 'Magic fingers.'

'I hope so,' she said, laughing.

'Saucy,' he replied. What was the matter with them? They were acting like teenagers out on a wrecking spree. 'We'd better get serious, Laurel.'

She nodded.

'For goodness' sake, put your gloves on.'

The wing in which Beattie was the only occupant was a mirror image of the south wing, where Carlton had lived. Frank pushed open the first door on the left. This was obviously Beattie's room, with similar furniture to Carlton's. He sniffed.

'What is that smell, Frank? It's a bit like bleach,' Laurel said, moving her head from side to side, reminding him of a lioness scenting the air for a tasty gazelle.

On Beattie's bed was an opened suitcase, half-full of clothes.

'Looks like she's planning to leave when she gets back from wherever she's gone to. Look, there's a passport on the top,' Laurel said.

Frank gritted his teeth. 'I've got a horrible feeling about this.' He started to carefully remove the clothes, laying them in order on the bed. At the bottom of the suitcase was a black leather book. He looked at Laurel.

Her eyes were wide, her mouth open. 'What do you think it is?'

'We'll soon find out.' He picked it up and turned it over. Embossed into the leather in a flowing script were the gilt words: *Diary 1973*. He flipped it open. There was no clue to the owner, no name written on the flyleaf, but in an elegant hand in black ink, someone had written:

*January 1st, 1973* on the first page.

'It must be his,' Laurel exclaimed. 'She must have killed him.'

'Let's read the relevant days before we jump to conclusions, but this is proof of another link between her and the Judge.' He pulled two chairs side by side, placed the diary on the table and turned the pages until he came to:

*Friday, 13th April, 1973.*

*The weather was pleasant today, sunny and warm in the morning, but a little chilly later. This morning I completed my newest painting and I am happy with it. The light in this part of the world seems to bring clarity and colour to objects. I will always love this special stretch of coast, but how I wish I did not feel like a prisoner here. I do miss London and my old friends. I'm glad Pamela is nearby; it is always a pleasure to see her.*

*She told me she was hoping to employ The Anglian Detective Agency to find out who is stealing her plants. It is disgusting how low some people will stoop. I do hope the Agency is successful as I know she is worried by the losses of some of her most precious plants. There is also the problem of Keith; why she ever married him I cannot imagine, but I suppose they were young, in love, and he wasn't such a heavy drinker then. It is sad to see the people you like aging; each day I find it harder to look in the mirror. I must admit I still find pleasure in looking at the young with their unblemished skin, clear eyes and supple bodies.*

*Today there were children rowing on the Mere. One of them a beautiful young boy. Then I saw David Pemberton, another handsome young man. I can see he hates me. I wish I could tell him I had nothing to do with the terrible happenings at Tucker's house. I don't think he'd believe me, and if he read this diary it would only reinforce his hatred of me.*

'We don't want Revie to see that,' Laurel said, pointing to the relevant sentence about David.

'Keep reading,' Frank said.

*I believe he had a friend at the school he went to, who was killed by those vile men. I wonder if they were ever brought* to justice. They never made the courts. Perhaps he thinks I was one of them. If the Establishment thought I knew their names, which I don't, I think they'd . . . It wouldn't just be exile here in Thorpeness.

So many things to worry about. I hope I am not being over-concerned by the appearance of Beatrice Mavor, but I clearly remember the trial. I saw the looks that passed between her and the man in the dock as she was about to give evidence, of complicity and lust; and the look of triumph at the end of her testimony, when she had bettered the counsel for the prosecution. I did not believe her, but the jury did. There was a recklessness about her. What is she doing here? Why am I worried by her presence? Am I becoming paranoid in my old age?

I telephoned The Anglian Detective Agency when I came back from my walk, and arranged to go over to their headquarters at Dunwich on Monday; what a strange, out-of-the-way place to have a detective agency!

Now I am having second thoughts. Perhaps if I talk to Miss Mavor, and say her face looks familiar, she will be frank and explain why that is. If she does that, I will know she means no harm and I will cancel the meeting on Monday. I'll go to the Club before I eat my supper and see if I can speak to her. Perhaps I will invite her to come back with me and I can offer her a sherry.

We can have a frank discussion. I still have the ability to read and analyse people. I will know if my concerns are justified.

I won't invite her to share my supper. Mrs Hegarty has left me some sandwiches, I can't say I am looking forward to them. She is a good soul, but her cooking is not of the best. She cannot come on Monday as her sister has a hospital appointment in Ipswich and she has promised to go with her. It will be a lonely three days.

Frank closed the diary.

Laurel's eyes were full of tears. 'Poor man, he was dreadfully lonely. What an awful way to die.'

Frank got up. 'I'm not sure what to do. If we take this to Revie, can it be used in evidence? However, if we leave it here, and Beattie returns and leaves with it, we may never see it again.'

'We can't leave it. We'll have to say we found it somewhere else.'

'One way of getting out of it would be to post it to Revie. Would that work?'

'I think you're being very un-Frank like. He needs to know about it, and he needs to get over here and nab Beattie before she scarpers.'

'You're right, romance is affecting my brain.'

'Why do you think she kept the diary? Why didn't she get rid of it?'

'Perhaps it's something to do with the reckless streak the Judge wrote about. I think before we contact Revie, we need to look round a bit more. That smell, it's still lingering. It worries me.'

'Let's look at the other rooms, there'll be another living room for a second person and kitchen and bathroom. Shall I do the bathroom?'

'No, we'll keep together.'

She gave him an old-fashioned look.

'Don't be so sensitive, I've taken on board what you said, I'll allow you to meet danger head on.'

'*Allow* me?'

'Sorry, slip of the tongue.'

'Let's do the bathroom.'

It was in the same sad state as Carlton's; chipped enamel bath, yellowing putty round the tiles, and a cracked mirror over the sink. The medicine cupboard, looking as if it might part from the wall at any moment, contained nothing more sinister than shampoo, soap, talcum powder, mouthwash, and all the other minutiae for keeping clean. A towel hung over the bath; it was damp.

'Right, let's see what the kitchen reveals,' he said.

There was a small central table, cooker, fridge and wall cupboards painted a mustard yellow. 'Frank!' Laurel pointed to the table. On it were tools and a good-sized vice, screwed to the table. 'What on earth does she want these for?'

Frank picked up a hacksaw and carefully ran a gloved finger over the blade. He turned his finger over and showed its greyed surface to Laurel.

'What is it?'

'Metal dust, looks like steel.'

'She's been sawing steel?'

He picked up another tool; a pair of pliers.

'Frank, what are you looking like that for? What's the matter?'

'I'm not sure. Search the rest of the kitchen.' He bent down, and knelt on the tiled floor. 'Is there any paper around?'

She rushed out and came back with a writing pad, tore off a sheet, and passed it to him.

He carefully brushed bits from the floor onto it, and holding the paper gingerly, got up and put it on the table.

'What have you found?'

'More fragments of steel and bits of electric wire.'

'This doesn't make sense.'

'I'm afraid it does. We need to search the cupboards and drawers.' He looked round the room and went to the metal waste bin, and pressed down a pedal. He lifted out the plastic liner and brought it to the table. 'Can you see anything I can tip this lot onto?'

Laurel rummaged in a drawer. 'Tea towels?'

'Just the job.'

Laurel laid out two overlapping white towels, patting them down to make a smooth surface.

Frank carefully tipped the contents out. 'Could you find a fork, or knife, Laurel?'

She opened three drawers before she found the cutlery. 'I feel like a nurse to your surgeon,' she said, passing him a fork.

He started to push aside the contents, bit by bit. Laurel sat down; her eyes focused on the rubbish. There was a crisp packet, plate scrapings, which looked like baked beans and the edges of burnt toast, till receipts, orange peelings, an empty margarine tub. He tensed, and moved something away from the unpleasant-smelling waste.

'What have you found?'

'More wire, a longer piece, and some nails.' He pointed to the twisted coloured strands.

'Was she wiring something? An iron?'

He looked up at her. 'I think she's made a bomb.'

Laurel flinched.

# Chapter Thirty-One

'A bomb!' Laurel gasped. 'You mean all this,' she pointed to the vice and tools, 'has been used to make a bomb? But why would she do that, Frank? How would she know how to make a bomb?'

Frank looked grim; she'd never seen him so worried. 'In the newspaper cutting she was shown as a, shall we say, *friend*, of the man accused of being part of the illegal terrorist group, Retribution. Let's suppose she had associations with the group, perhaps was even a member, she could have learnt how to make bombs then. From what I remember, they made quite primitive bombs, mainly targeting buildings, not people; the group disintegrated, and several of them are still serving prison sentences, but there might be members of a sleeper cell, biding their time.'

This was terrible. 'Who can she want to harm?' She put a hand to her mouth as she thought of someone Beattie had tried to hurt before. 'Frank, you don't think she could be planning to hurt Winifred Underwood, her old headmistress?'

He frowned. 'That incident was quite a few years ago. I would have thought it might be someone in her more recent history, but we can't rule it out.' He looked at her. 'I think we should contact Revie straight away. If I'm right, and Beattie has made a bomb, it isn't here. It's with Beattie and she may be on her way to plant and detonate it.'

'No! But we don't know where she's going!'

'Could you contact Revie, and I'll continue to search the rooms to see if I can find any clue to where she's gone.'

'What will you be looking for?'

He sighed. 'I doubt she'll have left any obvious signs like maps, addresses or sketches with X marks the spot where I'll plant a bomb. I really don't know, Laurel, and we might not find anything, but we must look until Revie takes over.'

She shook her head. 'No, *you* must phone. Go to the nearest house with a light, hopefully they'll have a phone. Revie is more likely to pay attention to you than me. Tell him about Miss Underwood, persuade him to send someone over there, or get her to move to a friend's house. I'll search for clues.'

He nodded. 'Yes, sir.'

She slapped his hand.

'Can you remember Miss Underwood's address?' he asked.

She put her fingers to her temples, concentrated and then told him.

'Thank you, Miss Memory.' At the doorway he turned. 'And what will you do if Miss Mavor comes back?'

She pulled a drawer open, and took out a rolling pin. 'David's not the only one who can use this as a weapon. Her VW engine has a most distinctive sound. I'll hear it if she comes back. I'll be behind the door and I won't have any qualms about banging her on the head.'

'I'll be as quick as I can. It looks as though she's planning on returning, so keep your wits about you. If she's a bomber, she's as ruthless as any of the men we've bumped into these past three years.' Then he was gone, running footsteps gradually disappearing.

She looked around her. She couldn't remember seeing anything that would give them a clue to where Beattie was planning to bomb, but they hadn't been looking for that, they'd been searching for clues to her connection with Judge Hanmer. She needed to search logically, and put any possible evidence on the table. She decided to go back to the bedroom and search it again.

She examined every drawer, surface, flicked open books and magazines, stripped the bed, looked under the mattress, pulled out furniture to make sure nothing was behind them, but there wasn't a map in sight, or anything else.

Next the bathroom. They'd searched there, but she gave it

284

another look over. The unoccupied room, with its stripped bed, showing a saggy and stained mattress, yielded nothing apart from dampness and a mouldy smell.

Why wasn't he back? Perhaps he couldn't find a house with a phone. Back to the kitchen. Where hadn't they looked? Quite a few places. They'd been taken up with the discovery of the vice, tools and Frank's theory Beattie had made a bomb. God, for once she hoped he was wrong.

She systematically searched every drawer and cupboard, removing items to make sure there was nothing underneath cutlery trays, or the paper lining the drawers and shelves. Nothing at all.

She sat down at the table and waited for Frank to return. If he was right, Beattie could be anywhere. She might have detonated the bomb already.

She looked down at the rubbish on the tea towels. She might as well put some of it back in the bin and get rid of the smell of rotten food, leaving just the evidence of bomb-making for the police to examine later. She picked up the fork Frank had used and pushed nails, wire and shards of metal to one side. She shivered, imagining shrapnel exploding into the air as the bomb case shattered, nails piercing soft flesh, gouging deep wounds as they penetrated bodies. The woman was evil. How could she have talked to her, played tennis with her, even drunk tea with her and her dead brother, without sensing the depth of her depravity? She poked at the rubbish with the tines of the fork; the more she sifted through the contents of the bin, the surer she was Frank was right. There was no other explanation.

She pushed a till receipt to one side. Her hand hovered over it. She picked it up. It was from a garage for the sale of petrol. She squinted at the details. A garage in Ipswich. Why did Beattie go there? The address was Cliff Road. She frantically pushed the fork through the rubbish they'd gone through, and found another receipt; it was from a small neighbourhood supermarket, in Duke Street, Ipswich. Why Ipswich? What was there to attract Beattie? She continued her search. Another! A different petrol station. Raeburn Road, Ipswich.

She put the three together. It was difficult to make out the dates they were issued, but it must be at least two different dates; it was unlikely she'd buy two lots of petrol on the same day. She held the receipts up to the kitchen light. Grease marks obscured the dates of two of the receipts, but one date looked like 10 April, three days before the Judge was murdered.

A door opened. She shot up, grabbed the rolling pin and darted behind the kitchen door.

'Laurel, it's me. Don't hit me.'

She lowered her arm. 'Thank God you're back. I think I've found something.'

His cheek was cold as he hugged her close. 'Miracle worker! Show me.'

She put the receipts in front of him and explained their significance. 'Frank, can you remember where any of these roads are in Ipswich?'

He bit his lip. 'Names are familiar. Cliff Road . . . Raeburn Road, I think that's . . . Duke Street, that's near to Neptune Quay. Cliff Road, I think that's the one that's almost a continuation of Duke Street, running south, where the river Orwell widens and deepens.' He blinked rapidly. 'Raeburn Road, that's near Landseer Park. They're all close to the docks.'

'Why on earth would she be interested in that area?'

He gripped her arm. 'When you were with Miss Unsworth, she told you where Beattie started work after her degree in chemistry. Where was it?'

Her eyes widened. 'Why, it was in Felixstowe, my home town. Portman's. What can that have to do with Ipswich docks?'

'That's where Portman's have their chemical plant. They make superphosphates for fertilisers. It's a large site, employs lots of people.'

'You think that's where she plans to bomb? Why?'

'Do we know why she left Portman's?'

'No. Miss Underwood didn't mention that. I'm not sure she knew what Beattie did after Portman's.'

'Supposing something happened there and she still bears a grudge?'

'But she worked at the Felixstowe branch. Could that be where she's gone?'

286

'Those receipts are the only clues we've got, and they point to at least three trips to the dock area. There could be more.'

'What should we do? Had you better tell Revie what we've found? What did he say when you talked to him? I was so excited finding the receipts I haven't asked you.'

'I was lucky, I got through to him quickly. He was won over when I told him about the diary. He's sending someone over to Miss Underwood's.'

'That's a relief.'

'He's put out a call to all mobile units to look out for all VWs similar to Beattie's and hopefully soon they'll have the registration number.'

'Do you think we should stay here in case Beattie comes back?'

'No. I think we'll make for the docks, and ring Revie from the first phone box we come across.'

'Have you enough change?'

Frank rattled his jacket pocket. 'Enough. Right, bag up the evidence, we'll take it with us and the diary. Just in case.'

'Revie could get to the docks before us if you can get through to him.'

Frank grimaced. 'That may not be possible, he may check on Miss Underwood himself.'

'We could leave a message with her, and ask him to ring the station.'

'Come on, let's go. Too many loose ends.'

'Got enough petrol?'

'Bloody hell, Laurel, stop it.'

'I can't, that's the way my mind works, always looking ahead, searching for the problems.'

'Don't forget the hacksaw and wire-cutters.'

'Will we need them?'

'They're evidence, but you never know, they might come in handy.'

Frank revved up his Avenger GT. It was going to be a scary ride. She could tell by his determined mouth and the tense hands positioned on the steering wheel. They skidded out onto The Benthills and Frank took the right-hand turn at speed.

'I'm taking the B1353 to Aldringham, then left until I hit the A1094. That's the quickest way to the A12.'

'Don't forget to stop at a phone box,' she said, as she grabbed the door handle, trying not to slide off the seat.

Frank groaned.

'Do you know what kind of bomb she's made?'

'I think she's made a pipe bomb. It's literally that. Made from a section of steel water pipe filled with explosives. You close the ends with steel or brass caps.'

'But how is it detonated?'

'Usually, a fuse is put into the pipe with wires running from it out through a hole in the side of the pipe, or the capped end. To set it off you might use an electric timer, with wires leading to it, and a battery, or it can be a common fuse you light. My bet would be it would have a timer.'

'But where would she get explosives from?'

'She wouldn't be able to get hold of high explosives, such as TNT, at least I hope not. It'll be any explosive mixture the bomb-builder can find: gunpowder, match heads, or a chlorate mixture. They're all dangerous to build bombs with, as they can go off when they're being packed into the tube. Things like nails, as we saw in the rubbish, or broken glass, can be packed in with the explosive, or alternately in an outer shell.'

She remembered the unexploded phosphorus bomb on Orfordness, triggered by the escaping Hinney, and how Frank had narrowly escaped being blown up or horribly burnt. The thought of a bomb terrified her. She hoped they wouldn't find Beattie Mavor's VW at the docks, or that the police would get there first. Cowardly thoughts, she knew, but the thought of a bomb detonating, killing, or maiming either or both of them, didn't bear thinking about. She wondered if Frank was having the same thoughts. She didn't ask him.

# Chapter Thirty-Two

Beatrice Mavor, dressed in black with her hair tucked into a woollen hat, drove slowly up the A12, in her VW camper van, towards Ipswich. Her throat was tight, her muscles tense, her mind awash with darting thoughts. She was taking a risk doing this, she might be caught, but she didn't think that was likely. Who'd be expecting a provincial factory to be bombed? This would be her last opportunity to pay them back. If she didn't do it now, she'd never be able to have the satisfaction of revenge. When they sacked her, they'd started off a chain reaction. What she'd wanted was a career as a chemist, a position of authority, power, leading a team to scientific discoveries, fame, and recognition. Her achievements would make her parents see her in a new light, no longer second best to Carlton; all he'd achieved was coaching tennis in a second-rate club. They'd robbed her of that. Now they could pay.

The greater risk was the organisation she'd joined and would soon be part of; they'd be appalled by her actions if they found out. Not so much by the number of people she'd kill and maim, and the destruction of the factory, but the fact she had acted on her own, to satisfy her need for revenge. They might reject her, as other organisations and individuals had, or even worse eliminate her, as she knew too much about them. Hopefully, they wouldn't connect explosions in a Suffolk factory with her, although they knew Suffolk was where she was keeping a low profile until she joined them. They would think it was some other organisation, like the IRA, or perhaps Retribution raising its head again.

When she joined them, she would have the power, the influence, and the respect she deserved. They'd contacted her in London, when she'd been at her lowest point. After all she'd done for Retribution; perjured herself, helped them to understand the foibles of different chemicals, shown them how to make explosives from everyday, easily purchasable ingredients. Despite this they'd chucked her out. Their reasons? She was a disruptive influence – she stirred up jealousies. What rubbish. She was glad to leave them. A tinpot terrorist movement, with no greater ambition than to bomb Boots and Woolworths, she sneered. Soon they'd hear on the terrorist grapevine of her daring exploits.

As for that shit, Clive, the fucking leader of Retribution, when Veronica came on the scene he'd dropped Beattie like a hot brick. She was sure the bitch had been the cause of them splitting up. When she and Clive had been a couple, there were no complaints then about her behaviour. Bastards.

The man who'd approached her in London seemed to know her history, both academic and political, from her degree in chemistry, her left-wing radical views, her work for Portman's, her dismissal, the move to Germany, her membership and subsequent falling-out with the Baader-Meinhof group, her return to the United Kingdom and her membership of the terrorist group, Retribution.

He called himself Ali, and over several meetings – the second one ended in his bed – he'd gradually unfolded his real reason for contacting her. Would she be interested in joining a group of like-minded people, based in the Middle East? This was not a political group, they did not have an ideology, they did not target particular nations or religions. This was to be a purely for-profit-based group. This meant they could operate in many countries. But always for money. They needed a chemist and someone with a knowledge of Western terrorist groups and how they operated. They would welcome her involvement. She would find them generous employers. They'd talked through many nights, with pauses for sex, usually long pauses; he was an imaginative and daring lover. She'd thought about his offer carefully. The rewards would be great, but balanced against

290

that was the fact she'd never be able to return home, see her parents. At that point she hadn't known she'd need to get away, she might be arrested for the murders of the Judge, and ... if she stayed. Fear grabbed her insides as she thought of him, her brother ... her mouth filled with acid as she imagined the faces of her parents when they were told she'd killed him. Thank God she'd agreed to join The Ring of Fire.

She stopped at a red light and thought of the three bombs hidden in the coolbox on the right-hand side of the van. She'd made a good job of them, each carefully wrapped in towels, the fuses not yet attached to the wires. They would go off tomorrow morning as the workforce came into the factory. By then she would be driving to Dover to catch a ferry to France, followed by a journey through France to Italy. Ali would meet her at Brindisi, where they would board a ship for the headquarters of The Ring of Fire. Then the work would start. There would be piracy in the sky, newspaper and television coverage would ensure there was panic and fear throughout the world, but especially in the rich Western countries of Europe and the USA. Vast sums would be paid for the release of hostages, or to prevent planes from exploding over crowded cities. She squirmed with excitement at the thought of the power she would have.

# Chapter Thirty-Three

Frank leapt out of the car and yanked open the door of the red telephone box. He dialled Revie's number and pushed as many coins as he had into the slot, each one slowly clanking its way down into the metal box, raising his frustration levels and making his heart beat even faster. He drummed his fist on the top of the box. It was ringing. Come on, you old bastard, pick up the bloody receiver.

'Yes.' Thank God, it was him, sounding tired and grumpy.

'Nick, it's Frank.'

'What do you want? You've given me enough trouble already tonight. No sign of our Miss Mavor at Blythborough. Put the wind up the old headmistress, they tell me. By God, I hope you're wrong and you've sent us on a wild goose chase. Otherwise, Mavor could be anywhere causing mayhem.'

'For God's sake, Nick, shut up. I think we may know where she's headed.' He explained. 'You need to get not just the best officers you've got down to the docks, but also ambulances, fire engines and somehow notify the bomb squad.'

'Whoa! I haven't got the authority to do that – all on a couple of petrol receipts?'

'Nick, you must. She's made pipe bombs. She's got them with her. This is the best clue we've got. Lives are at risk.'

There was silence from the other end of the line.

'Nick, are you there?'

'I'll talk to the Chief Constable. Not sure where he is, I talked to him at home after your last call. He said he was coming to the station. It'll be up to him. It's the best I can do. Where are you?'

Frank slammed the phone down and raced back to the car.

# Chapter Thirty-Four

Beattie swore as she approached another roundabout on the A12, she hated having to slow down, give way to traffic from the right, then carefully accelerate. The distinctive clattering of the VW engine, usually so reassuring, now took on a sinister tone, seeming louder than usual, as if saying to every car and lorry that overtook it on the dual carriageway, 'Look what I'm carrying.' She'd be glad when she'd planted the bombs and was on her journey to freedom and success.

If it hadn't been for that interfering judge, she wouldn't have had to rush this job. She wouldn't have had to . . . she gulped. She mustn't think about what she'd done. He could have gone peacefully. He needn't have gone at all, but he'd given her no option.

That blasted Judge Hanmer. Stupid old goat. She'd seen him staring at her. She'd wondered why. She didn't know who he was, sitting on the terrace of the Club, sipping a drink. She'd noticed he looked at Carlton too. She'd asked Carl his name. He told her he was a retired judge, and he couldn't stand him. Dirty old poof. He'd said his name and she knew why he was staring at her, looking puzzled and worried. She hadn't recognised him without his wig and gown; she wasn't expecting to see him here, in sleepy Suffolk. He knew she was involved with Retribution. His summing-up had been as close to asking the jury to bring in a guilty verdict as he dared. Luckily the jury were not swayed by him. She decided to ignore him. What if he had recognised her? What harm could he do?

Then he'd stopped her at the Club one Friday and asked if she would care to join him for a drink before dinner. There was something he needed to ask her. She was tempted to say no, but if she did would he be suspicious and take some action? She would soon be away from these shores, but not before she'd completed her own task, making people pay for the way they'd treated her. She couldn't afford the Judge to mess it up. If she was forced to, could she do it? She'd never taken a life before. Retribution didn't believe in killing people, they concentrated on causing damage to important constructions and buildings. Lily-livered swine.

She'd made sure no one saw her going into the Judge's house. He'd been old-fashioned courtesy itself. Offered a sherry, which she accepted. Then after he took a few sips of his own drink, he'd politely asked her if they'd ever met before?

She looked puzzled and said she didn't think so, although she'd heard a great deal about him from the people at the Club. She'd laughed and said she didn't move in such high circles as his.

He explained he thought she'd been a witness at one of his trials. She looked puzzled and asked if he was sure?

He rubbed his chin and frowned, as if uncertain. 'I need to check something upstairs,' he said. 'I won't be a minute.'

She waited a few seconds, took a pair of gloves from her pocket, put them on, and silently followed him up the stairs to the first landing. She could hear his footsteps in a room above. She hid in a bedroom, so he wouldn't see her as he came down.

He slowly descended, and when he was in front of her, at the top of the staircase, she gripped his shoulder, swung him round, and punched his face as hard as she could. He staggered, crying out. She grabbed him again, forced him to face the stairs and threw him down them. He screamed as he sailed through the air, sickening cracks as his body ricocheted against the bannisters, until he thudded onto the hall floor and lay silent.

She raced down the stairs, making sure, as she had when she went up, she didn't touch the bannisters or the wall. She knelt down beside him and checked he was dead. No, he was still breathing. Could she risk leaving him? He might not die before someone came.

She didn't know if he was expecting anyone the next day, or even this evening. She'd have to finish him off. But there was bound to be a post-mortem. She hesitated, her mind a whirl. She'd have to do it. She went into the kitchen, grabbed a tea towel and pressed it over his mouth and nose. Hard. He didn't move. After a few minutes all life left him.

She replaced the tea towel where she had found it. What had he gone upstairs to check? Was it something incriminating? She looked at his hands, nothing, the pockets of his jacket, but all she found was a handkerchief. She didn't have time to search upstairs. She retrieved her sherry glass, took it to the kitchen, washed it and wiped it dry with the same tea towel she'd used to kill the Judge. A nice symmetry.

She glanced round the sitting room. Was there anything here that might incriminate her? There was a painting on the easel, which she was tempted to slash with a knife. She pulled down the bureau door. A fountain pen lay beside a black diary. Could he have written anything about her in there? She didn't have time to find out. She must get away. She must establish an alibi, in case the police decided this was not a case of an old man falling down the stairs. She'd take it with her and check through it later.

She took a handkerchief and carefully cleaned all the places she'd touched. She'd made sure they were as few as possible. She could have worn the gloves from the beginning, but even the doddery judge might have suspected something. Then she looked round, and with the diary under her arm, she carefully opened the front door, and stared out into the night. There was no one in sight, and all she could hear were the pounding waves and the rustle of the stems of last year's grasses.

# Chapter Thirty-Five

Laurel caught glimpses of Frank's face in the passing streetlights; his jaw was hard as he concentrated on driving as fast and as safely as he could. As they bypassed Wickham Market it started spitting rain, and the tarmac roads gleamed ahead of them. The windscreen wipers hypnotically moved in slow motion over the windscreen. It would be better if it rained properly, rather than this, she thought, as all the wipers did was smear the screen.

'Try the washer, Frank, I can't see very well,' she said, getting more jittery by the minute. 'I don't know how you can drive so fast with such poor visibility.' To her own ears she sounded naggy.

Water and suds blocked her vision. 'Oh!'

He laughed. 'Satisfied?'

The wipers speeded up, and the screen was clear. If only what lay ahead was as clear. 'What's the plan? I presume you have one?' She turned her head and looked at his profile, one second a dark silhouette, next a green eye gleamed, lit by the lights from the streetlights on the dual carriageway. She'd never desired anyone as much as she did this strange, infuriating man. Why had this had to happen now? She was sure something was going to prevent them from being together. They'd faced danger before, both coming within a whisker of losing their lives. Deep inside her she was dreading what would happen when they got to the docks. She didn't want to lose him. She remembered how she'd felt on Orfordness, when it looked as though he'd been killed by the explosion of a phosphorus bomb. Now she knew he loved her, it would be worse. She couldn't bear the thought.

'We'll cruise round the area looking for Beattie's VW van. It's distinctive, we'd be very unlucky if there was another one like it in the area. If she's still in the van, we'll have to hope she doesn't recognise my car. I don't think she knows what I drive.'

'She'd certainly recognise my Ford Cortina, she's passed remarks about it.'

'Complimentary, I hope?'

'Not really. I must say I do like her camper van.'

'You wouldn't catch me driving one of those, almost as bad as a caravan.'

She glanced at the speedo; it was touching eighty. 'What then, when hopefully we find it?'

'If she's in the van, obviously waiting for a suitable time to go about her business, we'll stay put until she makes her move. Then we'll tackle her before she can do any damage.'

'What about the bombs, Frank? Will it be safe to physically attack her?'

He shrugged. 'Let's hope she's a good bomb-maker, and had planned to set the fuse when she'd positioned the bombs.'

She gulped. 'Any tips? How should we stop her?'

'I can probably take her down myself, Laurel. You can wait in the car, and help me when I've separated her from the bombs.'

Her fear drained away, replaced by love and courage. 'Sorry, Frank, I can't do that. I love you too much. We'll go together.' There, she'd said it.

His left hand left the wheel and caressed her face, the car veered left as well. He pulled it back in a straight line. 'Sorry about that. I might as well tell you, I'm torn between speeding on, or stopping in the nearest lay-by and ravishing you.'

She threw back her head and laughed.

'I'm serious.'

298

# Chapter Thirty-Six

Beattie's shoulders were hunched with tension as she continued the journey to the Ipswich docks. The A12 seemed to stretch out interminably, and driving at such a slow speed, with everyone else shooting past her, was immensely irritating; several times she started to press down on the accelerator in her impatience to get the journey over with.

Too much time to think. Somehow, she knew if Carlton hadn't been born, her life would have been different. Better. Her parents hadn't planned for his conception, he was a surprise. She didn't want a sister or brother. She was the centre of her parents' universe, praised for her prettiness, her cleverness, her facility for all games and sports.

Then along came another baby. A boy. So much more important than a girl. She often heard them talking about all the different opportunities Carlton would have, the possible careers, which university he could go to, how it was important to make provision now, when he was a baby, to set aside a goodly sum of money for his education.

She'd sit and look at him as he slept in his cot. 'Look how Beattie loves him,' one of them would say. She'd heard lots of babies died when they were young from diseases. Perhaps Carlton would die. When others weren't in the nursery she'd pinch him, digging her nails into his flesh. When he cried, she'd shout out, 'Mummy, Carlton's crying again.' Her mother would rush into the nursery and hold him close, rocking him until he stopped crying. She did it once too often, and her mother looked at her suspiciously. 'Why does Carlton only cry when you are in the room, Beatrice?' her mother asked. 'I think you had better stay out of the nursery unless I'm with you.'

She would often creep down the stairs when they thought she was safely tucked into bed and eavesdrop on their conversations. She did that night.

'I found suspicious marks on Carlton. I think Beatrice has been pinching him, deliberately making him cry.'

A horrified noise from her father. 'Surely not, my dear. I think your imagination is running away with itself.'

She heard sounds; a chair pushed back. 'Come and look for yourself, you can see the nail marks.' She fled back to bed.

After that it was difficult to do anything to him, although once, when he was out in the garden in his pram, with the hood up against possible rain, she managed to sneak out. Her mother was in the kitchen, baking. She pulled down the hood, and by the time her mother saw what had happened, Carlton was soaking wet and he developed a chill. From that day on her brother was guarded against her, until he was old and big enough to defend himself.

On another night she heard them talking about her; whether they could afford to send her to a private school, or would the local grammar school be good enough? She seethed with anger. They'd planned the very best education for Carlton. She was as clever, probably cleverer, and good at sports, why shouldn't she go to a good school? In the end she won a scholarship to St Mary's, and that helped her parents to make the decision to send her there.

At first, she'd loved the school; her achievements were praised, her abilities recognised, but there was always someone who took away from her the things she craved most. Always someone to hate and to try and pay back the hurt they'd caused her.

Her jaw, and her grip on the steering wheel, tightened, as she thought how she'd been robbed of a place at Oxbridge. She wanted to go to Cambridge, but she was prepared to accept an Oxford college. She didn't believe it when she was rejected by both. Why? Look how good she was at sports? She'd been sure her prowess in all sports, but especially tennis, would make all the difference. Girls in the year above, who were not as good as her, had got into one of the two universities.

It had to be Miss Underwood. From the first year she knew Miss Underwood didn't like her, all because of that silly girl who broke her arm. So what if I did put a foot out and trip her up? The clumsy oaf should have seen it coming. When she challenged Miss Underwood, she refused to discuss it, or let her see the report she'd written to the two universities. She wished she'd thought of her before. Pity she didn't have time to pay her a visit before she left this shitty country.

# Chapter Thirty-Seven

Frank slowed down as he approached the outskirts of Ipswich; the last thing he wanted was to be pulled up for speeding, with the delays that would cause. He didn't think a traffic cop would buy a story about rushing to the docks to prevent a factory being bombed. They'd probably haul him out of the car and see if he could walk in a straight line.

At the Woodbridge roundabout he turned into Main Road. Laurel had been silent for the last ten minutes. What was she thinking? Her reaction to his offer of tackling Beattie by himself had shot warmth through his heart. He *was* in love for the first time in his life; he'd been thrilled by her refusal to let him go it alone, and even more to hear she loved him. He didn't want to put her in danger, but he didn't see how he could stop her, short of knocking her unconscious, and he wasn't going to do that. She'd never forgive him. Well, she might, but he wasn't going to risk it.

'Are we near the docks?' she asked, her voice calm and measured.

'Not too far.' At the next roundabout, he turned into Heath Road.

'I recognise this part of Ipswich, there's a school to the right. We used to play matches against them, when I was teaching here. Copleston. Good school, and friendly staff,' she said.

'Aren't schools always friendly?'

'Not if we regularly knocked the stuffing out of them.'

'You're a violent woman, Laurel Bowman.'

'You'd better believe it.' She lapsed into silence again.

Heath Road merged into Bixley Road. His stomach tightened.

302

He hoped Revie had got hold of the Chief Constable and twisted his arm. They'd need back-up. He wasn't a bomb expert. He'd learnt fundamentals on a course when he was a detective inspector, but he wouldn't like to have to defuse a bomb. But he might have to. The wire-cutters might come in handy; the best way would be to cut through the wires leading to the battery, assuming that was how she'd constructed it. Supposing there was more than one bomb? He hoped they'd catch her waiting in her van. If she was already on the site, and had planted a bomb before they got to her, things were going to be difficult. He exhaled.

'Having second thoughts?' she asked.

'And third and fourth. I'm trying to visualise all eventualities. Pretty difficult.'

'We don't know what we'll face, but tell me what you're thinking. Don't worry, I won't go into a blue funk. If I know what might be coming it'll help me, and I might be able to add something to the mix.'

Her matter-of-fact logic and calmness filled him with pride. She was a woman in a million, possibly more. 'OK, this is what I've been mulling over.'

# Chapter Thirty-Eight

Beattie sighed with relief as she turned into Nacton Road. Not far to go now. She'd chosen a spot where she could safely park until the streets were completely deserted, and she could get into the factory. A few more hours, then off she'd go, mission accomplished. She gloated as she thought how much she'd enjoy hearing on her radio about the bombings, and better still, hopefully see some of the damage she'd done on TV. She'd have to stop herself from boasting of her work. She'd want everyone to know how clever, brave and accomplished she was. She frowned; she hadn't thought of that before. When she joined The Ring of Fire and began her work with them, people at home would never know of her triumphs, her standing in the organisation. Would she ever have a special name attached to her? Like Carlos the Jackal. How she'd love to be feared; to see terror in the hostages faces, as they recognised who she was, and what that meant. Their resolve would crumble, and they would whimper and plead for their lives. Then the money would roll in. But if it didn't, what then? If the ransoms weren't paid, they must be killed, so any future hostages and their nations would know for certain if they didn't cooperate, it would be death.

She'd killed twice. The Judge's death didn't bother her at all. She was surprised at her own reaction, or non-reaction. No, that wasn't true. She'd enjoyed the power of taking a life, even if it had been that of a feeble old man. It hadn't been physically challenging.

But Carlton. She hadn't wanted to do it, but it was his fault. He would insist on acting properly, telling the police they weren't together when the Judge was murdered. She tried to make him see it wouldn't help to go to the police. When he said he was going to talk it over with Laurel Bowman, she had to stop him.

They were sitting in his room, when he said, 'Beattie, I shouldn't have let you persuade me to give you an alibi for the time the Judge was murdered.'

'But, Carlton, I gave you an alibi as well. If you tell them we weren't together, you may come under suspicion; after all, you're the stronger candidate for his murder, everyone knows you hated him.'

He stared at her. 'I didn't kill him. I didn't like him, but you know *I* wouldn't hurt anyone.'

She hadn't liked the emphasis on the I; he obviously remembered some of the things she'd done to him when he was a child.

'Another thing, Beattie, what are you doing in your rooms?'

'What do you mean?'

'I went in there yesterday to see if you had any new tennis balls, the door wasn't locked. Why have you got all those tools in the kitchen? What are you up to?'

She laughed. 'Whatever do you mean? I'm only fixing some old tennis racquets. Re-stringing them, mending the frames in some cases.'

He looked at her dubiously.

'What time are you meeting Laurel?'

'Eight thirty.'

'Then you've plenty of time for a bite to eat and some tea. What would you like? Poached eggs on toast?' She ruffled his hair. 'Go ahead and tell her if it will make you feel happier. Both of us have nothing to fear.'

He looked relieved. 'Do you mean that, Beattie? I've been worried about telling a lie, but thank you for making up. I hate it when we quarrel.'

'Shall I make us something to eat?'

He smiled. 'Thanks, it's a long time until eight thirty, but I don't fancy poached eggs. I thought I might buy Laurel some supper, so I don't want much.'

'Where are you meeting her?'

'The Cross Keys.'

'I tell you what, I'll pop back to my room, I think I've got some chocolate cake. Would you like that?'

His eyes lit up. He was her little brother again. Sometimes, not very often, during his childhood, she'd felt warm towards him. It was when he'd said something nice to her: how she was terrific at tennis, could she teach him how to serve properly, he wished he could be as good as her. Then she would buy him a chocolate bar and his eyes would light up. Just as they were doing now.

'I won't be long. Put the kettle on.'

In her room she took the bottle of Rohypnol from its hiding place at the top of her wardrobe; a souvenir from her days with Baader-Meinhof. She hoped it hadn't gone off and lost its potency. She put it into her jacket pocket. In the kitchen, she opened a cake tin and placed two slices of chocolate cake on a plate.

In his room, Carlton was putting some teabags into a brown teapot.

'Here I am. This looks good, doesn't it?' She waved the plate at him. 'You sit down, I'll make the tea.' She placed the cake on the table, found some plates and two forks and placed them on the table.

'This looks good, Beattie. Thank you. I'm glad you can see we must tell the police about not having alibis. I feel so much better now.' He gazed at the cake.

'Don't wait for me, Carlton, go ahead, help yourself.'

He did, and forked a piece of cake into his mouth. 'Yummy.'

She poured the tea, added milk, poured some of the Rohypnol into one cup, gave it a good stir and placed it in front of Carlton. He was looking at the other slice of cake.

She laughed. 'Go ahead, have the other piece, I don't feel hungry at the moment.'

He turned to look at her, his sea-green eyes, so like hers, smiling.

Sometimes he looked so young. She moved to him, and stroked his cheek. 'I know you love chocolate cake. Eat it up. But drink some tea first. To wash away the last slice, then the next will taste even better. I don't know what it is, but tea always tastes better when

306

you've had something sweet to eat. I'll pour you another cup as soon as you've finished that one.'

'Thanks, Beattie, I'm glad we're on good terms again.' He swiftly downed the tea in a few big gulps and started on the second slice of cake.

She stood by the sink watching him. She didn't know if she'd given him too much, or too little. She hoped it was enough, she didn't want him to suffer. She sipped her tea.

He put a hand to his head. 'Beattie.'

'Yes, what is it, Carlton?' She moved towards him.

'I feel awful, my head's not working.'

'Not working? What do you mean?'

'I think I've caught something. Or the chocolate cake?'

'Oh, has it made you feel sick? I'm sorry, I shouldn't have encouraged you to eat two slices.'

'I don't know. Help me, Beattie.'

She moved her chair and sat beside him. 'I think you'd be better on the bed. Let me help you.'

'Lie down, yes, I need to lie down.'

'That's right. I'll help you into your pyjamas. Do you remember, I sometimes did that when you were little?' Only if her mother was supervising.

'No. I've got to meet Laurel – I mustn't undress.'

'You'll be comfier if you do. You've got plenty of time to get ready to go out. You'll want to change before you see her, won't you?'

He nodded and let her help him.

It took all her strength and flexibility to get his clothes off and the pyjamas on. She pulled back the top sheet and blanket, propped him up on a chair near the bed, then, putting her hands under his armpits, she managed to drag him onto the bed, heave his legs up from the floor, and cover him up.

'There you are, Carlton. Have a sleep; you'll feel better soon.'

He tried to lift his head; it flopped back onto the pillow. 'Laurel . . . I'm meeting Laurel.'

'Not until eight thirty. I'll wake you in time, don't worry.'

'Feel so ill.'

'If you can't make it, I'll drive there and tell her what's happened.'

He managed to get a hand above the sheets and touched hers. 'Thank you, Beattie . . .'

He didn't utter another word, his eyelids closed, and his breath became ragged.

She sat looking at him. Had she given him enough? If she left him, would he recover? Suppose someone found him and got him to hospital? She grimaced. She'd have to smother him, then place the bottle by the side of his bed. In the morning, she'd act as normal – she had a lesson booked for ten. Carlton had one at half ten. When he didn't turn up, either someone would look for him, or they'd ask her where he was. Then they'd find him.

She'd say he was worried about life; he was a homosexual and couldn't bear living a life of sin. Something like that. It wouldn't matter if the police became suspicious; by then she'd be gone. Gone for good.

She looked at her watch. Half an hour. His breathing was shallow, but seemed steady. She went to her room and took a pillow from her bed, hesitated, then from the kitchen picked up one of the surplus sections of steel piping she'd cut to make the bombs.

She turned him on his back, he was snoring, saliva dribbling down his chin. She swallowed hard. It was more difficult doing it in cold blood. The Judge had enraged her, she despised him for his courtesy, his easy manners, his sharp intelligence, and his aging body. He meant nothing to her. Carlton was different. He was a male version of herself, but without her brains and ambition. She hesitated. Then shook her head vigorously. She'd never see him again, anyway. It was his own fault for being stupid. She carefully placed the pillow over his mouth and nostrils. She mustn't leave any marks. As gently as possible she must stem his breath, leaving as little evidence of a suffocation as she could. Hoping the post mortem would not show signs he hadn't killed himself.

She kept her hands over the pillow, pressing down with a firm but gentle pressure.

He started to cough, she pressed harder. His hands shot up above the covers, scrabbling, he made gurgling noises as he tried to push the pillow away. She grimaced, and pushed down hard. 'Die, you bastard, die.'

His hands reached out and grabbed her shoulders, pushing her away. His right hand circled her neck, squeezing hard. She hadn't given him enough. Panic ran through her. She abandoned the pillow and gripped his wrist, pulling it from her throat.

His face was bluish, his eyes open, terror in those sea-green eyes. 'Beattie!' he screeched.

She picked up the steel pipe from the table.

He was trying to get out of bed, the tangle of clothes preventing him.

He leant over the bed, head down, retching.

She raised her arm, her face screwed up in concentration, and hit him as viciously as she would put away a volley at the net. Again, and again. At the base of the skull. Where the vital areas of the brain lived. He collapsed, dragging the sheet and blankets with him.

She grabbed a tea towel and wrapped it round his head to prevent the blood spreading, but some had already sprayed onto the pillow and sheets.

'God damn you, Carlton,' she hissed. 'Now what do I do?'

She sank back onto the chair. He was dead. No doubt about that. But she'd have to think what to do for the best. She bit her lip. Think. Think. She needed to buy time. First get rid of his body. Where? There was only one place – the sea.

Her heart was racing. This was going to be dangerous. She was strong, but he was tall, and though slim, he must weigh thirteen stone. She gulped. It was risky. Could she leave him here? She looked at his head, blood seeping through the towel. She got up and found another towel and wrapped it over the first.

She'd wait until she was sure there was no one about. She dragged his body from the bed, and dumped him on the floor, his flesh still warm. She ripped off the sheet and removed the pillowcase. The pillow itself was stained, but if she replaced the pillowcase . . . She filled the sink in the bathroom with cold water and put the pillowcase and the parts of the sheet stained with blood, into the water. She shook her head. She wasn't thinking clearly.

What about Laurel Bowman? How long would she wait at the pub? Would she give up and go home? Supposing she decided to come here, looking for Carlton? She groaned. She looked at her watch. How long would she give him? Half an hour? An hour? It would only take her a few minutes to drive here from Aldeburgh. She must hurry. Just in case.

She scrubbed the bedclothes, then wrung them out as best she could, and spread them over the chairs in front of the small electric fire. It would have to do. She'd deal with the blood-soaked towels when she came back.

She went to the front door and slowly opened it, and stepped outside. The Club was in darkness. She walked by the side of the building and peered round the corner up and down The Benthills. There was no one to be seen. She'd have to risk it. She cursed him. He'd made her kill him. Why hadn't he gone quietly, without pain, never to know his sister had committed fratricide? It was almost as bad as killing your mother or father; if she was found out she would be reviled. What would the hierarchy of The Ring of Fire think? Even criminals had their own codes of conduct. The thought of a life in prison horrified her. Enough thinking. Let's get it done.

She went back, leaving every door wide open. She turned him onto his back, and after taking a deep breath, she planted her feet squarely on each side of his head, bent down, grasped him under the arms and heaved, dragging him towards the door. She moved as quickly as she could, over the road, then down the beach, his bare heels bouncing off the pebbles. When she felt safe, she stopped, exhausted, and took several deep breaths.

Voices. She crouched down over Carlton's body, looking back towards The Benthills. In the fading light, a couple were walking their dog, chatting, strolling northwards. She froze with terror. The dog wasn't on a lead. It was running backwards and forwards, now in front, now behind the couple, stopping to sniff at a clump of grass, lifting its leg against sea holly. It stopped, raised its head, looking towards her. Was it scenting dead flesh? What should she do if it came towards her? Sweat was running down her back, as she tried not to breathe. The dog started to slowly approach, as though it was unsure of what was ahead of it. Go back, she wanted to scream. A low growl made her intestines contract.

'Rover,' a woman shouted. 'Come here!'

Rover stood his ground, giving another menacing growl.

'What is the matter with that dog? Rover. Come here AT ONCE.'

With a curl of his lip and a guttural sound, Rover reluctantly turned tail and rejoined his owners.

Beattie collapsed over Carlton's body, swallowing hard to stop herself being sick. She lay there, at first unable to move, then slowly managed to control her shaking body. She clenched her hands, driving fingernails into palms, the pain distracting her from the terror still coursing through her body. She staggered up and continued dragging him until she was at the place where water met sand and gravel.

Was the tide going out? She tried to clear her addled brain; yes, each wave retreated a little more than the last. No, it was coming in. His body would be washed away. It was the only piece of luck she'd had so far. By the time his body floated to the surface she would be long gone.

She dragged him as far as she could into the sea; waiting between waves to move him a little farther down the beach. She'd need to dry herself off, then she must make the bed with the damp sheets and try and establish an alibi. She'd go to the Dolphin; she often went there of an evening. She'd make sure she was seen. Talk to the landlady.

She stood looking at his body, the waters washing over him, claiming Carlton for themselves. A wave of fear washed over her mind, like the one caressing Carlton's body. She was a murderer. A woman who'd killed two men.

# Chapter Thirty-Nine

Laurel waited for Frank to tell her how they would try and stop Beattie Mavor from planting the bomb. He was chewing his lip, possibly trying to put his thoughts in order. She knew how his mind worked; off-the-cuff remarks as quick and as sharp as lightning, but when there was a problem he didn't know the answer to, he'd retreat to his cottage, with paper, coloured biros and several pots of coffee. Slowly and logically, he'd review all the evidence and come to a conclusion. He didn't have time for that now. She needed him to tell her his newly minted, and possibly incorrect, thoughts. He wouldn't like that – a perfectionist?

She hoped he wouldn't expect perfection from her; especially when it came to making love. It was a few years since she'd had sex, although it had been a close-run thing with Oliver. She was sure Frank had more practice recently. Stop this, she thought. There are more serious matters to deal with. Good job he didn't know what she was thinking.

'Stop me if you disagree, or want to add anything,' he said. 'First, we have to find Beattie's van. I propose when we come to the end of the Felixstowe Road, we go up Bishop's Hill, then into Fore Street, turn left into Duke Street, continue down Cliff Road and then find a place to park.'

'You've still got a good knowledge of Ipswich, Frank. I know my way around the centre, and where the different secondary schools are, but I don't remember the names of many roads.'

'When I was stationed here, we covered a wide area. It isn't going to be easy finding her van, we'll do a logical search, no good driving around like headless chickens. I'm presuming she'll park reasonably close to the factory. She's got to carry the bomb, or bombs – I'm not sure how she'll do that, but she'll have to conceal them. She'll also need to cut her way through the perimeter fence. If we find the van and she isn't in it, we'll search the perimeter and look for a forced entry.'

She groaned. 'This is going to take too long.'

He glanced at her. 'So, how would you make it quicker?' he said.

'I don't know – I can't. It's the thought we have to tackle her and she's got live bombs. Would it be better if we waited by the fence where she'd got in, and nab her on the way out? At least we wouldn't be blown up.'

'Good reasoning.'

'Does that mean you agree?'

'Not necessarily. I'd prefer to catch her before she plants it. It would be difficult and dangerous for anyone, including the experts, to find the bomb and safely defuse it. Let's see how it goes, we'll have to modify our plans as we go along.'

She hadn't won that one. A few days ago, would she have come up with that thought? Probably not. Does love make you a coward?

'This is Duke Street, I'll turn left, we can park somewhere near Holywell Park.'

She remembered this area; she and Simon, her ex-fiancé, had sometimes walked round here; she'd liked the names of various places: Flint Wharf, the Old Customs House, Wherry Quay, Neptune Quay. It seemed a lifetime ago, and she was a different person now.

Frank parked in Cliff Lane, south of the park. He turned and switched on the inside light.

She blinked. 'She might see us.'

'Don't worry, she'll be parked nearer the site. The factory is at Cliff Quay. Could you open the passenger box? I think there's some paper and biros in there.'

He was right. 'Are you sure you weren't a boy scout?' She passed them to him.

'I'll make a rough sketch of the area from what I remember. Chuck me a map, I can lean on that.'

She found the thickest map in the passenger door well.

He leant towards her. 'We're here, this is the beginning of Cliff Road. Instead of parking and exploring by foot, I think we need to keep driving. I suggest we go down Landseer Road, then turn right into Greenwich Road. If we don't find her, we explore some of the roads coming off that one, and then if we have no joy, turn right onto the road leading to Cliff Quay, until we come to the factory.'

'And then?'

'Let's assume we find the van. We drive past it trying to see if there's anyone inside. If there is we keep driving, park out of sight and approach by foot, wait for her to get out of the van, and attack before she can remove the bomb.'

'Sounds good. If she isn't in the van?'

'We drive back, park nearby, look inside the van for clues, then go directly to the factory and try and find where she's gained entry. Take the wire-cutters with us, and if needed, cut our way in.'

'Is it a big site? I've never been there.'

'Unfortunately, yes.'

She blew out a stream of air.

'I just hope we get some back-up. I'm sure Revie won't leave us in the lurch, but if the boss has cold feet, we could be on our own right the way through this.'

She squeezed his arm. 'We'll manage. We always have before.'

He pulled her to him and kissed her. 'Time for a snog?'

She laughed and punched his arm. 'Drive!'

He drove slowly down Landseer Road. 'If the cops see me, they'll nick me for driving too slowly, say I was on the pick-up.'

'This isn't a red-light area, is it?'

'Not that I know of.'

'It's certainly deserted.'

'Not much going on once the factories and businesses have finished for the day, especially on a Friday night, when everyone will be off for a night on the town.'

There was no sign of the blue and white VW van.

He turned into Greenwich Road; she gripped his arm. 'There.' She pointed up a side road. Between streetlights was a blue and white camper van. It was in darkness.

'I'll drive past, you try and see if she's in it.'

He drove the Avenger as close as possible to the van, without actually scraping it. She stared through the windows. She couldn't see anyone inside.

'Well?'

'No one as far as I can see, but she might have dodged down when she heard a car coming.'

'She's well ahead of us, Laurel. We'll go back and make sure she's gone.' He did a five-point turn, and drew up behind the van. He leapt out, ran up to it, and pulled at the driver's door handle.

She rushed after him.

He turned back. 'She's gone. I wish we had a torch, I can't see much inside the van.'

'I don't think we came well prepared.'

'You can say that again. Right, let's get on with the next part of the plan. We'll leave the car here.' He got the wire-cutters from the back of the car where he'd chucked them. Then pulled the release for the boot. 'Let's see what we've got in here.'

He lifted a tartan blanket, and rooted around in the interior of the boot. The light was poor, she couldn't see what was in it. He passed her a spanner. She whacked it against her hand. 'Haven't you got a bigger one?'

'As the actress said to the bishop,' he muttered.

She had to admire his gall; never let a terrible situation get in the way of a double entendre.

'Not much here in the way of weapons, I'm afraid.' He waved a tool for unscrewing wheel nuts. 'I'll take this, you'll have to make do with the wee little spanner. Right, let's go.'

He banged down the lid of the boot, locked the car and they ran off towards the factory.

# Chapter Forty

Beattie gently put down the rucksack by the side of the factory fence, and shone the beam of her torch onto her wristwatch. One fifteen. She'd made a map of the area she wanted to target, and this was the nearest point to it.

Although it was a vast site, there was only one night watchman, and she knew from her surveillance of the factory he was regular in his times of checking the area. He walked round from midnight to roughly one o'clock, then retreated inside the administration block until three.

The hours she had spent in her van waiting until she'd have a safe run had been mind-numbing. Every minute she expected someone to knock on the window and ask her what she was doing parked here at this time of the night. It had actually happened when she was surveying the site. *And* it had been a police car that had stopped to check the van. She'd said she was on her way to her parents' in Kent and had stopped because she was tired and was afraid of falling asleep at the wheel; they'd moved her on. But this time she was carrying three pipe bombs and the thought that the van might be searched was terrifying.

She took the wire-cutters from the rucksack, cut a hole in the wire near the ground, large enough for her to get through, and pushed back the square of wire fencing. She squeezed through to the other side, pulling the rucksack after her. Then she pressed back the wire.

She heaved the rucksack onto her shoulders; it seemed heavier every time she shouldered it. She walked gingerly, shining the light of her torch onto the ground in front of her. She couldn't afford to trip; she hadn't set the fuses, but she'd learnt how fragile explosives can be, and the thought of crashing to the ground with three bombs strapped to her was sending rivulets of sweat down her back. She wiped a hand over her forehead, but she couldn't deal with the trickle running down her backbone.

She reached her targets; they loomed over the River Orwell like beasts from *The War of the Worlds*. At the first one she carefully slipped the rucksack from her shoulders and lowered it to the ground. She knelt beside it, fumbling with the straps and buckles to open it. She swallowed hard, and rubbed wet palms against her trousers. She carefully took out the first bomb, unwrapped it from its towel covering, and checked it over. Its steel case was as cold as death. Each bomb was made of three lengths of steel tubing strapped together, the tubing filled with explosives and nails. The fuse needed to be connected to the battery and timer which were taped to the outside of the bomb; she'd do that once she'd fixed the bomb in place.

She removed the other two bombs from the rucksack and gently placed them on the ground. She wrapped the first bomb up again and put it back into the rucksack, with the torch. She gently eased the rucksack onto her shoulders, her heart thudding, her breathing restricted. For the first time she thought: Why am I doing this? I could be blown to pieces. No. She remembered all the people who'd messed up her life: her parents, the girls and staff at St Mary's, the people she'd worked with, the groups who'd rejected her. This was for all of them, but especially for the chemical company who'd blighted her life. Dismissing her had thrown her into the arms of radicals. There was no escaping them now. Would there be more rejection? From members of The Ring of Fire?

What she wanted was to be recognised. To be seen as a leader, an innovator. To be respected. To be the dominant female. To belong to the dominant male of the group. That had briefly been her position in Retribution. The lover of the leader. She'd sat on his right-hand side at meetings. The rest of the group had looked up to her, deferred to her. She'd loved the feeling of power, and the look of envy in the eyes of the other women.

It had been short-lived. A new member, younger, sure of herself, charming to the others, had replaced her. When she'd made a scene, throwing wine over her rival, she'd been ostracised. Then more flare-ups and she'd been told to leave, with the threat that if she informed on them, she would be hunted down and eliminated. If they went down, so would she.

Anger and hate filled her mind. Time for her own retribution.

# Chapter Forty-One

As they approached the factory, Frank realised the impossibility of their task. The site covered several acres. Beattie could be anywhere.

'Frank, what do you know about the factory? All I know is it makes agricultural fertilisers,' Laurel said, as she ran by his side.

'Tell you when we get there.' She had more puff than he did. He wondered if the factory bosses had heeded the warnings for the need for greater security because of the actions of the IRA? Revie would be aware of that. But the IRA weren't active in this part of the UK as, apart from the nearby nuclear station, there were no obvious targets in this area. No big populous cities, where a bomb could cause maximum damage. Perhaps the factory owners hadn't thought it necessary to beef up their security.

They reached the perimeter fence. It hadn't been constructed to withstand a determined saboteur; although ten feet high, it could easily be cut through with a good pair of wire-cutters. He crouched down and signalled to Laurel to join him; she wasn't breathing heavily. He peered at his wristwatch; the luminous figures showed it was one thirty-five.

'We'll start at this end and work our way round, pressing against the fence; she probably pushed it back and the opening may not be obvious,' he whispered.

'Where do you think she'll make for?'

She could be anywhere. He racked his brains for any scraps of information. 'It's a processing plant, making superphosphates for the agricultural industry. I know they own part of the Somerset Levels and extract peat from it. It's shipped here and they make Growbags for tomatoes and other plants.'

'Any idea how they make the phosphates?'

'I've only a sketchy knowledge. The quay here has deep water, so good-sized ships can dock; they bring in minerals rich in phosphate. It isn't soluble in its raw state, they use a chemical process to turn it into soluble superphosphates. Something like that.'

'Are dangerous chemicals produced? That might be where she's headed. If she blew up whatever they're contained in, that would be awful.'

Frank blew out a stream of air. 'Are you trying to frighten me? I know they make sulphuric acid and use it to dissolve the raw rocks. I would imagine there'd be high security in those plants. We're talking dangerous stuff. I'm not sure she'd risk that. But I could be wrong; if the bomb is on a timer, she wouldn't run much risk of getting acid burns.'

Laurel shivered.

'Cold?'

'No, it's the thought of acid bursting out of whatever its kept in.'

'Let's start searching the fence. If we think about what might happen, we'll lose the will to live.' He stood up. 'We'll work together. I'll examine the fence, you follow behind checking I haven't missed anything. I'll go slowly.'

If only they had a torch. There was some lighting on the site, even at this time of night, but none near this part of the perimeter fence. He pressed on the wire at ground level, working up to about five feet, as he couldn't see she'd cut any higher, that wouldn't make sense.

At the third fence section the wire gave way under his hand. 'Found it,' he whispered.

Laurel pressed against him, her breath hot and sweet on his face. 'Jolly good.'

She sounded like a PE teacher remarking on a goal scored in a hockey match. He put an arm round her shoulder. 'That's what I like, a keep calm and carry on foiling the bomber approach.'

'Let's get in.'

'Yes, ma'am.' He pushed the wire back and crawled into the site, Laurel following him.

'Where now?'

'I presume, since she obviously did some surveillance of the site, she knows where she's going to plant the bomb.'

Laurel gripped his arm. 'Then she could be near here?'

'Correct. We're close to the river and the docks. There may be ships anchored waiting to have their cargo taken off. We'll try that area first.'

The new crescent moon and a sky full of stars gave enough light to cast coal-black shadows. Laurel tripped and stumbled, crashing down onto her knees. He put an arm round her. 'OK?'

'Bashed my right knee. Shit, it hurts. Stupid fool.'

'Me or you?'

She pushed him away. 'I'm all right. Let me go.'

'For once you're going to do as I say.'

'I'm not leaving.'

'Did I ask you to? We'll support each other until we get to a place with some lighting. I'm as likely as you to take a fall, there's quite a lot of debris around.'

'I agree.'

'Right, let's make towards the river.'

They walked along concrete roads, grey shapes looming up out of the darkness – huge round metal containers. What where they storing? He pulled Laurel tighter to him as he imagined a terrible explosion, acid pouring towards them, engulfing them in a wave of corrosive fluid. They stopped and listened. The wind rattled overhead wires, making a strange melody, like a song from a distant planet. No sign of Beattie.

They moved past white-painted containers, reflecting what light there was. Crossing a road there were more buildings, but there didn't seem to be any order. There were huge sheds, small sheds, more round containers – it was a jumble, as if the factory had grown like Topsy.

'There doesn't seem to be any logic,' Laurel whispered.

'I think that's because there's been a factory here since the thirties, and it's expanded out of all proportion.'

'Doesn't help us.'

The river came into view, running dark and deep, a few lights from Wherestead Road glowed from the opposite bank. A wide concrete road ran the length of the dock area, with sporadic streetlights shedding pools of yellow. Near to the river, overhanging the deep water, like a row of praying mantis, were a multiplicity of cranes, each one supported by four giant legs, the crisscrossing steel girders making them seem like the internal structure of the bones of a giant bird. Each crane had two platforms, the first had only a shallow ridge for an edge, the second had a safety fence round a cabin. On the land side of the concrete road were more buildings, including a tall tower block with a pitched roof.

'I hadn't realised the factory was so huge. There's a ship moored near the third crane,' Laurel whispered.

Frank's muscles tightened. 'Look.' He pointed.

Laurel stiffened.

Halfway up one of the giant legs of the first crane, the outline of a figure, looking like a giant beetle. She was climbing slowly towards the first platform, her hand stretching out for the next girder.

Frank pulled Laurel down. 'It's her,' he whispered in her ear. 'Look at the base of the crane – there's more than one bomb.'

'What do we do?'

'Approach silently. She'll be too involved getting to the platform to see us. We'll check if the other bombs are armed. If not, you move them, hide them out of her sight.'

'What are you going to do?'

'I'll climb up after her. Try to stop her arming the bomb she must have in her rucksack.'

Her already rock-hard arm hardened a tad more. 'OK. What if she comes down and you don't?'

'Take her. Then get away as far as you can.'

There was no reply.

'Don't climb up after me. That's an order. Do you understand?'

'I understand.'

He wasn't sure she'd obey; in fact, he was damned sure she wouldn't. He gave her a bear hug. 'Do as you're told. Right, creep forward on your belly.'

He moved as fast as he could, the concrete scraping at his elbows and knees as he wriggled towards the crane. Laurel's breath was to his right. He kept glancing up, noting Beattie's slow progress. She had bottle, climbing a crane with a bomb strapped to her back. What if she lost her grip, and tumbled backwards, hit the concrete road and disappeared in the resulting explosion? If that was going to happen, he hoped it would be before they got into range.

At the base of one of the legs were two packages wrapped in towels. He unwrapped one. There were three pipe bombs strapped together. 'They're not armed. Safe to move, but be careful.' He pulled off his jacket.

She nodded, and waved the spanner in front of him. He swapped it for the wheel-nut changer and tucked it into his trouser belt. Better choice of weapon. Good thinking, Laurel. He moved to the base of the leg and looked up. Beattie hadn't reached the platform. He started climbing.

# Chapter Forty-Two

Laurel grimaced as she carefully picked up the bomb nearest to her, slowly walked to the other side of the road and placed it gently on the ground, round the corner of the nearest building. She ran back towards the crane. Beattie had disappeared. Frank was nearing the first platform. She took the second bomb and hid it in the same place. She knew she should separate them, but she needed to get back to see what was happening.

She stood back to get a better view. Frank had one hand on the platform's edge. Was Beattie climbing to the second platform? The machinery for operating the crane must be there, in the hut. Or was she already arming the bomb?

A scream of rage from above. She stepped further back, hands to her face, horror running through her veins. Looming above Frank was a black figure, its arms raised, fists clenched, shaking the air – it was Beattie.

'You bastard,' she shouted. She kicked and stamped on Frank's hands. 'Die. Die,' she howled.

Laurel rushed to the nearest girder and started to climb. Pulling herself up, arm over arm, feet searching for footholds. She reached out for the next girder. Her heart jumped as she missed, she was swinging by one hand, her body crashing into metal. She managed to catch hold of another girder, and for a moment she clung to it, her heart racing, deep breaths racking her body. She gritted her teeth and continued to climb.

'Fuck you!' screamed Beattie.

No! There was a sickening cry. A body tumbled towards her. He was trying to reach out his arms, clutching wildly at thin air. She hooked a foot round a girder, gripping another with her left hand and stretched out as far as she could. She snatched at him as he passed, grasping a handful of clothing. Trying to hold on, the weight of his body wrenching her shoulder. She silently screamed. He was too heavy. She couldn't hold him. The material ripped from her grasp. He plummeted through the air, now in a ball shape, and landed with a sickening crash on the concrete below.

She scrambled down, jumped the last five feet, and rushed to him. He was lying silent, in the foetal position, arms round his head. Tears of fear and anger clouded her vision. 'Frank. Frank,' she implored, as she knelt beside him. Had she lost him? Was he dead? All thoughts of Beattie and the bomb disappeared from her mind. Her insides were knotted, her heart racing, her mind flooded with grief. Her body seemed to be dissolving into a pool of death.

She tried to pull her mind back from the pit it was in. Deep breaths, deep breaths, she told herself. Help him, you idiot. Try to find a pulse. Please God, she prayed, don't let him be dead. She slid a hand under an arm, touching the skin of his neck. It was hot.

A groan.

She leant close. 'Frank. Frank.' He was alive. Joy swept through her.

'I'm OK. Think I've broken my left arm,' he croaked.

She rained kisses on his face.

'You saved me – broke my fall.'

Everything was wonderful. He was alive. Then the realisation. He could have died. She'd tried to kill him. Anger. In the distance, sirens, the whining of police cars.

'Revie's coming,' she said.

'About bloody time,' he whispered.

She looked above. No sign of Beattie. Laurel got up. Beattie would be arming the bomb. She went back to Frank and ran her hand round Frank's waist until she found the spanner, still wedged tight into his belt. That must have hurt, she thought, as she pulled it free, and tucked it into her waistband. He groaned. Normally there'd be a suggestive comment at her behaviour but all she got was, 'No, Laurel. Stay here.' She kissed him. He groaned again as he tried to grab hold of her.

She started to climb, full of cold anger. This was personal. She'd never climbed so quickly, or so recklessly, but it seemed to take forever before she reached the top; she pushed her upper body above the narrow rim of the platform. Beattie was crouched in the centre, a torch on the floor, shining on whatever she was doing.

Gripping the edge of the platform, she levered one leg, then the other, over the edge. She pushed with her arms, until she was upright. Beattie still had her back to her. She hadn't heard. She must eliminate her before she primed the bomb. How would she know if the bomb was live? If the wires were unconnected, she was in time. If they were attached? She'd deal with that if need be.

She needed a silent, decisive attack. No Miss Nice Bowman. She took the spanner from her waistband and wished it were heavier. She might need several blows to knock her out. Moving slowly and carefully, with her arm raised, she crept towards Beattie.

'For fuck's sake,' Beattie muttered.

Hopefully she was having trouble arming the bomb. Laurel was within striking distance. She steeled herself, biting her lip, summoning up courage to hit an unprotected head. Crack! Shit! She'd trodden on something.

Beattie's back went rigid. Clank. Something dropped from her hand. As Laurel brought down the spanner, she turned her head and Laurel hit her square in the face.

Beattie screamed and fell backwards towards the bomb. Laurel dropped the spanner and caught hold of her clothes, pulling her forward. Beattie grabbed one of Laurel's legs and pulled. Laurel fell backwards, thumping onto the platform floor. Beattie scrabbled on top of her. Laurel gasped with pain. Beattie grasped Laurel's neck, blood from her nose dripping into Laurel's mouth. She spat it back at her.

'You fucking bitch. I'll kill you,' Beattie grunted, spitting out a tooth.

'Never!' she hissed back.

She grasped Beattie's wrists, trying to lever her hands from her throat. They were almost an equal match. She pulled, Beattie squeezed, digging her thumbs deep. Laurel channelled her anger into a white-hot rage. This woman was not going to win. This was for the Judge, for Carlton and most of all for Frank.

She pulled up her knees and jerked them up into Beattie's midriff. Ouf! Beattie's grip loosened. Laurel levered up her knees again until they were tight against her body, the soles of her shoes finding Beattie's abdomen. She put every ounce of energy and muscle power into an explosive push with her legs. Beattie shot backwards, her arms in the air. She staggered towards the edge of the platform.

Laurel jumped up and lurched after her. Beattie's foot caught the edge of the platform. Laurel reached out, and tried to grab her. Beattie tottered backwards, out of reach, her hands scrabbling the air, and with a terrible scream she disappeared over the edge. There was a thud and a crack as flesh and bone met concrete.

Laurel staggered to the edge. There was a dark shape on the ground, arms and legs splayed, only a few yards from Frank. He was sitting up, grasping his left arm with his right. She was shaking, it felt as if every muscle in her body was vibrating. She took an enormous breath and tried to bring her quivering body under control. She steeled herself, put a leg over the edge of the platform and climbed down to Frank.

She went to him, and kissed him so hard, he groaned.

'I would have given you a round of applause, but I couldn't put my hands together.'

'I'm going to move you away from here. I don't know if she'd armed the bomb. I didn't stop to look.'

'Help me up. I can walk.'

'Sure?'

He nodded. Summoning up the last of her energy, she pulled him upright and they staggered across the road. 'Not there,' she said, 'that's where the other bombs are.'

'That's far enough,' Frank said and with groans and grunts they levered themselves to the cold concrete road.

She supported him, until a fleet of police cars, fire engines and ambulances arrived. Revie dashed to them, and crouched down. They were holding each other tight.

'Thank God,' Revie said.

'Possible armed bomb on the first platform,' Laurel said.

Revie shouted the information back, then patted them both on the head. 'What about her?' He pointed back to Beattie; a dark shape surrounded by a dark pool.

'Probably dead, I didn't check,' Laurel said.

'Fair enough.' He waved an ambulance crew over. 'Let's get you two out of here before we send up the experts.'

When they were in the ambulance Revie came to the door. Frank was being attended to by a nurse, another was wiping the blood from Laurel's face with a damp flannel.

'Good work, you two. I'll come to the hospital and you can tell me everything then. See you later.'

The door closed. Frank was grimacing as the nurse placed his left arm in a sling. She'd nearly lost him. Those seconds when she'd thought he was dead had seemed like a timeless warp. The relief when she heard his voice, the overwhelming joy, those conflicting emotions; suddenly it all hit her. She tried to control the tsunami of feelings welling up inside her. She couldn't hold it back. She burst into tears.

'Now don't take on,' the nurse wiping her face said. 'You'll soon have a nice cup of tea.' She turned to Frank. 'Not for you, of course, you're nil by mouth until the doctor checks to see if that arm needs an operation.'

Laurel looked at Frank, tears cascading down her cheeks. His face, like the proverbial clown, fluctuated between mirth and pain. She took hold of his good hand and wept tears of happiness.

# Chapter Forty-Three

Friday, 11 May, 1973

In the garden at Greyfriars, Laurel helped Mabel take the used crockery back to the kitchen, Bumper hopefully following behind, wagging his tail, seemingly happy with the constant invasion of visitors over the past days. Visitors meant cake, or biscuits, possibly even both at once. Today, he'd cleaned up the crumbs under the garden chairs and table and, like all Labradors, he assumed the best, and hoped for more goodies when they got to the kitchen.

'You're going on a diet,' Laurel said, as she laid the tray onto the kitchen table.

Mabel peered out of the window. 'You'd better go back, I think the Pembertons are about to leave.'

As she approached them, Adam Pemberton was shaking Frank's hand, then Ann bent over and kissed his cheek, David followed up with another handshake. She bit her lip. Frank was looking uncomfortable, but was managing a smile. He was getting progressively grumpier as each day passed. After he'd been discharged from hospital, with a plaster on his left arm for his broken radius, Dorothy had insisted he must stay at Greyfriars. He seemed grateful for their care, but impatient to get away from Dorothy's and Mabel's ministrations; they fussed over him as though he were a sick child.

'Laurel,' Adam said, 'no words can thank you and Frank enough for what you did for David. Once more we're in your debt.'

Ann came up to her and took her hand. 'All I can say is thank you from the bottom of my heart.' She turned to David who stood at her shoulder.

He was pale and withdrawn; he'd said very little while they were having tea.

Laurel smiled at him. 'I hope we're never called upon again, David. You deserve some peace. I hope you won't let the actions of an evil person stop you from trusting other people. You've been very unlucky to have met so many ruthless criminals. Remember, most people are basically good. Don't lose your trust.'

His deep blue eyes held sadness.

'I've been meaning to ask you, what did you mean when you asked me not to let you down again – you said it when you were in the cell in Ipswich Police Station? I wasn't sure if I had, but if it's true, I apologise.'

He bit his lip. 'I'm sorry I said that. I was so sure you'd do something to bring the men who killed Peter to justice. It was wrong of me, none of us could do anything. Please forget I said that.'

Now she understood. 'I thought it might be that. It's forgotten already.'

David picked up a leather document case he'd brought with him. She'd been wondering what was in it, but didn't like to ask. He took out an A4 sketch pad. 'I did what you asked, these are drawings of people I saw from the window at Thorpeness. I know it's a bit late, but would you like to see them?'

'Yes, please, let's show them to Frank, as well.' They walked over to where he was sitting. 'David's brought the sketches I asked him to draw,' she said.

David knelt down by Frank's side, Laurel looking over his shoulder.

'I know they're no use now, but I thought you'd be interested.' He flicked the pages over, pausing until they'd made a comment, or laughed. There were drawings of people who'd walked past his window: an elderly couple, clutching each other's arms, bodies tilted against a strong wind, the woman clutching her hat with the other hand, the man's white hair swept back from his face; children with buckets and spades; a teenager licking an ice-cream cone; a pair of lovers in a tight clinch, their bodies seemingly welded together. David paused. Then slowly turned a page. There they were, Carlton and Beattie Mavor, standing apart, face to face, Beattie with her hand raised as though she was about to strike Carlton, he backing off, terror written over his face. Hatred was painted over her features, her lips parted, almost snarling, teeth sharp as honed chisels.

'I didn't know who they were, I just remembered them stopping outside the window; they looked as if they were quarrelling. It was a few weeks ago, before the Judge died. I thought she was a terrifying person. Now they're both dead.'

'You've brilliantly caught their relationship, David,' Frank said. 'Inspector Revie will be interested in seeing this.'

David smiled and turned another page.

Laurel burst into laughter, joined by Frank. 'I'm not sure if you should show him this,' she said.

It was a wonderful likeness; clothed in his raincoat, lapels standing up, he looked like someone from a James Cagney mobster film, his eyebrows scrunched into a single line, his small eyes as hard as boiled sweets, but there was a twist of the mouth that spoke of self-deprecation and acknowledgement of this parody of a tough guy.

'I disagree with Laurel. If you can bear to part with it, David, I'd present it to Inspector Revie. I think it would have pride of place on his office wall.'

'Really? Then I'll do that.'

Laurel put out a hand to him, and helped him up. He blushed.

'Do you think you'll get your trust in people back?' she asked.

'I think I'll find it difficult. I trust Dad and Ann, and I trust you and Mr Diamond.'

'What about Inspector Revie? Do you trust him?'

His lips parted in a smile. 'He apologised to me, said he was sorry he'd arrested me, and hoped I would understand.'

'And did you?'

'I'm trying to. I'm going to send him the sketch I drew of him.'

Adam came up and put an arm round his son. 'One thing I would like to know, Laurel, if you can tell me, is how did you discover Beattie Mavor killed Judge Hanmer?'

Laurel smiled. 'If we hadn't been involved with the case at Yoxford Gardens, we wouldn't have made the connection.'

'Really?' Adam said. 'I'm intrigued.'

'When Frank was talking to Mrs Gage, she mentioned the Judge kept a diary, but the police didn't find a diary at his home. We found the diary in Beattie's rooms, and what the Judge had written incriminated her. But before that happened, Frank wondered why Beattie said she took arts A levels, but when I talked to her old headmistress, she confirmed Beattie took chemistry, physics and maths. It was that fact that started Frank's suspicions of Beattie.'

'Remarkable! Thank you for telling me. We'd better be on our way.' He turned to Dorothy who was sitting at the table, smoking a cigarette. 'Thank you, Miss Piff, for an excellent tea.'

'My pleasure, Mr Pemberton. We're all pleased things turned out well. As for the tea, you must thank Mrs Elderkin, she did all the work.'

Frank was watching everyone, looking fed up; his seven-day stubble made him look like a dangerous pirate. The Pembertons made their goodbyes, stopping at the kitchen to thank Mabel.

Laurel scraped at his stubble with a fingernail. 'Would you like me to shave you?'

He glared at her. 'You and who else? The whole world seems to want to take a razor to my throat. As soon as I get back to the cottage, I'll do it myself.'

'I hope you aren't going to use a cut-throat; remember you've only got one good hand.' He snarled. 'And remember no showers, you mustn't get the plaster cast wet.'

He used his one good hand to pull her down to his level. 'We need to talk, and we can't do that here. I'm going back to the cottage tomorrow, and if you won't drive me, I'll walk.'

'Nurses Dorothy and Mabel won't like you escaping from their clutches.'

'There's only one person I want dealing with my bodily parts – and that's you.'

He wasn't the only one feeling frustrated. 'We'll go tomorrow. I can stay and look after you – if you like.'

'I like.'

'We'll tell the others at dinner.'

He smiled at her. Goodness, his white teeth against the swarthiness of his face was intoxicating. She bent down and rubbed her cheek against his. 'Frank, I think you'd better keep this beard.'

'Really? Why?'

She whispered in his ear, 'It's fantastically erotic.'

He roared with laughter.

'What's the joke?' Dorothy asked.

'She said I looked like Popeye.'


'That was a lovely meal, Jim,' Laurel said, pushing away her pudding plate.

'Och, thank you very much, but I did'na cook the sweetie, that was Mabel's confection,' he replied.

All members of the Agency were seated round the dining table, including Mabel, who was having a night off from cooking.

'It was an excellent meal, Jim,' Frank said, 'your chips were out of this world.'

Jim laughed. 'It's one thing the Scots know about, the frying pan.'

'When you first started cooking, I thought we might get some fried Mars Bars,' Frank said.

Jim started to clear the table. 'I'll put that on a future menu, if you like.'

There was a chorus of noes.

'Before we retire to the sitting room, I must tell you, tomorrow I'm going back to the cottage. I can't thank you enough, all of you, for looking after me so well, but I think I can manage, and Laurel has said she'll help me,' Frank said.

There was a pregnant silence. Laurel smiled at them all. Mabel looked worried, Dorothy nodded, implying it was time, Stuart was resisting giving his plate to Jim, as there was invisible food on it that only he could see. Jim glowered darkly at Frank.

'You can always come back, if things get difficult,' Dorothy said.

Laurel wasn't sure who she was talking to, and what she was implying.

# Chapter Forty-Four

Saturday, 12 May, 1973

In the kitchen at Greyfriars, Mabel poured out two coffees and put one down in front of Dorothy, who was seated at the kitchen table. 'Biscuit?' She waved the barrel at Dorothy.

'No, thanks, I'd like a cigarette, but I know they're banned in here.'

Mabel sighed. 'Go on, just this once. I could do with something myself, but I don't know what. I'll make do with a Penguin.' She fished one out from the biscuit barrel, unwrapped it, and munched rapidly. She patted her stomach. 'Can't say that's worked. I'm still worried about them, especially Laurel.'

Dorothy picked a strand of tobacco from her lower lip. 'We've got to let them get on with it. Either it'll work or it won't.'

'How can you be so calm? We've all seen how things have changed between them, and you can see they're madly in love, and I'm all for that. But what if, you know, happens, and Frank decides, as he usually does, he won't take it to the final stage? Laurel's a different kettle of fish. I've never seen her like this. She's been let down by one man. I don't know how you can sit there, as calm as a cucumber, and not be worried.'

'Mabel, you're getting yourself in a state. It isn't up to us. Let them have some happiness, they both deserve it.'

'But will he ask her to marry him?'

Dorothy laughed. 'I think they've got other things on their minds, at the moment.'

'Dorothy Piff! I'm ashamed of you. I was a virgin when I married, and I certainly didn't let Stuart . . . you know, before we were wed. I know things have changed, but not for the better. All this free love and no bras.'

Dorothy took a long draw on her cigarette and gave Mabel a long look.

'What are you looking at me like that for?'

'As you know, I never married. I'm going to shock you now, Mabel Elderkin—'

Mabel gasped. 'You didn't!'

'It was the war, with every mission I never knew if he'd come back. We'd planned to marry when the war was over. We loved each other, and we wanted each other, as only two people deeply in love can. I'm glad I have those wonderful memories of the time we spent together.' She swallowed hard, and took another drag on her cigarette.

Mabel's eyes were swimming with tears. 'Oh, Dorothy, I'm too puritanical. You're right, there's nothing like being in love when you're young, when you realise for the first time what love is. Let's hope it's the same for Laurel and Frank. I love both of them, and I want them to be happy.'

Dorothy reached across the table and took hold of her hand.

The kitchen door opened, and Stuart came in.

'Ay, ay, what's going on here? Holding hands? Have we got a crisis? Or have you two decided men aren't needed any more?' He roared at his witticisms.

'Oh, Stuart, we've been talking about Laurel and Frank. I was being silly, but Dorothy's straightened me out.'

'Don't worry about those two, they're made for each other. If Frank gets out of line, she'll soon settle his hash. He'll be too scared to even look at another woman.'

The two women looked at each other, sighed and shook their heads.

Frank and Laurel came back from their late-afternoon walk over the heath as the sun was sinking behind the woods on Minsmere

Bird Reserve. Laurel was quiet, thoughtful, occasionally making a comment about a bird, or asking him the name of a plant. Was she having second thoughts? During the walk they hadn't done more than occasionally hold hands, as they trod the narrow, sandy paths, Bumper scampering in front of them, pausing to look back, as though saying, 'Are you all right?' Or possibly, 'Hurry up, you're too slow.'

Back in the cottage Laurel cooked mussels she'd bought from the fishmongers in Aldeburgh followed by Dover soles sautéed in butter. He'd tried not to interfere, only giving advice when she asked for help. The space between then seemed to be laden with unanswered questions, uncertainty, also with desire, certainly on his part. After coffee and a whisky, he decided it was now or never.

'I'd like to go to bed, Laurel.'

'It's quite early, are you tired?'

'No.'

'Oh.'

He let the silence go on.

'Do you need help to get undressed?'

'I've been waiting for those words for a long time.'

She laughed and the tension disappeared.

He got up and pulled her to him.

'Careful, Frank. Your arm.'

'Bugger my arm.'

He took her hand and led her to his bedroom, a room she'd never been in until today. She looked around, taking in the large double bed. She gave him a worried look.

'I have never shared this bed with another person,' he said.

'Mind-reader! Where are your pyjamas?'

'Tonight, I will not need pyjamas.'

'Oh.'

'But I'll need some help.'

'What do you want me to do?'

'That's a leading question.'

'Frank Diamond, I don't know what to say.'

'Then don't say anything.'

She helped him get out of his shirt; one sleeve had been cut off. She turned her back to him. He managed the rest and got into bed.

'I've got a lot of bruises,' she said.

'Ditto.'

She'd turned away from him and started to undress. He watched, mesmerised as the body he'd first seen running, nearly naked, down Minsmere beach to the North Sea, risking her life to stop a murderer escaping, emerged from her clothes.

He pulled back the bedclothes.

'Frank, your arm?'

'We'll improvise.'

She slipped into his bed, and at last, her warm skin and lovely body were against his. They matched each other, length for length. She looked at him, her pupils almost obliterating the blue of her eyes; fathomless pools of desire. She smiled, reached up, and ran her hand through his long hair and pulled his head down to hers.

'Frank Diamond, I love you.'

# Author's Note

I first went to Thorpeness as a nine-year-old child on a Sunday School trip from Felixstowe. I was enchanted as I was rowed over the crystal-clear waters of the Meare; the green fronds of water-crow foot undulating beneath the water as the boat cleaved its way round the many islands; swans and ducks sharing the lake with us. That magical childhood memory is still vivid today.

Thorpeness, where this novel opens, is a unique fantasy village, built by a railway magnate before the First World War; it is one of the jewels of the Suffolk coast, and a popular destination for holiday-makers today.

The Country Club, originally named the Kursaal, was one of the first buildings. It's a wonderful example of the architecture of that time, and occupies the best site and sea view in the village. I have used artistic license to modify its internal structure to suit my story.

A fascinating book, *Thorpeness*, by W. H. Parkes, originally published in 1912, and republished in its entirety, including original advertisements, in 2001, gives a fascinating insight into the building of the village and Edwardians at play by the sea.

The chemical factory in Ipswich is fictitious and owes its structure to my imagination.

It was a great pleasure to recently visit Thorpeness again, and to meet people who lived there in the 1970s. They talked with great affection of Thorpeness and their life at that time.

# Acknowledgements

My thanks to the following people:

To all my writing friends, who over the years, by listening, reading, and making useful comments, have helped to inspire me to write The Anglian Detective Agency series.

Especially, Margaret Tomas, my first listener and dear friend.

The members of The Dunford Novelists, who meet annually in a hotel in Bournemouth, to read and listen to each other's first chapters of their new novels, to offer helpful criticism, so hopefully, those first words capture a publisher or an agent's interest. Every year at least one member becomes a newly published author.

The South Chiltern Writing Circle. A small group of friends and writers who meet weekly and listen, and helpfully criticise, each other's work, and also catch up on all the gossip! Stalwart friends.

To all the people at Headline who have helped to bring this novel to fruition, especially my editor, Bea Grabowska, who deals with all my problems and periodic frothings with patience, kindness and efficiency.

To Rhys Callaghan for the superb production of the book; to Phil Beresford for the dramatic and brooding cover. Who would have thought the Suffolk coastline could look so chilling? To eagle-eyed Jill Cole for her meticulous proofreading – it's a great comfort to have your work checked by such a hotshot.

To my other editor, Jay Dixon, who has worked on all six books, and continued to weave her editorial magic as she nit-picked her way through *Death by the Sea*. She's so efficient, reliable and likeable. I've enjoyed working with her.

To Mary James, of The Aldeburgh Bookshop, for the splendid, almost permanent display of my crime novels, and for her help in finding people who were willing to talk to me about Thorpeness in the 1970s, assisting with my research into the village and especially the Country Club.

To Caroline Boxall, for her help and advice and for putting me in touch with Maggie Boswell. I was assured what Maggie doesn't know about Thorpeness isn't worth knowing!

To Maggie Boswell, for telling me about life in Thorpeness in the 1970s, and her own extraordinary life.

All mistakes, both deliberate and unintentional, are mine.

Join Frank, Laurel and the rest of The Anglian
Detective Agency as they embark on more cases . . .

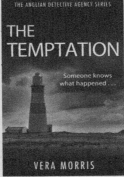
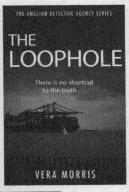
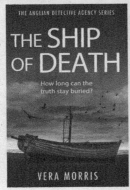
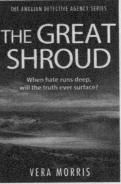
Available to order

ACCENT